You never
know
how dangerous
someone
can be…

BURIED MEMORIES

"Just tell me what you remember from that day," Sam said. "I need to find out what happened on that boat. Why my brother's dead."

Jules tried to remember, everything. But the details were elusive, the bits of memory lying beneath the fog.

"You don't remember anything about that boat trip?" Sam asked.

"No. I just . . . I remember getting on the boat, that's all." She told him of the quick flash of recall she'd just had. Shaking, her fear palpable, she stared at the house, her home, and felt herself shrink inside. "Something happened here . . . somebody came. . . ." She felt she was getting close to some kind of breakthrough and her breath came fast. The gray curtain was pressing down on her, hurting her head.

"Who?"

"I don't know. I'm afraid to know," she admitted. "I just know we had to get away. . . ."

"Away from what?"

"I don't know!"

"Think, Jules!"

"I'm trying! I'm really trying."

"Someone threatened you?"

"Yes. I think so. I don't know!"

"Well, what do you know?" he demanded in frustration. "Jules, I know you're trying, but I need you to remember!"

Books by Nancy Bush

CANDY APPLE RED

ELECTRIC BLUE

ULTRAVIOLET

WICKED GAME

WICKED LIES

SOMETHING WICKED

WICKED WAYS

UNSEEN

BLIND SPOT

HUSH

NOWHERE TO RUN

NOWHERE TO HIDE

NOWHERE SAFE

SINISTER

I'LL FIND YOU

YOU CAN'T ESCAPE

YOU DON'T KNOW ME

THE KILLING GAME

DANGEROUS BEHAVIOR

OMINOUS

Published by Kensington Publishing Corporation

Dangerous Behavior

NANCY BUSH

ZEBRA BOOKS
KENSINGTON PUBLISHING CORP.

http://www.kensingtonbooks.com

ZEBRA BOOKS are published by

Kensington Publishing Corp.
119 West 40th Street
New York, NY 10018

All Kensington titles, imprints, and distributed lines are available at special quantity discounts for bulk purchases for sales promotion, premiums, fund-raising, educational, or institutional use.

Special book excerpts or customized printings can also be created to fit specific needs. For details, write or phone the office of the Kensington Sales Manager: Attn.: Sales Department. Kensington Publishing Corp., 119 West 40th Street, New York, NY 10018. Phone: 1-800-221-2647.

Zebra and the Z logo Reg. U.S. Pat. & TM Off.

First Printing: May 2017
ISBN-13: 978-1-4201-4289-1
ISBN-10: 1-4201-4289-5

eISBN-13: 978-1-4201-4290-7
eISBN-10: 1-4201-4290-9

10 9 8 7 6 5 4 3 2 1

Printed in the United States of America

Prologue

"I can tell the future," she said.

He slid a look over to the woman two seats down at the bar.

Tiny Tim's was the kind of shitkicker place that hung its hat on expensive microbrews, like the rest of Greater Portland, but its decor was strictly blue-collar beer signs, scarred wooden chairs, booths, and sports channels. Tiny Tim, whose bald pate and center girth made him look a little like Humpty Dumpty, his nickname, was pulling a Deschutes black porter from the nearest tap and jawing with a guy sitting at the far end of the bar.

"Nobody can tell the future," he said, friendly-like. He'd had his eye on this one since she'd slipped into the room in a gust of wind and water. Outside the window he could see the light rain trickling down, visible in the sodium vapor lights that illuminated the strip mall's parking lot, although it was black as Satan's heart beyond these walls.

She moved to the seat next to him. He could smell her cologne, fresh and light. He thought she might be thirty-something, but she could pass as twenty-five. He felt his cock stir and smiled to himself. He was a little buzzed. Just enough to make everything shine a bit brighter.

"I can prove it," she said, gazing directly into his eyes.

"Yeah? You want my palm or something?"

"What's your name?"

"Tom. But if you can see the future, you probably already know that."

"Well, Tom. I can see things that are about to happen. And I see you and me out in your truck, moving to a rhythm all our own. Some call it love, some just call it sex. . . . I call it inevitable."

He laughed. He couldn't help himself. "I have a sedan, but that's a good line."

She slowly moved her head from side to side. She was a good-looking woman. Sure, a faint hardness showed through the facade, but her hair was long and lustrous, brushing her shoulders, and her eyes were dark and sultry. Her lips were plump, probably pumped up with some sort of product that they would find out was deadly cancerous twenty-five years from now, but they sure looked good enough to eat right now. He noticed the dusky valley between her breasts as she leaned into him.

"Should I put my hand on my wallet?" he asked.

"You've been watching me. I could feel it as soon as I walked in. Before, really. You saw me outside, too."

He tilted his head, thought about it a moment. "That was you with that guy?"

"My husband," she said. "He left. Don't make too big a deal of it. We go to a bar together and he thinks everyone's trying to pick me up. We fight. He drives off mad and I go home with the guy I want."

"It's like that, huh?"

"It's like that. Except . . . you don't look like the usual clientele around here." She ran a hand inside his black over-coat and pressed hot fingers against his silk shirt. Almost absently she played with his nipple, which made him go rock hard. "You dress nice, but some guys wear their best after work. . . ."

"Meaning?"

"Who are you, Tom? What's your day job? And what are you really doing here?"

Tiny Tim shuffled toward them, polishing a glass and giving a poor imitation of being disinterested in their conversation. Tom ignored the barkeep and said, "You're the 'seer.' You tell me."

"Were you following me and Ricky? I doubt it's Ricky you want."

"Ricky your husband?"

She nodded.

"I don't want Ricky."

"Good."

"Does Ricky beat you?" he asked curiously.

She withdrew her hand, which was a pity, but there was no way Tom could afford the kind of trouble she was offering. A jealous husband, spoiling for a fight? He didn't need everyone in the bar remembering him, especially, as she'd pointed out, since he didn't look like the usual clientele.

"Ricky loves me a little too much, that's all," she said with a dismissive shrug.

"That's what you call it?"

"It pisses me off and makes me want to fuck every man I meet." Her lips tightened. "You gonna buy me a drink, or what, Tom?"

"I'm thinking about it."

"Maybe I should be working on somebody else?" Her dark eyes sparked with challenge.

"The guy at the end of the bar looks available."

Her gaze narrowed and her expression turned to granite. "You lose," she said, moving past him to sidle up to the guy he'd pointed out. She leaned in and started talking close. Whatever she was saying brought a bright smile of good fortune to her next mark's face.

Tiny Tim said quietly, "Don't know you, man, but that one's trouble."

"You know her?"

"Never seen her before around here, but you can smell it on her. Maybe I should warn him." He looked down the bar where the woman had her hand out of sight beneath the bar. Her arm was rhythmically moving up and down and by the dull look of bliss on the mark's face, it was clear just what that hand was doing.

Tom dropped two twenties on the bar, a nice tip without being too showy, then walked past the woman and the mark and shoved his way out the back door into a damp June night filled with rain and fog.

His gray, midsize Honda sedan hunched at the edge of the lot, barely visible. A rental. He looked at it for a moment and thought about the sure thing he'd turned down inside Tiny Tim's. He craved a cigarette, but those little cancer sticks would ravage your lungs, so he steered clear of them. A vein pulsed near his ear. He could feel it. He pictured the woman inside the bar naked on a bearskin rug in front of a stone hearth filled with smoldering orange embers and dancing flames. He pictured himself on top of her, ripping off his own clothes, cock hard, nearly bursting, driving into her.

The back door of the bar flew open and banged against the wall. He automatically took a step back.

And there she was, locked in an embrace with the guy at the end of the bar, climbing all over him. They fell out together, nearly to the ground, but the mark braced himself with his hand against the rough, cedar siding, just barely.

It took a couple of moments for them to realize he was standing there.

"What the fuck you lookin' at, asshole?" the guy panted. One hand was in her waistband, the other was clutching her butt, bringing her crotch toward his.

"I guess the future was a little different than you predicted," Tom said to the woman.

"Go fuck yourself," she said, but there was a smile on her face. She was getting off on it all, too.

"It's a shame we couldn't get together. Maybe next time."

"How about right now?" She opened her mouth and rimmed her lips with her tongue.

"Get lost, asshole," the guy growled, burying his head between breasts that had practically sprung out of her blouse.

"Maybe we could go to my car?" he suggested, jerking his head in the direction of the sedan. Man, he was horny. She was really doing it to him.

"NO," the mark grunted in fury. His hands came free and he clasped the front halves of her blouse, yanked hard. *Scritch!* He ripped the damn thing apart.

"Hey!" she protested, slapping at his hands and backing up.

"You shouldn't have done that," Tom told him.

"We ain't having no ménage a twat," the mark snapped.

The woman slapped him hard, right across the face.

He cried out and fell back, holding his cheek, shocked at the sudden about-face. "You bitch! You bitch!"

"No cameras," she said, looking around.

"Nope," Tom answered, reaching into the pocket of his long, black coat. He pulled out a hypodermic needle and uncapped it.

The mark blinked at them, staggering and swaying. He reached for the handle of the back door, but she stopped him with a swift kick to the groin. He shrieked and grabbed his crotch, groaning and swearing and pleading as he collapsed onto the ground.

"Ugh," Tom said with a grimace. "Makes my balls hurt."

"Wha'd you do that for?" the man whined, sounding teary. He squirmed on the ground, squinting up at her.

She gazed down at him a thoughtful moment, then came

over to Tom and slid a hand gently over his crotch. "Love you," she purred.

"Love you more," he answered.

Stepping forward, he plunged the hypodermic into the man's neck. "Sorry, Denny," he said. "But on the craps table of life, you just rolled snake eyes."

Denny gazed up at them fearfully. "You know me?"

"Oh, yeah. We do." She smiled.

"Whoo—why?" Denny chattered.

"You made bad choices," Tom said.

"Karma," she agreed.

Denny opened his mouth and tried to scream, but she swiftly bent down and clasped him by the throat. His only sounds were garbled glugs until he was a wallowing mess.

"We'd better get him outta here," she said.

Tom carefully recapped the hypodermic needle and put it back in his pocket. Then he grabbed Denny's limp form beneath his arms and dragged him to the sedan. She helped him toss Denny into the trunk, then Tom climbed behind the wheel and she slipped into the passenger seat. They looked at each other.

"Good thing he Ubered it from that ratty apartment he now calls home," she said. "No car to deal with."

"Yep."

"We still have other problems back home," she reminded.

"I'm going to take care of 'em."

"How?"

"I'm working on it."

"You need to tell me," she insisted. "You don't think things through like I do."

"Bullshit. You're not the only brains here."

"Yeah, well, you gotta stop shopping us around. I don't like anybody knowing about us, no matter how much they pay."

"The next one's for us as much as the man."

"The man," she sneered. "As soon as this whole mess is

taken care of, we're not taking any more jobs, you understand? It's too dangerous, and I like my life."

"Me too." He inclined his head in agreement and focused on her lips. "How'd you get 'em so big?"

She ran her tongue around them. "Actually I bit the hell out of 'em. Hurt like a bitch."

"I was thinking about them from Tom's point of view when we were in the bar. Tom thought it was Botox and it wouldn't be good."

"Collagen, but no. I didn't have time for that," she said. "Tom didn't like them?"

"Tom's got a rod up his ass."

"Except when Bridget's around," she said, pulling back the shreds of her blouse and unsnapping the front clasp of her bra. Her breasts tumbled out and he cupped one and rubbed the nipple.

"Tom turned Bridget down tonight."

"Well, he's not going to now, though, is he?"

"No . . ." With a groan he bent down and drew one nipple into his mouth, sucking hard, until she was arching and moaning and damn near yanking out his hair.

"I thought about you . . . naked . . . in front of a fire. . . ." he gasped.

"God, I wish!"

By unspoken mutual consent he pulled reluctantly away from her and she redid her bra clasp and tucked her blouse back together. "Jesus," she said in disgust at the ruined garment.

"I liked the bit about Ricky."

She shot him a sideways smile. "Love a good backstory."

"Maybe we should stop at a motel," he said as he pulled out of the dark lot and headed slowly through fog-shrouded streets toward Sunset Highway.

"Don't let your cock be your guide. We've got Denny and we're going to be late as it is," she said.

"I know."

They drove in silence for half an hour, climbing up the foothills of the Coast Range to where the fog was ghostly wisps. Ten minutes later he turned onto a narrow side road and bumped along for about a mile. They got out, popped the trunk, hauled Denny's body out and dumped him onto the ground. Then they both dragged him into the underbrush.

She leaned over Denny as Tom pulled a bottle of bleach from the trunk.

"He's dead," she said.

He doused Denny from head to toe with the bleach, rolling him over and doing the same to his backside, just in case there was any of her DNA anywhere.

They returned to the car, backed out of the rutted road, and pulled onto the dark highway. There was no traffic; everyone was already wherever they wanted to be.

She said, "God, I want to fuck."

"Me too."

"Oh, hell. Pull onto that side road just past the summit."

"You sure . . . Bridget?"

"Get that rod out of your ass, *Tom*. The only one I want to see is the one that hits the G-spot."

"Oh, baby," he groaned.

He found the turnoff and bumped and banged over tree roots and river rocks. But when he threw the car into park and grabbed for her, she put a finger to his lips and lifted her cell phone to her ear. He froze as she waited for the connection, then she said, "Hi, it's me just checking in. I'm afraid I'm delayed again. Everything go okay?" He heard the voice answer though he couldn't make out the words.

"You're the best. See you soon . . ." she said, clicking off.

"Kids okay?" he asked.

"Of course."

Then she slipped her hand around the back of his neck, pulling his facedown to hers. She ground her lips to his, her tongue delving deep into his mouth as he settled himself over her, fighting the gearshift and the steering wheel, but it was still the best sex in the world.

Chapter One

The woman on the beach slowly came to consciousness, the frigid water sliding up and over her, then receding. Sand beneath her fingers. She curled her nails into it, trying to focus, trying to wake up. She needed to remember something.

Get up or you'll die.

Apart from her fingers, she couldn't move. Everything was weighted down. She couldn't even open her eyes . . . but . . . yes . . . one sand-crusted lid lifted. She was on a beach. And there was something just there . . . beside her on the beach . . . hunched.

She worked to open both eyes and looked right into—

The wide open blue eyes of a dead man.

She shrieked, but it came out as a whimper, and then the next wave hit and it was bigger, lifting her up, slamming her into the dead man, his arm tussling with hers until they tumbled back into the surf.

I can't . . . she thought.

And then the world faded to black.

Sam Ford rattled his truck along the jetty, scanning the western horizon. The ocean was gray today, restless under a low July sun. A line of smoke could still be seen, drifting above the water the same color as the sand. A boat had caught fire and sank. Was it his brother's boat? Was *she* on it? Sam was still waiting to hear.

The back of his throat was gritty and raw, as if he'd been in the way of the smoke, and yet it was a mile from shore. He threw the truck into park and climbed out, grabbing his binoculars. The coast guard helicopter was hovering near the boat on a northwest trajectory from where Sam stood.

The text from Joe ran across his mind, like it had a thousand times since he'd received it: *Meet me at my dock at noon.*

Sam had been surprised by the message. He and Joe . . . the rift between them had grown over the years and they didn't speak much any longer. Their father had thrown up his hands that they couldn't reconcile, though now his mind seemed to be playing tricks on him, so who knew what he thought anymore. Their mother had divorced their father and remarried, stepping away from her sons and starting a new life. She'd had an inkling that things were not well between her two boys, but she'd chosen to pretend everything was fine, right up until breast cancer stole her away.

Meet me at my dock at noon. . . .

Sam gazed up at the sun. It had started its descent to the horizon hours ago, though it was long after Sam had texted his brother back and told him he couldn't make it, even though he could have. He'd come up with a dozen excuses, but Joe had never sent another text, which kinda pissed Sam off. Joe ordering him around? Playing passive-aggressive? Nope. That wasn't the nature of their relationship.

But Joe texting him at all was pretty unusual. His brother usually left him alone, and vice versa. Was he imagining the imperative note to the message? At first it had just seemed autocratic; his older brother making demands on him just because he could. But that wasn't Joe's way. If anything, he tended to leave Sam be, and that was just fine with Sam. But that text had wormed its way into Sam's brain, circling around, and he'd started thinking it was something more. A desperate plea? Why had his brother sent the message?

He'd tried to call Joe to ask him. He wasn't going to go racing down the mountains from his parents' old cabin to the beach without a good reason. Of course Joe had no way of knowing he wasn't at the condo he'd been renting, or for that matter that he could be at work. Sam hadn't told Joe that he'd quit the Seaside PD in favor of a job in Portland, which, in the end, hadn't materialized—a job that would have been a step up to detective, one Sam was more than ready for. But just as soon as he'd quit at Seaside there'd supposedly been shifts within the Portland PD—a lot of double-talk from everyone involved—the upshot being someone with political ties was slotted into the open position in Portland and Sam was out. He could've gone back to Seaside, maybe should've gone back to the old job, probably, but instead he'd taken time off to think things over. And he really wasn't sure he wanted to go backward anyway. Returning to his job as a general cop—Seaside wasn't big enough for departments—felt like that's all it would be. Also, his relationship with Dannella had fallen apart because he couldn't commit, or so she said, although it hadn't taken her long to find someone else and the last he'd heard she was married with a new baby. He'd felt a twinge of regret over that, but like his job, he'd decided to just wait and let things happen. There was nothing to do about it anyway, and really, Dannella moving on had been a good thing.

Joe hadn't answered, and he'd never responded to Sam's further texts. The morning had slipped by and finally Sam had just thought, screw it, and had driven the hour from the cabin to his brother's house on Fisher Canal, an offshoot of the Nehalem River. He'd braced himself for a run-in with

Joe's wife, but the house had been deserted when he got there. He'd rung the bell and peered in the front windows, able to see through the living room and sliding glass door to the back deck and across the narrow inlet to the house on the opposite side. The neighbor's boat sat outside their dock, which had made Sam realize Joe's was gone. To make certain, Sam had tramped around the side of the house and, sure enough, there was no boat beneath the gray canopy over the boat slip, nor had it been tied to the silver cleats gleaming in the sun against the weathered boards of the dock.

While he'd been there a woman had come out from the house across the river and waved at him. Sam reluctantly waved back, aware she probably thought he was his brother, even though Joe was eight years older than Sam.

She called over to him. "Who's got the boat?"

"I'm not Joe. I'm his brother," he yelled back.

"Oh!"

She'd clearly been taken aback, and Sam suspected Joe had never mentioned him to her. No surprise there.

"You didn't see him leave?" Sam asked.

She shook her head and motioned behind her. "Just got home," she yelled.

Sam had nodded and waved a good-bye as he headed back around the house to his truck. He walked up to the garage and cupped his hands over his eyes, looking through the narrow garage window. Two vehicles were inside. A black Explorer and a light blue Subaru Outback. He surmised Joe's was the Explorer, a Ford. His brother probably didn't hear the same grief as he did about driving something other than a Ford when your last name was Ford. His Chevy pickup had been a good deal, period.

With both cars accounted for, he'd asked himself: Are Joe and his wife together on the boat? Maybe on their way back now?

He'd checked his cell phone. Eleven fifty. If his brother was returning by boat, he was pushing it pretty hard to make noon. There were houses on both sides of the narrow waterway that led into Nehalem Bay and further to the ocean. When he shaded his eyes and gazed down the ribbon of water to the sharp bend at the southwestern end, all he saw were the houses. But Sam could tell by sound alone that no boat was approaching.

He'd waited until twelve forty-five, then had climbed back into the cab of his truck and reversed out of the drive. Punching the accelerator, he'd headed toward the bay. As he'd approached he'd seen a crowd of onlookers outside their cars in the marina's lot who were all staring toward the edge of the horizon where a line of smoke and faint flashes of orange light were a pinpoint to the naked eye.

"Boat's on fire," a gravel-voiced man had stated, his baseball cap bearing the name of a local hardware store.

Sam's heart had clutched. There was no reason other than timing to think it was Joe's boat, but still . . .

A young woman in shorts that were completely covered by an oversized sweatshirt had said, "Coast guard should be there."

"Don't hear the whirly-bird," Gravel Voice had pointed out, frowning.

At that moment the *whup-whup-whup* of the approaching helicopter had reached their ears. Gravel Voice gave a quick nod and said, "Thar it is."

Sam had reached for his cell phone. He'd tried Joe one more time, then sent another text: Where r u? On the boat? Call me.

He'd waited another five minutes, but no answer. With growing alarm he'd gotten back into the truck and put a call in to his ex-partner, Griff.

"Hey, man," Griff had answered lazily. "I'm off today. Catch a beer later?"

"Griff, you hear about a boat accident south of Salchuk? Looks like one's on fire, out on the horizon."

"Coast guard chopper's out there," he'd answered after a minute.

"I know." Sam had debated on mentioning that it could be his brother, but Griff wasn't known for keeping things to himself. "Let me get back to you on that beer. Got a few things to do."

"You on the scene?"

"Yep. Gotta go."

"Okay, I'll be at the Gull."

Griff spent a lot of time down at the Seagull, a decrepit pub overlooking the Necanicum River in Seaside, another of the feeders to the Pacific on this stretch of coastline but thirty miles north of the Nehalem. Sam had lifted more than a few pints with his partner during their five years together on the force. Griff had been against Sam's decision to quit and was hopeful Sam would return. Maybe he would and maybe he wouldn't. He'd been tentatively offered a job with the Tillamook County Sheriff's Department, further south down the coast, as well. He knew people there, too. He just wasn't certain what he wanted yet and wasn't sure that job was still on the table, either.

He'd slid his phone back in his pocket, cursed under his breath, and then beaten down the fears that had assailed him . . . told himself his brother was okay—he had to be—then had driven north to a section of sharp cliffs that reached into the ocean, a treacherous spot between Nehalem Bay and the small town of Salchuk, a sleepy ocean village that had recently become the newest, hottest place to be. The cliffs created an isolated beach that was only approachable at low tide around a pair of sheer stone arms that clawed into the Pacific. He'd parked, then half walked, half ran down the sharp, small rocks that tumbled off the massive stone walls. It wasn't a popular place to come. The beach was too narrow, the view north blocked by the cliff, the stretch of sand on the south end disintegrating into larger rocks that were arduous to cross. If you were a thrill-seeker, then you might attempt a swim around the rock arm to the sheltered beach, but the frigid water, even in the dead of summer, might give you pause.

Now, Sam's gaze moved across the horizon. He liked this stretch for all the reasons others didn't. Its inherent loneliness appealed to him. What that said about him he was pretty sure he didn't want to know, but Joe had been aware how Sam was drawn to the place, so maybe . . . ? The beach itself was deserted except for an enterprising seagull who eyed him with a baleful eye. If it came to a turf war, Sam thought he might win and he strode across the sand. The gull let him get within a foot before it screeched loudly, hopped a few steps away, and flapped its wings.

Sam pulled his gaze from the haze of smoke and that's when he saw the shoe bobbing among the waves. A woman's tan, slip-on sneaker. His heart clutched again, and he could almost feel the blood pumping through his veins.

Without serious conscious thought he dropped his cell phone and wallet on the sand and ran toward the surf, meeting a wave as it was coming in. He kept his sneakers on as he dove into water cold enough to stop his breath, and he battled the surf and turned northward as soon as he could to round the stone cliff, glad for the shoes that saved his feet against the rock face.

He caught a mouthful of seawater on his mission and spat it out as he clawed his way around the last part of the jagged stone wall.

He saw the woman's body immediately. It was being teased by the incoming tide. Soon it would be sucked back out to the sea.

Jules!

He let the next rush of waves hurtle him toward her, then

battled the receding waters, staggering up the beach, falling down to his knees and stumbling up again. He grabbed her as she tumbled back toward the waiting ocean, clamped his hands onto both of her arms, and pulled her up the sand. The waves rushed back and he lost his balance and his grip on her. Her brown hair was a mermaid's floating crown around her head.

"Shit . . ." he whispered.

He grabbed her again and this time he hauled her as far up the beach as he could. He rolled her onto her back. She wasn't breathing. Immediately he started CPR, rhythmically pushing on her chest while his head jerked around from side to side. Where was the coast guard? Where was Joe? God, was it *his* boat? Had to be. Why else would Jules be here?

She wasn't responding. Even though it was no longer protocol, he leaned over her, opened her mouth, blew air into her lungs, then pushed on her chest some more.

"Come on, Jules, come on," he gritted through his teeth. "Where's Joe? Come on, come on. Breathe . . . *breathe* . . . Where's Joe?"

It seemed like forever before her body lurched and she hawked up a rush of fluid from her lungs. Sam immediately turned her onto her side to help her.

Her lips were blue but her eyelids fluttered.

"Where's Joe?" he asked, unable to help himself. "God, Jules. What happened? Where's Joe?"

"Joe?" she warbled, shivering.

"Were you on the boat? Did it catch fire? Was he with you? Jules . . . *was he with you?"*

Her gray eyes regarded him dully. She was shivering all over and he gathered her close, aware how cold she was.

"I'm going to give you my shirt," he said. "I've got to call nine-one-one. Let them know where you are. My phone's on the other side of the rock."

"What . . ." she whispered.

"Stay warm. I'll just be a minute. You're safe here." *For now*, he thought. But with the tide coming in, maybe not for long. This whole area would be underwater soon.

He raced back into the water, calculating how much time he had. If worse came to worst, he would swim with her around the rock, but it would be harrowing. For now he just needed the chopper or a rescue boat.

He worked his way around the cliff face again, was slammed into it by a sudden, powerful wave, banged the side of his head. His vision spun for a moment before he gathered the strength to push himself around the last jut of stone, then let the waves shove him up the beach. He stumbled to his feet with an effort and staggered to where he'd left his phone. Thank God it was still dry. He dialed 911 and spoke to the dispatcher calmly, telling them exactly where they were.

Then he left the phone again, but slipped his wallet into his back pocket. It would be soaked, but he wanted the identification, just in case.

Just in case.

His trip back around the rock seemed to take forever. Inch by inch, holding on to the sharp edges, trying to gain purchase with his feet, every movement was sluggish, every stroke felt as if he were losing ground. His vision swam, his head throbbed. Aching, he realized he was hurt. A concussion, possibly. Well, hell. He'd had a few in his time. Football . . . Maybe he shoulda stayed away from that game. . . . He forced himself forward, around the damned rock, bracing himself against the battering, icy surf. Gritting his teeth, he squinted against the spray and saw her.

She was lying on her side, still out of reach of the waves, though their fingers were reaching ever closer. The tide was coming in. He ran toward her; at least he thought he did. More like lurching, he dimly realized.

"Wake up, Jules," he ordered sternly, seeing her eyes were again closed.

He leaned down to her, alarmed. She was breathing raggedly. But alive. From the corner of his eye he saw it: a sneaker wave that suddenly jumped up the beach, racing across the sand to snatch at her. It splashed over both of them, arctic cold, dragging them both toward open sea. With a supreme effort of willpower he held on to her and pulled against it, muscles straining, strength waning, until the wave finally reluctantly released its death grip and receded.

She'll die of hypothermia. . . .

He pulled her up to the base of the cliff, as far up the beach as he could possibly, then lay down atop her, warming her, making sure his weight didn't interfere with her breathing. He had to find Joe . . . had to . . . But Jules beneath him . . . ? All he could think about was her dove gray eyes, her ironic smile, the feel of her silky skin. . . .

Just like old times, he thought.

In a strange twilight consciousness, he remembered making love to her. Being in love with her. Thinking of making a life with her, before everything happened. He'd been an asshole, he knew. But she'd proved her faithlessness in the end, just like he'd feared. She'd married Joe, for God's sake, and then—

Joe.

Where was Joe?

He awoke, startled to full consciousness. God, where was the ambulance? The EMTs? He was shaking violently. Another wave raced up the beach, climbing up his pant legs.

The woman beneath him stirred. Opened her eyes. He looked down into dull gray depths that stared back at him blankly. Then her eyes widened and she screamed with fear, though she could barely muster more than a whimper.

"Jules . . . Jules . . ." Sam said helplessly.

"What . . . what happened . . . ?" she choked out.

"I've called nine-one-one. They're coming."

"Oh . . . oh . . ."

Sam struggled to keep his wits about him. "Jules, where's Joe?"

"Joe . . . ?"

"Yes, Joe. My brother. Your *husband*," he snapped. He was filled with nebulous alarm. "Where is he?"

She stared past his ear, into some distant horror. Just when he thought she wasn't going to answer, she said, "You're dead," and her eyes rolled back in her head.

Far in the distance, he heard a faint *woo-woo-woo*, the welcome wail of a siren. They were coming. He hoped they had a rescue boat. Had he told the 911 dispatcher he needed a boat? A wave inundated them up to their waists, then receded. His ears were full of the ocean's roar. His face was wet with spray.

As the wail grew louder, Sam looked down at Jules. She was still unconscious but breathing. He realized an ambulance had pulled up on the southern side of the arm of rock. He felt relief when he understood they were using an inflatable to circumvent the cliff. He *had* told the dispatcher and now the boat was riding the waves, growing closer, two rescuers guiding the craft toward the shore. He tried to get to his feet and help them but felt too lethargic. When he rubbed a hand across his head it came back bloody.

"We're here," he chattered, as if the two men in wet suits who'd materialized from the surf with a stretcher could hear him. "For God's sake, hurry. . . ."

"We've got you," one of them said as if from a distance, and Sam rolled off Jules and reached a hand to be helped to his feet.

* * *

She awoke in what appeared to be an ambulance, looked around, didn't have a clue where she was. There was a mask on her face, regulating her breathing. *I've been injured*, she thought. She tried to lift her right arm and pain stabbed her.

An attendant looked over at her and said, "Try not to move. We're on our way to the hospital now."

"What . . . happened?" Her head hurt like a son of a bitch.

"The doctor's meeting us in the ER."

"I was in the water," she murmured, feeling a gray numbness descend on her like a shroud.

"You're safe now," the voice said, but it sounded wavy and far away and she didn't believe it.

They put Sam in an ambulance, a different one from Jules's, even though he protested that he was fine. He wasn't fine. He didn't think he'd ever be fine again. He wasn't sure he had ever been fine.

"My brother," he choked out, struggling upward from the gurney.

The EMT put a light hand on his chest. "We're looking for him. The coast guard's alerted."

"The boat . . . the one on fire . . ."

"Sir, we just need you to lie down."

"My phone was on the beach on the other side of the rocks."

"Someone will find it," a confident male voice told him.

"Was that Joe's boat? Was it?"

You're dead.

Had Jules said that? Were those the words, or had he imagined it?

Half an hour later the ambulance screamed into the hospital drive and swept beneath the portico outside Emergency.

The EMTs leapt out and yanked open the back doors. They pulled Sam out and he wanted to protest that he could walk on his own, but no one was listening. Jules's ambulance was in front of his, and she was already being pulled out. They snapped the gurney's wheels down and pushed through the automatic doors into the hospital's ER.

As soon as he was on the ground, Sam once again tried to get off his own gurney. A young female nurse warned, "Sir? Sir? We need you to lie back. We'll be there soon."

"My cell phone," he said again. "Can you find who has it? Or any phone, for that matter. I need to call the Tillamook County Sheriff's Department."

"The doctor will see you and decide," she answered.

It kind of pissed him off. No, it *really* pissed him off, but he let it stand because his head hurt and he felt dull. But his mind was also on fire, full of questions and fear. Was Joe on that boat? Did he survive? *What happened?*

He was given a cursory check over by an ER doctor who looked to be in his early thirties, about Sam's same age, then he was deposited on a hospital bed in a cubicle with curtains for walls. He could hear them working with Jules. He lay staring at the ceiling for about five minutes before throwing off the covers. He was still in his pants, shirt, and sneakers, which were damp and uncomfortable, but he scarcely noticed.

"I need a phone," he said.

"Sir . . ." A young woman in blue scrubs frowned at him from across the room.

"Sam Ford," he told her. "I'm a policeman and I need a phone." *Was* a policeman, but she didn't have to know that.

An older, heavyset woman, also in scrubs, lumbered his way, her thighs making a scritching sound as she walked. "Mr. Ford, please go back to your bed." She made a shooing motion. "We're doing everything we can for your . . . wife? Or sister . . ."

"Julia Ford." He didn't want to waste time on explanations.

"Yes."

"How is she? Is she all right?"

"She's in good hands."

"Is she alert?"

"She's been communicating. Now, please?" She held out her arm toward his cubicle. Sam hesitated briefly before complying and returning to his room.

Though her words had been a request, her tone had held a warning that Sam was unlikely to miss. Authority trip, he decided. He was too quick to judge; he knew that about himself. But he also knew he was generally right, so he didn't much care.

He suffered through nearly an hour of waiting, his mind searching for answers when there wasn't enough information to find any. He could hear Jules's voice occasionally, which mostly eased his fears where she was concerned, but he was sick with worry over his brother.

And then the doctor—the senior one with decision-making capabilities, apparently—checked him over and pronounced him able to leave, as long as someone drove him home. "You've suffered a minor head injury, and I'd like you to be monitored."

"I'll call my sister," he said, "but I don't have my cell phone." He also didn't have a sister.

"I think the police brought it in. One of the EMTs said you were missing it."

"Do you know where I can find it?"

"Ask Jan at the desk on your way out. She knows all." The doctor gave him a brief smile. "We're still assessing your wife, but you can see her for a few minutes. But you should go home and take care of yourself. Can you call someone?"

"I will . . . my sister," Sam said, thinking hard. They thought Jules was his wife and that gave him a kind of access to her and information about her he might not be granted if they found out he was her brother-in-law instead.

On slightly unsteady legs he walked toward her cubicle. The curtain was closed on his side, but open on the other. As he came around, he was a bit startled that she was sitting up and very much awake.

"Hey," he said. "How're you doing?" His shirt was tossed on the chair and he picked it up and shrugged into it.

"I have a cracked collarbone . . . clavicle." She said the words slowly, as if testing each one out separately. He could see the bandage peeking out from the hospital gown she'd been issued. Even wet, bedraggled, her skin abraded, and having just escaped drowning, there was something about her that was, and always had been, captivating. He ignored it. Told himself he was immune.

"What happened out there? Do you know where Joe is?"

"Joe?"

"Yeah, Joe," Sam said tightly. "He was on the boat with you, right?"

"I don't . . ."

He waited, but she trailed off and didn't start again, so he pressed, "Joe called me and told me to meet him at noon at your house. But you guys were gone. What were you doing out there? Did something happen?" He lowered his voice and moved in closer. "Was Joe with you?"

She shrank back into the pillows.

He was scaring her. She'd been through a tremendous trauma and he was scaring her. He had to pull himself back, but he didn't want to. He wanted to keep hammering at her because time was ticking away, like blood seeping from a wound, each moment bringing Joe closer to death.

"What did you mean 'you're dead'?" he whispered. There were too many people outside the curtain and he didn't want any of them to hear.

She stared at him helplessly. "What?"

"You said, 'you're dead,' when we were on the beach."
When she didn't respond, he pressed. "When we were on
the beach, when you'd washed ashore before they brought
you in. Remember? For God's sake, Jules—"

"I don't know!" she cried out.

The curtain shot back, caught in one strong fist. "Mr. Ford,
it's time for you to leave," the battle-ax said through taut lips.

The senior ER doctor—Dr. Metcalf, Sam now read on
his tag—was right behind her. "We're taking your wife to
her room now. Did you reach your sister?"

Jules was looking at Sam with trepidation, as if he was a
complete stranger. He wasn't ready to leave, but Battle-Ax
and the doctor exchanged a look, and Sam knew he was
about to be tossed out.

"No . . . uh . . . my brother's missing. I think he was on
the boat with Jules. The coast guard's searching for him,
but—"

Battle-Ax interrupted, "Then check with the coast guard.
You can talk to your wife later."

Sam half expected Jules to set the record straight about
whom she was married to, but she'd closed her eyes and,
well, her pallor was ghostly. Scarily so. He allowed himself
to be ushered away from the ER's inner sanctum. He found
his way to the reception area where he picked up his cell
phone from Jan at the desk, a petite, older woman with gray-
ing hair stylishly cut. He thanked her, and the gods that had
found his phone and given it back to him. It was a bit sandy,
but turned right on. As he headed for the outside doors and
some privacy, he put through a call to the Tillamook Sheriff's
Department.

"Detective Savannah Dunbar," he requested of the
female dispatcher who'd answered the phone.

"Detective Dunbar's not here," she said. *Probably Brenda*,
Sam thought. He was familiar with a number of the

department employees. "Would you like someone else, or to leave a message?"

He stopped short at the sliding doors, which opened, then whispered shut again when he didn't walk through them. "How about Stone?" Sam asked, thinking of the other detective whom he was familiar with.

"Detective Stone is on another line. Would you like his voice mail?"

"Jesus Christ. Who's available, Brenda?" Sam snapped.

"Who is this?" she responded frostily.

"It's Ford. Sam Ford. My brother Joe's missing. Possibly in the ocean. A chopper's already been sent out, but I need to talk to someone. If it's not Dunbar or Stone, who the hell is there?"

"Deputy Hartman's on duty—"

"I need a *detective,* Brenda." He was practically shouting and it wasn't doing any good with her or the other people milling around. It wasn't like him to be so desperate, but this was his brother . . . whom he'd blown off when he'd asked for Sam's help . . . and now he was gone. *Missing*, he reminded himself. *Not gone.*

"Mr. Ford, could you please turn off your phone or go outside?" Jan asked loudly. Her earlier smile had disappeared completely.

He lifted an apologetic hand and headed through the exterior sliding doors as Brenda said, "I can contact the coast guard for you."

"Please. Yes. Thanks. And would you leave Detective Dunbar a message that Sam Ford called?"

"Yes."

He phoned Griff again, though it was more likely they would hear something through the Tillamook Sheriff's Department before the Seaside Police, based on the proximity of the boating accident. Griff answered, but knew nothing more than when Sam had called him earlier, since he wasn't on duty. Sam considered calling the Seaside Police Department, but the accident was too far south for them to be involved.

Stymied, Sam stared toward the western horizon. His pickup was still parked at the jetty lot. His head ached, but he could live with it. He was torn between wanting to get a ride to his vehicle and ignoring all protocol by returning inside to interview Jules again.

The one thing he wasn't going to do was go home and have his "sister" take care of him.

Chapter Two

After five minutes of deliberating with himself, Sam decided against going back into the hospital and fighting the red tape to see Jules again. Instead he called Griff right back and asked for a lift to his truck. It took his friend about thirty minutes to pick Sam up outside Emergency, and then he shot Sam a concerned look as they climbed into his black Tahoe.

"Jesus, man," Griff said, looking over Sam's bedraggled state. "What the hell happened?"

Sam's partner was about forty pounds overweight with a wide, approachable face and genial manner. He was a serial dater who really wanted to settle down with a wife and family, but the right woman hadn't crossed his path yet.

Briefly Sam's thoughts turned to his ex-wife, Martina Montgomery, and he grimaced. She hadn't been the right woman, either, and Sam had made the colossal mistake of getting involved with her when things were going sideways with Jules. He'd been young and stupid and impressionable, and Tina had radiated sex and availability. Jules had been involved with family problems and she and Sam had been at odds. He'd let himself be lured into a few dates with Tina, who was rich and sexy and ready to party. When Jules found out, she and Sam were through. Stung, Sam told himself that he'd dodged a bullet. He even half believed it, for a while. They all knew each other, having gone to rival high schools, and Tina and Jules had been on the same cheerleading squad. Sam's eye had initially landed on Jules, though Tina was flashier, but years later, one hot, summer night, he found himself sitting beside Tina in her BMW, the top down, coastal air making her red hair fly around her face as she drove him down the coastline. What started as trips in her car became makeout sessions behind Digby's Donut Shoppe, and from there to full-on sex atop the gearshift knob after Jules broke it off with him after he'd confessed to kissing Martina.

He'd been deep down angry. Selfishly angry. Jules's mother had some kind of early-onset mental disease that her father couldn't cope with, and Jules was doing all the heavy lifting, so to speak. She'd lost her only sibling, her brother, when he was little more than a toddler, so she was alone. Sam had initially tried to tell her the thing with Tina was nothing, but she let him know it was over. He wasn't there for her in her time of need, so she never wanted to see him again.

Her attitude had pissed him off and made him feel guilty. He kept seeking to salve his conscience and injured pride. Tina was somehow fascinated by his decision to go into law enforcement, something Jules never was. He told himself he was better off. He told himself that a romance that began in high school couldn't pass the test of time, completely ignoring the fact that high school was how he knew Tina. He and Jules had outgrown each other, that was all. So, he'd pushed aside memories of laughing with Jules, making love with Jules, sharing tender moments with Jules, and stuck with Martina.

And then Jules moved to Portland, and Sam, fresh out of the academy, returned to the beach, landing a job with the

Seaside Police Department. His mother had remarried and moved out of state long before, then kept her cancer a secret from both Sam and his brother until the very end of her life. Sam saw her once before she died, guilty as hell about not being there for her, though that's the way she'd wanted it. He'd determined he would make up for it by taking care of his father, who'd recently left the financial world, leaving a job in Portland for semiretirement in Seaside. Sam moved in with him at the cabin in the woods and quickly learned his father's mind was developing some strange quirks as well. Donald Ford became unreliable. One day completely in tune with the world and his place in it, another day lost in a wisping fog that he seemed to slide in and out of. Sam and Joe discussed the situation and Joe aided with Dad's care as best he could, given that he lived in Portland, he was still married to Gwen at that time, and he was buried in his fledgling financial business. Whenever Joe came to visit their father he would talk with him about business and finance, which always perked Donald up, nearly seemed to bring him back, in fact. But when Joe would leave, the on-again, off-again nature of their father's condition returned, and the job of caring for their father mostly fell on Sam's shoulders. Ironically, he was in the same position Jules had been when they broke up because he was the one who stayed.

Stitch it on a sampler, write it as an epitaph: *I was the one who stayed.*

Now Donald Ford was in an assisted living facility and Joe was missing . . . maybe even dead.

"Got wrapped up in the rescue," Sam said shortly, staring through the windshield. His clothes stuck to his skin and his shoes squelched when he walked, but he had other things to worry about than minor discomfort.

"The boat? Whose was it?"

"Don't know yet."

"But you got an idea."

"Not anything I want to talk about."

"Suit yourself." Griff lapsed into injured silence.

They pulled up to the jetty twenty minutes later. Griff parked near Sam's dusty pickup, then leaned an arm on the steering wheel and turned to stare hard at him. "Gimme something here, old friend."

"I can't yet, Griff. Sorry. It may be . . . my brother's boat."

He whistled. "Oh, shit, man."

"I don't know yet. I just want to figure things out."

"You need any help from me, just ask."

"Thanks."

"Is your brother . . . okay?"

"Griff, I don't know." Sam reached for the passenger door handle.

He nodded, but his curiosity couldn't be contained. "And the wife?"

Griff didn't know all the ups and downs of Sam's history with Jules St. James Ford, but he was aware that Jules and Sam had once dated. "I'll let you know as soon as I have more confirmation."

"Okay . . . You going back to the cabin?"

"After I hear about the boat."

Sam thought about Jules, her white, frightened face. What had she seen? Why wouldn't she tell him?

Why did you ever let her go?

With an effort he dragged his thoughts from Jules and immediately thought of his ex-wife. Martina Montgomery Ford, a beautiful, expensive mistake. She'd damn near sucked the life out of him during their short-lived marriage, and once it was over she quickly returned to the circle of her own wealthy kind, while Sam breathed a sigh of relief. Whatever he'd thought he'd seen in her, all the shallow pieces that had seemed so important in high school, popularity being top on the list—*if all your friends want her, she must be worth having, right?*—proved to be as insubstantial as dreams. Tina was beautiful, haughty, and mean spirited, and never had enough. Her parents had received Sam into the family with open arms, which had surprised him because his own family was several tiers down the financial ladder from their upper echelon social circle, but he'd learned soon enough that their happiness was because they were glad someone had taken her off their hands. When the marriage ended, they actually sheepishly apologized, in their way. They'd known what a workout their daughter was, hadn't told him—not that it would have mattered, probably, because he'd made his choice and was damn well sticking to it, by God—and subsequently felt guilty about it.

He didn't blame the Montgomerys. He actually liked Conrad and Cecile, even now. He might have stayed friends with them, but Tina had made them choose—her or Sam. They'd really had no option, and so that door had been closed to him. But by then he'd had his own issues to deal with anyway—his mother's death and his father's decline—and was too busy putting out fires to worry about it too much. He'd let the friendship lapse, and in a strange twist of fate, it was Joe who'd connected with the Montgomerys through his business, and they'd become his clients.

He got my girlfriend, and my ex-wife's family.

But you were the one who let Jules go. . . .

Sam reached for the passenger door handle as Griff asked, "Not planning any more swims in the ocean, are you?"

Sam shook his head. Griff was just one of those guys who loved to talk, and Sam wasn't ready to tell him about Jules, or his fears over his brother, because he wouldn't keep it to himself. The news would be out as soon as the media got hold of the story.

"It was a rescue, right? Not a recovery," Griff tried again.

A recovery . . . The idea made Sam's gut tighten. "A rescue, so far. I'll tell you more as I learn it."

"Okay, good. I'm going to be lifting a few at the Seagull, in case you decide to join me later. Get some dry clothes. You make me cold just looking at you."

"I will. Thanks."

"And don't mess with a head injury, Sammy." His gaze took in the side of Sam's head. "You should have Sadie look at you. I could tell her to stop by the cabin later, if that's where you're headed."

"Thanks, I saw a doc. I'm all right."

Sadie McClesky was Griff's older sister, who had a way of undressing Sam with her eyes, whenever he saw her. She was tall, blond, and severe, and Sam steered clear of her as a matter of course. He always fell for a certain type: slim, athletic, beautiful, smart, and sexy. But there was more that he wanted, too—a warm smile, a sense of humor, compassion. Tina had failed all of those last ones; Dannella, most of them. Like Griff's sister, Sadie, both his ex-wife and his ex-girlfriend were determinedly and doggedly on their own paths to achieve whatever goals they felt were paramount. Tina wanted money, social standing, respect, and a husband to float on her arm, and Dannella wanted marriage, a family, and maybe also social standing and wealth. He figured they'd picked him because they liked the look of him, and only later decided he wasn't really checking all the right boxes.

Griff finally gave up and turned out of the lot as Sam swung himself into his Chevy pickup and backed it away from the jetty. His headache was a dull pain that was manageable. Instead of taking Griff's advice, he drove straight to his brother's house again. He did not have a key, but on his first trip he had seen that there was a window partially open in the back. He didn't much like the idea of crawling inside in view of all the neighbors who lived across the narrow inlet, but one of them had already thought he was

Joe, so maybe he could get away with that, if anyone was looking.

He slid the window all the way back. It moved smoothly, and Sam wasn't surprised. Joe was tidy and careful and kept things in good working order, whereas Sam had a tendency to go by the seat of his pants. He wasn't as organized as his brother in any way. He operated on gut instinct and a kind of management by crisis, which worked for him, but had been another of Dannella's many complaints.

He climbed through the kitchen window and had to lever himself onto the counter and then down to the tile floor. The kitchen was white and gray: white painted cabinets, white counter, stainless steel appliances, and gray slate on the floor. There was a vase of maize flowers on the peninsula that separated the kitchen from the dining nook. It looked like someone had moved the sunny flowers from the center of the white melamine table, as there were also several light gold votives shifted as well. A pen had dropped to the slate floor, along with a piece of scratch paper that Sam picked up. A sticky note, as it turned out, that simply read: "Cardaman file."

The name was familiar. Ike Cardaman had been arrested for financial improprieties. He was in the same business as Joe, but unlike Sam's brother, Cardaman had played fast and loose with the legalities and wound up in jail, and there were scads of people who'd lost their savings as a result.

Sam walked into the living room and sat down on the couch. His shirt had dried and his jeans were getting there. He slipped out of his shoes, then pulled out his phone, setting the timer for twenty minutes. He just needed to lie down for a while.

It felt like he'd just closed his eyes when his phone rang. Not the alarm, but the loud and jingly default ringtone. Sam had to lift his head to remember where he was. He threw a hand out for the trilling phone, snatching it up from where he'd left it on the coffee table. "Hello?"

"Mr. Ford? Langdon Stone from the Tillamook Sheriff's Department. I understand you called for Detective Dunbar earlier. She's not in today."

The other detective from the TSD. Sam had met Stone a number of times before. The last time he'd seen him was when he'd interviewed at the Sheriff's Department. Stone had been friendly enough. A compatriot, of sorts. So, his formal tone now made Sam's heart clutch a bit. "I called about the boat that caught fire this afternoon . . . you know whose it was?"

"Haven't had that confirmation yet."

Stone's careful tone told Sam he knew something, though, something he just wasn't saying. Time to lay it out for the detective and get some answers. "I'm looking for my brother, Joseph Ford. His boat's missing and his wife's in the hospital. I found her on the beach. Joe's boat is *The Derring-Do*."

There was a hesitation. Sam counted his own heartbeats. This was not good.

Stone said soberly, "The coast guard picked up a male body in the bay."

A body. Not a living person.

Recovery . . .

Sam closed his eyes and swallowed hard. He climbed to his feet and walked a bit unsteadily toward the white table, staring out across the inlet toward the other houses' back decks, seeing nothing but his brother's stern visage imprinted on his retina. "It's Joe?"

"Not confirmed yet. The body wasn't near the boat that caught fire. It was closer to shore."

"Is that body at the county morgue?"

"Yes." Another hesitation. "I may ask you to come in and identify it. I'll call you back soon."

"Okay," Sam managed to get out, then pressed the off button. He didn't need to wait to hear more about the body from Stone. The recovered body was Joe. He knew it. Had known it from the moment he'd first smelled the drifting smoke and seen the burning boat on the horizon. Had understood the danger in his brother's careful text even before that.

Meet me at my dock at noon.

Not Joe's regular way.

Sam put on his damp sneakers and drove back toward the hospital especially carefully, even though every nerve was screaming at him to *hurry, hurry, hurry.* But he ignored the signals. There was no hurry anymore. Joe was gone.

A man in blue scrubs was pushing a cart loaded with covered meal trays down the hall as Sam walked to the reception desk. It was dinnertime. Sam knew he, too, needed to eat, but he had no appetite.

"What room is Jules . . . er, Julia . . . Ford in?" he asked the woman at the desk.

She didn't have to check her computer as she said, "Two-twenty-one. It's down this hall and—" She cut herself off then, her eyes on the monitor. She'd been pointing to a hallway that veered toward the right, but abruptly dropped her arm. "I'm sorry. She has a limited visitor list," she apologized. "I didn't see that at first. What's your name?"

His instinct was to lie, but he decided to play it straight. "Samuel Ford."

Her brows knit together. "You're a relative?"

"Her brother-in-law."

"They're only allowing family, but I don't have your name on the list."

"I was with her when she was brought in. Dr. Metcalf saw us both."

"Let me call Roxanne. I think she's still here." She punched in a number and conferred with someone on the other end.

Sam had the room number, but he waited while she ran through her protocol. Apparently Roxanne was unavailable, and the woman asked Sam if he would take a seat while she made further calls.

Sam agreed, but when someone else walked up to the desk and shielded him from her direct vision, he slid out of range and headed in the direction she'd pointed, looking for room two-twenty-one.

He found it easily enough. There was a security guard posted outside, currently in conference with a doctor. He walked past them down the hall, catching a bit of their conversation.

". . . who put you in charge?" the young Asian doctor with the stern look was asking.

The guard was also young, Hispanic, and wore the same stern look. "Tillamook County Sheriff's Department."

"Specifically? Could you give me a name, please?"

"Will Detective Langdon Stone do it for you, Doc? You can call and talk to him if you want."

The doctor bristled and Sam moved on, bypassing this little war of authority. The fact that Jules had a guard and was on a limited visitor list told him there were questions about the boating accident.

What the hell had happened out on the water? Why had Joe asked Sam to meet him?

With a heavy heart, Sam decided to take a pass on fighting it out with the guard just now. He chose a different corridor and turned back to the main reception room of the hospital, crossing in front of the desk and heading out through the sliding doors to a cloudy July evening, now heavy with the threat of rain. He climbed into his truck and sat behind the wheel, his mind full of questions, his thoughts ping-ponging all over the place. Leaning back on his spine, he let his chin drop to his chest. He was still tired. His whole body was shutting down. He suspected Joe was dead and he couldn't grasp it. A lot of guilt mixed in with sadness and an overall feeling of low-grade dread. Something was very wrong. Something he should have prevented.

He pictured his brother: tall, tough, with a rare smile that occasionally broke through, shining like the sun after days of rain. But he couldn't hold the thought, wouldn't take the trip down memory lane. It was too raw.

Instead his mind shifted to Jules. Easier to focus on her. How he'd tried to forget her. How much he'd hated her for marrying Joe. How she'd never left his thoughts even when he'd tried desperately to forget about her for his own well-being.

No good thinking about Joe. Better to think about his first love. Easier. Julia . . . Jules . . .

He'd met her a million years ago at a high school football game. A rivalry between her school and his. He'd been standing on the sidelines, ostensibly watching the game but mostly looking at her . . . and yes, Martina, too. There were other Triton cheerleaders jumping around on the sidelines, but it was Jules Sam had been drawn to. He learned enough about her to know that her name was Julia and all the kids called her Jules, that her family was as wealthy as the Hapstells and Montgomerys, who owned most everything from Seaside to Tillamook and beyond, and that she looked damn good in a tight sweater.

He watched as she leapt into the air screaming for her team, wearing black and gold, her school colors, her dark hair pulled into a high ponytail and fastened by a shiny gold ribbon. Beneath her Triton sweater her breasts bobbed up and down. Nice breasts. He could imagine cupping his hand around one. He told himself to stop fantasizing, but he couldn't pull his gaze away.

She and the other cheerleaders were a tight band of girls in sweaters and short, pleated, black skirts with gold insets, leggings, and sneakers. Football season. An orange October moon hung low over the blaringly bright stands. The crowd was roaring with glee because the Tritons had pulled ahead. Not for long, though. Their rivals, the Hawks, Sam's team, hadn't lost one game this season and everyone at his school constantly bragged about how they could easily play a division higher. That was a total no-go, he knew, but the Hawks were a whole helluva lot better than the Tritons. So far Jules's team had just gotten lucky.

Sam was a football player himself and just the month before he'd been a running back. But then his own teammate, Brady Delacourt, had lumbered into him just as Sam was dodging a tackle. Brady's two hundred and fifty plus pounds had collapsed onto Sam's ankle, crumpling it, ripping tendons and cracking bone. Sam had been sidelined on crutches ever since and there was no hope that Jules St. James would notice him. There was no chance anyway. Everyone in both schools knew she was Walter Hapstell Junior's girl. Hapstell was the Triton quarterback and though their team was just a shade or two above mediocre, "Hap" was the best player on it. Good enough to play college ball, maybe. He was also a wealthy son of a bitch, the Hapstells being in the same league as both Martina Montgomery's family and Jules's.

Not that Sam Ford gave a damn about any of that, but it was just a known thing. Something the guys talked about in passing. "Hap's loaded," was the general consensus. Sam knew who had money at his school as well. Brady's family, the Delacourts, were right up there. There were no secrets along this section of the Oregon coastline. The fact that most of the wealthy families sent their children to the local high school rather than the nearest private school in Portland, a good two hours away, just proved good parenting, according to the locals.

Sam had learned all about the Hapstells and Montgomerys from his father. Donald Ford had been a one-time stockbroker and financial advisor who'd quit that slugfest, as he called it, for a simpler life away from Portland and the hubbub of investments and finance. He'd followed his dream to "retire" to the coast, keeping only a few clients whom he'd advised up until just a few years earlier. That was about the time Sam's mother divorced him and moved away. Joe had already chosen the financial road their father had veered from, living in Portland and working on making his own fortune. He was eight years older than Sam and engaged to be married to Gwen, a woman with a toddler from a previous marriage.

Sam had been in his last year of high school and found it hard to imagine what it would be like to settle down with a woman and begin a life together. At the time all he could think about was sex . . . and Jules St. James . . . and maybe that haughty bitch, Martina Montgomery . . . and sex, and sex, and sex. Sam had wondered if Jules was doing it with Hap, and it made him feel slightly ill whenever he thought of them together.

As he watched from the sidelines that night, his eyes had strayed from the cheerleaders back to the game. Walter Hapstell Junior was running backward with the football held high aloft as he looked for a receiver to pass to. Sam was on Hap's left side, and he saw the wide receiver, number eighty-eight, break right. At the same moment Hap threw a bullet to the receiver, who caught it in a wild reach toward the sky that sent the Triton fans stamping the bleachers and screaming with excitement as the receiver pulled it in and ran another twenty-five yards, making it to the ten-yard line before being brought down.

Great catch. Mostly because of a great throw.

"Damn," he muttered to the fates, looking down at the cast around his right ankle.

But on the next play the Triton running back fumbled the ball and it was the Hawks' ball. Hap looked ready to have an aneurysm as he strode stiffly off the field, hands clenched.

The Triton cheerleaders were huddled together, colluding with a couple of guys dressed in similar outfits. Honorary cheerleaders? They'd only just appeared and the game was well into the second half. The newcomers arranged themselves to hike the girls into the air, offering their threaded palms as a launch pad. Sam watched as Jules placed her hands on the two tallest guys' shoulders and stepped into one of their woven fingers. The male cheerleaders hefted her up to their chests, their taut arms holding her in place, her fingers linked through theirs. Sam swallowed at the thought of what they might be able to see beneath that short skirt once they tossed her skyward, as they were preparing to do.

Then she was in the air, twirling twice, her arms hugging her torso, her body rising to the crest of the parabola before falling back, down, down, down, then caught neatly in one of the spotters' arms, a tall boy with Michael Phelps arms. He swung her to her feet and she bounced onto her toes, raining a bright grin of thanks on him.

Sam dragged his eyes away from her with an effort, concentrating back on the game. The Hawks' quarterback, Tim Stanton, threw a shovel pass to the running back who'd taken over for Sam. Sam gritted his teeth as the guy tucked the ball from Stanton and ran over ten yards for a first down. The two of them made two more first downs, and then they were at the fifty-yard line, marching down the field. It was hard for Sam to acknowledge that the team didn't need him, that the sophomore who'd taken over for him was as good as he had ever been, but hey, that was the nature of the game. Didn't mean he had to like it.

Sam could feel the momentum going the Hawks' way, and he was just sorry he wasn't a part of it. The Tritons were losing ground and desperately trying to halt the Hawks' relentless attack, but it was no use.

Less than a minute later the Hawks scored a touchdown on a quarterback sneak and the score grew to 28–10.

Not enough time for the Tritons to recover. That, however, didn't faze the Triton cheerleaders, who were shouting and furiously shaking their gold pom-poms.

What would it be like to kiss Jules St. James? he wondered.

"Sam."

He looked around to see Zoey Rivera smiling at him. She was cute. One of the cutest girls at Oceanlake High, and she'd never shown him the slightest interest.

"Hi, Zoey."

"You going to the party tonight?"

"What party?"

"Come on." She slapped at him playfully. "At the Hapstells'."

Sam gave her a long look. What was this? "Not on the invite list."

"No one's on the invite list. There is no invite list. All ya gotta do is bring something to drink, and I don't mean Red Bull . . . unless it's got a little extra kick to it."

"Where are the parents?" he asked, figuring if there was a party, Mr. and Mrs. Hapstell were unlikely to be on the premises.

She shrugged. "Not home. Everybody's going. You gotta come."

He nodded toward the scoreboard. "You think Tritons are going to want some Hawks around after this?"

"Who cares? Just want to get drunk, you know? Come on, Sammy. Let's go together."

He hardly knew what to think. She'd never shown him the least little bit of interest. She was too pretty, too petite, too popular. And yes, he'd felt her gaze on him a time or two, but she had an on-again, off-again relationship with a college guy two years Sam's senior, and he'd steered clear of her. Some girls were trouble. You just knew it, and the best thing to do was to avoid them. Zoey was one of those.

He held out his palms apologetically and looked down at the cast on his foot. "Sorry. I can't drive. Getting picked up by my brother."

"You have a brother?"

"A lot older than me."

"Maybe he'd take us," she suggested hopefully.

"A *lot* older," he reiterated. "Almost like a parent older. He's just here for the weekend."

"No fun," she murmured, but she didn't go away. She watched the final few minutes of the game at his side, mostly looking at her cell phone, but when the Hawks' cheers filled the stadium after their predicted win, she clicked off and turned to him again with a smile.

"So, I'm on the outs with Byron," she said. "He thinks I was with Rafe Stevenson. You know him?"

Sam nodded. Rafe was a Hawks lineman. He glanced back toward the now empty field. Rafe was a big guy. One of the biggest on the team. Sam suspected that Byron wouldn't mess with Rafe, even if he was supposedly seeing his girl.

"So, take me to the party. I don't want to walk in alone. It would be nice to be with someone who . . ." Here, she stumbled, and Sam waited, pretty sure they were going to get to the crux of things. "Well, you're hurt. And you're not on the team anymore, so it would be okay."

Ah . . . he wasn't a threat. He was on crutches and he was no longer a Hawks football player. He'd been neutralized by Brady Delacourt's crushing friendly fire, so now he was a safe guy to show up with. It should have pissed him off, but it mostly amused him.

"You'd have to drive," he told her.

"No problem." Zoey beamed at him. "And I've got a

surprise for you. A fifth of Grey Goose under the seat. We can drink it together."

"Grey Goose."

"Yeah, the good stuff. Byron got it for me months ago and we were supposed to celebrate together tonight, but now that's all shit." She added a little too brightly, "It's our six-month anniversary, but it looks like I'm going to be spending it alone."

Sam pulled out his cell phone and phoned Joe to tell him he'd made other plans. His father had insisted he come home right after the game because they were leaving early the next morning to drive to Seattle to look at the University of Washington, but though Sam had reluctantly agreed to the stipulation, he had no interest in U-Dub or college or pretty much anything at the moment. So, he was going to call Joe off, who was staying at their dad's place with Gwen for a couple of nights, an impromptu trip for a weekend at the beach, even though the Ford cabin was really nestled in the Coast Range foothills.

Joe answered on the second ring. "You ready?"

"Uh, no. I think I'm going to hang out with some friends."

"Dad won't like it," he said, but there was a faint tone of amused conspiracy to his voice.

"I'm not going to U-Dub. I won't get in, and I'm not going anyway."

"You need to tell him that."

"He knows it already," Sam snapped. Zoey was right there, able to hear every word, so he said with more restraint, "I'll get a ride home so you don't have to pick me up."

"Dad'll be calling you," he warned.

"Fob him off somehow, okay? Better yet, tell him the truth. If I go to college, it'll be in state, not Washington or anywhere else."

"If?"

"Yeah, *if*," he declared, then hung up.

"I'm going to Oregon," Zoey offered.

Sam nodded but didn't respond. He was interested in law enforcement and was thinking of applying at an academy in Salem, about an hour's drive from Portland. He wasn't convinced campus life of the ilk available at the University of Oregon or Oregon State, or any number of large colleges, was really for him. As an alternate plan he was thinking of Portland State, a commuter school in the heart of Oregon's largest city. He had a vague plan to see if he could live with his brother and his soon-to-be wife, but one way or another he was going to follow his own path.

He walked beside Zoey to the parking lot and her car amid a tide of happy Hawks and disappointed Tritons. Several guys called out to Zoey, asking about Byron, but she simply smiled and shrugged. Her ride was a Mercedes sedan. "My parents'," she told him as Sam slid his crutches through the back door and across the seats. He then worked his way into the passenger seat as Zoey switched on the ignition.

"I still love Byron," she said plaintively. "And don't believe anything you've heard about me and Rafe. It's a bunch of lies." She drove onto Highway 101 and began heading north up the coast. "I didn't have sex with him. I mean, not everything," she amended, as if he'd asked for a complete confession.

"Not my business," Sam said.

"Bullshit. Everything's everybody's business. You know how it goes at school. God, I can't wait for college. So sick of it."

He was mildly surprised. Zoey seemed to be the girl from his school who had it all.

The Hapstells, Montgomerys, and St. Jameses lived along a curving stretch of beach that had once been summer cabins but had slowly changed over to McMansions with yards that turned into sand and surf, those cabins having

been bought up by Walter Hapstell Senior, who'd split the
lots and filled them to capacity with monster homes, dou-
bling the original capacity. Sam's father had said Hapstell was
doing the same thing in Portland, where large residential lots
were being subdivided much to the fury and freak-out of
old-time residents who were desperately trying to keep their
neighborhoods from losing their character. Across the city
there was much local teeth gnashing over the teardown of
rambling ranch homes and daylight basements to make way
for two multistory houses on each lot, homes that ate up
most of the acreage, turning streets into lines of tall, expensive, look-alike boxes, making the area resemble a planned
community. This did not go over with the city's obsessive
desire to be unique, but Walter Hapstell Senior didn't give
a shit about that and kept on bulldozing ahead, also according to Donald Ford, and would continue to do so until there
was a law against what he was doing.

Zoey slowed and turned off the highway. The Hapstells'
home outside Seaside was down a private drive lined by sea
grass and trees so tortured by stiff ocean winds they looked
like gnarled old men bent at the waist, desperately stretching toward something just beyond reach. At the end of the
drive lay a wide parking area currently choked with cars
parked every which way.

"Hmmm," Zoey said, trying to make another spot at the
edge of a sandy ledge.

"If I were you I'd turn around, park somewhere else, and
walk back," Sam said. He was already rethinking his choice.
What would happen if they were arrested for underage
drinking? Maybe it wouldn't be an end to his desire to join
the force, but it sure wouldn't look good. And what did he
care about teen parties anyway? He just wanted to get laid.

At that moment Jules herself bounced into view, ponytail
swinging as she whipped around the front of the house and
down the side at a run. She was no longer in cheerleading

gear. She wore tight blue jeans, sneakers without socks, and a gray sweater that came over her hips. At first he thought she was into some kind of high jinks, but the tension in her face said otherwise.

"Wait. Stop," Sam ordered.

"What?" Zoey asked. "Thought you wanted me to park somewhere else."

"Let me out first. I can't walk." He was already opening the door.

Zoey said, "Fuck," in a fuming voice as Sam stepped out, barely snagging his crutches from the backseat and slamming the door before Zoey hit the gas. As he stumbled backward to avoid being hit, the Mercedes squealed around and she headed back out as another car eased its way toward the house. They nearly collided and Zoey shrieked and the other driver swore at her. She slammed her foot to the accelerator and wheeled around the approaching BMW.

The cops'll be called, Sam thought, but he worked his way forward in the direction Jules had disappeared. Music was blasting from speakers on the second or third floor—it was hard to tell from his angle. Tom Petty's "American Girl."

He silently cursed his lumbering gait. And Brady Delacourt for causing it. And the whole set of circumstances that had brought him to the Hapstells' beachside home. He managed his way down a set of stone steps that curved around the house, hanging on to the wrought-iron handrail like a scared little girl, he was so unsteady on his feet, which pissed him off even more.

At the bottom was a stone patio and beyond and down about five feet, the beach itself. Sand had blown onto the rough stone surface and no one had bothered to sweep it away as kids from both schools, and probably more as well, crammed onto the outdoor furniture, sand and all, covering every inch of the patio. Loud voices and loud music drowned out the roar of the ocean, but the waves, black and frosted like icing, raced up hard-packed sand to lap ever closer to the revelers dancing on the slate surface.

At that moment Walter Hapstell Junior shouldered his way through the crowd from inside the house, his face set in a glower. "Damn it!" he screamed, trying to be heard above the noise. He faced the back of the house and looked upward to the second story, waving his arms madly. "Turn it down! Turn it all down!"

Sam followed his gaze to where a window was wide open and most of the music was blasting. The dancers on the patio weren't paying a lot of attention, but when the sound suddenly cut out, they protested loudly.

"Jesus, Hap," a swaying, drunk guy grumbled.

"Put it back on!" a girl yelled, which earned her a hard stare from Hap. She mumbled, "Just not as loud," then stumbled into a table and smacked her shin. "Shit!"

"Keep it off," Hap hollered up at the window. "You guys want to get raided? C'mon. Take it inside." He turned to a guy Sam recognized as one of the Triton running backs and said, "Get 'em outta here. And where the hell's Jules?"

Sam had thought she'd joined in with the partiers, but when the running back swept his arm toward the ocean, Sam turned to scan the dark sand. His heart began beating hard. The tide was coming in and it was black as pitch outside the range of the Hapstells' outdoor lighting. Where was she?

"Goddamn it," Hap growled. Sam glanced back at him. "She's pissed and probably doing something stupid," he added, shouldering his way past the running back and pushing at the mass of bodies trying to squeeze as one through the French doors.

Martina Montgomery, leaning against the rail, waved a hand at the crowd. She was wearing a red bikini top and low-cut jeans. "Somebody bring me a jacket before I freeze my ass off," she called.

A male voice answered suggestively, "Bring that ass over here. I'll keep it warm."

"Fuck you," she said on a smile, shivering.

Sam thought about giving her his jacket, but before he could negotiate the steps back upward, another guy was eagerly hauling a blanket from inside the house. He helped her wrap it around her shoulders and then she looked at him and pleaded, "And now do you think you could find me a drink?"

The guy immediately turned back to the house.

Sam focused his attention to the beach once more, trudging and stumbling down the short dune to the packed sand in search of Jules. He was immediately chased by an incoming wave, and he tried to keep away from its swift, wet water but was too ungainly. He damn near fell over trying to avoid the eager wave that soaked his sneaker, the cloth boot on his injured ankle, and the hem of his jeans.

With a sigh, he looked down the edge of the surf and saw nothing but dark waves and dark sand. In the light of day he knew he would be able to see a long stretch of beach. Glancing to his right, he wondered if she'd headed north instead of south. He kept looking both ways, and was about to give up, when he saw something ahead, in the ocean. Was that a person standing in the receding water? As he peered through the gloom, another larger wave charged forward.

"Jules?" he called, yelling over the rush of the ocean.

Movement. She tried to dash through the water toward him, but it was halfway up her calves. He sloshed awkwardly toward her through the now receding wave, hoping a big one wasn't on its heels. She let him come for about ten steps, then, when her bare feet were almost free of the water, she quickly pivoted away and began walking south.

"Wait! Jules!"

She was carrying her shoes and she stopped short for a

moment, looking back. "Who are you?" she demanded, the words sounding sharp but faint, snatched by the wind.

Sam was having a helluva time navigating, especially with the fits of gales that came off the ocean and damn near toppled him. "Name's Sam Ford," he called.

She waited, but he sensed she was ready to leap away from him. "Hap sent you to find me?"

He wasn't sure what answer she was looking for, so he settled on the truth. "No."

"You're not a Triton," she observed as he drew nearer. She seemed to be debating whether to leave him to his crutches and race away, or stick around and find out what he was about.

"No." He was close enough now to see the wariness in her eyes. "I'm a party crasher, I guess."

"What happened to you?" she asked, looking at his injured foot.

"Football."

"Really? Huh. What team are you on?"

"You played us tonight."

"You're a Hawk?" That seemed to take her aback. "How'd you get to the party so fast? You had to have gone to the hospital for that." She motioned to the soaked, cloth-wrapped ankle.

"This happened in an earlier game."

"Ahh. Well, your team still won."

"Yeah. I'm not as irreplaceable as I'd like to believe."

That netted him a fleeting smile. "So, how did you hear about this party?" she asked. "You and Hap friends?"

"I don't even know him."

"That makes two of us," she said with a grim smile. She hitched her chin back in the direction they'd just come. "The cops are going to come and I don't want to be any-where near that party."

"Then let's leave."

"That's what I was about to do."

"I'll come with you," he invited himself.

"You'd only slow me down—no offense. I've got a long way to go, and no cell phone. My father bought me one for Christmas and I dropped it in the toilet and so now I'm phoneless, and well . . . I gotta go."

"You walking home?" He knew her house wasn't that far from where they were standing.

"Nah . . . not yet. Too easy to find."

"You hiding from Hap?"

"You ask a lot of questions, Sam Ford."

He shrugged. Nothing much to say to that.

Jules looked past him to the north, toward Hap's house and her parents'. Then she continued in the opposite direction and Sam struggled to keep up with her.

"I don't want to go home yet," she admitted after a while. "I'd rather go up to the highway and get something to eat."

"Kind of a ways from any restaurant," Sam observed.

"Yeah . . . eventually someone'll come by that I know from the party and pick me up. Unless they're all busted."

"I'll come with you," Sam said. He had a phone and could make some calls, find someone to give them a ride somewhere, but he didn't want to give that away for fear she would use it to leave him and meet up with friends.

"Suit yourself, but I'm not waiting around." She picked up the pace and Sam gritted his teeth and kept up with her, though it was no mean trick. A frisky little wind was blowing off the ocean and whipping her ponytail to and fro, stinging Sam's eyes. Luckily for him, the wind threw sand at her as well, so she had to keep turning around, her eyes squinched shut.

"Damn sand," she said.

"Yeah," he said, but he really didn't care. When a particularly hard lash of sand hit them both, he said, "C'mere," and held his arms out, his crutches tucked beneath his armpits, offering her shelter.

She came without hesitation, which both surprised and delighted him. He could feel the warmth of her body as he wrapped his arms around her, balanced on one leg, the crutches teetering. They stayed that way for long minutes and in that time Sam decided in his teenaged heart that he was in love with Jules St. James.

Chapter Three

Ling-ling-ling-ling.

Sam's cell phone woke him from his reverie. He'd been sitting in his truck, hands loose on the wheel, focused unseeingly on the horizon, lost in memories. Now he witnessed stripes of orange light knifing through layers of gray clouds, the setting sun. It felt more like fall than summer. Or, maybe he just felt cold.

Glancing at the cell's screen, he saw it was the Tillamook County Sheriff's Department. Stone again. Dread ran through his veins. "Sam Ford," he answered.

"Stone here."

"The recovery . . . It's my brother, isn't it?"

Stone exhaled heavily. "We believe it's likely. The boat fire is under control and it is *The Derring-Do.* . . ."

Meet me at my dock at noon.

It was Joe's boat. He'd planned on taking it out. That's why he wanted Sam to meet him at his dock.

"We recovered a male body. It's at the morgue. I could meet you there."

Sam felt ill. His head ached. "I'll be there in half an hour," he said, realizing dully that he would have to let his father know about Joe sometime soon. Donald Ford was not in complete command of his wits, however, so Sam didn't know how much would actually penetrate into his functioning mind. He wasn't looking forward to trying to explain to his father that his eldest son was gone.

Later, he told himself.

He drove to the morgue with no memory of the trip. In fact, he didn't remember much of anything until he was at the hospital, in the basement, and shown into a cold, sterile room where a body lay on a stainless steel gurney, covered by a white sheet. Langdon Stone had been waiting for him and had led the way into a viewing area. An attendant in scrubs had lifted the sheet off the deceased person's head, and Sam stared down at the man's face for a long, long time. He could hear seconds ticking off inside his head, though there was no clock in the room.

Stone cleared his throat. "Is this your brother, Joseph Ford?"

Sam nodded slowly. "Yes. That's my brother." He swallowed. Still wanting to disbelieve. *God, Joe . . .*

"Cause of death?" he managed to get out.

"Drowning. There's a head injury, but the lungs were full of water. Do you want an autopsy?"

"No. I don't know. Not yet."

"The sheriff may order one if there's a question of foul play," Stone said, "so it might not be your choice."

"Yeah, I know." Sam turned away and headed toward the door. "I'll connect with the sheriff," he said over his shoulder.

Stone asked, "You okay? You want to sit down?"

"Nope."

"Where're you going?"

"To have a talk with my sister-in-law . . . and then my father."

* * *

She was dreaming.

It had been a beautiful day. She and her father were walking along the shore and had stumbled across a small collection of sea glass. Beautiful blues and teals and greens. A collector's dream. Nobody found much sea glass anymore. The practice of people burning and burying their trash in the sand had gone out with the days of recycling, and sea glass was mostly litter, forgotten pieces of glass honed and polished by the waves. Worthless. Abandoned. Still, the pieces were more precious than jewels to her. Absolutely gorgeous and good luck to boot.

She took her bounty home and showed her mother, who managed a weak smile, but didn't show much more emotion of any kind. She never did. Life had worn her down, like the sea glass, until there were no more edges, just smooth corners that let everything pour over them, nothing sticking.

Her good mood disappeared and she began to cry. Why was Mama always so distant? Why didn't she care? Dad cared. He took her everywhere and told her that she was his princess and she believed him. But what was wrong with Mama?

"She's sad," Dad said. "You understand."

Did she? She didn't think so. "She doesn't love me like you do."

"Of course she does. She just loved Clem. . . ."

More, she thought jealously. *Mama loved Clem more.* That stung, though she knew it to be the truth. Clement, her little brother, had been swept away by a sneaker wave and drowned. She had been there and screamed and screamed, but he was gone. She wanted to miss him now, but he'd been gone a long time and she scarcely remembered him. Still, it kind of made her mad that he was gone and Mama was still boo-hooing about him.

"I don't love her," she declared, and her father suddenly put his hand over her mouth and pressed it hard.

"Take it back," he told her sternly. "You take it back."

She screamed and screamed, but her voice was muffled by his strong fingers. She tried to remember why she'd been feeling so good, but all of that was gone. She just knew that Mama loved Clem more than her and it wasn't fair.

And then she was somewhere else. And Mama was there, except she wasn't. She was seated in a rocking chair but she wasn't moving. Her eyes were staring, staring, staring at something, but there was nothing there.

"Mama?" she asked, turning to look at whatever Mama was seeing. She saw the other side of their living room and through the window to the ocean. She squinched her eyes, struggling to see. Outside, way out at sea, a buoy with a red flag snapping in the wind, a warning that the wind was up. Was that a body out there? Was that an arm? Was someone *dead*?

Her eyes flew open and she gasped with fear. No more ocean. There was a television across the room, above her head, its blank eye staring in the dim room light, and blankets and a pillow and the smell of disinfectant. A hospital room?

Someone *was* dead.

Her hands covered her mouth. Her heart was beating madly. She saw the mound of her feet beneath the covers. She was in a hospital bed? Why? What had happened?

Beside her bed was a tray with a water glass and flexible straw. She reached for it with her right arm and a wrenching pain shot through her shoulder. Moaning, she dropped her arm, belatedly aware it was in some kind of sling. She was strapped to an intravenous line at the back of her left wrist. She followed the line with her eyes and wondered what fluid she was being fed. She was suspicious of hospitals, suspicious of doctors, ever since—

She blinked, froze in the act of reaching for the water glass with her left hand.

There was something niggling, twisting just outside her peripheral vision. Something about her dream?

She broke out in a cold sweat.

Outside the room she heard the clatter of a gurney or cafeteria cart. Soft conversation in hushed tones. The sound of approaching footsteps.

"Sir . . . sir!" A woman's voice called out and then bunny quick footsteps followed after a stronger, heavier tread.

It was a man's stride, she realized. Coming her way. Fear swam through her veins, and if she could've, she would have leapt to her feet and run out of the room. But she was tethered and she hurt all over, especially her head . . . and her shoulder.

A moment later a man blasted into her room, his clothes rumpled, his face haggard, his hair in need of a serious combing. It was a nice face. Concerned. Dark eyes searching for hers, though their color might have been a trick of the light, and a set, grim mouth, as if it were forcibly holding his lips together.

There was a twitch in her brain. A memory? It shut down so fast she wasn't sure it had even been real. And it was followed by a heavy weight that fell over her like an iron shroud.

"Hey," he said tautly.

A nurse shot into the room on his heels, her body stiff. "No one is allowed here unless their name is on the list!" she declared. "The guard just left for a moment. If you don't leave I'm calling the desk."

"I'm her brother-in-law," he growled. "If you want to kick me out, give it your best shot."

"The guard will be right back!"

"She's allowed family."

"You're not on the list!"

"I don't give a good goddamn. Put my name on it. Samuel Ford." His gaze swung back to the bed and he stared at her. "You're awake."

She tried to answer but the words wouldn't come. The nurse looked infuriated and anxious, ready to launch herself between this man and her bed. She could see the woman's valiant effort to pull herself together and it was anyone's guess if she would manage it.

The man was still staring at her hard, so she cleared her throat and managed a raspy, "Yes. I'm awake."

The nurse, after a tight moment of indecision, spun on her heel and marched back out the door.

"What happened?" he demanded.

She stared at him helplessly. Her brain hurt. The iron shroud had eased a bit, but the hovering gray mass seemed to be just over her right shoulder, affecting her thought. She tried to turn to look at it, but it disappeared. Pain shot through her skull. Something wrong there.

"Joe texted me to meet him at your dock at noon," the man was saying, "but he wasn't home. You took the boat out. Both of you. Why'd you go on the boat? Where were you going?"

His questions were rapid-fire and accompanied by sharp looks at the door, as if he were expecting the nurse to return with reinforcements.

She shifted position and her shoulder jabbed her. "I can't think," she murmured. The pain in her head was evolving into something harder, a hammering throb that was narrowing her vision. With a tortured inhale of breath, she closed her eyes.

"I know you don't want to talk to me, but we don't have a lot of time. Joe wanted me to meet him because something was wrong. Why did you take out the boat? How did it catch fire? Something happened, something dangerous? What started it?"

"Something dangerous," she repeated. That gray mass was behind her, reaching into her skull.

"And now Joe's . . . gone." He stopped, his voice tortured.

She lifted one lid a teensy bit. Gone? Did he mean *dead*?

"They're going to kick me out of here. I can already tell. Give me something to go on. Joe asked for my help, and I want to help him."

She squeezed her eyes shut tightly again. He kept saying Joe . . . *Joe*. . . .

"Was it just the two of you? Or was someone else there? Was it really an accident? How did it catch fire?"

The grayness converged on her, an enveloping cloud, muffling his voice.

"For God's sake, *what the hell happened?*"

His voice grew far away, disappearing. She wanted to help him. She really did. She tried to speak, but her breath was caught in her chest, her lungs ready to explode. She struggled with all her might, but all she got out was, "Who's Joe?" before she faded back into blessed twilight.

Sam stared down at his brother's wife in disbelief as the nurse with the grim countenance suddenly charged back into the room, accompanied by the previously missing guard. Sam let them hustle him out of the room without protest, mostly because Jules was unconscious again and he was too tired to fight. Seeing Joe's frozen face had knocked the stuffing out of him. Getting back to normal was going to take a while, and it didn't help that Jules wasn't tracking yet. Or, maybe she just didn't want to talk to him, for a whole lot of reasons. He got that, but he hadn't even gotten to say much about Joe before she'd retreated back into unconsciousness. It didn't bode well for the future.

The guard had been shooting questions at him, which he'd ignored. Now he held up his hands and cut in, "I'm her brother-in-law. I'm a cop . . . ex-Seaside PD. Call it in. Find out. But back the hell off."

"A cop," the guard repeated.

The nurse said, "This patient is under protection ordered by the Tillamook Sheriff's Dep—"

"Talk to Detective Langdon Stone from the Sheriff's Department," Sam snapped. "I was just with him at the county morgue. Identifying my brother's body."

That stopped them both for a moment. Then the guard said gruffly, "If that's true, we still need to see some ID."

Sam opened his wallet. "Take it all. I don't give a damn, but I need to find out what happened."

"The Sheriff's Department is sending someone to interview Mrs. Ford," Grim-face started in, but Sam didn't give a shit.

"I know Jules . . . Julia. I know her well."

That was the truth; at least it once was. He knew her mother was dead, a victim of a wasting mental disease, and that her father had jumped or fallen from a bridge over the Columbia River. Peter St. James had never learned to swim, was despondent over Jules's mother's passing, and had talked of joining her. One day he made good on that promise, plunging from the bridge into the river far below. Unfortunately, his body was never discovered, washed out to sea, which only added to Jules's grief and torment. Rudderless after her father's suicide, that's when she'd accepted Joe's offer of marriage.

At least that's what Sam told himself in his bitterest moments. He didn't want to believe she'd fallen in love with Joe, but maybe she had. Maybe he'd been just kidding himself all these years.

"I'm probably her closest next-of-kin," he said to the guard, who was still blocking his way.

"We'll wait until we hear from the Sheriff's Department," the nurse answered for him. She wasn't backing down.

The guard, however, was looking at Sam out of the corners of his eyes in a way that suggested he might be starting to realize he wasn't a threat to Jules's safety. The man didn't relax his vigil on her behalf, but something had subtly shifted.

At that moment rapid footsteps approached and a young, male doctor with an open lab coat that billowed out cape-like behind him entered the room. He glanced at Sam. "You're Mrs. Ford's next-of-kin?"

"She's my sister-in-law." He held out his hand. "Sam Ford."

"Ron Lillard," he said, offering a firm handshake as Sam read Dr. Ronald Lillard on the tan name tag pinned to his white coat. "We were instructed by the Sheriff's Department that a guard would be placed outside Mrs. Ford's room. Until we hear differently, no visitors are permitted. Not even family," he said as Sam opened his mouth to protest. "If you could come with me down the hall . . ." He held out an arm to Sam while pointing to the door with the other. "Maybe we can expedite you seeing your sister-in-law."

Sam wasn't going to get anywhere by bullying, so he let himself be led out of Jules's room and down the hall to where a couch and two chairs were clustered in an alcove around a square coffee table.

"She acted like she didn't remember Joe," Sam muttered, glancing from the doctor to the western windows where a half-moon was rising, a line of quivering moonlight visible against the ocean.

Lillard gestured to one of the chairs, but Sam shook his head. He didn't feel like sitting.

The doctor remained standing as well, glancing out the window to the small, well-lit quad below with its frame of sidewalks and benches surrounding a central fountain. A woman was sitting on a bench in the lamplight, staring down at the toes of her flip-flops as if she could decipher all of life's mysteries if she just tried hard enough.

"Your sister-in-law's had a head trauma," Lillard said. "I understand you're the one who found her."

"On the beach." He then spent a few minutes telling Lillard how he'd swum around the rock promontory to the secluded beach in order to reach her.

Lillard said, "You should rest, too."

"I know. But I'm not going to."

"Nothing's going to be accomplished tonight."

"Well, when can I talk to her? In the morning?"

"Possibly."

"Possibly?" Sam repeated, frustrated.

"The guard's there for her safety, but my main concern is your sister-in-law's continuing recovery."

"About that . . . how long will this 'amnesia' last?"

"She's had a trauma. A concussion. Give her a chance. She may not remember all the details of the accident that caused her injury. It happens that way a lot. She's still recovering and will be for a while."

"Okay, but how long does it *usually* take to remember?"

"She needs to heal. She's physically exhausted and may be unable to help you right away."

"My brother died, Doc. I need to know how this happened. Do you understand?"

"If I could help you, I would, and so would your sister-in-law," he said sincerely.

They stared at each other. Sam understood the doctor was being patient with him. He didn't want anyone to be patient with him. He wanted to hit something, or someone. He wanted to yell long and loud until his lungs gave out.

Instead he turned on his heel and stalked away.

* * *

The bar was full of city people taking a weekend at the beach. Lots of tank tops, bare midriffs, and flip-flops. The man idly watched a group of young women who were all from some sorority, he thought, as he could overhear snatches of their conversation: "Kappa" this, "Dee Gee" that, and "Phi" whatever the fuck. They were partying on like school was in session, not like it was the middle of summer. A tall, blonde woman with the broad shoulders of a swimmer and chlorine-stiff hair, probably from too many hours in a pool, pointed at another one and declared, "You can't beat last year's rush, you just can't! Carrie put on the best one ever." She smiled at another girl, who was shit-faced to the extreme.

The shit-faced girl—Carrie—responded with a deep nod that almost took her off her bar stool. "We got good pledges."

"Like I said. You can't beat that, Ingalls," Broad-shoulders said, still addressing the first girl.

"I wouldn't even try," Ingalls declared, smiling a bit uncertainly at Carrie. "Nobody beats Carrie when it comes to recruiting."

Both girls were clearly vying for Carrie's attention and endorsement, and he found the whole fake-lovefest interesting. Sorority girls, you had to love 'em. Carrie herself wasn't half as cute as Ingalls, or even Broad-shoulders for that matter.

Still, all those young women with half their clothes on . . . His cock twitched expectantly. He thought about screwing one of them senseless. He had a vision of taking one on the boat and down in the cabin. Her legs up over her head, her mouth open in an O of ecstasy. Moving in and out of her, watching her. Jesus . . . He had to shift in his seat to get comfortable again. He wondered if they would be interested. Maybe if he offered money? It was surprising how venal those hot little snatches could be.

Or . . . maybe he wouldn't have to ask? Just let one of the drunkest stumble off for a while and he might be able to talk her into his car.

Immediately he shut that thought down. He already had the hottest piece of ass available anytime he wanted it, so there was no need even to fantasize. He needed to drag his gaze away from that tight butt in the blue shorty-shorts that seemed to be beckoning.

With an effort he concentrated on his beer, cooling his thoughts. Besides, he'd discovered a better thrill than sex . . . killing . . . with a partner. And then sex. Hot, hard, no-holds-barred sex.

"Need somethin'?" the bartender asked, and he realized belatedly that he'd groaned.

"Nah."

The bartender gave him a knowing look—the asshole—then wandered down the bar toward the girls. He asked them the same question and they all ordered more, staggering toward the bar in a group. Damn. He knew he'd better pull it together when even the bartender could read his mind.

So, he turned his thoughts to when they'd killed Denny, letting himself relive every moment of the game they'd played on him. Man, he itched for another night like that one. In fact the need was swelling inside him as it had since last month when they'd taken him to the woods and doused the body with bleach. He knew it was probably too soon to go for another. Dangerous. Extremely dangerous . . . but goddamn, the rush . . .

He exhaled and took another long hit from his beer. Denny's body hadn't been discovered yet, so maybe they could pull off another one. Zero in on another victim. *Not victim*, he reminded himself with a grimace. *Friend.* Maybe they could find another friend to join in their fun. If they were lucky, maybe that friend would want to embrace the game, thinking it was make believe. That would really draw it out in a delicious, slow burn. That would be great, and it had happened once before, a few months before "running into" Denny, so he knew it could. That sly, little bitch who'd said she would fuck them both till they were sore for a price had thought she'd had them, not the other way around. She'd assumed they were a couple of dumb tourists.

Rest in peace, slut.

Thinking of her stirred his blood some more, and of their own volition his eyes traveled back to the coeds. The girls were well past the point of reason, yet the asshole bartender kept serving them. Maybe he was looking to get lucky himself.

Unfortunately his partner wasn't as eager to go for girls. She liked men. He'd watched her having sex with that guy with the big cock, a short guy but his tool was pretty damn impressive, he had to admit. But he wasn't interested in any male parts. Just not the way he was made. That mark had been chosen because he'd gotten in the way, too, just like Denny. They'd planned to just take care of him. No fun and games. Just a straight kill. But in the end they'd become Bridget and Tom for him, too, just because they could, and once he'd pulled his penis out of his jeans and she'd gotten a look at it . . . well, she just couldn't say no. She'd swung her gaze his way, silently asking, and he'd thought, fine. Go for it. So Bridget and Tom had taken the schmuck to a motel where she'd put him on his back and ridden him like a bucking Brahma bull. Just before they'd finished, Bridget had slipped a scarf around the dumb ass's neck and Tom had moved in on the guy, too. They'd strangled him together, watching his eyes pop wide, hearing his gasping breaths, feeling his desperate fingers clawing at theirs. Too late. His eyes had rolled back and he'd sunk into oblivion, but not before his last happy ending. Asphyxiation right at the time of climax! Man, he'd heard it didn't get any better than that. He'd like to try it himself, but the danger of going too far held him back. He wasn't interested in dying, and well . . . *Bridget* seemed a little too eager to help him out, and sometimes she kind of forgot who she really was.

And actually, he reminded himself again, she was all he really needed. She thrashed and moaned and screamed and clawed like the wild woman she was. Sometimes, just occasionally, Tom dreamed of snuffing her out, but he couldn't let that happen. He loved her too much.

He drew a breath and slowly exhaled it. The single most important thing was that they couldn't get caught. They had to be careful. And this one today—that had been pure business, no fun at all—was bound to stir up all kinds of notoriety. There was a connection to Denny, which could be trouble, but no one knew about Denny and if they were lucky, maybe never would.

Maybe they should have done a better job of burying Denny. The site was remote, but they'd left him in a kind of humped up mound. He felt anxious about it, and today's job hadn't assuaged any of that building anxiety. It had been strictly for the cash and he wasn't even sure how successful they'd been. Ford was dead. He'd made sure of that. But the wife . . .

He jiggled his knee and struggled not to snap his fingers, needing to release nervous energy. The sorority girls were now downing shots and dancing with each other. One had perched on the edge of a bar stool, the crotch of her Daisy Dukes wide enough for him to ascertain she was going commando. His cock, which had softened a bit, immediately *boinged* upward, painful in the constriction of his jeans. Damn. Where were the girl's panties, anyway? Didn't her mama raise her right? What the hell was wrong with the youth today?

His phone silently vibrated in his pocket, unexpectedly adding to the thrill. Annoyed, he yanked it out. "Yeah?"

"Where are you?"

It was her. His partner. The best piece of ass ever. "Waiting for you," he said, practically panting.

"Well, I've been a little busy," she snapped.

"I know."

"And you've been just . . . loafing?"

"Fuck, yeah," he retorted. "Just loafing around after swimming in the ocean for an hour and then hiking ten miles up the beach!"

"It wasn't ten miles," she said coolly.

"Close enough."

"I've been playing my part, keeping everything cool. Where are you now?"

"Seaside." He wasn't going to name the bar. Some things were his alone.

She sighed and her voice finally turned to a purr. "Maybe we need to meet at one of our rendezvous."

Oh, baby, yeah, he thought. Was it too dangerous, too close to the killing? They could just go back. They didn't need to risk having sex somewhere public. They *should* go back, he determined, but he heard himself ask, "Where?"

"Can't be anywhere on the coast."

"Where then?"

"The rest stop."

"That's fifty miles inland! You want to do it in the car again? There could be a lot of people around."

"Bring a blanket and we'll hit the woods." She was terse. He could hear her own expectation building in her voice and it made him want to groan again. "Better yet, I want you to lift me up while we're standing and settle me on that hot prick of yours. I'll wrap my legs around you and I'll slide up and down and we'll get all wet and sticky and howl at the moon and—"

"Goddamn it," he breathed, throwing some bills on the table for his beer.

He was out the door and unbuttoning the top of his jeans for relief, sporting one serious boner.

Chapter Four

Sam's eyes popped open and he stared around the dark bedroom in confusion. Once again he heard the tones of his default ring, something chimey that he needed to change but never got around to, and levered himself off the bed. He was in his bed at his dad's cabin—and he'd fallen asleep in the sweatshirt and pants he'd changed into after the long hot shower he'd taken when he got back from the hospital yesterday.

Ling-ling-llliiiinnnnnggg.

He ran his hand over the nightstand, knocking over a glass of water in the process, swearing to beat the band. It was early morning, by the time on the clock, but he'd drawn the blackout shades and it was still dark as a tomb inside the bedroom.

He switched on a bedside lamp, righted the water glass, only to realize he'd left his phone across the room on the dresser. Stumbling from the mattress, he lunged forward and grabbed up the cell. The house was a two-bedroom cabin with a loft where Joe, Gwen, and Gwen's daughter, Georgie, had slept the times the Ford family had gathered for the holidays. When Joe's first marriage broke up, he'd still shown up with Georgie, and then later with Jules. By that time Sam was with Martina and everyone being at the cabin together like one big, happy family was a no-go, though Donald acted like they should all get over it. Dad had always liked Jules and didn't seem to mind or even notice that Sam's onetime girlfriend was now with his oldest son. Donald's cavalier attitude had angered Sam, until he'd recognized there was something else at play with his father's mental faculties.

Now, whenever Sam visited his father they didn't talk about Joe, Jules, Georgie, or anything besides how Donald was getting along and if he needed anything. Sometimes Donald still talked on the phone about would-be financial deals, but those deals never materialized; they were just dreams and memories from a fading past.

Now Sam read the screen of his cell as he answered the call. Tillamook County Sheriff's Department. He steeled himself. "Hello?" He waited, then said, "Sam Ford," but he'd missed the connection. Sighing, he looked around the room and ran his hand through his hair, which was sticking up all over the place. A soft *ding* told him the caller had left a message. He then listened to his voice mail, surprised to realize the caller was Sheriff Vandra.

". . . come into the station this morning," the sheriff was saying, "to go over further developments in the case. Detective Dunbar is with your sister-in-law now. If you come in around eleven she should be back. The guard that was posted outside your sister-in-law's door . . . I want to talk about that, too." There was a slight hesitation, then he added somberly, "I'm very sorry about your brother."

Sam clicked off. Thought about Joe. Shook his head and concentrated on the here and now. So, Detective Dunbar was interviewing Jules. Well, maybe now they would let him see her. It kind of pissed him off that they were keeping him in the dark, even though he understood all the reasons. He was next of kin and therefore on a need-to-know basis only. But he was—or had been—a cop and he wanted to know everything that was going on. Every last goddamn detail.

He sopped up the spilled water then headed to the bathroom, stripped down, then stood under a hot, needle-sharp spray, needing to clear his head. After last night's shower he'd thrown on sweats and dropped onto the bed, asleep instantly, almost in a comalike state.

He remembered the therapist he'd briefly seen after his mother's death, the one he'd practically been forced to meet with by the Seaside Police Department after he'd beaten up a perp to an inch of his life after the man attacked him with a knife. "People handle grief in all sorts of ways," the shrink had told him. "Lucky for most, they aren't attacked, otherwise there could be a lot more tragedies."

Sam had listened silently and never offered up much. Grief. He understood he was in the throes of it, though what he mostly felt right now was numb.

Half an hour later he stepped into morning sunshine and climbed into the pickup, aware that he needed to go see his father and let him know about Joe before someone else did. Sam had pushed thoughts of his old man aside yesterday, but now he pulled out of the fir needle–covered lane that led to the highway and turned north rather than south to head to Sea and Sunset Retirement Living.

He fiddled with the radio for a moment, then turned it off. His head felt heavy and achy—no surprise there—and his body seemed like a stranger's. Definitely a disconnect going on inside him. His mind shied from thoughts of Joe, entirely. He felt guilty about being estranged from his brother, knowing a good percentage of the problem had been on his side.

Once more he went back to thinking about Jules. Far easier now, though it hadn't been while Joe was alive.

While Joe was alive . . . Past tense.

He just couldn't think about that now. Instead he thought of Jules. . . . Remembering. Whether he wanted to or not . . .

"We should get off the beach ASAP," he'd told her that first night when they'd been standing in that embrace, shielding their faces from the blowing sand. Sam had glanced toward the nearby houses at the top of the dune. It wouldn't be a terribly long walk up to the glass-fronted structures from here along the beach. From the homes they could take driveways to the highway, but the trek would be arduous with the fierce wind slinging gritty sand at them.

"I wish I hadn't ruined my phone," Jules said against his shoulder. "We could really use it now."

His cell phone was likely to burn a hole in his pocket, but no way was he reaching for it now, not with her warm body pressed to his. "You have any brothers or sisters?" he'd asked, deliberately changing the subject.

"Not anymore."

"What's that mean?"

"I had a brother once, but he's gone. . . ."

He'd waited for her to continue, but she just stopped. Vaguely, in a forgotten hallway in his mind, he remembered a rumor. Something about a kid who'd drowned when he was really little. Jules's sister or brother. When she didn't go on, he offered, "If you want to go somewhere, I have an older brother who's in town who could come pick us up."

"How're you going to reach him?"

"Well, I have a cell phone," he reluctantly confessed.

"What? You have a phone?" She pushed back from him at that and swiped at the hair escaping its ponytail and flying around her face.

"I was going to tell you. I just liked . . . like walking with you." It was lame, but the truth.

Jules had bent her head to keep further sand from getting into her eyes. He'd been afraid she was about to stalk away from him, pissed that he'd played such a dumb game. But all she said was, "This sand sucks!" Then she'd cupped her hands over her eyes and staggered forward toward the houses, aiming for a path between the two nearest ones. Sam struggled to follow after her, swearing in his mind at his ungainly gait. He was somewhat gratified when he caught up with her near the road, both of them hugging the cedar-shingled house that was sheltering them from the blasting, wind-propelled sand.

"So call your brother," she ordered. "Have him take us somewhere."

Us. "Okay."

"Let's go somewhere and get something to eat," she added, music to Sam's ears. He'd thought the night was over, but maybe not. Unfortunately he was pretty sure Joe would resent playing chauffeur unless he was bringing Sam home, like his dad wanted. But if it meant extending a little time with Jules, Sam was sure going to give it a try.

"I'll never get the sand out of my hair," she declared.

"You can be prematurely gray."

"Funny. You're a funny guy."

Sam was faintly embarrassed. It was a dumb line. He'd never been great with girls. He had no idea what they wanted to talk about.

"You got a lot of sand on your face," she observed.

He put a hand up to his cheek and felt the grit. Jules swiped at her own face and said, "God, I'm starving. French fries, huh?"

"Yeah."

Sam tried calling Joe but the cell rang and rang. "He's not answering."

"Then come on." She tucked her head down and headed away from their sheltered spot and toward the street. The wind howled and flung sand at them as they moved between two of the big houses. What had started as a breeze was fast becoming a gale. "Geez," Jules protested. "Wonder how Hap's party's going with all this."

"They've gotta all be inside now, so maybe the cops won't come."

"The house is gonna be a wreck. I told him he was an idiot, but he doesn't listen to me."

"You told Hap he was an idiot?"

"Maybe not those exact words, but . . . yeah," she said.

"You're going with him, though, right?"

"No. Not right. We just hang out. Who told you that?" She shot him a look.

"Guys on the team know who the cheerleaders are," he explained. "They talk about 'em and who they've hooked up with."

"Yeah? They said I was with Hap?"

"You're not?" he questioned.

"I don't know. Not really. All we do is fight about stuff. What else do the guys on the team say?"

"Just stuff."

"What stuff? About the cheerleaders?"

"Some."

"Well, what? Come on. Tell me!"

"They talk about your looks mostly, I guess. This one's cute. That one's tall. That one's got a great set of . . . she's got a great smile, personality, that stuff."

"A great set of . . . ?" she repeated.

"I don't know."

"Bullshit, Ford."

He was both delighted at the familiarity of his name on her lips, and worried that it sounded like she'd already relegated him to the friend zone. "A great set of legs."

"Sure. That's how guys talk. You were going to say 'boobs' or worse. . . ."

"No." But he had been. He'd cut himself off at the last minute.

"Don't lie."

"I'm not lying."

"Yes, you are."

"Okay, fine. Great boobs."

"They were talking about Jilly Dolittle or Tina Montgomery, I'll bet."

"Well . . . you got me."

"Double-D?" she asked, eyeing him as if searching for the truth.

He was a little embarrassed that she knew Jilly's nickname. "Well, you know how guys are."

"Yes, I do." Her tone was dry. "Do I have a nickname?"

He shook his head.

"Don't make me pull it all out of you."

"I've never heard a nickname for you," he told her seriously.

"Then make one up for me," she challenged.

"What?"

"Make one up for me. Right now. A good one. Not like Jilly's."

They were walking down the road, leaning into each other to keep the wind and sand out of their faces, yelling to be heard.

He looked into her eyes, dark, in the uncertain light, and watched her swipe hair from her face again. "Sandy," he said after a moment.

She broke out laughing. "Because of this?" She threw an arm out and they were peppered with grit. "I could call you the same thing!"

"Okay." He kinda liked it. "Glad to meet you, Sandy."

"Back at 'cha, Sandy." She grinned at him.

He was in love with that smile. He was in love with her.

"Try your brother again," she said.

"Sure."

He fumbled with getting his phone out of his pocket. When he put through the call it went directly to voice mail again. He tried once more with the same results. "He's not picking up. Maybe there's someone you can call?" he asked reluctantly, holding out the phone to her.

She considered for a moment, then shook her head. "Nah, let's just go for a while. Unless you're tired."

"Nope."

"There are some shops down that way." She pointed southward to where the road turned a corner and disappeared. Sam knew the area well and nodded as she added, "There's a restaurant that I think stays open late."

"The diner . . ." Sam said.

"Brest's." Jules laughed shortly. "Hap calls it Boobs. Every time we drive by. Like it's news, or something. 'Look, Jules. There's Boobs.'"

Sam's opinion of Walter Hapstell Junior dipped even further, though Hap wasn't the only one who called it that. Lots of guys did, himself included. Sam just didn't want to like Hap.

Jules headed down the road and Sam worked to keep up with her again.

"I've got about three dollars," she said.

"I've got a twenty."

"Well, then hobble a little faster, Sandy, and you can buy."

"You got it, Sandy."

And those were our nicknames right up until we split up.

He thought about that, the pain of it all and the outcome. God, it seemed like a million years ago . . . yet it felt like yesterday.

He'd hooked up with Tina after feeling ignored when Jules was dealing with her mother's illness. He'd felt like a heel—he *had* been a heel—and he'd then doubled down on his mistake by sticking with Tina, for no good reason he could think of now. A year into their relationship she'd wanted to marry him and that had finally woken him up. He'd tried to see Jules again, seeking . . . what? . . . some kind of absolution? The chance to repair what he'd broken? Maybe make things right?

Not a chance. It was déjà vu when he showed up at her parents' home; he'd stood in the same spot when they'd broken up and this time Jules had assessed him through the screen door, cool and disinterested. He knew she'd been seeing his brother, but he'd thought it was merely a friendship. Joe was not only in the same business as their father, he was in the same business as Peter St. James as well. It was only natural that he and Jules ran into each other.

By that time Jules's mother was in a deep, almost comatose state, and Peter, Joe, and Walter Hapstell Senior were working on several real estate deals both in Portland and in communities along the Oregon coast. Jules's father had thrown himself into his work, unable to deal with his wife's illness, so Jules was the one to help her.

"Congratulations," she'd announced to Sam through the screen, when he'd managed to choke out that he and Tina were talking marriage.

"It isn't decided," he assured her. "I just wanted to see you, and see how you are."

"Well, I'm just fine."

"You're taking care of your mom?"

"Yep."

"Is there any chance you and I could go out for coffee sometime? Talk over some stuff."

She stared at him a long moment. "Nope."

He'd flushed in embarrassment. He'd deserved everything she dished out, had pretty much expected it, but to see her and realize how little she cared about him, how clearly there was nothing left, had dug into his gut and heart. Somewhere inside he'd apparently harbored the hope that she could forgive him, that maybe they could be friends again, or something, but that was clearly not to be.

"Well, it was good seeing you again," he managed to force out as he turned away.

"Same," she said without inflection, then she closed the door.

A year later he and Tina were married. Right after that, Lena St. James passed away in her sleep. Six months later, Peter St. James left a good-bye note and then made his way to a bridge over the Columbia River. He spoke to a woman before he threw himself into the river, and she witnessed his fall, hysterically saying she thought he'd dived in. Sam's own marriage had begun its death spiral, and he was already heading for divorce court when Joe and Jules said their "I dos."

Now he exhaled heavily. Directly ahead was the familiar wooden sign, painted in tan, gray, and white, with sandpipers carved into its face, that always welcomed him to Sea and Sunset Retirement Living. He pulled into an asphalt parking lot that ran beneath a portico where a short bus with another sandpiper painted on its side was waiting for passengers. Sam parked in an empty spot that had writing painted into the asphalt: "For Future Sea and Sunset residents."

His father's studio unit was at the end of a short hall. A Lucite sleeve had been attached to the wall next to the door and the day's newspaper lay in its embrace. Sam pulled it out and looked at the headlines. BOATING ACCIDENT RESULTS IN DEATH.

Swallowing, he knocked on the door but didn't wait for it to be answered. "Dad?" he called as he stepped inside the room. The bathroom door was closed, the only other door in the room. He could hear his father inside, brushing his teeth. He walked farther into the room. His father's bedcovers were thrown back and his clothes from the night before tossed over the back of the visitor's chair, the only one in the room besides his dad's recliner. Sam perched on the cushion and opened the paper, scanning the article, his chest tight. The reporter did not name the victim, just described him as male, and there was no mention of Jules. Sam had a moment of new respect for the Sheriff's Department. They'd kept a lid on things.

And placing the guard outside Jules's room said something about the accident; they hadn't ruled out foul play.

Neither had Sam.

His father came out of the bathroom clad in a pair of striped pajamas that looked several sizes too big for him. The old man was shrinking. Age was shrinking him.

"Joe?" he asked in a voice that warbled slightly.

"It's Sam, Dad."

"Sam?"

"I came to see you. I want to talk to you."

Donald pulled back at Sam's serious tone and shuffled to his dark brown recliner. With a flap of his hand he motioned Sam to go on. Still holding the newspaper, Sam picked up the chair and positioned it directly in front of his father's. The old man was barely seventy, but he acted a decade older, maybe even more. His in-and-out dementia was so random that at times Sam thought he was faking. It just seemed a little too convenient sometimes, because his father tended to fade out whenever the discussion turned to something he didn't want to talk about.

"It's about Joe," Sam said, handing his father the paper.

"Are we going to breakfast?"

"No, Dad. I'm going to say this. I just need your attention."

"We have to eat sometime. I think I might be too late."

"Joe's dead, Dad. He died in that boating accident yesterday." Sam inclined his head toward the paper.

Confusion filled his father's face. He looked at the newspaper and his face drained of color. His mouth opened in shock. Then he closed his jaws with a snap and said angrily, "Joe was just here."

"Maybe yesterday . . . or the day before . . . not today. Because, Dad, he's gone. I went to the morgue yesterday and identified the body. I saw him and I . . ." The wave of emotion took Sam unawares, sweeping over him, drowning him.

His father's eyes moistened. "You're lying!" he cried, but he knew . . . he knew.

Sam swallowed several times. His chest was tight. His eyes burning.

Meet me at my dock at noon.

"I'm going to find out what happened," Sam stated. "I don't believe it was an accident and I'm going to prove it."

He hadn't known what he was going to say. The words just popped out of him, but once said, he knew they were right.

His father's jaw trembled, but then it grew rock hard. He shot Sam a hard look and said, "It's about the money."

"What?"

"It's about the money. They all think Joe swindled them, but he saved them. They killed him for it. They killed my boy."

Sam stared at his father. He seemed stone-cold sober and in the present. Sam almost didn't want to spoil the moment.

"You check with his partner," Donald said grimly. "If Joe's dead, like you say, then it's because of the money."

"His partner? In his company?" Sam asked with dread. He didn't like the sound of where this was going.

"That's right." He leaned forward conspiratorially. "And if you've invested with Joe, sell everything."

"I didn't know he had a partner."

Donald waved a dismissive hand. "Your friend. You know."

"Hapstell? He wasn't a friend. He was a—"

"That's the one," he interrupted.

"You always said not to have a partner," Sam reminded.

"I heard you say that a hundred times. I heard you tell Joe that."

"Partner, schmartner. They worked together, that's all. Did some deals. Sometimes you need money to make the deal work, even if it's a bargain with the devil." His face clouded over. "Sometimes you get burned."

Sam gazed at his father in a kind of suspended disbelief. His older brother had been the one who'd made good in Donald's eyes. It was Sam who was the screwup. Sam who'd chosen a career in law enforcement and not the heady, elite world of finance.

"I'm not invested with Joe. What about you?" Sam asked him.

"Joe pulled me out months ago. The cabin's free and clear, and I've got enough savings for this place." He sank back in his chair and turned his eyes toward the ceiling, staring for several minutes, then he let out a long, drawn out sigh and asked, "Why did you come by again?"

Sam was still processing his father's sudden sentience. Now he was snapped back to the moment. "You really don't remember?"

His father frowned. "Something about Joe?"

Sam got to his feet. "I came to tell you he died in a boating accident yesterday."

"Joe's dead?" His father gazed at him in horror.

Sam turned toward the door. He didn't know what to believe any longer. He saw a notepad and pencil on the small kitchen counter. Grabbing up both, he wrote: "Joe died in a boating accident yesterday." Then he added his cell phone number, signed it, and handed it to his father.

Donald stared down at the words as if committing them to memory. "Does Georgie know?" he asked.

"Not yet," Sam said. Georgie lived with Gwen in Portland. They needed to be informed, but Sam had wanted to tell his father first.

"What are you gonna do?"

"I don't know, Dad. I don't know what to think. But I'm going to find out why Joe died. I don't think it was an accident," he repeated.

This time his father was silent, and he seemed to shrink even further into himself. Sam asked him if he wanted to walk with him down to breakfast, but he shook his head and waved a hand to the counter where a stack of energy bars waited. Sam was too tired and his head too achy to argue the point.

He left a few moments later, reflecting that he couldn't trust that his father would even remember their conversation, and he hadn't had a hell of a lot of luck with Jules, either. Maybe today would be better.

His stomach rumbled, making him realize he couldn't go much longer without food. He drove out of Sea and Sunset Retirement Living and turned the pickup south, heading toward the Tillamook County Sheriff's Department. There was a McDonald's in Tillamook, if he could wait that long.

But then he spied the sign for Digby's Donut Shoppe and he wheeled into the lot for a cinnamon cruller or two to tide him over.

Chapter Five

She woke up slowly, cautiously, opening one eye first to test the surroundings. No one in her hospital room. She swallowed, focused on the fluid being dripped into her vein, and realized vaguely that she must have a catheter, otherwise she'd be wetting the bed, because it felt like days since—

Nothing.

Panicked, she told herself to calm down. Days since . . . the boating accident. There'd been an accident. The man with the nice eyes seemed familiar, but he'd said Joe was gone.

Joe.

Her head ached like a son of a bitch. Hurt worse when she attempted to recall anything. But a blistering thought blasted through the pain: *I can't remember anything!*

Not true, she told herself immediately. Not true. You know you're in a hospital and something happened to put you here. You know you've been hurt. You know you're a woman with brown hair and . . . freckles?

Who am I?

She cried out in shock, the sound seeming to echo off the walls. Fear ran like ice through her veins and she started shivering uncontrollably.

A young nurse peeked into the room and stared at her. "Did you want something, Julia?" she asked uncertainly. "You can push the button attached to the bed frame. Do you see it?" She stepped over to her right side and showed her the button inset into the white plastic box attached by a cord and wrapped around a bed rail to keep it from falling out of reach. "One of us will be here right away."

"Thank you."

You're polite. . . .

"No problem. Are you hungry? You've been sleeping awhile."

"Not really."

"We should get you something to eat. I'll check with Laura. She's the head ER nurse, but she wanted to know when you woke up."

"Okay."

The nurse disappeared and she lay back and stared at the ceiling, working hard to keep full-blown panic at bay. *You're passive. Accepting. Even though you want to scream your head off that something's very, very wrong, you keep quiet. You're scared to death because you can't remember anything, even your OWN NAME.*

"Julia," she whispered aloud. That's what the nurse had called her. Julia.

Ju . . . li . . . a.

Heart beating fast, she ran the name around in her head, but nothing clicked. He'd said he was her brother-in-law. Was she married? Did she have a sister and he was her husband? What was the connection?

Tears formed in her eyes and she buried her face in her pillow and cried softly, not wanting any of the staff to come to her aid and ask too many questions. *You're private . . . you may have secrets. . . .*

What had he said? Sam Ford. The man who claimed to be her brother-in-law?

You have to talk to me . . . don't have a lot of time . . . Joe wanted me to meet him . . . something dangerous . . . how did the boat catch fire? . . . were you and Joe alone? . . . was someone else there . . . ?

Something shifted in her mind and she strained to reach for it, increasing her headache till she had to stop and cover her head with her hands. She encountered a bandage, wrapping half her head. *Oh, God. What do I look like?*

Moments passed and she worked hard to pull her emotions under control. Her own thoughts resonated through her brain.

What do I look like? Brown hair . . . freckles?

That's all I remember? That's it? she asked herself, feeling suddenly furious. *That's IT?*

She turned her head to spy the call button, reached forward and pressed it. A few minutes later the young nurse returned. "We have scrambled eggs with ham this morning. It's pretty good. I'm going to bring you a tray as soon as I can."

"I'd like a mirror."

The nurse inclined her head toward the full-length cupboard that was mounted on the wall by the door. "There's a mirror on the inside of your closet." She walked over to it and pulled open the door. A mirror was indeed hung on the inside of the door, but from the angle of her bed, she couldn't see herself.

"Is there a hand mirror?" she asked.

"I'll see what I can find," the nurse said dubiously, looking around the closet. "I don't see your purse. Do you carry a compact?"

"My purse is gone," she said without thinking, then felt a leap of joy. She knew it was gone! Lost at sea . . . but she still had more questions than answers. *How do you know that? Where is your purse? Why is it gone?*

"Let me see what I can come up with," the woman said again, with a quick smile as she left.

Why do you know your purse is gone? Why do you know that but you can't remember that your name is Julia?

"Julia," she said again.

The gray presence hovered over her, pressing down, a warning. It made her head hurt even worse. It didn't want her to remember.

She closed her eyes. She couldn't think about it anymore today. She needed to rest . . . recover . . . get better.

The young nurse returned to find her sound asleep again. She laid the hand mirror on the table beside her patient. She'd borrowed it from cranky Margie for an indefinite period of time, so there was no need to return it until cranky Margie started bitching, which would come, but maybe not for a few hours.

Sam sat down across from Sheriff Burton Vandra, feeling like he'd been called into the principal's office. He'd met the newly elected sheriff on several occasions, not sure what he thought of the fifty-ish man with the short, silvery hair and military bearing. O'Halleron, the previous sheriff, had retired at the end of the year, a surprise and loss to the department, according to what he'd heard, and the jury was still out on Vandra. Sam couldn't complain, however, as the sheriff had seemed interested in having him come on board when he'd tested the waters for a job. It was Sam who hadn't jumped on it, so maybe the older man was holding a grudge. More likely it was just that he was running the show and this was his normal demeanor—a hard man who had little time for pleasantries.

Both Detective Savannah Dunbar, auburn-haired and somber, and Detective Stone, also somber, had been invited into the sheriff's inner sanctum. Stone leaned against the wall, his arms crossed, his brows furrowed, and Dunbar, who was very visibly pregnant, stood up straight beside him.

Feeling Sam's eyes on her, Dunbar said, "I'm sorry I wasn't here yesterday when you called."

Sam had only asked for her because she'd been friendly when he'd met her a number of months earlier when he'd first applied for the job. "You saw Jules today?" he questioned.

"Yes. I tried to interview her, but she didn't have any memory of the accident."

"None?" the sheriff asked.

"She doesn't even know who she is. I talked to her doctor, Dr. Lillard, who says she took a hard blow to the head and is working to put her memories back."

"She has to know who she is." Sam's voice was full of his disbelief.

The sheriff looked as skeptical as Sam.

Dunbar said, "Right now she's having trouble with all her memories. I asked Dr. Lillard when they would return and he said to be patient." She made a face and pressed a hand to the small of her back. "He said she needed to physically heal first. I got the feeling he thought she was . . . I don't know, holding back because she maybe doesn't want to remember. Once she's healed, then we'll know more."

Sam wasn't buying it. Jules was faking. Maybe not on purpose, exactly, but she was deliberately not facing the truth of her memories. There was no way she wouldn't remember who she was. Sam felt angry and frustrated. The longer they delayed, the more it was going to take to get to the bottom of what happened.

The sheriff said to Sam, "I'd like a full accounting of what happened yesterday. How you ended up finding your sister-in-law."

"I was first on the beach."

"How?"

Vandra's voice was tense. The man was genial enough on the surface, but there was a whole lot going on underneath. Sam briefly asked himself if he still wanted a position as a deputy and decided he might, if it was still available. But he wasn't ready yet. He had a lot of questions about his brother's death and, though he could use the department's help, he would be stonewalled from the investigation because he was family. But he needed to give them the facts.

Sam said, "I got a message from my brother. A text. He wanted me to meet him at his dock at noon. It wasn't how we usually communicated. In fact, we usually didn't communicate much at all, at least lately. I thought the message was . . . odd. It put me on edge. When I got to his house, there was no one there and the boat wasn't there. I figured he'd taken it, so I went to the jetty and that's when I saw the smoke on the horizon. . . ."

"How did you know the boat was your brother's?" Vandra asked.

"I didn't. But his text seemed imperative, and I started worrying. And then I started wondering about the beach north of the jetty that's hard to get to, so I went in the water." Sam went on to explain about finding Jules, and then the hospital and going back to Joe and Jules's house.

He did not mention the note about the Cardaman file, nor his father's warning, "It's about the money." Until he knew more, he wanted to do some lone wolf investigating. He could tell the Sheriff's Department what he learned later, after they determined whether Joe's death was an accident, or not.

"Why were you and your brother not communicating?" the sheriff asked.

Sam had an image of Jules as he'd last seen her at the

hospital: thin, scared, and confused. "Just fell out of the habit," he lied. "He had his life and I had mine."

"When was the last time you saw him?"

"I'd have to think. . . ."

It was when Cardaman was first arrested. Joe had called Sam to reassure him that he wasn't involved with the man, not that Sam had asked. It was like his brother forgot he wasn't part of his financial circle. Cardaman had been accused of being part of a Ponzi scheme, illegally "selling" and "reselling" the same property many times over to different investors, all of whom believed they owned a particular tract of real estate when none of them did. Cardaman had pocketed the money at each transaction, while the blithely unaware investors believed they'd invested in something real.

"What?" Langdon Stone asked, and Sam realized the detective must've read something on his face.

Did this accident have something to do with Cardaman after all? Was Joe involved at some level? Had he gotten involved in some shady transactions, illegal transactions? Sam didn't believe it. Not Joe. Not straight-arrow Joe.

Yet . . . maybe . . . Joe had texted him about something and now he was gone.

Could Jules know?

"Mr. Ford?" the sheriff demanded impatiently.

"The last time I saw Joe was at my father's assisted living place about a month ago. Sea and Sunset Retirement Living in Seaside." That was the truth. After Joe's phone call, they'd run into each other, both visiting their father at the same time.

"Does your father know about your brother's death?" Dunbar asked.

"I told him this morning. I stopped by there before coming here."

"That last time you and your brother visited your father,

what was your take on your brother? Anything unusual?"
Vandra questioned.

"If you mean was he nervous or acting different, no. We
were just there seeing Dad. There wasn't much of a conversation. My father kind of talks about what he wants to talk
about and we just listen."

*But Joe was preoccupied. You noticed it and wondered if
it had anything to do with Cardaman.*

Sam wished he'd tried harder with Joe. He should have
gotten over the Jules thing two years ago, when she and Joe
got married. He should have stayed close to his brother.

His head started aching again. The pain had pretty much
receded, but his grief kept bringing it back.

"Any other family members that need to be told of your
brother's death?" Savannah asked.

*Georgie. Joe's stepdaughter . . . no, adopted daughter.
God, he wasn't even sure. Georgie used to be closer to Joe
than her own mother, maybe still was, unless Joe's marriage
to Jules interfered with that relationship. His father had
brought up Georgie this morning, but she wasn't a blood
relative.* He rubbed his forehead and grimaced, deciding he
needed to talk to Gwen first. "No."

"Do you have any thoughts on why Joe wanted to see
you yesterday?" the sheriff asked.

"No. But it was unusual enough for me to drop everything and come. I tried calling him, but he didn't answer his
cell. I don't suppose you found his phone?"

Vandra shook his head. "If it was on the boat, it could be
in the ocean. There wasn't much left of the vessel. It burned
hot and fast. We've towed in the hulk. We'll see what forensics has to say."

"You think it wasn't an accident, though. That's why you
posted the guard."

"I posted the guard," Stone interceded. "Strictly precautionary. We don't know enough yet to say."

The sheriff's weight shifted in his desk chair, causing the spring beneath to squeak in protest. "Might be that we pull that guard. At this point all we've got is a boat accident. No real evidence of foul play."

Sam could see Stone's lips tighten, but the detective merely nodded his head.

"We want to make sure everyone's safe, that's for certain," the sheriff went on, as if talking to Stone. "But we're stretched pretty thin around here as it is and Detective Dunbar isn't up to full capacity just now. She's going on maternity leave soon, so I'm going to tell Ramirez to come back to the station."

"When will we hear from forensics?" Sam asked.

"The *department* will hear fairly soon, I'd think." The sheriff was drawing his line in the sand, letting Sam know that he wasn't part of the team . . . yet.

"What about an autopsy?" Sam asked. He hadn't been interested, when asked about it earlier, but he'd been in shock, hadn't yet gotten his bearings . . . maybe he still hadn't.

"We'll run toxicology and see what else was going on," Vandra answered. "You don't know anything more about your brother's state of mind? Something that might have led to this?"

Sam shook his head. The sheriff seemed like he was fishing, but Sam stayed mum.

"We want to be sure the fire was an accident. Not deliberately set"—the sheriff went on—"by anyone."

The other shoe dropped. The sheriff was hinting that Joe had started the fire himself. Sam said, "My brother wasn't suicidal."

"Not suggesting he was." Vandra sat back again, a line forming between his brows. "Just looking for information. Anything at all that you remember or might know that could help."

This was his time to bring up the note about Cardaman, but he kept his mouth shut because his instincts still told him to wait. He didn't like the way Sheriff Vandra seemed to be angling to blame Joe. Maybe the fire was an accident. Maybe the whole thing was just an unfortunate and terrible tragedy, but Sam wanted to make sure himself. What he needed to do was go back to Joe and Jules's house ASAP and do some searching of his own.

"I wish I could help you," Sam said.

The sheriff studied him a moment, then turned to his two detectives. "I want to keep Ford's name from the media as long as possible. That damn Phoenix Delacourt has been like a plague around here today, and I want to keep her shut down until I'm ready."

"She left a while ago," Dunbar informed him.

The sheriff snorted. "Thinks she's an investigative reporter for the *North Coast Spirit.* Deluded hippie should stick to arts and crafts and beer festivals."

Neither the detectives nor Sam responded to his remark. The *North Coast Spirit* was a small newspaper that chronicled local news, and Phoenix Delacourt, Sam's onetime lineman Brady Delacourt's aunt, wrote about local happenings up and down the coast.

Vandra added, "I talked to the television people this morning and that's all they're getting for now."

The four of them talked for another half hour with nothing more of import being said, then Sam left Sheriff Vandra's office with detectives Dunbar and Stone.

Dunbar confessed, "My leave from the department may be permanent. I have a little boy at home, too, and I can't believe I'm saying this, but I may be retiring, at least for a few years. The deputy job's still open, and the department hires from within."

She was telling him that he could be on a fast track to detective, if that's what he wanted. A part of him felt like jumping at the opportunity, but another part was still holding back. Right now he didn't want to be yoked by the rules of law enforcement. A far cry from how he'd felt when he'd first become an officer.

"Thanks," he said, shaking both of their hands.

He headed up the highway back toward Jules and Joe's house, stopping off at the jetty to look out toward the ocean once more. The day was filled with fluffy, white, cumulus clouds and the sea sparkled in diamonds beneath the sun. Its beauty made him feel melancholy and for a moment his throat was hot.

Joe . . .

They should have had time to repair the breach between them. He ached inside to make it right, and now it was too late.

And Jules?

He turned his head to the south, thinking of her lying in the hospital. Temporary amnesia? He didn't believe it. The doctors could all walk around with long, serious faces and speak gobbledegook theory all day long, but *he didn't believe it*. He was angry at her. Really mad at her. If that was transference, so be it. He wanted to shake her and demand answers.

Instead he got back into his truck and headed north to their home on the river, across the highway and about five miles from the small but well-monied town of Salchuk. He got to the house about thirty minutes later and pulled into the drive. He didn't have a key, but the same window was a little bit ajar.

Looking around, he saw the neighbor woman who'd waved at him sitting on her back deck, staring across the river at him as he moved to the back of the house. She waved again and he lifted his hand, not sure how he was going to explain climbing in the window.

She cupped her hands over her mouth. "You're Joe's brother," she called.

He did the same, hollering back. "Yep. I'm Sam. I'm locked out. Gonna climb in this window."

"Where's Julia?"

He debated for a moment. The guard outside Jules's door was a precautionary measure, so it didn't seem like information he could just yell at a neighbor even though the names of the people involved in the boat accident would probably hit the news by this evening, no matter what measures the sheriff took. "She's gone for a few days. So's Joe."

"I've got a spare key," she yelled, and then headed into her house. A few minutes later she held it up for him to see, then climbed into a kayak and paddled her way over to Joe and Jules's dock.

Sam helped her out of the kayak. She was about five foot seven, with rounded curves and a moon-shaped face carved with dimples. She wore tan shorts and a white tank top and had a solid, muscular shape. "I'm Tutti, like tutti-frutti," she said, handing him the key. "Glad to meet you, Sam Ford. I've known Julia and Joe since they moved in a year and a half ago or so. My husband, may the bastard rest in peace, and I built our place about six years ago."

"You're a widow?" Sam glanced over at her house, recognizing signs of neglect now that he was looking: weathered boards; shaggy bushes and landscaping that had gone to seed; gutters that hung a little too far down and maybe hadn't been cleaned in some time.

"No, I just wish him dead." She smiled, appraising him with frank appreciation.

He got the sense she uttered that line often, looking for a reaction.

"Dirk and I are separated and have been for years. Been meaning to get that divorce, but that would mean sharing assets and I don't like to share. He found himself someone else, and so I did the same, and for a while we just screwed our brains out with whoever we could find, just to get back at each other, y'know. But then, that got old, at least for me. I decided I wanted a real relationship next time, but that next time just hasn't quite happened yet."

"I see."

She laughed. "I'm making you uncomfortable. Don't mind me." She waved a hand down the river, encompassing the two rows of houses facing each other over the water. "They all've heard every little detail about my life, so I thought I'd just get it out there first. What about you? Have you taken the plunge into the waters of marital bliss? You look single."

"Divorced."

"Joe never mentioned he had a brother. If you didn't look so much like him, I wouldn't give you the key."

"We hadn't been in touch for a while."

"He also didn't mention they were leaving. When did they go?"

"Yesterday. They took the boat out in the morning."

She glanced down at her kayak, which was tied up next to the empty boat slip. "I was in Seaside. I work part-time at Elite Designs on Holladay. You know it? The furniture store?"

"I've seen it." Holladay Street was one of Seaside's main roads.

She cocked her head. "Usually they say something if they're going to be gone overnight. When will they be back?"

He thought about telling her the truth. She seemed to know quite a bit about Joe and Jules and might be a source of information. But he debated with himself too long and she held up one arm.

"Enough questions. You look like you want to get rid of me. Okay. I can take a hint." She offered an enticing look at her backside as she maneuvered into the kayak. "Some of the other Fishers are coming over to my house for an afternoon barbecue later today. Join us? You can tell us why we've never met you before, and where the hell Joe and Julia are."

"Fishers?"

"That's just what we call each other. This is Fisher Canal, you know."

"Ah, yes."

"So, are you in?"

"I've got some things to do, but I'll try." Her frankness reminded him a little of when he'd first met Jules.

"Don't let me scare you now." She had climbed back into the kayak and held the paddle over her legs, making no effort to immediately leave. "I'm good friends with Julia. We talk, y'know? Don't know your brother quite as well. He's always working. In fact I have some investments with him. So does Dirk, I think, but he's an asshole, so who cares. Come on by. You'll find their canoe inside the garage, I bet. Otherwise you can drive around, but it's a couple of miles by road. So close, but yet so far, right?" She picked up the oar and headed back across the narrow river. "Six o'clock. Bring a bottle of wine."

"Okay."

He tried the key to the back slider and it worked. Stepping inside the yellow and white kitchen, he watched Tutti reach her property and nimbly climb up the couple of rungs of the ladder that led to her wooden dock. She looked back, saw him staring through the window, and waved.

Sam waved back, lost in thought. It had been nearly a day since the boating accident and the discovery of Joe's body. Time to move forward. He pulled out his cell and placed a call to Gwen Ford, Joe's ex, Georgie's mother, whose number was still in his contact list. It had been there since she and Joe were first married and he half expected it to have changed. But he recognized her voice when she answered impatiently, "Hello?" That's what he remembered about her, her impatience.

"Hi, Gwen, it's Sam Ford."

"Sam. Well. This is a surprise." Then, "What's wrong?" as her radar clicked in and she jumped to the right conclusion. A call from Sam was unusual.

"There's been a boating accident. . . ."

Her breath swept in. "Oh, my God. I saw it on the news! That was Joe's boat? Georgie said it looked like Joe's boat!"

"It was Joe's boat." He found his throat tightening.

"Oh, God . . . oh, oh, God . . . Is he all right?"

"It was a recovery mission, Gwen."

"What does that . . . oh, shit. Hell. Recovery . . . not . . ."

"Not rescue."

"Joe?"

"Yes."

A pause. "And Julia?"

"Jules is all right, but Joe didn't survive."

"Damn. I can't . . ." She gulped in several deep breaths and it gave time for Sam to steady his own emotions. "He's dead?"

"Yes."

"Oh, God. How did it happen?"

"It appears they were on *The Derring-Do* together. Jules is . . . recovering."

"Is she in the hospital? Which one? Tillamook?"

It'll all be on the news tonight, he reminded himself, but he only said, "She has a head injury and her shoulder's in a sling. There should be more answers when the forensics are in."

"Sam, who'll take over his company? He had investments for Georgie. Oh, Lord. Who should I talk to? I need to talk to someone."

"I don't know."

"He has—had—a lawyer."

"Then they'll be getting in touch with you."

"They'll be getting in touch with you, too," she said.

"I don't know about that."

"Don't you know you're a prime beneficiary? Unless Joe radically changed since he married Julia, you're going to get a windfall. It's me who loses, but oh, well. I've got a good man in Evan now. The estate'll be divided between you and Julia and Georgie."

It's about the money.

"I don't think Joe would do that," Sam said.

"Then you don't know your brother."

He glanced at the counter where he'd set the note about Cardaman. Not seeing it, he looked underneath the table and chairs, then all around the counters.

The note about Cardaman was gone.

Chapter Six

Sam stared at the place where the note had been while his mind sizzled. It was gone. *Gone.* Someone had moved it, or taken it. Someone who had access.

He managed to disconnect with Gwen somehow, but his mind had moved on. He looked all over again, knowing the note had been *right there.* After a few fruitless minutes he headed down the hall, veered first toward the master suite, then immediately backed away from it and went into one of the spare bedrooms. The walls were painted a lilac color and there was a dresser filled with bottles of perfume and various and sundry makeup items. It stopped him cold for a moment, before he realized it was probably Georgie's room.

He went into the third bedroom, which had a daybed and a chest of drawers, the look of a guest room. He sank onto the edge of the bed and thought hard.

Someone had been inside the house. Tutti-frutti whoever the hell had given him a key. She'd just *handed over a key* like no big deal, without asking for ID. Sure, he looked like Joe, but Tutti knew nothing about their relationship. She'd even said she didn't know he had a brother, yet she'd just plopped the key in his palm. Way too trusting.

Someone had been inside their house and moved the Cardaman note.

There was something there. Something financial. He'd been walking around like a sleepwalker. Saying he believed it wasn't an accident, but not really coming to the logical alternative, his mind shying away from the fact that foul play was involved. Someone had killed Joe, and tried to kill Jules. Joe was dead. *The Derring-Do* was a burned-out hull. Sam had been slightly concussed—was still feeling the effects—and dull as dirt because of it.

But now he had to do something.

Now.

Immediately Sam shot to his feet and headed into the den. Joe's den. There was a desk in the middle of the room, a big, oak one. A monster that had been their father's, a gift to Joe. The surface was clear except for a lamp. No computer. Sam opened every drawer, resisting the urge to dump them out on the floor. Instead, with an increasingly aching head, he went through every file, searching for anything about Joe's financial dealings with Cardaman or anything else.

There was no Cardaman file inside. Joe had an office in Seaside, though Donald had told him that Joe had moved to Salchuk, closer to Fisher Canal. It was likely the Cardaman file was in one of those two places.

The smaller drawers held pencils, stamps, paper clips, a pair of reading glasses, a pocket-sized cassette player from when they were kids, a magnifying glass, and a number of other small office supplies. The file drawers weren't locked, but all he could find were personal papers, nothing to do with Joe's business.

He left the office and headed back to the kitchen, his eyes still searching for the missing note.

He needed to talk to Jules. Really talk to her. Ask questions. Get answers.

No memory?

"Bullshit," he muttered angrily.

He suddenly realized he was thirsty and he walked back to the kitchen. He opened the cupboard by the sink, looking for a glass, and found a bottle of aspirin. Shaking two out, he then spied a row of neatly arranged blue glasses on an open shelf on the opposite wall. He grabbed one, filled it with tap water, swallowed the two tablets, while he gazed through the window to the houses on the other side of the canal. Tutti's was directly across and a little north, the end home on her side as Joe and Jules's was the end one on this side. Next to Tutti's was a farmhouse style house with grayed shingles and white trim. On the composition roof stood a cupola out of the same shingles, capped by a wrought-iron weather vane in the shape of a porpoise. It was currently pointing east. An east wind brought hot air. He hadn't thought about it, but it was warming up. A beautiful summer day with temperatures in the seventies and only the faintest breeze. Good boating weather.

What had happened out on the water yesterday?

He went back to the daybed, wanting to be out of sight of the neighbors without having to draw the curtain, which smacked of secrecy. He lay back and stared at the ceiling. He hadn't been paying enough attention yesterday. He hadn't been himself. He'd walked around in a daze—pain, grief, shock, disbelief, call it what you will—but it had made him feel like he was slogging through quicksand.

But now he felt razor sharp. Joe had called him because he was in danger. He'd gone out on his boat and taken Jules with him. Was that a usual occurrence?

He closed his eyes. He was still tired, but his mind was buzzing. He needed to know more about Joe . . . and Jules. What was their life like? What were they into? Who were their friends? Tutti? Other people along the river? People from work?

His heart clutched as he thought about something his father

had once said, something he'd dismissed at the time because the old man was unreliable even on a good day.

"You should give up that damn cop thing. Your brother's doing good. Work with him. Make some money. Joe's made some good connections, you know. The Hapstells. They got it growing on trees, y'know. That's who they are. . . ."

Walter Hapstell Junior . . . Hap . . . Jules's old boyfriend.

The first night he met Jules they'd found their way to Brest's. They'd ordered French fries and split a burger. It was like they'd known each other for years. They teased each other. The Sandy thing really got going. In the end he'd reluctantly called Joe to come and pick them up, and he'd made the mistake of bringing up Hap again while they were waiting.

"He's not my boyfriend," Jules had said with more force than earlier. "We went out a couple of times, but I'm just a conquest that he can't have. That's Hap. It's all about what's the next best thing. He's okay. But it's over. We're all going to graduate and never see each other again anyway."

"I'll still be around here," he'd protested. "Your family's here."

"Yeah, well . . . maybe."

He'd almost told her he wanted to see her again but couldn't quite get the words out. Didn't want to spoil the nice evening they'd had. He was still trying to work out how to make future plans when Joe wheeled in front of the restaurant in his black Explorer and he and Jules climbed into the backseat.

"Hi," Joe said to Jules. "I'm Joe."

"I'm Julia."

"Nice to meet you."

Sam noticed that she hadn't called herself Jules, which was what she went by in high school. She didn't know Joe, and with people she didn't know she was apparently Julia. She and Joe were acquaintances, nothing more, and that's what Sam had always expected them to be. In truth, he suspected that's what they'd always expected they would be, too, if even that. Joe had been in the throes of wedding planning and he didn't have tons of time for Sam and any of his high school friends. Jules didn't pay much attention to him, either. She was more concerned about the dark house they pulled up to. Her house.

"Everyone's asleep," she said, worried.

"Maybe you can sneak in?" Sam suggested.

"You don't know my family."

Sam gallantly walked her to the front door, leaving the passenger door open. Under its interior light Joe was on his phone, smiling, talking to Gwen.

"Thanks for the fries, burger, and ride," Jules said, but her eyes were on the door.

"When you get your phone back, I'd like to call you. Make sure everything turned out okay."

"Okay."

"What's your number?"

She dragged her attention back to him and reeled off the digits, which he committed to memory, running them through his mind like a litany, inputting them into his phone as Joe drove him back to the cabin.

He'd called her the next week, but she hadn't picked up. He'd tried again the next week and the same thing happened. He was thinking she'd shined him on when she suddenly called him.

"Hey, Sandy," she said, a smile in her voice. "Let me take you to Brest's. My treat. Fries and half a burger. Just got my phone back. Long story."

"When?"

"Today?"

They met at the diner after school. She wore jeans and a green blouse that picked up hidden flecks of teal in her gray eyes. A dusting of freckles lay across her nose. She wore nearly nude lipstick that nevertheless made her lips look luscious.

"How'd you get here?" she asked.

"I drove. Awkward, with this ankle, but doable. You?"

"Hap brought me."

"Hap?"

"Argued with me all the way here, then sped off in a cloud of dust." She looked long suffering. "I told him we were just friends and that's all it would ever be, but he's so predictable. Even though he was with Martina."

"Martina?"

"Yup. While I'm fighting with my dad to get my phone back because he all of a sudden decided I was spending too much time on it. Acted like we would go back into the dark ages of no communication. I had to stop making him dinner and ignore him. I just helped out Mom. Finally, he came around. But we were talking about Hap. . . . He's been with Martina all along. They're like codependent. Can't leave each other alone."

"You okay with that?"

"I told you. Hap and I weren't ever really together." She dunked a fry in ketchup and munched it down. "But I acted like I was broken up and upset. He hung his head and said he was sorry, but it was really what he was looking for. A sign that I couldn't live without him. Now he can go be with Martina, knowing my heart is broken. Bet he's telling Martina right now, burying his sorrows in her arms."

"You sure you're okay with this?"

"I've been trying to unhook for weeks. It was never anything anyway, but you couldn't tell Hap that. Better to act like it matters more than it does."

"Psychology."

"Exactly." She grinned. "That's what I'm going to study. Psychology. I think I have a knack for it."

"He dropped you off here. Does he know you're meeting me?"

"Yes. I told him you were just a friend, which is the truth."

Those words had deflated Sam some, but he'd already decided he would take friendship if that's all there was . . . for now. "Okay. Just wanted to know if I had a target on my back."

"Nah. Hap's all talk. He won't do anything. That's too much work." Then she slid her hands across the table and linked her fingers through his. A small gesture that later ran through his mind over and over again. "I don't want to talk about him anymore."

"Neither do I."

"So, what're we gonna do now?"

He'd stared at her, aware of her brightness, aware that something special was happening to him, aware that he was a little bit scared. "We could drive up the coast."

She looked at him and he'd sensed that she was really examining him, too. "Okay."

And that's how it started. Friendship . . . then a first kiss on the beach, some exploration in the car . . . first lovemaking the day his ankle was unwrapped for good. Even now he could remember Jules pulling his mouth down to hers on the cabin couch after his father had gone to bed, the DVD player playing one of her favorite romantic comedies, the television flickering over their moving bodies, the soft gasps and moans that issued from her lips, the taste of her skin.

Throughout that fall, winter, and spring, through graduation and the next summer, and into college, she'd been in the forefront of his mind.

And then . . . Thanksgiving weekend. Everyone home and Sam feeling anxious and impatient. Jules was busy. Couldn't see him. Dealing with a sick and difficult mother and a disengaged father. Everyone else their age meeting at various houses or down on the beach. The weather unusually warm for November. The rains holding off.

And around a campfire one night, Martina made a play for him.

"Jules's sure been a ghost," she observed. "Too good for us."

"Yeah, that's it. She's too good for all of us."

"Don't be an ass. What's the deal with her?"

Sam shrugged. "Family stuff."

"And she's leaving you all alone here with the rest of us? Dangerous. We might corrupt you."

"You might," he'd agreed.

And the night had gone on from there. He'd been happy to be with the old high school group, happy not to deal with real problems, happy to revert to his teenage self. He drank too much and Tina gave him a ride home. She kissed him good night and he let her. He let her a little too long.

The next day he went to see Jules and told her about his night with the old friends. She was distracted. Her mother's illness had reached a crisis point and decisions were having to be made. Jules's father was too distraught to make the decisions, so they'd been left up to Jules. When he admitted Martina had kissed him, at first she didn't seem to hear him. But as he was leaving, she asked, "Did you kiss her back?"

He could've said, "No," but it seemed like a chickenshit kind of response. A half-truth to make himself feel better when she was really asking something else. So, he said instead, "I didn't push her away."

At some level he'd thought she would understand. He'd expected he'd be in the doghouse for a while, but that things would go back to the way they'd been, the way they should be. But that wasn't how it turned out. In that moment she just stared at him, as if she'd never really seen him before and didn't much like what was there. She said, "We'll talk later," and headed into her house.

He couldn't reach her on the phone the next day, or the next, or the next. He finally went back to her house, more than a little pissed that she'd gone dark on him. He banged on the door and waited on the porch, and it took her so long to answer that he was back on the sidewalk, stalking to his car, before she cracked the door open.

"There you are," he greeted her, but his tone was accusatory.

"Yep. Here I am."

"I've called you a bunch of times. I'm sure you know."

"I've been kind of busy."

"Too busy to answer the phone?"

"Sam, I really don't want to do this now."

"Well, neither do I, but what the hell, Jules?"

"If you want to talk, it's going to have to be later. Much later. I've got . . . I just can't see you right now. So, if you want to spend time with Martina, have at it."

"Jules," he protested.

"Just . . . leave me alone," she said angrily. Then she whisked back inside and locked the door behind her.

Well, that really pissed him off. He'd wanted to bang down her door, demand that she come back and have it out with him. Luckily, he'd turned away and peeled out of her drive. He stewed for a while, expecting her to call. When she didn't, he took her advice and went to be with Martina.

And that was the end of it all.

Somewhere in the back of his mind he'd always thought they would be together in the end. Even with everything, it hadn't killed his romantic dream for the two of them. But it didn't happen and Jules moved to Portland, while Sam returned to the coast and joined the Seaside Police Department. He kept seeing Tina, drifted into marriage with her, then after the tragedy of her father's suicide, Jules had tied the knot as well. With Joe.

Now he wished he would have tried harder to put it all behind him, get over it, make peace with Joe. He should've accepted their marriage. He should've reconnected with his brother.

And now, if someone had deliberately set out to harm Joe, *kill him* . . . Sam was going to find the bastard and get some payback.

"Julia?"

She lifted her lids slowly. She'd been poked and prodded all day and her shoulder was hurting. Rest and not jarring it would supposedly put her collarbone back together, but all she felt was weary.

Luckily she no longer had a catheter.

Dr. Lillard was at the foot of her bed, looking expectant. She murmured, "You're not going to make me do another test, are you?"

"No. I just have some test results for you, and they're all good. You've had a concussion, but you're recovering well. I have the results here." He held a sheaf of papers in his hands. "I'd like to go over a few things, and then we'll make the final decision."

"What final decision?"

"Whether to send you home tomorrow."

The news hit her like a hammer. Home? Where was home? She had no memory of it, and when she struggled to visualize it, the gray entity that seemed to shroud her mind pressed down on her, making her head ache and blocking all thought.

"I don't think I'm well enough." She could hear the unshed tears in her voice.

"We won't send you before you're ready. Mind if I go over some of these reports?"

"Sure," she said.

There followed a detailed report of her injuries, from the trauma to her head, which appeared to have happened when her skull encountered a blow of some kind right behind her right temple, to the break of her clavicle, which appeared to be more of a crack than a break, which could make her recovery quicker, to the scrapes and abrasions that ran along her arms and legs.

She listened to the rumble of his voice, but the words faded away. All she knew was that she felt deep down scared. She sensed that there was something just beyond her grasp that was really important, but every time her mind probed its own dark recesses, the gray entity bore down on her, crushing her thought process, ratcheting up her fear, affecting her breathing.

"You all right?" Lillard asked, pausing in his delivery, as she struggled for air.

"Yes."

He dropped his clipboard by his side and said, "I don't see anything here that will hold you back."

"Okay."

"How are your memories coming?"

"They're . . . coming . . ." she lied, closing her eyes.

"Good. You might not remember the accident itself. . . ." His voice traveled on, covering the same information he'd told her before. She moved her eyebrows in response but didn't open her eyes, and eventually she heard him say, "I'll check in on you later."

His footsteps departed and she told herself to open her eyes, but she didn't want to. She just wanted to retreat, to be left alone. She didn't like hospitals. She didn't like the smell, the feeling of hopelessness. . . .

Hopelessness?

She probed her mind carefully and had a sharp impression of being in a hospital once before . . . the medicinal odors, the soft whirs and clicks of machinery, the uncontrollable sobbing and anguish. . . . But no, it wasn't for her. It was for . . . a little boy . . . kept alive by a ventilator, and then the ventilator was stopped.

". . . *No brain function* . . ." someone had said.

And then a woman's wails and screams. A finger pointed at her. *It's all your fault! Where were you? You were supposed to be watching him!*

"I was?" she said aloud to the now empty room. Her eyes flew open and she squinched them closed again, carefully trying to search for other memories, aware she could inadvertently turn over a hot coal and get burned. But there was nothing more. The gray weight hovered.

So frustrated she could cry, she buried her hot face in the pillow. And then there was a man's voice. *Don't listen . . . She's just upset. . . . There was nothing you could do. . . . She loves you very much.*

Her father consoling her. Talking about her mother. She knew it was a true memory, which gave her hope that she would remember something else. She tried to concentrate on her father, but the gray entity swarmed in, forcing her to shut off her mind.

She drifted off to sleep, but she was restless, her mind circling the same questions. *Why can't I remember?* Finally, she fell into exhausted slumber, and when she awakened she was surprised to see Dr. Lillard had returned.

"I just thought I'd check on you again," he said.

He was worried about her.

"I lied earlier. I can't remember anything. This isn't usual, is it? I should have remembered something by now."

"Every patient's recovery is different and—"

"Have you ever had anyone like me before?"

"I've had patients with head trauma who've had great difficulty remembering things in the beginning."

"Their name? Their husband, their *whole life*?"

"I had a patient who suffered a head injury, more severe than your own, and his recall came back within the week, except for the trauma of the car accident, which he never fully remembered."

"Did he know who he was?"

The slightest hesitation. "Not immediately."

"What?" she asked, sensing he was holding back.

"It was a very different situation. He was in a difficult situation in his personal life and didn't want to remember. So, he found a way to block his memories."

"He did it on purpose, that's what you're saying." It felt like there were bands around her chest, squeezing the breath out of her.

"He had all his memories back in a matter of days."

She swallowed several times, then opted for honesty. "I have a block. And if I try too hard, I get a headache and there's this *shield* that comes over my brain and I can't think!"

"Headaches come with the territory, I'm afraid. I've got a prescription for you and I got a message to your personal physician, Dr. Werkel, who's on vacation and was unable to come in. She's aware of your injuries and will follow up with you at home."

"I don't know any Dr. Werkel," she said unevenly.

"Maybe we should get another MRI. Make sure there's no change."

She was almost glad to hear it. She didn't like hospitals, but the prospect of being sent home scared the bejesus out of her.

Bejesus. That word sounded familiar.

"Meanwhile, Laura, the floor nurse, will get your paperwork ready. Dr. Werkel's office sent over your history."

"Can I see it?"

The words just popped out. The doctor thought about it

briefly and said, "I don't see why not. I'll tell Laura to bring you the file."

"What if they don't come back? My memories?"

"I'm going to go out on a limb and predict that they will. Most of them, anyway." He was reaching for the door handle. "Try having a friend go over events from your past with you."

"I feel kind of short of friends right now," she said, forcibly keeping emotion out of her voice.

"What about your brother-in-law? Or whoever's picking you up tomorrow."

"I . . . don't have a phone. I can't call anyone. . . ." She was alarmed to discover she couldn't think of anyone, anyone at all, other than Sam Ford, and she only knew him because he'd come to see her.

"I'll check your paperwork from Dr. Werkel's office. See who you have listed."

"I don't have my brother-in-law's number. . . . Sam's . . . He said there's a guard outside my door."

"There was. I didn't see one just now. I'll check that out with the Sheriff's Department."

He didn't actually glance at his watch, but she got the feeling she was holding him up. He was anxious to get to other patients . . . and maybe away from her. She was being released because she had relatively minor injuries, but she was a problem. Her amnesia wasn't normal. And he thought she was doing it to herself.

Was she? Was there something she didn't want to face?

She tried probing her thoughts again, but carefully, hesitantly. Her heart started a slow, deep pounding that quickly became a gallop. *Had* she done something, something she was only too happy to forget?

Yes.

What? What did you do?

"I'll schedule that MRI," the doctor was saying. He nodded a good-bye and headed out of the room.

Her mind was feverish with worry. She wanted to remember. She needed to remember! But something . . . some *thing* . . . the gray entity . . . was intent on shutting her down.

Throwing back the covers, she stepped carefully toward the closet. She'd been up several times, always with the help of a nurse, but if they were releasing her she needed to see if she could walk.

And she could. Walk. Without pain. All right, then. Maybe she was getting better. She opened the closet door and looked at herself close up in the mirror. They'd unwrapped her head so she could see all her hair. Her arm was in a sling to protect her collarbone. "Clavicle," she corrected herself. Was her skin tone always this ghastly white? Like she'd seen a ghost? Or was in terrific pain?

"You could use a tan," she said aloud, and had a sudden sharp feeling of déjà vu. Someone had said those very words to her. She could almost hear that person . . . a man? This Joe who was her husband?

She tried to think about him and failed. She tried to think about her mother and father and her stomach tightened.

The boy on the ventilator . . . You had a brother who died.

Immediately the gray curtain closed off her brain and suddenly it felt like she couldn't breathe. She clutched the handle on the closet for support. She couldn't be doing this to herself, could she? How? What was this thing that wouldn't let her probe the recesses of her mind? What kind of governor was it?

What did you do?

"What are you doing?" a voice snapped at her.

She gasped and nearly fell over. Hard arms caught her and held her rigidly, then righted her onto her feet. Sam, she saw. Her supposed brother-in-law. She wanted to melt into him, absorb his strength, but the way he was looking at her told her that would be a bad idea.

"Vandra's fast. The guard's already gone," he said, sounding pissed off. Then, "You okay? You're not going to fall over?"

"I'm okay." Another lie.

He moved away from her, stalking across the room and pulling out his cell phone. "I want that guard back. We need to know more about the boating accident, before he's just taken away. Stone had the right idea."

She didn't know who or what he was talking about. While he scrolled through the screen on his phone, she headed back to her bed. "They're releasing me tomorrow," she said, falling into the pillows.

"What?" He stopped in the act of placing the call.

"I'm having another MRI, but the first one was fine, so if this one's good . . ."

"Do you remember Joe?" he asked, his expression tense and sober.

"I'm having some problems, but it'll all come back. My head injury isn't that bad, apparently. And my cracked clavicle will mend with rest."

"You don't remember him?"

"Umm . . . not really."

His cell phone rang in his hand, surprising him. He looked at it, then answered tautly, "Sam Ford," as he walked out into the hall. She strained to hear his side of the conversation. ". . . No, Griff, I can't. A lot of stuff has hit the fan. . . . Yeah, it was Joe. Probably be on the evening news. . . . Not keeping it a secret, but you know . . . Thanks . . . Tell Sadie thanks, too, but I'm just too busy right now. . . . I'll let you know. Yeah, bye."

He hung up and came back into the room a few moments later, eyeing her critically. "You don't look ready to be released."

"Tomorrow," she reminded him. She had the absurd feeling that she was about to cry, so she drew a deep breath and reached for her water glass. Her hand trembled as she sucked down a big gulp.

"Maybe I should get a nurse."

"No," she commanded, finding her voice.

His direct gaze was unnerving. She asked, more for him than her, "Have you heard any more about . . . Joe?"

"What do you mean?"

"I don't know what happened. I wish I could remember. I wish I could help you. I just thought . . . maybe you knew something more."

He stilled. "Detective Dunbar didn't tell you?"

"What?"

His jaw worked and he said heavily, "Joe's body was found about a mile from where I found you. I identified him at the morgue."

"I'm sorry," she said in a rush of shock.

"*The Derring-Do*'s being examined, but I guess it's just a burned-out hull," he went on as if she hadn't spoken. "The Sheriff's Department's working on it. A forensics team. They thought . . . there was a question of whether the fire was accidental or set on purpose."

"Set on purpose?"

"That's why you had the guard." He looked toward the door. "I'm not sure what happened there. I'll call the sheriff and see. I didn't think they'd come to that conclusion so fast. I was just there this morning."

"You think there's danger?"

"You tell me. What were you and Joe doing? He told me to meet him at your dock, but then he took out the boat."

She struggled once again, but the pain in her head intensified. "I can't. Not yet."

"What do you remember? Let's go with that."

"I don't. I think . . . I think I had a brother who died. . . ."

He stared at her. "Oh, come on."

"You think I'm faking," she realized with a spurt of anger. Who the hell was he?

"You don't remember Joe. Your husband. My brother. You remember Clem, who died when you were just a kid."

"Sort of . . ." *Mama blamed you. She always blamed you.*

"I don't believe you."

"I'm not faking."

"Good."

"I'm not!"

"Fine. Good. Whatever. I'm not going to argue with you, Jules. I don't have time."

Jules?

"My name is Jules," she stated positively. Finally. Something that felt right.

He swore between his teeth, then lifted his hands and backed away. "Okay, fine. You don't know who you are. You don't know anything."

He was heading for the door, and she called, "Please don't leave. I need help. I need someone to pick me up tomorrow."

His head whipped around and she saw realization cross his face. "What about your friends on the river? I have a key that you gave to Tutti."

"What's Tutti?"

"Who's Tutti," he corrected. "Your friend directly across the canal. One of the Fishers."

She just stared at him, almost afraid to ask any of the questions crowding her brain. She settled for, "The canal?"

"The river . . . canal . . . where you now live. Yesterday you took the boat down the canal to the river, then to the bay, then out to sea. I don't know why. I was supposed to meet Joe at *your dock*."

Hearing his frustration, she said, "You seem . . . kind of familiar."

"God, Jules . . ." His hands fisted and he relaxed them with an effort. "My brother's dead. I'm sure you're having some trouble remembering, and it's probably hard for you, but I can't play this game."

"It's not—"

"So, I'm just going to keep talking. I'll keep talking and I'll ask the questions. You and I have things to talk about, but I can't hear any of this right now, okay? Joe's dead. That's a fact. That's what I'm thinking about. Your friends across the river, canal, whatever, are going to need to know about Joe and the accident and you. I'll talk to them this evening. I'll let them know. You and I . . . we'll figure the rest out later."

"Will you come for me tomorrow . . . or get someone to?"

"I'll take care of it."

"Thank you."

After he left, she pressed her face into the pillow again and fought back a scream.

Chapter Seven

"Holy shit," Sam muttered, the same thing he'd muttered half a dozen times as he strode to his pickup. "Holy mother of—"

You don't actually believe her, do you?

Nope. Nope, he didn't. But okay, she was weak. And shattered, and she'd been through hell, and he was sorry he had to be the one to tell her about Joe. Joe. Her husband. Whom she said she didn't remember.

He called Sheriff Vandra as soon as he was seated in his pickup, staring across the parking lot to the hospital, counting the floors, his eyes searching out approximately where Jules's room was.

The receptionist answered and said the sheriff wasn't available. Sam left his name and told her it was urgent, which they probably heard all the time, but maybe Vandra would think he'd learned something of import.

He thought about calling either Detective Stone or Dunbar, but by the way it had seemed this morning, this case was the sheriff's baby. Why had Vandra removed the guard? Did he believe it all was just a terrible accident? What had made the sheriff decide that?

But why did Joe contact you, then? His brother didn't do stuff like that just for the hell of it.

Sam drummed his fingers on the wheel, his thoughts churning. He tried to divine what his brother had been thinking, but it was beyond him. Twisting the ignition, he thought some more. Maybe going to Joe's office in Salchuk would offer some results. The town was not as well known and populated as either Seaside or Cannon Beach, nor as much of a tourist mecca, but it was getting that way. A gem with a beautiful, somewhat private, stretch of beach just north of the twin headlands that reached into the sea where he'd found Jules.

Salchuk also had its own tiny police force, three officers who did everything from traffic control to working local crimes. Sam didn't know any of them personally. Their reach was too narrow for him to come in contact with them much. He hadn't bothered to apply for a job with the Salchuk Police because he hadn't wanted to go that small, nor would they have probably had an opening. Now, however, he wished he'd at least shown up and tried to hire on, just so that he would have some history with the officers. He wanted in to Joe's office, and he didn't know how he was going to do that without breaking in. He wanted to know what his brother had been working on. He wanted to know if the Cardaman file was on the premises.

He didn't want to think about Jules.

He drove into Salchuk, along the store-lined main street that sloped directly toward the ocean, which today glittered under a gray sky, the sun glaring down balefully on the restless water. Beside him were typical shops: beach togs and toys, caramel corn and saltwater taffy, art galleries that featured local artists, kitchy knickknack places, kites and sand bikes and skim boards. On the hill to the north, homes with expansive windows dotted the hillside, their glass fronts glimmering within the fir trees. These were the expensive houses, mostly owned as second homes by wealthy Portlanders and other out-of-towners. To the flatter south was less ostentatious housing. A few original cabins were tucked in among other residences, which had been, were being, or were soon to be remodeled, but they were in the minority as Salchuk had morphed into an "in spot." If you had the dough, and you wanted a sleepy, somewhat secluded, safe community, Salchuk was for you. Only the few homes along Fisher Canal, on the other side of Highway 101 and south of Salchuk, were considered on par with the Salchuk hillside McMansions. They might not be as impressive architecturally, but they were getting there, and the waterway was prime real estate with limited length. Sam's father had told him the price Joe and Jules had paid for their house, which had made Sam wonder if his father was lying or just plain wrong.

And Tutti had just handed over the key.

Sam knew Joe's office was on Eighth Street, and though he'd never been there before, he drove right up to it, seeing the sign for Joseph Ford Investments. He parked on the street and walked up a gravel path to the the small office, which had been converted and updated from one of the original cabins. Joe's investment clientele were from all over, again according to their father, which may or may not be the truth. Sam knew very little about his brother's business, by choice. The last time he'd seen Joe, when they'd run into each other visiting their father, there'd been some business talk between Joe and Donald. Donald didn't see Joe as much as he did his younger son, mainly because Joe's life was currently very busy whereas Sam was between jobs. There had also been that tension, though at the time Sam had put it down to the fact that Joe was closing his Seaside office and maybe business had dropped off some.

"Why're you moving to Salchuk?" Donald had complained. "If you're moving, you should go back to Portland. That's where the business is."

"Just seemed like the thing to do," Joe had answered.

Donald snorted. "You staying away from those Hapstells?"

"You know I don't like partners."

"Yeah, but they sure try to worm their way in, don't they?"

Joe hadn't responded, but he'd glanced Sam's way, as if thinking about what he might be overhearing.

"Don't mind me," Sam had said, lifting his hands. He felt uncomfortable around Joe at the best of times, and if his brother didn't want him overhearing, so be it. He'd left the room and let them keep talking.

Now he wished he'd stayed. Maybe he would have learned something that could lead him to the right answers. It was disheartening how little he truly knew about his brother.

He tried the handle. Locked. He cupped his hands to look inside and could see a desk and credenza in the main room. There was an old river rock fireplace gracing the wall opposite the desk, and some file drawers arranged in what used to be the nook. Sam walked around the building to the back entrance, finding it locked as well. No surprise. He looked inside and saw the remains of a kitchen with extra shelving for office supplies. He didn't think he'd get lucky enough to find a window that didn't close correctly, but he tried them all anyway, to no avail.

He was just walking back to his pickup when a Salchuk patrol car cruised up to him, a newish, dark blue Ford Explorer similar to the one Joe owned, and double-parked next to Sam's car. The officer left the engine running and climbed out, giving Sam a fake smile. "You looking for someone?" he asked in a genial tone, but Sam sensed he was being checked out very carefully.

"This is my brother's office." He was fairly certain Officer Kent Bolles, as his tag read, already knew the male body found from the boat fire was Joe. Vandra had said he was keeping a lid on Joe's identity, but word got out, especially in the law enforcement community.

The officer was in his midthirties, fairly short, about five seven, with dark wiry hair, cold eyes, and a faint paunch around the middle. The smile dropped from his face at Sam's words. "That right? Well, I'm real sorry about what happened. We all know Joe."

"His wife's in the hospital. She asked me to check the house and Joe's office." The lies came easily.

He nodded several times and pursed his lips. "Heard she was having some memory problems. She okay?"

"Who'd you hear that from?"

"Just heard it around."

Rodriguez, the guard, Sam guessed, who'd probably reported to Vandra. The fact that Vandra knew Jules was compromised and still pulled Rodriguez pissed Sam off all over again.

"She's being released tomorrow morning," Sam said. "It's going to take a while before I'd say she was okay."

Bolles nodded toward the office. "You have a key?"

"Nope. It may have gone down with the ship, so to speak. Wasn't on Joe's body when he was . . . recovered. We're hoping it, or a spare's, at the house."

"Well, you know your brother moved down here earlier this year. I heard he closed his office in Seaside. That would make this his main office. Bound to be confidential files in there."

Sam realized he hadn't seen a laptop or tablet or other electronic device. What did Joe do with his information?

"Your brother handled a lot of money," Bolles was saying. "Gonna panic a few people that he's gone."

"Yes . . . I would imagine."

"We all trusted him, y'know?"

"Joe was trustworthy," Sam agreed.

"You aren't the first one come sneaking around today."

"I'm not? Who else?"

"You know Phoenix Delacourt?" he asked with a sneer. The reporter. "I know of her."

"Thinks she's some kind of investigator these days. She wanted in to your brother's office, too, but I turned her right around."

Vandra had said she was hanging around the Sheriff's Department. Sam had no interest in talking to a reporter about his brother, but she seemed pretty fast on the trigger about Joe.

"Half the people around here invested with Joe," Sam said, more to make conversation and ease back to his car than because he really wanted to keep talking to Bolles.

"Half? You're not giving your brother enough credit."

Sam regarded him carefully, sensing something underneath his words. "You invested with him?" he guessed.

"I don't have the kind of money some people do, but I put a nickel or two in with him." The smile was back in place, just as phony as before.

"Okay," Sam said, for want of anything better to say.

"I didn't catch your name."

"Sam Ford."

"You have some ID I could look at?" he asked casually. "Can't be too careful in times like these."

Sam reached for his wallet. He moved very slowly and deliberately, picking up vibes he couldn't understand. When he showed his driver's license to Bolles, the man scrutinized it carefully, a line drawing between his dark brows.

"Bad business out there on the water," he said, handing Sam's license back to him and shooting a glance west. From Joe's office you could see over the tops of the houses on the downward side all the way to the ocean. The sun had broken free of the obscuring clouds for a moment, lightening up a strip of water that almost glowed in the light.

"I talked to Sheriff Vandra this morning," Sam said,

tucking his wallet into his back pocket. He decided to test the waters. "Forensic team's going over the boat. No word yet on whether it was an accident or the fire was set intentionally."

"Set intentionally?" He shook his head and squinched up his face as if something smelled bad. He walked back toward his SUV with "Salchuk Police" swept across the side in large white script. "I'll keep an eye on the place till you find that key. Don't want anybody breaking in now, do we?"

Sam climbed into his car and watched the policeman leave. "Couldn't have that," he agreed to himself.

His stomach rumbled. Glancing at the clock on the dash, he saw it was after three. His crullers weren't going to do it. Deciding to get something to eat, he drove down the main street to the Spindrift, a diner known for its huevos rancheros, though they were way past breakfast and lunch.

The place was full of tchotchkes that had something to do with the beach, the walls lined with shelves above four-top tables with plastic tablecloths, each shelf crowded with dolphin, seagull, and whale figurines, salt and pepper shakers designed like starfish and crabs, small framed pictures of waves and sand and sky. He was shown to a table in the back and his waitress swept a salt and pepper combo of dancing mermaids off her serving tray, plopping them on his table along with a plastic-wrapped menu. "The huevos rancheros," he said without opening it.

"Too late for huevos. That's the dinner menu."

He looked it over, then glanced at the only other diners at this hour, an older couple who'd split a fairly large cheeseburger and fries.

"How about that?" he said, pointing.

"Something to drink?"

"Water's fine."

He handed her back the menu and thought about Joe, which made him think of Jules, and then back to Joe. He'd gotten his cheeseburger and was just finishing up, eyeing the rest of the French fries but remembering that Tutti had invited him over—bound to be more food there, and he wanted to meet the other "Fishers"—when a wiry woman with long gray hair pulled back in a clip at her nape breezed in and walked directly up to him. Her gaze was direct and she had a weather-beaten, no stranger to the elements look that suited her.

"You looking for me?" he asked, wiping his hands on a napkin.

"I am if you're Sam Ford," she said, pulling out a chair. "I saw you talking to Officer Bolles." She stuck out her hand. "I'm—"

"Phoenix Delacourt." He shook her hand.

"Ah . . . yes." She offered a faint smile of acknowledgment. "I heard about your brother. I'm really sorry. I liked him."

"Sheriff Vandra was trying to keep Joe's name out of the press, but it clearly hasn't worked."

"It'll be on the news tonight in any case. Nothing to do with me." She held up her hands. "I'm coming at this from another place."

"What place is that?"

She eyed him carefully. Her eyes were very close to the color of her hair, a dove gray. "I've been doing some research on Joseph Ford Investments, among others. There're a lot of local people who have their life savings tied up with just a few financial companies up and down the coast. If one of them should go under, it could create a tidal that would drown people in debt. Good people."

"What's this about?"

"Do you know Dennis Mulhaney?" she asked.

"No."

"Never heard his name?"

"No. Why? Does he have something to do with Joe?"

"He worked for your brother up until a few months ago.

He wasn't happy with the direction the business was going and he said so. Pretty loudly. To anyone who would listen, myself included. He threatened to make a claim to the SEC about illegal use of money, and then he quit."

Sam didn't like talking to the reporter. Whatever else he felt about Joe, he believed he was a good businessman, an honest businessman, and that he wanted the best for people who invested with him, who trusted him with their savings. "Why are you telling me this?"

"I'm still working on the story. Denny came to me all fired up. He wanted to take your brother down, but there are . . . indications . . . that it was mostly a grudge on Denny's part. He'd made his own investments and they apparently went nowhere, but he blamed your brother."

Sam scooted back his chair, ready to get to his feet. "I don't know anything about my brother's business."

"He moved it here to Salchuk a few months ago, about the time Denny quit. You don't have any idea why?"

"I just told you, I don't know."

"Denny kept in contact with me. He moved to Portland and took a big hit in pay taking a job as a bookkeeper in a small firm, but he still wanted to blow the whistle on the whole 'financial corruption on the coast.' His words, not mine."

"I don't know him, but I know my brother," Sam said, getting hot under the collar. "And it sounds like this Denny is blaming Joe for all of his own problems."

"That's a real possibility," she agreed. "But now, y'see, Denny's disappeared. He's been missing for about six weeks. Just didn't show up for work one day and nobody's seen him since."

Sam stood and dropped enough cash on the table to pay for his cheeseburger and leave a healthy tip, but Phoenix stayed seated at the table. "What are you getting at?"

"Your brother just died in a boating accident and your

sister-in-law's in the hospital. Denny's missing, and those are the three people who worked at Joseph Ford Investments."

"Jules worked there?"

"Part-time, yes. I tried to see her yesterday, but there was a guard outside her door. Why is that? Is there a chance your brother's death wasn't an accident?"

"All I know is my brother's gone," Sam said, turning away. If she wanted to stay, fine, but he had things to do.

That got her to her feet. She had a suede, fringed bag of sorts that she slung over her shoulder. "Do you mind if I talk to you again later?" she asked, following him out.

"You're barking up the wrong tree. I might not know about my brother's business, but I know his character."

"And his wife?"

"What?"

"You know her character, too?"

"If you mean, could she have something to do with whatever financial conspiracy you're spinning, no. She's not made that way either."

Sam's chest was tight. In high school, Brady Delacourt had been proud of his aunt, who'd left the coast to go make her way in Portland, or Seattle, or some other big city. It had been a disappointment to the whole Delacourt family when their shining star returned and took a position at the lowly *North Coast Spirit*, which was really little more than a pamphlet of local happenings despite Phoenix's efforts to print more substantial stories.

"Officer Bolles told me that you were at my brother's office this morning, trying to get in," he said as they headed outside.

She lifted her face to the sunlight. "He's right. I would have loved to have poked around in there."

"To find the information to prove my brother's taking his investors," Sam said coldly.

"I'd like to prove against it."

"Sure. And you wouldn't mind breaking in to an office to do it."

She ignored the jab. "I understand your sister-in-law has some memory issues."

He gave her a hard look. He was beginning to understand Sheriff Vandra's aversion to the woman. She just kept lobbing the balls at him. "Where'd you hear that?"

She just shrugged and smiled.

He left her and fired up the truck, putting the phone on speaker and then placing another call to Vandra, only to be sent to voice mail once more. Frustrated, he phoned Detective Stone next, who answered but admitted the sheriff wasn't around. "Not sure where he is right now," Stone admitted. "Something I can help you with?"

"I'm not comfortable with the guard being removed outside Jules . . . Julia Ford's room. I don't think Joe's death was an accident."

Stone seemed to want to say a lot of things about that, but he chose discretion, which was too bad in Sam's mind. "Sheriff's still waiting on forensics."

"When that information comes back, I want to know it, too," Sam said a bit belligerently.

"I'll tell Vandra."

Sam hung up in disgust. When you were inside the police community, you were privy to all kinds of information. When you were outside, you were on a need-to-know basis only.

The problem was, he hardly knew which way to jump until he heard if the boat fire was arson. If that proved to be the case, he was launching his own investigation outside the Sheriff's Department. He needed to know what had happened to Joe. If the fire was not arson, he still had questions. Why had Joe called him? What had he wanted to say? Was there a money problem as Phoenix Delacourt suspected?

Sam shook his head, feeling like he was wading through a nightmare. Half the time he didn't think about Joe's death, focusing instead on what was going on in his brother's life directly prior to it. The other half he felt knee-buckling grief and guilt. If only he'd had time to make amends, to become friends again with his only brother, to get past the fact that Joe had married Jules.

But now all that was lost to him.

He allowed himself a few moments of grief, aware that if he took the reins off his emotions that he could actually break down. He thought of his brother's smile, one that had become rarer over the years. When had that happened? When Joe broke away from the huge firm he'd worked with in Portland and gone into business for himself? Joe had initially been close with Jules's father, but Peter St. James had taken his life somewhere in that first year of their marriage and left personal financial disaster in his wake, again, according to Sam's father. And it was a kind of strange twist of fate, too, that when Peter St. James lost the imposing family home on the beach, the Montgomerys and Hapstells weren't far behind. The three families with all the money moved out of their palatial houses within a few months of each other.

Maybe they'd all lost money in the same way.

Sam turned his truck toward Joe and Jules's house, and about a mile from the turnoff, he got another call on his cell. He didn't recognize the number. "Sam Ford," he answered.

A stuttered gasping reached his ears. "Who is this?" he asked.

"It's Georgie!" a young, female voice wailed. "Mom said you told her that Dad's *dead*! What happened? Oh, my God, *oh, my God!*"

The line went dead.

* * *

The café where they met was just outside Portland on the west side. It touted its homemade cinnamon rolls, which were small, dense, and tasteless. The result was, nobody of note patronized the place, and it was a perfect spot to rendezvous, whenever either one of them was ready to go back to the coast, away from their Portland killing grounds.

By unspoken understanding they eschewed the rolls and drank coffee strong as iron, staring across at each other in the booth. He reached a hand toward her, but she ignored it and kept on cradling her coffee cup.

"Bridget's not happy with Tom," she said, her eyes never leaving his as she sipped the hot drink.

"What the fuck. I did everything I was supposed to do."

"Except make sure there was no one to tell the tale."

He leaned back, pissed. "I took care of Joe. That was the deal. That was the payment."

"Plus any contingencies," she hissed. "And there was a pretty fucking big contingency that you *missed* and she's lying in a hospital bed just waiting to tell her tale."

"I'll take care of it," he snarled.

She wanted to reach across the table and slap him. She was the pragmatic one. He was a dreamer and she'd always known it. She'd had a good marriage once, but then she'd started sniffing around for adventure and there he was. Who knew she'd find someone with a like mind?

"And we have another problem, two actually, for a total of *three*."

"What are you talking about?" He tried to play with her fingers with his, but she pulled her mug of coffee toward her.

"Loose ends," she hissed. "Loose fucking ends!"

"I told you I'm on it. I'll take care of Julia tonight."

"And the other two?"

"The kid'll be easy. If you're hinting about Phoenix, that's gonna be trickier."

"No loose ends," she repeated. "That's what the man said. That's the mission."

"I like it better when it's just you and me, doing our thing. No jobs. No bosses . . . Just us having some fun."

"I want to retire from my job," she said. "I want enough money so that we can do what we want. That's why we have to hire out."

"Yeah, this one got more complicated than it was supposed to be. What the hell was that about taking the boat out? I about shit myself," he confessed. "Had to work really fast."

"You always planned to take him out at sea."

"Not yesterday! I wasn't really ready and then he took his goddamn wife with him."

"And you like her and don't want to hurt her. *But she's a loose end!*"

"I'm going to do it. Shut your beautiful mouth. Save it for more important things," he added suggestively.

"We just have to be clear, that's all. You need to do your job and I need to do mine."

"Remember the first time?" He gazed at the window into the far distance. "Gives me a hard-on every time I think of it."

She struggled to tamp down her anger. He always did this. Always went to the romantic, ignoring all the signs of trouble. He was a creature of sensation, but then so was she.

"I remember," she said shortly.

They'd been at a viewpoint overlooking the ocean with a split rail fence at the edge of the headland, a popular spot for tourists to take pictures. She'd stopped to assess her life, go over all the mundane pieces that had led her to where she was, try to figure out where she went wrong, where her road to "exceptional" had wound down to "mediocre." Stuck in a job and a marriage that were both going nowhere.

He'd been driving by and seen her and had pulled in. "Hey," he'd said, getting out of the car, and she'd been a little annoyed because she'd been trying to commune with herself.

They were the only people at the viewpoint apart from a middle-aged couple who were wearing matching shirts splashed with gaudy pink flamingos and matching virulent pink pants. They wore matching straw hats and had matching potbellies. They were taking pictures but couldn't get in the shot together. The man hollered over at them.

"Hey! Yoo-hoo! Can one of you take our picture?" He waggled the camera at them, a huge Nikon that had been around a few years.

Neither of them had responded. They were making small talk of their own. They knew each other well, but it was pure circumstance that they were standing there at that time. Neither of them wanted to deal with the tourists.

"Yoo-hoo! HEY!" Both of them were clamoring now.

Under his breath, he said, "Wouldn't it be nice if they just fell over that cliff and died?"

"The world would be a better place," she agreed.

"HEYYYY! OVER HERE!!"

They'd both turned reluctantly to look at the couple, who were waving at them frantically. Then they'd looked at each other and something happened. A sizzle of awareness that ran through her like an electric wire. She'd almost come just standing there, thinking about pushing the couple over the edge.

They sauntered over to where the couple was standing in front of the fence. Behind them was a sharp drop to jagged rocks below.

"Well, hi there," the portly man said, thrusting out the hand not holding the camera. "We're Jerry and Jeri Hofstetter. That's how we met, you know. Our names being the same and all."

"We went to grade school together," Jeri added, smiling at her spouse and the clearly oft-told story.

"What are your names?" Jerry asked.

They hesitated, and then she said, "Bridget." She'd always liked that name.

"I'm . . . um . . . Tom," he said.

"You married?" Jeri asked.

"No," she said.

"Yes," he said at the same time.

"We've been engaged so long sometimes it feels like marriage," she told the couple, smiling at Tom. She should have known right then he'd be the weak link in their partnership. "We're still searching for that perfect ring."

Jeri had scanned both of their left hands as they'd approached like the nosy old lady she apparently was. With that answer, Jeri brightened and said, "Oh, Jerry and me just went out and did the dirty deed with a plastic ring he'd saved from when he was a kid!"

"Got it in a cereal box," Jerry confided with a wink.

"Of course you did. That's adorable," Bridget said, smiling.

Jerry handed Tom the camera and he and Jeri scooched in together, their arms around each other. Tom aimed the lens at them and took a picture while Bridget stood beside him.

"I'll take a couple more, just to be sure," Tom assured them.

She could feel the excitement rising in him, rising in herself. Were they really going to do this? No. No way. It didn't happen that way. A random thrill-kill from two law-abiding citizens? Uh-uh.

Tom took one more shot, then pulled back and looked at Bridget through heavy-lidded eyes. He was feeling it, too, their eye contact hot enough to burn right through her. She was thrilled anew that she was about to come. With no body friction. Holy mother of *God!*

When he stepped toward Jerry and Jeri, she did, too. And then they took another step. And then another, crowding into them.

"Whoa," Jerry said. Looks of confusion crossed both of their fat faces.

And then, as if choreographed, they both put their right hands out and pushed them over. Jerry flipped over the rail and bumped once and was gone. Jeri's purse strap got hung up on the rail for a nanosecond, so Bridget picked up her foot and kicked her over. The Hofstetters' dying screams were cut off by a hard *thunk-thunk* as they landed, followed by a cascade of pebbles as their bodies bounced off the cliff-side into the ocean.

Bridget and Tom looked at each other. "Damn, woman," he breathed, and then they both dashed to their cars, he still with the old couple's camera.

They drove off madly, both in the same direction, Tom in front, Bridget following. She wanted him inside her and she called his cell and told him so. He warned her to slow down and he did the same. They drove as carefully as they could given that inside they were thrumming with sexual need. When he pulled onto a lane that led past a bed-and-breakfast on the east side of Highway 101, away from the ocean, then went on past the place and wound into deep woods, she was on his bumper, practically panting.

At a small clearing in the woods, miles above the ocean, they both stepped out of their cars. She ran to him. He opened the door to the backseat, grabbed her, and threw her inside. Her head banged hard onto the seat but she didn't care. They couldn't rip their clothes off fast enough, and then he jammed himself inside her and she screamed with pleasure so loud that he clamped his hand over her mouth. "Careful, 'Bridget.' At that decibel level someone might hear us."

Afterward they laughed like maniacs. He lay atop her on the seat, his pants down around his ankles, hers hanging from one still-shod foot. When their laughter broke they stared at each other with smiles in their eyes.

My soul mate. My love. My secret passion.

Now she looked across at him and had different thoughts. Yes, she could still feel the high and desire that had come after killing the Hofstetters, and a number of others since, but it was hard to reach that same level again. Her desire wasn't as high, wasn't as strong, wasn't as good.

And the Hofstetters had nearly been their undoing. Right there, at the very beginning! Some passing motorist whom neither of them had noticed had reported seeing a couple of sedans parked at the viewpoint and thought there'd been another couple with the Hofstetters. The search had gone on and on and on for several months she'd been crazy with fear that somehow they would be found out. The fear had served to heighten her sexual need and she'd rendezvoused with "Tom" in remote places several more times, always somewhere outside the area they lived.

And then time had passed and nothing had happened. They'd gone about their lives and the Hofstetters became a cold case. When she was with him the need, the memory, the desperate desire was reflected in his eyes. She knew he could see it in hers.

They decided to kill again, but somewhere else. The nearest big city was Portland, so that's where they went. It wasn't easy. Neither of them could get away for long and the excuses grew thinner and thinner, not to mention finding a mark they both agreed on. She didn't want to take out a mother with a young child, and he didn't want to kill any man supporting his family.

They agreed their kills should be singles, childless couples, or anyone over the age of fifty.

And then they found Monique. He/she—they never knew what to call him/her—was part of the LGBT community and therefore a perfect mark. Neither of them cared a whit about Monique's sexual identity. He/she could be whoever they wanted, for all they cared. But his/her sexual identity sure as hell was a great smoke screen to hide the blame for whodunit, and sure enough, as soon as his/her body was discovered, the media declared Monique's death was a hate crime. Everyone was riled up and the search was on, but Bridget and Tom were long gone. They'd wooed Monique out of a dark bar and into a back alley with the promise of a three-way, then Bridget had grabbed the baseball bat they'd planted earlier and had bashed in his/her head. Tom took off Monique's boa, and together they wrapped it around and around his/her neck until Monique's chest stopped rising and falling. They waited precious long seconds more to assure themselves he/she was really dead, then they racewalked to their respective cars, drove to the nearest freeway exit with a cheap motel, and screwed their brains out for a couple of hours before driving back the two hours to the coast.

After that, they claimed Portland as their hunting ground. There was no reason either one of them would be there, let alone want anyone dead. The homicides seemed unrelated and so they were.

But he—*Tom*—had a big mouth, something she hadn't foreseen. He'd hinted about their extracurricular activities to someone who had their listening ears on. He'd said that he knew how to commit murder and get away with it. And that person, over time, finally asked if there was any way he could have one whistle-blowing little shit taken out, once and for all—theoretically, of course—and Tom had told the man that anything was possible.

Luckily, he'd never brought her name into it, even as Bridget, but it had really sent her pulse skyrocketing with fear.

"Are you out of your fucking mind?" she'd screamed at him.

"I'm thinking of the future, darling. There may come the time that we need to run, and to do that we need cash."

She'd argued with him to the point of slapping and shoving

him, and then he'd done the same to her, and somehow they'd wound up screwing on the hood of her sedan. And she'd pushed her doubts aside and even gotten into it when they'd hustled Denny. She'd pretended she had a husband named Ricky who was a stone-cold killer. The bartender at Tiny Tim's might be able to describe Tom and Bridget. That had been a risk. But no one knew Denny was dead yet, or no one cared apparently, because it had been over a month and there'd been nothing. Not a word about him going missing. Nada. He was that much of a loser.

But then new panic. All of a sudden the man wanted them to take out Joe Ford. Had hinted that if Tom didn't take the job, he would be exposed. And that would mean Bridget would be exposed as well because Tom was basically weak. She'd wanted to throttle him for putting them in this position and yet . . . the man who'd hired him paid well. The rumor was the man had lost a ton of money through bad investments and he blamed Ford.

"Get rid of Joe Ford," the man ordered.

Tom had argued that it was too soon after Denny, but his worries had fallen on deaf ears. The man gave him three days and so he and Bridget had hustled around, putting a new plan into place. Their original one had included burning Joe's boat, but then yesterday, at the last minute, Joe had apparently gotten wind of what was coming down and had changed his own plans. He suddenly took the boat out himself, with his wife, and they were gone. Tom and she had been forced to scramble around and run by the seat of their pants. Plan B meant Tom had to intercept *The Derring-Do*, claim his motorboat had run out of gas, and ask if he could get a lift. Joe Ford had helped Tom aboard, but before he could ask what the problem was, Tom hit him with the gas can and sent him overboard. Julia had run, but he'd caught her and pushed her into the ocean as well. With that, he'd poured gasoline all over that boat, stem to the stern, then dropped the lighted match as he dove into the water. He'd watched the boat go up in a *whoosh* as he climbed back into his own boat, one he'd liberated from its mooring at the marina, and motored out to sea. Once he was several miles out, he turned north and kept going all the way to Seaside, where he ditched the stolen boat at a private dock where he knew the elderly vacation homeowners never came. He'd wiped the boat down, though seawater and the elements would probably take care of any DNA material he might inadvertently leave. It could be weeks before anyone found it. Meanwhile, she had purposely put herself in a bar at the entrance to the bay, in full view of people who knew her, so when the boat went up, she was one of the first to gasp, point, and shriek for help.

Tom had gone to a bar in Seaside afterward, which had kind of pissed her off for no reason she could name, but then they'd rendezvoused at the rest stop and trekked into the woods and that had all been good.

Now, however, the fallout was starting to concern her. The man who'd paid them for Denny, and who was paying for Joe Ford, had assured Tom he would be safe, but that was before Joe's wife saw Tom on the boat and survived. And that was just one of the problems that were popping up like mushrooms, all because Tom had gone rogue.

Yes, the money was nice, but getting locked up for murder would make that a hollow victory, wouldn't it?

"She has no memory," Tom said now. "I've got some time to take care of her."

"That's a rumor," she reminded. "And even if it's true, what about when she remembers?"

"She might not remem—"

"You want to bet your freedom on that? I sure as hell don't!"

"How'm I gonna get her in the hospital, hmmm?"

"You better figure out how."

"I said I'd take care of it, and I will."

"What if she recognizes you?"

"It won't do her any good, because it'll be her last few minutes of life."

"I mean, what if she remembers before you get to her."

"Stop worrying."

His lackadaisical attitude drove her *insane.* If he didn't take care of the problem, she'd have to, and was she supposed to do it alone? What if she failed? What if she was caught?

No fucking way.

"They're releasing her tomorrow," he said now

"How do you know? Did you get a call?" She glanced toward his cell phone, which lay beside his hand on the table.

"Sure did."

"What if she remembers *tonight*? Or, maybe she already has and we just don't know it. What about that?" Her voice was rising and he shot her a sharp look.

"You gotta take it easy."

"You've got to take it more seriously."

He sent her a ghost of a smile. "I got a dick that'll slide right into you and have you screaming for more."

"Oh, for God's sake."

"I'm coming over there."

"To my side of the booth? What are you talking about?"

"I'm gonna make you howl."

The place was practically deserted, but there was no way that was going to work. She started laughing. He was so easy to turn on. As pissed off as she was at him, the idea was turning her on, too, but she could handle the heat. He couldn't.

To her surprise, he jumped from his side of the booth and slid into hers, jamming his hand between her legs.

"Stop it!" she hissed, slapping at his hand. For an answer, he unbuttoned her jeans and slid his other hand inside, wiggling his fingers. She tried to squirm away, glancing around with wild eyes to make sure they were alone, but he was insistent.

She wanted to kill him!

"Okay," she gasped. "Okay!"

He pulled himself away from her but stayed on her side of the booth. "Don't worry about Julia Ford," he whispered in her ear. "I'll take care of her."

"All right."

She was all jazzed up in spite of herself. She wished she could be part of the killing, but it was too dangerous. Still, the thought of it made her blood run hot. She smiled to herself, relieved and a bit bereft when he slid back to his side of the booth, then threw some money on the table.

"We gotta go," he said.

She walked to her car, her head full of images of Julia Ford, imagining her wide eyes filled with sheer terror as she came at her . . . and then the image switched to Tom as she attacked him, the question in his eyes turning to horrified realization as she stuck a knife between his ribs once, twice, three, four, *five times*!

She shivered in delicious excitement.

In the end, her beloved Tom was going to be her best kill.

Chapter Eight

Sam pulled into Joe and Jules's driveway. He'd tried to reconnect with Georgie over and over again, but the call just kept going to voice mail. He tried calling Gwen, too, but got more of the same.

"Damn it," he muttered, glancing at the clock on the dashboard as he switched off the ignition. Five forty-five. He'd left Salchuk in search of a burner phone but had failed and would have to try again later. Salchuk was known for not allowing national stores within its city limits, and store owners were all local, which was nice but made shopping for items like a new phone inconvenient.

Climbing out of the pickup, he stretched his back and heard it crack. His head was loads better, but a tiredness had settled in his bones. He headed to the front door, slid the key into the lock, twisted the handle. He walked inside and strode directly to the kitchen and a bottle of water. Inside the refrigerator he saw Joe had a couple of Coronas. He debated on opening one and downing it. He was hot and tired and a little angry. He probed his mind for that anger, like a tongue searching for a lost filling, pretty certain he wasn't going to like what he would discover.

He landed on it pretty quick. He was mad at Jules that

she couldn't remember anything beyond her brother's death. She was married to his brother, had been for several years, and before Joe there was him. Sam. Sam and Jules.

She couldn't remember *any* of it?

And now Joe was gone and there was something really wrong inside Joe's business. Something his father had sensed and Phoenix Delacourt seemed to know about. It felt, in fact, like everyone knew things but him.

"Screw it," he muttered, reaching for the Corona, then opening and shutting several drawers, searching for a bottle opener.

Ding-dong . . . ding-dong, ding-dong, ding-dong!

Christ, who was this? He looked at the beer, felt guilty about it, and slammed it onto the counter. "Hold on!" Sam yelled. Someone had pressed the doorbell to the ringer and wasn't letting up.

He strode to the door and flung it open.

The man who stood on the steps was about his same age and same coloring, but carried a good thirty pounds extra. His shirt and slacks were expensive. Sam wasn't much good with clothing designers, but even he could tell they were some label that screamed money. A pair of Ray-Ban sunglasses covered his eyes. His hair was combed back and applied with product, and that watch . . . If it wasn't Rolex, it was one helluva imitation.

And then Sam knew him. Jesus . . . "Hap," he said, dumb with surprise. "What the hell?"

"Hi, Sam," Walter Hapstell Junior said with a forced smile. "Long time no see."

"What are you doing here?"

"Maybe I should ask you the same." He tried to look past Sam. "Where are Julia and Joe?"

"Uh . . . they're not here. They're . . ."

He debated on telling him the truth. It seemed like the worst kept secret in the world, but before he could answer,

Hap continued, "Tutti said as much. Are you going to her barbecue? She said she invited you."

"How do you know Tutti?" He looked past Hap to the white Mercedes convertible that was parked in the driveway next to his Chevy pickup. A long-legged redhead was just stepping out of the car.

Jesus, Mary, and Joseph. *Tina.* In a tight blue dress and matching high heels.

She waved halfheartedly, her smile little more than a grimace. "Hi, Sam," she said.

"What . . . ? What are you both doing here?" he demanded.

Sam's ex-wife looked from Sam to Hap, who answered, "Tina and I live on the other side of the canal. We're the gray house three down from Tutti's. Tutti said you were here and Joe and Julia weren't. Are you staying with them, or house-sitting or something? When will they be back?"

Sam stood silent in the doorway. He could scarcely process. He hadn't seen Hap since high school. He'd heard about him. Through Joe. Through his father. And from what he'd gleaned Walter Junior would inherit all of Walter Senior's investments, which meant a big chunk of Seaside and most of the rest of the coast south to Tillamook, including Salchuk. They may have sold their house in a down time, but they'd bounced back, higher than ever. Donald had said that Joe had done business with the Hapstells, and Sam had assumed more with Walter Senior than Walter Junior, but you never knew. Hap was on Joe's doorstep for a reason.

The fact that Martina was with him shouldn't have been a surprise. If Hap was back in the black and the cash was flowing, Tina was bound to be hovering nearby. It wouldn't suit her to lose money. She'd been in a complete state when her father had sold their house on the beach and his business had teetered on the edge of bankruptcy. She'd clung to Sam for all she was worth during that time, and he'd always suspected he'd been a safe choice in a scary world. He hadn't understood it then, and he'd once asked her why she'd chosen him. Her answer had been to hit him playfully on the shoulder and say, "Because you're as good as it gets, sugar."

A nice comment, but Tina had a way of complimenting you while she was planning to stab you in the back.

You were the one who wanted out, he reminded himself. Well, that, and the fact that fortunes had begun rising again with the Hapstells, Montgomerys, and his own brother. In the end Martina hadn't been all that heartbroken about their divorce.

And clearly she'd found her way to Hap.

"Aren't you going to invite us in?" Tina asked, coming up the steps to stand by Hap on the porch, slipping her arm through his.

As much as Sam would like to pose some questions to Hap, he didn't want him to pass through Joe's door. "It's not my house."

"Well, maybe it is," Hap suggested. "If there's been the tragedy I think there has. I know the boat that burned was *The Derring-Do* and that's Joe's boat. Is he okay? Where is he?"

In the morgue . . .

Hap didn't wait for Sam's answer. "Joe and I are associates, business associates—"

"And friends," Tina put in.

"—and have been for quite a while. You knew that, right? That we've been working together for a while on some deals? I really need to talk to him. Can you give me some idea when he'll be back?"

Sam remained silent. He didn't want to talk about Joe and Jules. He didn't want to say that Joe was dead, and he didn't want to say Jules was in the hospital. He didn't know how the boat had burned, what the circumstances were, but his gut told him it was no accident.

Hap eyed Sam closely. "Jesus, man. He's dead, isn't he?"

Tina gasped and her hand flew to her throat. A little overly dramatic maybe, Sam thought, cataloguing her reaction. But maybe it was real.

Sam's cell phone rang, giving him a momentary reprieve. "Excuse me," he said, shutting the door in their faces. He didn't want Hap in Joe's house. Too many questions that needed to be answered first.

Glancing at the screen, he saw it was the Sheriff's Department. "Sam Ford," he answered.

"This is Stone," the detective said. "Forensics came back on the boat. It was doused with gasoline and deliberately set."

Sam felt his stomach sink. Expected. What he'd known, but it still felt like a blow.

"Who set it?"

"We don't know yet, but the sheriff heard from a kid down at the marina gas station who says that . . . your brother brought in a can and bought about five gallons of gas about a week ago."

"No."

"The kid just volunteered it. He saw *The Derring-Do* being brought into the bay, but didn't put it together till he talked to Vandra."

Sam couldn't process. There was no way Joe did this. "Joe may have bought the gas, but he didn't do this."

"You want to talk to the kid?"

The invitation surprised him. He could already tell Sheriff Vandra wouldn't take kindly to any interference. "Yeah. But I'm telling you, Joe would never hurt his wife. And he wouldn't set his boat on fire. He loved that boat. There's no reason. He wouldn't do it."

The Cardaman file.

Sam leaned against the kitchen counter. Maybe there was

a reason. Something financial had gone terribly wrong. Some deal, or deals, or . . .

Bang, bang, bang.

Sam turned to the sound. The front door. Hap and Tina.

. . . Joe and I are business associates . . .

Dogs began barking frantically from the house next door, and Sam glanced their way. He hadn't heard them earlier, so they must have just gotten there. Jules and Joe didn't have a neighbor on the other side; they were at the end of the development of houses, the last one on the west side, though the canal meandered away north for several miles. Sam heard Hap yell at the dogs to shush, calling them by name, Less and More, it sounded like, but it only seemed to send the dogs into a further frenzy of barking.

The cell phone at his ear, he saw the bottle opener stuck to a metal knife rack tacked on the wall beneath the cabinets. Sam thought about opening his beer but he stayed where he was, thinking.

Hap wants in the house. Maybe he's already been in the house. Maybe he's the one who took the note. Did he have something to do with Joe's death?

He realized Stone had given him the kid's name. "What was that again?" he asked, snapping back to the moment.

"The kid's name is Ryan Mayfield. He's part-time at the marina. Vandra won't like it that I gave you the name, but I'd like some follow-up on Mayfield."

"You don't believe Joe burned his own boat, either," Sam realized.

"I'd like a little more corroboration," Stone admitted.

"Joe would have never set his boat on fire deliberately, and he would have never risked his wife's life."

"But he didn't meet you after he texted you."

"Something must have happened. Something that changed his plans. Something that changed everything."

Bang, bang, bang!

"I gotta go," Sam said, as Less and More ripped into more wild barking. It was lucky they hadn't been around when he was sneaking through the back window. Sam clicked off, then stared at the front door a moment, before stalking across the room and throwing the door open once more.

"Well, there you are," Tina said, piqued. "Jesus, when did you get so rude?"

"You're right, Hap. There's been a tragedy. That boat that burned today, that was *The Derring-Do*, Joe's boat. Joe drowned and Jules is in the hospital." His throat choked up.

"What? What?" Tina's eyes were stretched wide. If he didn't know what an actress she was, he would have thought she was in total shock. As it was, he couldn't trust her. He couldn't trust either of them.

Hap looked poleaxed. "Joe's really dead?" Though he'd posed the idea, he didn't seem to be able to comprehend the news.

Hearing it again affected Sam, as well. "Yes."

Tina wobbled on her heels and abruptly sank down on the porch step. "Oh, my God. Oh, Hap. Oh, my God. What're you going to do?"

Hap said to Sam, "May I come in? I could use a glass of water."

"Why don't we all go to Tutti's barbecue?" Sam heard himself saying. "It's after five already. I should tell Joe and Jules's friends. It's going to be on the news tonight, but I think I should be there. I'll meet you there."

He closed the door on them, locked it, and stepped back, half convinced they would still try to get in.

The last thing he wanted to do was go to a barbecue, but someone had taken that note. Someone had let themselves into the house. And Hap was one of the Fishers. It was an opportunity to learn more about Joe and Jules that he needed to take.

Joe hadn't set his boat ablaze. Joe hadn't harmed Jules. Joe may have drowned, but he'd also had a bash on his head. Sam had seen it when he'd ID'd his brother's body. Maybe it was from the accident, or maybe it had happened before the boat had burned. Something happened. Somebody attacked him and Jules, burned the boat, got away. . . .

Why did Joe purchase the gas?

Sam's gut tightened. No. He wasn't going to be dissuaded from his belief in his brother. He knew what Joe was capable of and what he wasn't.

He walked back into the kitchen, thinking, saw the Corona and opened it, drank half of it down, wiped his mouth. He felt like he was in a nightmare. Taking the beer, he walked into the bathroom, stared at himself in the mirror. Same dark hair, same blue eyes, same mouth, and chin, currently sporting five-o'clock shadow.

He rinsed his face and dried it off, decided against shaving. He wasn't trying to win any beauty contest, he just wanted information.

He went out to the garage and pulled down the canoe that was hung by hooks on the wall and took it through the back door of the garage to the dock. He returned for the oar, locked the garage door behind him, then, remembering Tutti's request to bring a bottle of wine, headed toward the refrigerator where an unopened bottle of Pinot Gris seemed to be waiting just for him. He hoped to hell it wasn't horribly expensive because he was going to have to pay them back . . . pay Jules back, anyway.

As he left he made sure the house key was still in his pocket, then manhandled the canoe into the water, dropped lithely inside. If Tutti had a key, it was highly possible someone else on the canal did, too. Someone had entered Joe and Jules's house after Sam had secured the window, and he sensed it was one of the Fishers . . . the friends. . . . Briefly he thought of Jules, hoping she was getting better. He needed her to remember what had happened on the boat, for his brother and for himself.

Jules wanted to fall asleep again and dream, but she was restless and achy. She pushed the swing arm table away from her—they'd brought her turkey and mashed potatoes and some anemic-looking peas—got up and used the bathroom. She lifted her right arm inside its sling—yeah, it hurt—then checked out her scrapes and bruises. There was an abrasion along her jawline and a bandage at her temple. She reached up with her left hand and pulled the bandage off. Her hair was stuck to her head and she sported a huge knot with a small cut. Gingerly, she examined the knot. Yep, that hurt, too. She tried to remember how she'd gotten her injuries, but it was a complete blank.

Frustrated, she returned to her bed but didn't climb inside. She wanted to walk. Wanted to do something.

She skirted the end of the bed and glanced at the meal that she'd barely touched. It was like Thanksgiving, sort of, only not as good. Not like her mom used to make.

She sank onto the only chair in the room, straight-backed with blue cushions and wooden arms. Her mind suddenly clicked on. She had a flash of recall so swift it made her dizzy. She was looking out the window of a cabin in the woods, surrounded by snow. Unexpected snow. Early and unusual for the coast. A dinner table with a cream-colored tablecloth and candles waving in the slight breeze from an interior door opening. The scents of cinnamon and brown sugar. A cornucopia spilling out dried corn cobs with multi-colored kernels, tiny pumpkins, hazelnuts, and pine cones. *Thanksgiving.* There were people in the shadows. Her mother and father?

She immediately had a mental picture of Mama. Sitting in a chair, staring out at the sea. Her mother had always blamed her for her brother's death even though she'd been a child herself when it happened. Where was her father? He'd been her champion once, but thinking of him, them, made her head feel like it was going to explode.

She eased her thoughts from them, desperate to hang on to the Thanksgiving scene. There were people with her, but they weren't her parents. One, she saw, was Sam Ford, and he was with . . . *Joe* . . . and *Donald* was there, too, their father!

Oh, God, I remember! I remember!

"What else? What else?" she whispered. There was a woman . . . Gwen . . . Oh, God, Joe's ex-wife and her daughter, Georgie, Joe's stepdaughter—no, *adopted* daughter. Joe had adopted her.

Why do I remember this? she asked herself. *Why this?*

It didn't matter. It was a true memory, teased awake by the traditional Thanksgiving meal. Her heart was pounding in her chest, making her head throb as well, but she didn't care. She wanted to shout for joy.

I remember Joe, she thought, trying to stay with the memory, though it was growing hazier by the moment.

But I was with Sam.

She stumbled to her feet, slamming her knee into the side table. The tray clattered to the floor, splattering potatoes and peas and turkey. The gray curtain pressed down on her, but she held on to the memory for all she was worth. Damn it. Why was this happening to her? Why couldn't she remember?

Because you don't want to. . . . You know you don't want to. . . .

"But I do want to."

A brisk, older nurse Jules hadn't seen before stepped into the room. "You all right?" she asked Jules, who was standing at the end of the bed.

"I just dropped my tray."

"Okay, I'll get someone to clean it up." She was gone in a flash.

You were with Sam first, then Joe.

Was that what she didn't want to remember? No. She could remember that now, and a lot more. It was coming back, just like Dr. Lillard said it would, though she had to be careful not to try too hard or her brain wanted to shut down.

But she and Sam were ancient history, she realized, rubbing her knee as she sank back onto the chair. She'd been with Sam as a teenager, when her mother's illness had begun to really manifest, but it was Joe who'd rescued her in those final dark days of her mother's life when her father had become a stranger to her, and she'd been left caring for her mother basically alone. After her mother's death, and then when her father killed himself, Joe was there for her. They'd reacquainted when she was taking some night classes at Portland State and he was getting an MBA and working at a prestigious Portland investment firm . . . she couldn't recall the name just yet . . . while she was working on a business degree that she never finished because she was called home to take care of her mother by her desperate father. She and Joe had recognized each other across the classroom and they went out for coffee at the break. Then it was a glass of wine, after the next class, and then they started hanging out together. Joe became a big part of her social life, and Georgie had been there, too, still just a kid, but she'd bonded tightly with Jules, mostly because her own mother was a cool customer whose time was taken up with her interior design business.

And then her father called, begging her to come back to the beach. "I can't take care of her," he said. "You need to. I can't be here."

Jules had left school and gone home. Her father, who'd been so good to her when she was a child, now was a stranger.

He spent as little time with them as possible. Money was tight. He'd sold their beach house, which had been too expensive to maintain, and he'd moved them into a rental. Jules had accrued quite a bit of debt in student loans, and suddenly she was her mother's caretaker, unable to work and unable to make payments.

It was Joe to the rescue. He offered to help her financially, through this crushing time. She refused, still believing her father would snap back to reality and help his wife and only child. But he left Jules to take care of everything, and she cried herself to sleep every night. She tried to help her mother, who couldn't do even the simplest thing for herself, and she railed at her father for emotionally abandoning them. The only positive was that her mother had deteriorated enough that she didn't remember who Jules was . . . and therefore stopped blaming her for Clem's death.

Julia was with her mother when she died, and finally her father seemed to momentarily snap out of his depression. Then six months later, he killed himself. Threw himself into the Columbia River

Joe to the rescue again . . . and Georgie. They had become her family. The people who cared about her. When Joe had asked her to marry him, she said yes. The only hiccup was her previous relationship with Sam, but she'd told herself it didn't matter. Besides, he was all wrapped up in Martina Montgomery—engaged, if the rumor was true— and there was no reason not to run to Joe with open arms, so she did. They went to a justice of the peace and she became Mrs. Joseph Ford.

For those few months after her mother's death, her father, who was a mentor to Joe, had seemed really happy that Jules had married him, and appeared to be coming around. But then he was gone, too. And then Sam married Martina and apart from one very uncomfortable dinner at Donald's cabin—Thanksgiving again—he'd made a point of staying away from them and they'd pretty much done the same.

Jules.

She'd almost forgotten he still called her Jules. No one else did but Sam. It bothered her that she'd latched on to that name over Julia. What did that mean? Was she still thinking about Sam, *pining* for him? It embarrassed her to admit to herself that she'd never completely gotten over him. It was—

She stopped and went cold. What the hell was wrong with her? Joe was dead and she was thinking about Sam? Joe was good and kind and had taken care of her. God, what kind of person was she?

Joe. She couldn't believe he was gone. It was a lot like when her father died, impossible to accept. It had taken her a long time to grieve for her father and she was struggling now with Joe. All the deaths linked to the water. Her brother, Clem, and the sneaker wave, her father who had jumped to his death near the mouth of the Columbia, and now . . . now Joe on the boat . . . Oh, God. She shuddered at the memories.

Snap out of it! You need to remember what happened on the boat. That's what matters now.

Forcing herself, she tried to turn her mind to yesterday's events and immediately broke into a cold sweat. The gray curtain hovered, felt like a guillotine ready to cut off her head if she remembered.

"You're nuts," she whispered.

She stood up again. Too fast. The room reeled. Immediately she sat back down and put her head between her knees. She felt anxious, tight. With a concentrated effort, she got herself to relax a little. She would remember it all in time. Even the accident. She had to. And Sam was going to take her to her home tomorrow, so it would all be okay.

A vision came to her of kissing Sam, him atop her,

making love to her at his father's cabin in the light of the flickering television, kissing her in an effort to stop her laughter and his while the Julia Roberts movie, *Sleeping with the Enemy*, played out on screen.

She realized instantly that this particular vision was one she'd pulled out often. A memory she'd clung to, even while married to his brother. A favorite memory, although there was something tainted about it now.

Because it's the wrong brother.

One of the aides appeared and began cleaning up the mess Jules had made. "I'm sorry," she said lamely.

"No problem," the aide said, then she gathered up the remains of the turkey, potatoes, and congealing gravy and stowed it all in a plastic bag, which she held away from herself in rubber gloves as she whisked off again.

It's not like it's radioactive, Julia wanted to mutter.

She caught herself up. *Maybe you're not that nice after all.*

For some reason she found that cheering.

The nurse came back in a few minutes later and asked if she would like anything else. "Some ice cream, maybe?" she suggested.

"Oh, no, thanks."

"You sure?"

The thought of ice cream suddenly had huge appeal. Maybe it was one of her favorites. "Well . . . maybe . . ."

"I'll go get it."

She returned with an ice cream cup, a swirl of vanilla and orange, and Jules sat back in the chair and ate it, feeling memories dart around like fireflies, impossible to grab as they lit up just for a moment or two before fading out.

She tried to watch television, but nothing appealed to her. She suddenly craved a book, but she couldn't think of anything she wanted to read. She couldn't, in fact, think of one title.

Well, okay, fine. It was going to take a while, but at least she felt that her memory might actually finally return. That was a relief. It had been bone deep frightening to think it might not happen.

She got back into bed, starting to feel glad she would be leaving the hospital tomorrow. The television was tuned to a sitcom that wasn't even close to funny, in her opinion, but her eyes were getting heavy. Good. She'd go to sleep and face the new day and maybe something good would happen. If not good, then better.

Maybe, just maybe, if she was lucky, she would recall what had happened on the boat.

She was dozing when she heard soft footsteps outside her door coming her way. Her eyes flew open and she was suddenly full of terror. Someone was coming for her!

"Get to the boat," Joe yelled at her, and she was scrabbling to climb inside.

She was halfway out of her bed when she came to and spied a woman with gray hair tied up into a bun appear in the doorway, carrying a small notebook and a gray cardboard carrier with two cups of coffee in paper cups.

"Hello, Julia," she said.

Jules froze with one leg out of the bed. "Who are you?" she questioned, instantly panicked. She wanted to run far away from her, an irrational and immediate reaction.

The woman tilted her chin and assessed Julia frankly. "You really don't know who I am?"

Yes, she did know. She couldn't quite remember, but she did know. And it was tied up with something else. Something she couldn't bear to know.

"I'm Phoenix Delacourt," the woman said. "And both of these are decafs, given we're past five o'clock. I don't know about you, but I can't handle caffeine this late in the day." She set the cardboard tray on the swing table.

Jules's mind had shut down. She fought the urge to flee and got back in her bed, pulling the covers up tight.

The woman, Phoenix, gazed at her thoughtfully. "Some kind of amnesia, I hear. Or, maybe you're faking?"

"What do you want?"

"It's actually what *you* want, Julia. I'm the reporter. The one you came to see. You found me, not the other way around, and it was you who gave me the file on Ike Cardaman. Remember that? You told me you wanted to make sure that the investors got their backs, no matter who swindled them. And that included your husband. . . ."

Chapter Nine

"No," Julia Ford said through lips that barely moved, but Phoenix could read the dawning horror crossing her face.

Maybe she was faking, maybe she wasn't. But she sure as hell was afraid Joe Ford had been wheeling, dealing, and cheating.

Phoenix took in the young woman trembling before her and decided in that split second that no, Julia Ford wasn't faking. She looked like the proverbial deer in the headlights, just waiting for the car to hit her. It was a good bet she had one helluva story to tell.

"Relax," Phoenix said. "I'm here to help. Mind if I take this chair over here?"

Julia mutely shook her head, so Phoenix chose one of the cups of decaf and one of the cups of cream nestled beside the cups and took a seat. Twenty long years as a reporter for the *North Coast Spirit* had taught her patience, something sorely lacking in her character when she'd first graduated from the University of Oregon with a degree in journalism and then had applied for jobs up and down the Willamette Valley and from California to Washington with no success. Too young. No jobs. Sorry, sorry, sorry . . . So she'd come home to the coast, her dreams dashed, her tail between her

legs, and old Mr. Templeton, who owned the paper and had
a soft spot for idealistic individuals who wanted to change
the world and had enough energy to do so, had hired her as
a gofer around the newspaper office, which was settled in
the right half of the lower floor of an old brick building in
Tillamook. The left half was originally a printing/copy shop,
which seemed a natural next to the paper, but it had only
lasted a few years. The space then turned over to a number
of businesses—shoe repair, computer repair, appliance
repair, whatever. Currently it was a coffee shop, which was
why Phoenix had come to the hospital with two cups of
coffee snug in a gray paper carrier the exact color of her
hair. She had never colored her hair in her life, even when
the first strands of silver had shown up in her late twenties.
It just wasn't her style, then or now. She'd always let her
mass of gray hair grow because she didn't want to fuss with
it. She also eschewed makeup of any kind, and when she
appeared in Jules's room, she looked like the aging hippie
everyone accused her of being, although she'd missed that
particular stage in American culture by about as many years
as she'd been on the planet.

"Joe would never do that to his investors," Julia said.

"You sound just like your brother-in-law, but that wasn't
what you said when you came to see me."

"What did I say?"

"You said, and I'm paraphrasing here, 'I don't know if
my husband's involved with Cardaman or not, but maybe
this will help.' And you handed me the file, which is locked
up in my office file cabinet."

"What's in the file?"

Phoenix could barely hear her, she spoke so softly. "A list
of names, mostly. People you wanted me to check out. I'm
about three quarters down the list, and no one's blamed your
husband yet. Of course, with his death, that could change, I
suppose, and if there's no clear head of the company, I'd

imagine those investors are going to be lining up to get their money back. Do you know who inherits the company?"

"No."

"Would you like your coffee?"

Julia turned blankly toward the table that held her cup, still in the cardboard carrier. Like an automaton she picked up the paper cup and removed the lid, peeled back the top of one of the miniature cream tubs, dumped it in. She put the lid back on and took a sip.

"I usually drink regular coffee," she said, as if testing out the idea.

"I tried to see you yesterday," Phoenix said, "but there was a guard outside your door. I thought he was going to be there for the duration, but he's not there now. Apparently you're no longer either in danger, or a suspect."

"A suspect!" She nearly dropped her coffee.

"I don't think you're a suspect," Phoenix said, "but yesterday I didn't quite know what was what. The general consensus was that boating accident was just that, an unfortunate accident that sent you to the hospital and took your husband's life."

"But you don't think that," she said, lifting the cup to her lips. Without makeup, she looked about twelve years old.

"You handed me the Cardaman file after Denny left the company. Your husband had just closed his Seaside office, and you were no longer working for him. You wanted me to see if there was any wrongdoing."

The blood drained from her face. "Who's Denny?" she whispered.

Once again, Phoenix thought the amnesia wasn't an act. "He was your husband's bookkeeper. There were a few other employees, off and on over the years, but he was the last one. He left around March. He complained to me about financial fraud."

"I can't . . . remember," she wrenched out.

Phoenix debated how hard to push. The answers were inside Julia, no matter what the cause of her amnesia, so it was a matter of unlocking them. "You know what happened, even if you don't have all the pieces yet."

"I don't have any of the pieces."

"Yeah, you do, and I think you know it. You just can't access them right now."

The last few years of her tenure with the *North Coast Spirit*, since Phoenix had diverged into her own kind of reporting—a decision made when old man Templeton died and left her a big chunk of the paper—she'd learned a few things about coaxing information out of reluctant informants. This was a little different, but along the same principles. Phoenix felt she was pretty damn good at her job, so it was just a matter of fitting the right key in the right lock. "How about I tell you all I know about you and then maybe that'll be the grease that gets things going, hmm?"

"I'm afraid I won't like what I hear," she said, swallowing.

"I wouldn't worry about it. Apart from what you told me, I didn't know much about you, so I did some research. I asked people about you. And everyone who knows you said you were good people."

Tears suddenly filled her eyes. "That's nice to hear," Julia choked out.

"But the question's about your husband and whom he was in bed with, financially speaking."

"You think he's sleeping with the enemy. I was just thinking about that movie," Julia said, her lips twisting.

"You were the one who brought me the file," she reminded gently.

Footsteps sounded in the hallway. Rapid. Approaching. Phoenix moved up to Julia's bed and said quietly, "You met me at the coffee shop next to my office. Perfect Cup, which

I think truly overstates their product, but it's handy. You were the one who set up the meeting. Do you remember that?"

"No."

"You said you wanted to know the truth about your husband, no matter what it was, and then you handed me the file. Do you still want to know the truth?"

A nurse pushed into the room, older, solid, with a take no prisoner's attitude. Phoenix knew she was about to be bounced out of Julia's room, but she kept her eyes on the girl, waiting.

In this Julia didn't hesitate. "Yes," she said firmly. "I want to know the truth."

Sam arrived at Tutti's a little after six-thirty, tying his canoe to one of the shiny, silver cleats on the dock, then swinging onto the ladder that reached from the dock into the water and hauling himself up it. Hap and Tina weren't there yet and he looked down the canal and saw Tina move out to their deck and look his way. Neither of them waved. It had taken Hap and her a good twenty minutes to drive from Joe's around the bridge on the north end of the canal and back down to their house, a much longer route than across the water. Hap came out to join her and they moved together to a motorized rubber raft floating near the attached boathouse. Beyond them sunlight glittered on the green waters of the canal, which took a sharp bend on its way to the main body of the Nehalem River, then the bay and eventually the ocean.

Sam's head was full of questions for Hap about Joe's business. He would like to get him alone for a deep discussion, but if it had to play out in front of the other Fishers, he didn't know if he much cared. He wanted results fast. He wasn't interested in finessing answers if it was going to take too long.

"There you are!" Tutti declared, spying Sam as he walked

up the five steps from the dock to the upper deck, which was on the main level of her house. The sun beat down on the back of his neck, but the breeze was cold, now coming off the ocean. No more east wind.

He let himself be propelled by Tutti toward an outdoor wooden table where a sweating, ice-filled bucket held bottles of wine and beer. Sam added his wine bottle to the mix, but chose another Corona for his drink, which Tutti immediately took from him. She stuffed it with a lime slice and handed it back to him with a flourish. Only one other couple had arrived thus far, and they were inside the house in front of the television. Sam could see them through the screen of the sliding glass door. The man had the remote in hand, aimed at the television.

Tutti was saying, ". . . and Jackie Illingsworth. They're on your side of the canal, or Joe and Julia's side, I should say, four houses down, right over there." She pointed and Sam dutifully turned to look. "The house next to the Illingsworth's is empty, just sold, and it's a second home, I believe. I haven't met the new owners yet. Then you've got Byron and Zoey, and between them and right next to Joe and Julia are Stuart and Bette. They've got the German shepherds." *Less and More.*

Sam's cell rang at that moment. The local news was just coming up on the television. "Excuse me," he said, glancing down at his cell.

"Sure," she said, but she didn't move.

The caller was Gwen. He gave Tutti a "just a minute" sign as he moved toward the steps that led back down to the dock. "Hey, Gwen. How's Georgie?" he answered.

"Fine. Better. Sorry about that. I didn't know she'd called you. She was in her room."

"I'm happy to talk to her."

"Yeah, thanks. She's finally resting. I had to give her one of my sedatives to calm her down."

"Okay." He sure as hell hoped she wasn't giving a prescription drug to her twelve-year-old. "She can call me anytime."

"It'll probably be tomorrow. She wants Julia's number at the hospital, too. Do you have it?"

"Call the hospital, they'll connect you to her room, but . . . um . . . Jules is having some memory issues, so don't expect too much." A collective gasp went up from inside Tutti's house. They must have just learned about Joe. "I gotta go."

"When you see Julia, warn her that Georgie is going to want to see her. Probably she'll talk me into that tomorrow. I just can't do it today. That kid sure can make life miserable when she doesn't get her way. You're lucky you don't have any."

Her attitude stunk, he thought as he jogged quickly to the upper deck. The screen door was open and Tutti was inside with the other couple, the Illingsworths, Sam reminded himself. Tutti turned to Sam accusingly, her hand to her mouth.

The hand dropped. "Your brother's *dead*?" she cried.

"I didn't want to say anything earlier."

"Oh, my God!" The TV screen showed a shot of the ocean and then the back side of *The Derring-Do*, the boat's name visible through the blackened charring of the stern.

"I wasn't planning on coming," Sam admitted.

"What about Julia?" she practically shrieked.

"She's in the hospital. She's okay. She'll be okay."

"Well, what happened? What did she say happened?"

"She . . . hasn't been able to remember the accident."

The man detached himself from his willowy wife, who was balancing a martini, looking stunned as she teetered on high heels. "Rob Illingsworth," he introduced himself as he stepped onto the deck and shook Sam's hand. He was just under six feet, muscular and wiry. He sported a close-trimmed beard, tan Dockers, and a dark brown T-shirt. His wife was in white capris and a shiny red top.

"This is Sam," Tutti said distractedly. "Joe's brother."

The woman sloshed her drink onto Tutti's carpet before joining them outside. "Jackie!" Rob snapped at her.

"Sorry . . . sorry, I'm so sorry," she murmured. She looked absolutely shattered, and she was clearly already less than sober.

"Why is Jules in the hospital?" Tutti asked Sam anxiously as she closed the screen door behind her. "Is she okay?"

"She's got a broken collarbone. Some head trauma."

"Can she remember what happened?" Rob asked, frowning.

From the corner of his eye, Sam noticed that Hap and Martina had arrived. Hap was tying up his raft before helping Martina out. Both of them had changed. Hap wore a black silk shirt and pressed denim jeans and Martina had changed into a different sundress, this one black, which showed off her tan legs and a pair of black high-heeled sandals. It took Sam a moment to realize they'd dressed in black for Joe.

"Are you staying at their house?" Rob asked Sam as Hap and Martina greeted everyone.

"No, I'm just trying to piece some things together."

"You're investigating?" Rob asked. "Tutti said you're a cop with the Seaside Police."

"That's what Julia told me," Tutti inserted quickly.

"Was. I'm in between jobs," Sam said at the same time.

"Jackie and I raised dairy cattle. My dad's farm outside Tillamook. Big farm. Too much damn work, so we sold a few years ago, and we've been looking for something else."

"We invested with Joe," Jackie gasped out tearfully. "Now what?"

Tutti grabbed Sam's arm again. "I'm so sorry," she declared again. "I'm just so sorry."

Tina, who had overheard the remark, said a bit huffily, "Your investments are safe, Jackie. Hap's going to take care of everything."

"How's Hap involved in Joe's business?" Sam asked her.

"Hap has his own firm. Well, with his father, but Walter isn't doing all that well these days. He's had some heart trouble, so Hap's taking over."

Jackie asked Tina on a gulp, "Did you know about Joe?"

"I heard earlier. It's terrible. Come on, let's get you another martini." Tina put her arm around Jackie and steered her back inside the house where apparently the hard liquor was kept.

Everyone kept commiserating with Sam and each other. Sam's throat grew tight and he had to cough to clear it several times. Two other smaller boats arrived, bringing two more couples.

The first couple docked their craft and headed up the ladder onto the dock. The man followed beneath the woman. He must have made some comment on her short, blue silk skirt because as soon as she was on the dock, she lifted it higher so he could get an unadulterated view. He laughed and she smiled and strutted away from him. He was carrying a plastic bowl of some potluck dish, balancing it as he got to the dock.

Then the woman spied Sam and he got a good look at her face.

He immediately was thrown back in time to the night of the Triton/Hawks football game . . . the night of Hap's party . . . the night he met Jules.

Zoey Rivera, he thought in surprise.

What the hell was she doing here?

Zoey saw him at the same time. "Sam!" she shrieked, then ran up the stairs to greet him.

Byron and Zoey. Sam hadn't clicked to it, when Tutti had said their names. He'd been thinking about other things. Now, as Zoey threw herself into his arms, he saw that her companion was the same Byron from high school, Byron Blanchette, her onetime boyfriend, the one who'd broken up with her because she'd supposedly been with Rafe Stevenson.

"Oh, my God, oh, my God. I heard about your brother," Zoey said, her whole body shaking. "I'm so sorry. Are you okay? How're you doing? It's terrible. Just terrible. What about Julia? Oh, my *God,* I'm so sorry!"

Byron came up behind her and diffidently offered Sam a hand, which Sam shook. "I'm Byron," he said. "I remember you."

"I remember you, too," Sam said. Byron was about Sam's same height, though he carried a few extra pounds on his six-two frame. There were faint touches of silver in his dark hair, but he looked fit and strong, as did Zoey.

"We all remember each other," Tina said with a tight smile as Zoey eased herself out of Sam's arms.

Hap added, "A lot's happened since then."

Zoey's eyes were teary. "I'm just so shocked. And so, so sorry, Sam."

"It's all right." Sam weathered Zoey's continued sympathy for a while. He learned Zoey and Byron both worked in Seaside. He was a real estate developer and she was an agent. Zoey wasn't wearing a ring and it came out that they were living together and had been for quite some time, but there were no wedding plans in the future as yet. Byron handed off the bowl to Tutti, who set about placing it on the outdoor table atop the red and white checked plastic tablecloth.

The other arriving couple was Stuart and Bette Ezra, Jules and Joe's next-door neighbors, the couple who owned the German shepherds. They were as shell-shocked over the news of Joe's death as everyone else. Stuart was in his late thirties or early forties and wore a black Polo shirt that emphasized the muscles in his arms. His hair was brownish blond and he sported a close beard a few shades darker. His wife, Bette, had large breasts and was stuffed into a black cotton tank dress that was beyond form-fitting and hugged her curves. Her skin was honey colored and she surveyed him critically through large brown eyes.

Stuart set the casserole dish, filled with some pasta and cheesy thing he'd carried from his rowboat, onto the table beside the bowl from Byron and Zoey, then came up to Sam. "Sorry, man. It's hard to believe. Joe's a great guy . . . was, I guess. . . ."

Bette's dark eyes were full of pain. "We really, really liked them," she said to Sam. "I can't believe this. You must be devastated. And Lord, what about Julia? How's she handling all this? She's so fragile. I worry about her."

Fragile? Not the Jules he knew. Sam explained about Jules's injuries to the crowd as a whole. They were all sober, all stunned. He did mention that she was having some troubles with memory, but they all took it that she simply couldn't recall the accident. He didn't correct them.

While they were all talking, Tutti buzzed around as the host, checking to make sure the guests had everything they needed. But she kept coming back to Sam, grabbing his arm and hanging on as if for dear life, maybe more for her support than his. Hap spent a lot of that time checking his phone, and Tina seemed to slowly relax a bit, chatting with Zoey and Tutti, while the Illingsworths stood to one side, in some kind of deep discussion.

Sam tried to catalog Joe and Jules's friends with a detached part of his mind, but their shock and grief renewed his own, and he found himself drifting out of their conversation. The one thought that kept circling was about the gasoline. Why had Joe purchased a can of gas from the marina gas station? Why had he taken it on his boat? The boat fire had been fueled by gas. How had that happened?

Who set the fire?

Tutti opened the bottle of wine Sam had brought and poured herself a glass, taking a large gulp. She then stopped for a moment and leaned her back against the warm exterior wall of her house. She'd changed into short shorts since he'd seen her earlier, which showed off a nice pair of legs. Her pink halter top barely kept her breasts in place, but she seemed oblivious to that fact. Her gaze, Sam realized, tended to fix on Stuart Ezra from time to time.

Huh. Sam glanced across the canal to the house next to Joe and Jules's, where the dogs, in the slanting sunlight, were now sleeping on the wooden deck. All of the houses on the canal were nestled close together, just a quick boat ride or swim from one back door to the next.

Zoey was going on about high school, a classmate of both Sam and Byron, and it was clear she kind of longed for those days again. Byron, however, made terse, snappish remarks to all of her reminiscences, which seemed to suggest he felt far differently.

When the subject of Joe's death and Jules's injuries was exhausted, the group finally moved to other topics, except when one of them was including Sam. If he was part of the discussion they wanted to make sure he was okay, so they kept asking him how he was. Though Sam's whole purpose for joining the barbecue was to learn anything he could about Joe, he couldn't get past the well-wishing. Finally Tutti, misunderstanding why he was so quiet, demanded that everyone stop making Sam feel bad, and then she took it upon herself to jabber away about anything under the sun, as long as it didn't have to do with Joe. It was frustrating, but Sam figured he'd let some time pass, then maybe direct some conversations himself back to Joe and the accident.

In the meantime he learned Tutti's real name was Kathy Anderson, but no one called her anything but Tutti. It was a nickname her ex, Dirk the bastard, had given her when they were dating because she'd ordered tutti-frutti ice cream on their first date to the fair and spilled it down his front, then had proceeded to lick it off his shirt, right in the middle of the fairgrounds, which had quickly led to their first sex in the fair parking lot in his Dodge Ram truck, right in front of God and everybody, had anybody been walking by at the time, which they hadn't.

"Got pregnant right away, wouldn't you know," she added at the end. "Sean was already here by the time we got married and Devon was the next year. Too bad Dirk turned out to be such a bastard. We had good sex."

Hap drawled, "The way I hear it, you have good sex with everyone."

Tutti threw him a surprised look. "Well, if it isn't good, why have it?" she asked.

"Amen, sister." Hap gave her a "just kidding" wink, and Tutti waved a hand at him, like he was such a wag. But Sam saw the set smile on her face as her eyes followed him the rest of the evening . . . except when those same eyes slipped a look in Stuart's direction.

Sam sipped his beer while Tutti went prattling on, explaining that Sean and Devon were thirteen and twelve, respectively, and they lived with their father. "Their choice," she said shortly. "You know boys that age. They think they'll have more freedom with him, but they should know better. They want to be here on the weekends, though. They like crabbing and fishing, anything to do with the boat, and of course that god-awful drone, also Dirk's idea. I make them take it down to the beach."

Zoey broke from Byron and came back to Sam. "Can I ask you a question about your brother?"

"Go ahead," Sam said, ready to get back on topic.

But Tutti popped in with, "Sam doesn't want to talk about it anymore."

"It's all right," Sam assured her.

"How did you learn that it was Joe's boat? Did the coast guard or Sheriff's Department call you?" Zoey asked.

"They didn't have to because I'd guessed before I knew."

"It's not all right," Tutti interrupted. She tried to steer Zoey away, but Zoey wasn't about to be moved.

Sam continued, "Joe asked me to meet him on his dock, but when I got there, *The Derring-Do*, Joe's boat, was gone. I figured he must be on it."

"Were you supposed to go with him?"

"Zoey," Tutti complained.

"Not that he said," Sam said.

"Well, why did he want you to meet at the dock, then?"

"I don't know," Sam answered honestly. The question had certainly crossed his mind when he'd gotten the text, but then everything had gone to hell. "He didn't say there was a plan to go in his boat."

Tutti gave Zoey a speaking look, so Zoey said, "I won't ask any more questions if you really don't want to talk about it any longer, Sam. It's just . . . it's so terrible and hard to believe."

"And that's why he doesn't want to talk about it!" Tutti declared.

Zoey ignored her, keying in on Sam, waiting to see which way he'd jump.

"Go ahead," Sam encouraged her.

"So, the Sheriff's Department found . . . Joe, or maybe the Salchuk Police?"

"The Salchuk Police," Byron declared loudly, coming

over to be with Zoey. "They're worse than useless. How'd their name come up in conversation?"

"We were talking about Joe," Tutti said shortly.

"The coast guard was there," Sam said.

"Oh, sure." Zoey shook her head. "I just was wondering how it all happened."

At that moment Rob Illingsworth called from inside the house. "Sheriff's on the news about Joe!"

Tutti sighed heavily. She turned to Sam and made a face. "I tried," she said as the group traipsed into the house.

"It's okay. It's all we're thinking about," Sam said.

On the television Vandra was relating the facts of the case to the media. He explained that Joseph Ford had drowned following a boating accident. There was a picture of *The Derring-Do*, up in flames, from either a chopper or a drone. The sheriff said it appeared Ford's wife was onboard as well, but she was alive and being treated for injuries sustained in the accident. She had been rescued by her brother-in-law, Samuel Ford. . . .

Bette Ezra turned to Sam, eyebrows high. "You saved Julia?"

"I was first on the scene," Sam said.

"But you saved her," Zoey repeated. "*You* did."

Tina drawled, "Well, of course he did. It was Julia."

Hap laughed. "You gotta find a way to hide that jealousy, honey."

"I don't know what you're talking about," Tina said, and shot him a hard glance.

Jackie Illingsworth had finished her second martini and was swaying on her feet. Stuart Ezra reached out and grabbed her elbow, steadying her. "You might want to sit down."

Tutti took over from Stuart, fussing over Jackie, helping

her into an overstuffed chair positioned near a river rock fireplace.

About that time there was a knock on the back slider—another guest, a single man, who had come around the side of the house and onto the deck. Leaving the slider open, he stepped inside, kissed Tutti on the cheek, and introduced himself as Scott Keppler "You're Joe's brother," he guessed, eyeing Sam. "Tutti told me she'd invited you."

"That's right."

"Sorry to hear, about him. Must be rough." He shook hands with Sam and said that he lived on the same side of the canal as Tutti and had decided to walk rather than travel by boat. He was a big man, about a decade older than the rest of them, somewhere in his forties. He gave Sam a long look, said he looked a lot like Joe, and offered condolences again, saying that he'd seen the earlier news report.

Bette Ezra watched Scott's back as he took his bottle of wine out to the dock to add with the rest. "He was Joe's lawyer," she said in an aside to Sam. "But something happened, and he no longer is."

Sam really examined Jules's next-door neighbor. There was something sultry about Bette that was arresting. "You have the German shepherds, Less and More." He hitched his chin toward the Ezras' house where he could see the dogs still sleeping on the deck, though clouds had crawled across the sky, blocking the sun.

"I just picked 'em up from doggy day care. They haven't bothered you, have they? How'd you know their names?"

From behind Sam, Stuart said, "Joe told him," in a tone that suggested Bette was slow on the uptake.

"Actually, I heard Hap call them by name," Sam explained.

"Hap?" Bette looked over at Hap, who was back to examining his phone. "The dogs don't like him."

"They're in fine company then," Stuart said. "Lots of people have issues with Hap."

"Yeah?" Sam asked, taking a sip from his beer.

Stuart shook his head and said quickly, "Just kidding."

Sam wondered. He sensed all wasn't exactly Norman Rockwell perfect on Fisher Canal. Despite the laughter and conversation, the pretense of congeniality, there was something more going on here.

Rob Illingsworth had been glaring down at his wife. Jackie's head was lolled against the back of the chair near the fireplace, her eyes closed. He said something under his breath, then as if realizing he wasn't alone, looked around the room. He focused on Sam and then lifted his own beer bottle to him.

"You're the guy whose ankle Brady Delacourt took out in high school, aren't you?" he said. "You guys were on the same team. The Hawks."

"Yep. It happened during the game against Astoria."

Rob left Jackie and joined Sam's group, who were all heading back outside. The clouds had taken over the sun completely, turning everything cool and dark. "I was good friends with Brady. My family had a summer place in Cannon Beach. He was a big son of a bitch. Even bigger now." He put down his empty and grabbed another beer, nodded to Scott Keppler, who'd poured himself a glass of red wine, a new bottle as the one Sam had brought was already gone. "Too much money, right?" He shot a good-natured glance toward Hap, who was leaning up against the rail, his dark hair teased by the breeze. "It's kinda going around."

Hap reminded easily, "You've done all right, Rob."

"Hell, I'm not complaining. No, sir. Everything's going pretty damned well. I have no complaints about Joe."

There was a loaded pause and a woman behind Sam cleared her throat. She came into view and he saw it was someone new. She looked around the group and focused in on Sam. "Hi, I'm Joanie, Joanie Bledsoe," she introduced herself, still studying his features and connecting the dots. "You must be Joe's brother. Tutti said she'd invited you. I'm really sorry about everything. Such a shock. I'm still reeling, and I'm sure you are." She wore very little makeup and her smooth brown hair was held at her nape with a tortoiseshell clip. Her dress was a blue pinafore over a white blouse, very earth-mothery.

"Traffic was a nightmare from Seaside. That's why I'm late," she went on. "The commute to work's gotten to be just awful. I came into Tutti's a little earlier, but you were all watching the news. My girls want to use the kayaks and stop by later, so I dropped them off before driving back here. So . . . sorry I'm late." She smiled faintly and looked around, to see if anyone had heard her excuse, then turned back to Sam. "I'm planning to go see Julia. I'm worried sick about her. Think I can see her tonight?"

"Maybe," Sam said, studying her. Joanie was all over the place. "Jules is being released tomorrow."

"Oh. I didn't know. You think I should wait?" She peered at him closely. "She's such a great friend of mine. I really want to see her."

"Leave it till tomorrow, Joanie," Scott Keppler said. There was something long suffering in his tone that said maybe he'd had more than a few dealings with her.

"I just want to make sure she's okay." Joanie pointed toward Hap and Martina's house for Sam's benefit. "I'm further down the way, on the same side of the canal. My two daughters are friends of Georgie. I'm so glad she wasn't on the boat with Joe and Julia." At Sam's silence, she said, stricken, "Oh, no! She wasn't, was she? Oh, God!"

"No, no. Georgie wasn't on the boat. She's with her mother. She's fine."

"She's with Gwen?"

Sam nodded, then realized Joanie had more to say on the matter. "Why?" he asked.

"Well, I'm not one to talk out of turn, I'm just surprised, that's all. Gwen's not . . . well, she's not exactly mother of the year, if you know what I mean. But thank the Lord Georgie wasn't here for this tragedy. You know—well, of course you do—Georgie's living with Joe and Julia, not Gwen. She hasn't lived with Gwen for years. I know it's summer, but honestly, they just don't get along. Mothers and daughters, sometimes . . . Luckily I've always been close to mine. What?" she demanded to the snickering that was going on between Hap and Rob Illingsworth.

"You're not one to talk? Oh, come on, Joanie," Rob said with a big smile.

Sam thought she was going to come unglued, but instead she just shook her head at him and dredged up a return smile. To Sam, she went on, "My daughters, Xena and Alexa, do everything with Georgie, but Gwen . . . well, she's got a life of her own. She and Joe weren't a good fit like he is . . . was . . . with Julia." Her face fell. "It's just impossible to think of Joe as dead. I'm glad, so glad, Julia is okay. I just feel terrible."

"We all do," Zoey said, unashamedly eavesdropping as she waltzed up.

"What are her injuries?" Bette Ezra asked. She dipped a cracker into an artichoke dip from the table and said, "I mean, specifically. Nothing super serious, I hope?"

"Broken collarbone. Head trauma," Sam said again.

"Somebody here said she can't remember the accident," Bette said, nibbling on her cracker.

"That's right." *And not much else, either.*

"How'd the boat catch fire in the first place?" Stuart

put in, eyeing his wife's cracker and turning toward the dip as well.

Sam had a vision of his brother stowing a five-gallon can of gasoline on the boat and his stomach clenched. "Unknown," he said shortly.

"Must have been a terrible accident," Joanie said.

"Well, yeah," Zoey rejoined. "What else could it be?" She looked over at Sam, the glint of challenge in her eye.

Everyone else turned toward Sam, too, as if expecting an answer.

Chapter Ten

Tutti moved closer to hear Sam's answer to Stuart. Hap and Illingsworth ceased talking, and Byron hovered by Zoey. The little group was tight around him; Sam was the center of attention and it made him more than a little uncomfortable. Despite the wind kicking up a bit and the party being outside, he felt suddenly claustrophobic. He'd come here searching for answers, but he, being Joe's brother, had been elevated to some kind of quasi-celebrity status and was the one being questioned.

"Any theories?" Stuart asked.

"What else could it be?" Sam said, echoing Zoey. He wasn't going to believe Joe had set fire to the boat himself.

"Maybe the engine caught fire," Tutti said.

No, it was a gas fire. Deliberately changing the subject, Sam asked, "Does anyone else have a key to Joe and Jules's house? Tutti gave me hers. I'm trying to lock things up. Make sure it's all safe, since Jules will be there alone when she gets home. Just want to know if there're other keys out there."

Bette said, "We have one. We exchanged keys with Joe and Julia. Georgie watches our dogs sometimes."

"And she damn near got her hand bitten off by that big one," Joanie said, crossing her arms.

"Less was just playing," Stuart assured her.

Bette was nodding and glanced across the canal where her dogs were both now standing at attention. "He . . . he wouldn't hurt a flea."

"He's a goddamn guard dog and he's fucking scary!" a woman's voice hollered furiously.

Everyone turned around to see Jackie standing belligerently by the back door, another martini in hand.

"Jesus, Jack," Rob muttered. He went to his wife, looking pissed. When he put his hand on her shoulder she shrugged it off and walked unsteadily back inside. Rob followed her in and some of the others who had clustered around Sam backed off a bit, turning their attention elsewhere.

"She's a mess," Zoey muttered, burying her nose in her own wineglass.

"No more than usual," Byron muttered. "A textbook case of why marriage doesn't work."

Zoey made a face, then said to Sam in a bored voice, "Byron loves any opportunity to put down marriage. Any opportunity at all. But that's not Jackie's problem. You know what it is?"

Sam really wanted to know about the keys, but he shrugged and waited.

Zoey glanced over to Bette and Stuart Ezra, who were talking to Joanie Bledsoe and Scott Keppler. Tutti was with them, too, though she kept fussing with her hair, as if she wasn't into the conversation.

"Jackie's pissed off because Stuart has no interest in her anymore. She came with money, and so that interested him for a while, but now he's moved on to . . . Tutti."

Byron groaned. "You're such a bitch," he declared.

"Oh, shut up. It's the worst kept secret on the canal."

Zoey lifted her chin. "You know it, I know it, everyone knows it. Sam might as well, too. Right, Sam?" She turned to him. "You're here because of your brother. You want to know what happened to him, and Tutti gave you an opportunity to meet us all. So, now you're thinking, which one of us did it, right? Like it wasn't just an accident, no matter what you say, and all of us are all up in each other's business? You want to know who's close to Joe and Julia, close enough to maybe use their boat or have a key or—"

"Jesus Christ." Byron stomped off from her as two ducks landed on the water and the dogs across the canal started up a ruckus.

Zoey watched him leave, her jaw set. "He makes me crazy," she said unhappily. "But I'm not wrong, am I?" she asked as Bette yelled across the canal and the dogs, surprisingly, shut up as the ducks, flapping and quacking their indignation, flew into the darkening sky.

"About Jackie? I don't know."

"About you, Sam."

"I want to know what happened to my brother, yeah."

"Was it an accident?" she persisted.

"You know, Zoey, when I find out, I'll let you know."

She snorted, then sent him a sideways smile. "Okay. Sorry. Sometimes I just want people to just say what they're thinking. And in answer to your question, *we* don't have a key, Byron and me. But around here with all those kids . . . Rob and Jackie's boys, and Joanie's girls, they're in and out of each others' houses all the time, y' know. And then there's Tutti's kids with their damned *drone*," she said disparagingly. "She says she makes them take it to the beach, but she doesn't. They don't listen to her. And that thing could drive us all fucking batshit, and those dogs . . . they go nuts." She shot Less and More an unkind look though they'd stopped barking and were now just sitting and watching the party in silence. "Luckily,

Tutti's kids are only here on the weekends. But none of them would give a shit about who has whose keys."

Sam made an executive decision and decided to be upfront with Zoey. "The first time I went into Jules and Joe's house, there was a note on the counter. It said 'Cardaman file.' Like it was a reminder of something. I went in later and it was gone. Someone came in and removed it."

"Cardaman." Zoey frowned. "Well, couldn't it have just fallen down or something? Got stuck somewhere?"

"That was my first thought, but I searched. It's not there."

"The Cardaman file," she said again. "Huh. You should ask Hap about that. He's the finance guy."

"What do the Ezras do?" Sam asked, given the opportunity.

"Bette's all into yoga and fitness and all that namaste stuff. Stuart? He's in sales of some kind, I think. Maybe cars. Last week he was talking about the new Mercedes truck, or whatever, like he could have an orgasm over it."

"Is he really seeing Tutti?" Sam asked.

Zoey lowered her voice. "I don't know for sure. I was just kind of being bitchy to Byron. Ask Julia about Stuart. She never said, but I think she caught him with someone. Stuart's kind of a horndog. But Tutti? She's still in love with that asshole Dirk, no matter what she says. The bastard. Jackie . . . she's another case altogether. She might've been with Stuart. Joanie said she saw her in Seaside with some older man, but Joanie always goes for the drama. Jackie's problem is she drinks too much. Period."

"Huh," Sam said. It all sounded like just gossip, but Zoey seemed fairly tapped in to the goings-on on Fisher Canal. "How was . . . Joe and Jules's relationship?" he asked diffidently.

"Good, I guess." She smiled faintly. "How did that happen? I've always wanted to know. You were with her and then you married"—she glanced over at Martina, who was out of earshot but seemed to be watching them like a hawk—"*that.* And then your brother's with Julia."

"Things happen," Sam said, tipping up his bottle and finishing his beer.

It was as if some silent command had been issued because everyone began moving toward the barbecue en masse. Even Jackie came back outside, with Rob Illingsworth's hand firmly clasped around her upper arm to keep her on her feet. Sam filled his own plate with ribs, a scoop of upscale macaroni and cheese from the Ezras, and a healthy helping of Byron and Zoey's mixed green salad, heavy with kale, dried cranberries, jicama, and sunflower seeds, and dressed with something lemony and light.

Sam had been living on fast food and diner fare for so long that it was a pleasure to have a real meal. He took his plate down to the dock, sank into one of the chairs, and just ate.

Martina came down the steps, plate in hand, mostly salad. "May I join you?"

He silently gestured to another chair. He didn't actively dislike his ex-wife, but he wasn't seeking out her company, either.

"I heard what Zoey said. About why you came here tonight."

"Tutti invited me because I'm Joe's brother and I was at the house, and she thought I'd like to meet some of the people who live on the canal, you know, get out a little bit."

"Yeah, but you came to learn about Joe and Julia. I don't blame you. I want to know what happened, too. So does Hap."

Sam had questions of his own and Martina seemed to want to talk. He asked, "What's the true financial connection between Hap and Joe? Is Cardaman somehow involved?"

"Cardaman. Ask Hap. I don't know. I don't think either of them had anything to do with that man. His clients are screwed." Her face set harder. "My dad's one of them."

Sam said in some surprise, "Your father?"

"That's right. Mom and Dad moved to Portland, and they're renting a place. They have to be careful now."

"I'm sorry. What about . . . Walter Senior?"

"Oh, Hap's dad's still okay. He knows how to hang on to a dollar. He's not handing over anything to Hap, no matter what everybody says. Hap's gotta do the dance for his father. He never paid attention to the company when he was younger. Just wanted to play football. But he got injured right away in college and that was over. Now he has to beg for every little crumb. What an idiot."

"Huh," Sam said.

"Oh, Hap's an ass. He's always been an ass. He'll always be an ass. Why don't you ask what's really on your mind?"

"What's really on my mind?" Sam wondered.

"'Tina, why are you with Hap, if he's such an ass?' The answer is, I don't know. He's not a horrible guy and I've met some horrible guys. After you and I split up, I went to Seattle, and I met horrible guy after horrible guy. Now, I just want to settle down and have things be better." She gazed at him frankly. "Wish things had worked out for you and me, sugar."

This was definitely dangerous territory. "We weren't good for each other," Sam said carefully.

"*I* wasn't good for you, not the other way around. And I wasn't good for myself, either. But I'm better now."

This new Martina worried Sam, so he simply nodded and let the subject lie. The Tina he'd met earlier in the day, the one standing beside Hap on the porch outside Joe and Jules's house in the clingy blue dress, heels, and smart attitude . . . that was the one he recognized.

"I also overheard you tell Zoey there was a note about Cardaman that disappeared. If I were you? I'd check with the teenagers," Martina advised. "Tutti's boys, Sean and

Devon? They popped in and out yesterday. Maybe they did it. They're troublemakers, but then, hey, weren't we all back in the day?"

"I thought they only came on weekends."

"Yeah, well, I saw them on this very dock. Dirk came and picked them up, and I heard Tutti invite him to the barbecue, but of course he wouldn't come."

Sam had seen Tutti on her deck when he'd first gotten to Joe and Jules's, then again later. Both times she'd been alone. "Maybe because she calls him the bastard."

"He is the bastard," Tina said, shivering a little at a kicky evening breeze. "He left her for somebody in his office."

"What kind of office?"

"Chiropractor. Guess they were using the tables for more than just 'adjustments.'"

"Zoey inferred that something might have happened between Tutti and Stuart."

"Maybe . . ." Martina made a face. "Stuart thinks he's all that. But rumor has it he was really with Jackie. Maybe he's the one who drove her to drink." She laughed shortly. "I don't know how Bette stands it. She just kind of ignores it all and hopes it goes away, I guess. But Stuart and Tutti . . ." She shook her head. "I don't see it, do you?"

Sam looked over to where Stuart was still talking with his wife and Scott Keppler, who was putting out a cigarette into an ashtray Tutti had set out on the deck rail. Tutti was a few feet away, looking at Stuart, but Sam wasn't sure what her expression meant. She seemed to be thinking hard about something, but it didn't seem like . . . lust.

"So, what about you?" Tina asked. She had moved the lettuce leaves around on her plate but he hadn't seen her eat a bite. All she'd done was lift her wineglass to her lips. "I mean, I know this is a terrible time and all, but what are you doing? You quit the force and . . . that's where you are?"

"That's about it." Sam had finished eating everything but the barbecued ribs and now picked up one of them, biting into the meat and effectively cutting off conversation . . . until some of the other Fishers decided to join them.

Hap was first down the stairs, a bottle of wine held loosely in one hand, his glass in the other. He poured himself a drink and said, "So, Sam, you're not moving into the house?" He nodded across the canal.

"Nope," Sam mumbled.

Stuart, Bette, and Scott Keppler followed behind with Joanie and Tutti on their heels. Rob and Jackie were still on the upper deck, and it appeared Rob was giving his wife a serious talking-to.

Hap sauntered over and refilled Tina's nearly empty glass. "Maybe I'm talking out of turn here, Sam, but I know a thing or two about Joe's personal finances."

"Well, there you go. We were just talking about what your financial arrangement is with Joe," Tina said, offering him a smile, and as he lifted the bottle, said, "Don't be stingy."

"Truth?" Hap poured a little more into Martina's glass. "Mainly it's just Summit Ridge. We're still trying to buy those houses out of the Cardaman shit bucket. They're all good properties."

Sam set down his last rib, wiping his mouth with his napkin, then cleaning off his fingers. "The houses in Salchuk? The ones that Cardaman sold over and over again. I thought they were never finished."

"They're not," Stuart said.

"Some are," Hap insisted. "Nobody ever really owned 'em, so nobody ever lived in 'em. They're just waiting there, and they're great houses. They just need to be cleaned up, or finished. They've got sweet views."

"They'll be tied up forever in legal red tape," Scott Keppler said dryly, and reached into his shirt pocket for a near empty pack of Winstons.

"Where're you getting the money to finish them?" Bette asked.

Hap gave Stuart's wife a long look, like he resented the question. "I'm in the business, Bette. This is what I do."

Tina caught Sam's eye and shook her head very slightly.

Tutti said, "Ah, ah, ah. I feel like you guys are going to get in a fight over money again. Let's not do this."

"They're not going to be tied up forever," Hap said to Keppler as Scott lit up. "Joe and I were both interested in saving and finishing those houses. It's good for everybody."

"Except the investors Cardaman screwed over," Stuart pointed out.

"Not my problem," Hap told him coldly.

Tina put in, "Sam said there was a note about Cardaman on the table in Joe and Julia's house yesterday, but when he went back it wasn't there."

Everyone looked at Sam. He was a little irked at Martina, but he just went with it. And actually, the more people who knew it, the better. "I think someone took it from the house."

"Georgie?" Bette suggested.

"She was still with her mother," Sam said.

"You sure it's not just lost?" Keppler asked. He'd walked a few steps away to keep the smoke from his cigarette out of range.

"Maybe," Sam said, in a tone that made it clear he didn't believe it.

No one had anything more to say about that.

Hap put in, a bit grumpily, "Two years I'll have those Summit Ridge houses finished and they'll sell in the millions. Better be nice to me, Zoey, if you want the listing."

"I'm always nice to you, Hap," Zoey responded, but her eyes were cool.

It's about the money. Donald had been right. Sam decided he needed to talk to his father again, hit him with the specifics of Summit Ridge. Hope that Donald was having a good day. Tomorrow. Maybe before he picked up Jules.

Keppler couldn't let it go. "I warned Joe about Summit Ridge. Told him not to go in with you on this. Sorry, Hap, but like Cardaman, you have investors you need to do right by. That's what I told Joe."

"I know," Hap said tightly.

Sam wondered what had happened between Keppler and his brother, why the lawyer and Joe had parted ways. Keppler and Hap sure didn't seem to like each other much.

"Stop it," Tina said, lightly slapping Hap's arm as he'd walked over to stand right beside her. "You'll give Sam the idea that all we do is fight, and that's just not how it is around here. We're all friends."

Stuart ignored Tina and said, "A lot of people lost their shirts on those properties."

"You talking about Summit Ridge?" Rob called down to them.

"Yes, Rob," Tina responded in a loud, bored voice.

"Anybody need another drink?" Tutti asked.

"I'm good." Drawing on his cigarette, Scott Keppler moved past them and back up the stairs to where Rob Illingsworth was hanging over the rail, listening to the conversation below. His wife, Jackie, was staring across the canal toward Jules and Joe's house. Sam's eyes followed hers and he saw a light had come on. He started, half got out of his chair, then relaxed when he realized the light was on an automatic timer.

"Sam," Hap said. Now he was between Sam and Tina, his back to the rest of the crowd. "When are you getting together with Joe's lawyers? People are going to be calling when they learn Joe's . . . gone. Somebody needs to take over."

"Not me," Sam said.

"Joe told me he split his estate between you and Julia. That includes the house and Joe's business. Some of these deals need to be looked at ASAP. Sorry, but that's just the way it is."

"Oh, God, Hap, really?" Tina muttered, with a roll of her expressive eyes. She took another sip from her glass.

Joanie Bledsoc had moved nearer just in time to hear what Hap said. Now she asked on a half gasp, "Does Julia know?"

"That can't be right," Sam said. Surely his brother had left his estate to Jules. It annoyed him that Hap was blabbing about his brother's finances in front of the Fishers, and thinking about Joe was making him feel low.

Hap urged, "Talk to the lawyers. I think Joe moved to Fairbanks and Vincent in Salchuk."

Salchuk again. Sam was going to have to get into Joe's office and soon. Maybe there was a key in the house somewhere. Gathering up his plate, Sam decided it was time to leave. "Did any of you see Joe's boat leave yesterday?" he asked.

They all looked at each other and shook their heads. Bette Ezra said, "We were all probably at work except Tutti."

"I work," Tutti sputtered, as if Bette had specifically offended her. "I just was off yesterday. I don't work Wednesdays."

"So, did you see the boat leave?" Joanie asked.

"No. I had to meet Dirk to pick up the boys. He needed me to take care of them for a few hours. The sitter was sick and he knows I don't work Wednesdays." Tutti sounded slightly defensive. "Joe must have taken the boat while I was gone.

I saw Sam around noon on Joe's dock, when I got back. The boys were playing video games and I was outside."

They'd all moved to the upper deck. Jackie was finger-combing her hair and looking a little closer to sober. Her gaze trailed after Stuart, who seemed oblivious.

Twilight was upon them and people were beginning to clean up the food. Tutti said, "If Julia's coming home tomorrow, we should all make a meal for her."

Joanie pounced on that. "I was just thinking the same thing!"

At that point all of the women started discussing what menu items to make, although Jackie, Tina, and Zoey were listening with only half an ear. A cool breeze had cropped up, blowing off the ocean and rippling the waters of the canal. Sam said his good-byes and was heading for his canoe when Scott Keppler caught up to him. In a lowered voice, he said, "Hap should have kept his trap shut about Joe's will. Born with a silver spoon, it sure's never kept him from talking too much."

"Why did Joe switch to Fairbanks and Vincent?" Sam asked the lawyer.

"Well, we had a parting of the ways, and . . . I'm taking some time to do something I've always wanted. I'm doing some commercial fishing. Got the biggest boat on Fisher Canal. Look down there."

Keppler pointed down the waterway to a two-story house stained dark brown with a large trawler docked behind it. Sam figured the canal must be a hell of a lot deeper than he would have credited it to accommodate the size of the boat. "Fishing's hard, uncomplicated work, which is just what I want. Cleans the palate, if you know what I mean. But I took a page or two from your brother's book and bought some income property. Lost the wife and the house during the downturn, but hung on to most of my savings. Joe helped me out. I'm renting the house and I got the trawler.

Own a couple of small properties south of Nehalem, and the kids come and see me, so it all worked out okay."

Sam thought about his brother, about his business, his finances, his whole life. He knew so little about him apart from the basics. He knew Joe had married Gwen and that Gwen's child from a teen relationship that hadn't lasted became Joe's adopted daughter. Then, that relationship had disintegrated, though Joe was still close to Georgie. He hadn't known much of anything else other than that Joe had married Jules, of course. He certainly hadn't known Georgie mostly lived with Joe and Jules.

Sam drifted out of his conversation with Keppler as Martina strolled his way again, wineglass in hand, the red liquid swaying with her hips as she approached. "I think you should stay at the house with Julia," she said. "She's going to need help and Lord knows Georgie can't do it."

"Georgie's with her mother right now."

"Well, then, you're the only one. It's terrible about Joe and that's going to be hard for Julia, too. Besides, it would be nice to have you in the neighborhood. We could use someone like you." Was there a bit of come-on in her eyes as she looked up at him through her lashes? With Tina, you never knew.

"I'll figure out who can stay with Julia."

"If it was you, maybe she'd be nicer to me."

"Jules isn't nice to you?"

"Don't be dense, sugar. I was married to you. She never forgave me for that."

"She married my brother."

"Big fucking deal. I was the girl who took you away. And when she married Joe, that about killed you, too."

"That's not—"

"Shut up, Sam. It's true. You and Julia . . . Jesus. Joe knew it, too, but we all acted like it wasn't there. You should've gotten over it long ago, but you didn't, so here we are.

And," she added, when he tried to break in, "I'd normally be the last person who would tell you to stay with *Jules*, but these aren't normal times. Your brother's gone, and he was a good guy. I'm going to miss him, too."

Sam couldn't find anything to say to that.

"I miss you, too, Sam, but you were never really present when we were together anyway. And you weren't with Dannella, either. Only with Julia."

"You talk to Dannella?" Sam was taken aback. He hadn't been aware his ex-wife and ex-girlfriend even knew each other.

"Oh, sugar." She shook her head at him as if he were a lost cause. "I saw Dannella strolling her new baby down to the beach in Salchuk. She's happy now. Has a husband who's *present*."

"Well, good. I'm glad."

"Are you?" She swallowed a gulp of wine and peered at him through narrowed eyes. "Dammit, you probably are. Give everybody a hand and say how great they are while you're running away."

Once more Sam looked across at Jules and Joe's house. He wondered if he'd learned anything here tonight. He was damn tired all of a sudden, and he wanted to be alone. His head was full of information and he needed to sift through it all, winnow it down, separate out anything that might aid him in his investigation, throw the rest away.

"It was good seeing you, Tina. But I gotta run."

"Asshole," she murmured as he climbed into his canoe, but there was a note of amusement in her voice as well.

The Illingsworths' two boys were just arriving, having been summoned by their parents. They showed up in matching kayaks, the sleek crafts slicing easily through the waters of the canal. The boys were in the late tween stage somewhere, eleven to thirteen, and starting to fill out. About Georgie's age, he realized.

"Sam!"

He looked around to see Joanie hurrying up to him. "You're leaving?" she asked him, but her eyes were on the Illingsworth boys.

"I'm tired," Sam admitted.

"Of course you are. I'm so sorry. And I'm sick at heart about Joe. You sure you can't have another drink? That wine you brought is yummy."

"Actually, it was from Joe and Jules. And thanks, but I gotta go."

"You're picking up Julia tomorrow?"

He nodded.

"Ask her about Georgie, please. I know my girls are going to want to know when she'll be back. *If* she'll be back," she amended. "She's really a pretty good kid."

"Okay."

"And be careful," she added as an afterthought, which he didn't know what to make of.

Sam paddled back across the canal. As he neared Joe's dock he caught a glimpse into the house next door, the Ezras. The dogs had gone inside, probably through a dog door or one left open. Now they pushed their heads through the curtains, noses up against the glass sliding door. Upon seeing Sam, a stranger, they emitted loud, low-throated growls that could freeze the blood.

Across the canal, Bette yelled, "SHUSH!!" which this time they ignored completely.

They kept it up until Sam had entered the house and walked through, making certain everything was secure. Then he turned out the lights except for the one on its timer. After double-checking all the doors and windows, latching the one he'd climbed through before, he went out the front door, locked up, then drove back to the cabin.

* * *

He stood outside Emergency, watching through the sliding glass doors. Nothing happening tonight. No ambulances screaming in. No injured or sick would-be patients arriving. Quiet and slow.

Which wasn't working for him. He needed the craziness and bedlam of trauma in order to sneak inside. All the other doors were locked for the night, and the way in was through Emergency.

He sat in his killing vehicle, the gray, five-year-old Honda Civic that was registered to an older man he knew who'd moved to Alaska and was, he'd learned recently, in a nursing home and at death's door. He'd stolen a few license plates since then, making sure there was a lot of time left on the tags, and he kept the Civic parked down by the marina where there was an empty lot that had become a place you could leave your vehicle with a For Sale sign in its windshield. He always made the phone number smudged enough that it was impossible to read, and he kept the would-be price on the high side. Even so he'd had interested buyers leave him notes under the windshield, asking if he'd take a little less and leaving their phone numbers. He gathered those phone numbers for future use. He even knew the name of one potential buyer, a man named Corey who was kind enough to give his address in Seaside, just in case he might need it someday.

But tonight was a problem. He was tucked into his hoodie, his face pointed downward to make sure the cameras couldn't capture his features, the hypodermic in his pocket. This wasn't like killing Denny, which had been a sheer blast. That had been dangerous, sure, but no one had even missed the unlucky bastard. Tiny Tim from the bar might remember Bridget, if it ever came to that, but neither of them was a regular, like Denny had started to become, and no one knew their true names.

Should he try to get inside and take care of Julia tonight?

It was dangerous. Foolhardy. The kind of thing that gave him a hard-on. She'd seen him on the boat and she could identify him, that was for sure, so he needed to make certain she was gone for good. It was crazy that he wasn't more concerned, but then he'd heard through his sources that she might not ever remember the accident. Didn't mean she wouldn't in the future, but he felt lucky about the whole thing somehow.

Or maybe that was just his cock talking because he'd like nothing better than to stick it to Joe Ford's widow. He'd always kind of had a thing for her.

But no, that was too risky. He needed to remove her. Remove the problem. That's what Bridget wanted him to do, and she always thought she knew best.

She does know best, you asshole. You know she does.

But Julia Ford . . . mmm-mmm . . . luscious in that girl next door sort of way. She'd been in the back of his mind when he'd been eyeing those college girls. They'd been sloppy, sexy, and sweet, but dirty in a way he really liked, but he dug Julia's strangely virginal appeal, even though he knew for a fact she'd fucked both of the Ford brothers, even more.

Sam Ford . . . He thought furiously about him for a moment. Ex-policeman, ex-husband of Martina Montgomery . . . How had that loser gotten two of the best-looking women on the whole coastline?

"He couldn't keep 'em, though, could he?" he growled aloud.

He looked again at the black, hulking hospital with its brilliantly lit Emergency Room.

Fuck her or kill her . . . or both. . . . Now was the time.

He got out of the car and headed for the doors, head down.

* * *

Jules came to suddenly, fully awake. She was lying in the hospital bed, had been dozing rather than dead asleep after a hard afternoon going over and over Phoenix Delacourt's words. She'd given the woman a file that could prove, or disprove, her husband's involvement in financial wrongdoing, and worrying about it had worn her out. Finally, she'd fallen into a fitful sleep, but now she was awake again and full of unnamed fear.

She'd heard something, hadn't she? It was dead quiet tonight except for the faint hum of the air ducts, the heating and cooling system holding the temperature.

There it was. Footsteps and the soft *thunk* of the elevator doors closing. Someone on the floor, coming her way.

Without conscious thought her fingers found the call button and she depressed it. A faint chime sounded, way down the hall. Was that her bell? Probably. But what if no one heard her?

Pulse rising, she climbed silently out of her bed and moved toward the closet, then realized that wasn't going to work. Not enough room. Quickly and quietly she lay down on her back, feeling a twinge in her arm, a throb in her head, then she slid herself under the bed, pulling the bedcovers down on the side nearest the door, hiding herself from view, she hoped with all her heart.

Whoever it was was taking his sweet time. She pictured him peeking in rooms, checking the beds. Why she was so certain he was after her she couldn't say. Some primal awareness that rose beyond the gray veil.

He tiptoed to her door; she sensed the light quickness. She held her breath, counting her heartbeats. *Please come . . . please, please come,* she silently begged the hospital staff.

If he yanked back the draping covers she would be exposed and then . . . what? She had no alternate plan.

Except screaming. Screaming for all she was worth.

He took a step inside, then a second. A moment's assessment. She was dizzy with fear.

Then, in the hallway, another sound. Strolling footsteps making no effort to disguise themselves. Some employee working graveyard, heading down the hallway. Had that person heard her call? God, she hoped so!

The man in her room—she was pretty sure it was a man, though she had no reason to know—took a couple of steps. She envisioned him peering out the door, waiting for the employee to disappear. Her own pulse was damn near deafening her. Over its roar she heard those casual footsteps approaching, then . . . *no, no, no!* They were growing fainter! The person had turned down some other hallway or gone into some other room.

Oh . . . God . . . oh, God . . .

The man exhaled softly, tensely. Then to Jules's relief he tiptoed back out. Was he leaving? Or, was he just checking to make sure he was still safe?

Her head pulsed with the stress and her shoulder ached.

Jules stayed where she was, not trusting that he'd truly moved on. Time passed. . . . She was nearly frozen with fear. An hour must have gone by.

Finally she dared peek around the bedclothes to realize he was gone.

Her cell phone vibrated on her nightstand in the darkness. Quickly she swept it up, holding her breath.

"Bridget?" his voice asked.

She glanced to the other side of her bed, then back to her cell where she saw the time. A little after midnight. The moon was high in the sky and a finger of moonlight slipped through the curtains, making it easy to see as she tiptoed out of the room and gently closed the door behind her. "Is it done?" she asked softly.

"Two things," he said tightly. "One. The only way into the hospital is through Emergency, this time of night. I went in and made it without being seen, but I didn't have the room number, only the floor."

"And?"

"She wasn't in any of the rooms I went into."

"What do you mean?"

He snorted in disbelief. "What do you think I mean? She wasn't *there*. Not on the fourth floor. There was one guy walking around beside the nurse's station, and I almost shit myself when he came down the hallway. I'm probably on every fucking camera, too."

"You were seen?" Her voice was a choked screech.

"Hoodie covered me and I kept my head down, but if that fucking orderly or nurse, or whatever the hell he was, had seen me, he would've thought it was weird. And there was a nurse coming, too. I had to get the hell out."

"You promised you would take care of her!" she hissed, infuriated and scared. "You promised!"

"I *know* . . . but we've got something else anyway."

"What do you mean?"

"The man has another problem he wants us to take care of."

"Oh, fuck." She could feel herself going into the danger zone and held on to her cool with an effort. "Julia will recognize you. You've got to take care of her tonight!"

"I'll take care of her when she's at home, and anyone else who gets in the way."

"Oh, big man."

"Yeah, big man," he agreed, ignoring her sarcasm.

"And what about that . . . Cardaman note Sam Ford was talking about? You took it, didn't you?"

"Shut up and let me tell you about this new job."

"You took it! *Why?* This is exactly what I'm talking

about when I tell you to stop going rogue. Stick to the plan. Now you've made Sam Ford suspicious!"

"I didn't know he was going to be there, did I? I just saw the note and took it, so there wasn't any evidence left. You're the one always bitching about loose ends!"

"Fuck you, *Tom.*"

"Fuck you, *Bridget.*"

They were both breathing hard. She wanted to reach through the phone and wring his worthless neck.

"The man's offered an extra piece. One hundred thousand dollars in cold hard cash. No banks. No IRS. No nothing."

"Yeah? What do you have to do for it?"

"We have to remove an obstacle. The kind we like to remove." A smile crept into his voice.

"Who's the mark?" she asked, unable to stop herself, then, "No, don't tell me. I don't want to know."

"Yeah, you do," he chuckled. "It gets you going like nothing else."

"Fuck you," she said again, and clicked off in disgust.

But she did have that jazzy little buzz going, he was right about that. Made her want to click her fingers and dance around a little. Made her want to screw.

Still, he was becoming a big, big problem. And the Julia Ford issue was getting bigger every day, too. Julia *would* recognize him. And he *would* buckle under pressure if he was caught. Right now Julia was still in the hospital, still contained, but what about when she was back on the canal? She would recognize him, for sure. Luckily, Julia still didn't know that Bridget was involved in the boating accident.

But goddamn, there was no telling what *he* would do or say if he got caught.

She couldn't have that. Couldn't. He was a liability that was growing bigger and bigger every day.

And he was untrustworthy. She wasn't the only woman in his life, no matter what he said. Or, at least she hadn't been. Didn't matter. She was going to have to start thinking in the long term and this . . . this period of lunacy would have to end. She hated the idea of giving up the killings. There was absolutely nothing like it. *Nothing.* But she was into self-preservation a hell of a lot more than thrills.

Tom's days were numbered.

She just needed to figure out how to get rid of him . . . after they got the hundred thousand.

Chapter Eleven

Sam strode down the main hall of Sea and Sunset Retirement Living to his dad's apartment. He knocked on the door and tried the handle. Locked. Knocking louder, he called, "Dad? It's Sam. You in there?"

There was no answer, so he waited a couple of minutes, wondering if his father was in the bathroom. It was barely seven a.m., a little early for a visit, maybe, but Sam didn't have time to waste. He was heading to the hospital next, though he knew discharges tended to take a while. No one had given him a time to pick up Jules. For that matter, no one knew he was going to be the one to fetch her.

"Dad?" He rattled the handle.

An older woman with a walker was just coming out her door, and she looked at him askance. "Who are you?" she warbled.

"I'm Donald's son. Sam."

"Donald said his son died."

"His other son. He has two."

"No, he only has one." She slowly wheeled herself past him, heading down the hall where he'd just come.

"Dad?!"

"Hold your horses," came the irked and muffled voice

from Donald's room. About a decade later his father opened the door and Sam stepped inside, closing it behind him.

"What're you doing here?" Donald asked. "You know what time it is, son?"

"I need to talk to you about Joe, Dad. About his business. What he was doing. You know the financial end of things. You're the one who got Joe interested in the business in the first place. . . ."

"Hang on there. Don't blame me. He was always interested in making money." He trundled back to his chair, throwing over his shoulder, "Can't say the same for you."

Sam paced past his father to the far end of the room and looked out the window, struggling to get a handle on his composure. He normally wasn't so undone, but Joe's death was a bolt of lightning that kept striking from the sky, catching him unawares and reverberating through him long after he thought the chance of getting hit was over.

In the presence of his father, Sam felt the grip on his emotions start to cave. He bore down on his feelings, aware that if he succumbed he could break down completely. Only the desire to find out the truth kept him from being overcome by grief. Still, he thought of his brother's smile, one that had become rarer over the years, and his heart ached. When had that happened? When Joe broke away from the huge firm he'd worked for and went into business for himself? Or was it something else?

"Breakfast is at eight," Donald let him know.

Sam sat down in the only extra chair in the room as his father worked to adjust his La-Z-Boy recliner. Once Donald was settled, Sam pulled his chair up closer so they were looking at each other, eye to eye. "I need some help, Dad. I need to find out about Joe."

"Joe?"

"Yes, Joe. Your son. He died in a boating accident the day before yesterday."

"You told me."

"Yes, I told you. That's right. I need you to focus now and tell me about Joe's business. I've talked to some other people, but no one seems to know exactly what was going on."

He *tsk-tsked* and waved his finger at Sam. "That's secret stuff, you know. Other people's money."

"You specifically said 'it's about the money,' when we were talking about Joe, and I think you're right. Joe's gone, and I'm working on finding out what happened. And to do that, I need to know as much as you do, and probably more, about Joe's company. A lot of people invested with him, trusted their funds to him."

"You didn't."

"Dad, please. Bear with me."

"Joe was good to you, Sammy. He left you everything. And his wife. He left you his wife, too."

That was just crazy, about leaving Jules to him, and the rest, what he'd heard at the party from Hap, he'd dismissed as speculation or gossip.

Sam shook his head, frustrated. "You mean, he left his wife everything. I'm not a part of his will."

"How do you know?"

"Dad, Joe and I weren't . . . I will be meeting with Joe's lawyers. Jules needs to see them, and I'll take her. She's just not ready yet."

"Well, then you'll know."

"Does the name Cardaman mean anything to you?" Sam asked, hanging on to his patience with an effort.

"Ike Cardaman." He snorted. "He was running that Ponzi scheme before he got caught. Yeah, I know him. He in jail?"

"Yes. I believe so."

"He talked your brother into some stuff he never shoulda got into. He put investors' money into Capitol College, that online one, y'know? Then the government shut 'em down, stopped the student loans. It was all a racket. No money from the government, so the college goes belly-up and who's left holding the bag?" Donald was getting riled up as he jabbed a gnarled finger at Sam and answered his own question. "Joe's investors, that's who. And who're they blaming? Joe, that's who. Luckily Joe's smart. He had 'em diversified, his investors. Capitol College was just some of it. He was trying to get all the money back for 'em. But that damn whistle-blower brought it all down. Joe had to defend himself, but people were really mad."

"What about Summit Ridge, in Salchuk?"

"Everybody moving to Salchuk," Donald said on a sigh.

"I ran into Hap—Walter Hapstell Junior—and he said he and Joe were working on a deal to buy those houses from whomever's holding them."

"Cardaman's houses?" He looked at Sam like he'd lost his mind. Bushy eyebrows drew together. "Bah. That's gonna be years. Government's gotta untangle all Cardaman's messes and put on a trial. Too long to wait. Houses'll be termite dust by then."

"It sounds like it's Hap's big deal."

He flapped a hand at Sam, as if wanting him to stop talking. "He wants to get into Salchuk before it's too late, but it's already too late for Summit Ridge. Salchuk's supposed to be the next big deal on the coast. Been a sleepy little town far too long. Got a great, private beach. Might be that it's the big money maker. I put some money there, too, through your brother." He paused, his face clouding over. "Where'd you say Joe was?"

Sam didn't answer. He just couldn't get caught in that kind of loop with his father. "Did Joe ever tell his investors to go with Cardaman?"

"Nah . . . Joe just inherited some clients who'd invested with Cardaman."

"He inherited them?"

"They were all real upset 'cause they'd lost money with

Cardaman and they wanted Joe to save 'em." A frown line etched deeply between Donald's eyes. "Maybe Julia knows."

"Was Julia that involved in the business? I thought she just worked part-time."

"Mighta been they were her dad's clients," he mused. "That St. James . . . stupid man." He shook his head. "What a way to go. Couldn't swim and jumps into the Columbia."

"You think Julia knew about all this?" *When she could remember things* . . . Sam reminded himself grimly. Dealing with Dad's altered reality and Julia's loss of memory was only making things more difficult.

"Ask Joe," Donald said. "He'd know."

Sam gazed at his father in consternation. "Joe's gone, Dad. *The Derring-Do* was set on fire and Joe didn't survive. He drowned. And you know what they're saying, Dad? That Joe burned his own boat. That he purchased the gasoline that was spilled on the boat and set fire to it. They're intimating that he committed suicide and that he tried to take Jules with him."

Donald reared back as if Sam had hit him. "Get outta here!" he roared.

"*I* didn't say it, Dad. That's just what the sheriff thinks. And I'm going to prove him wrong."

"Those assholes don't know what they're talking about!" He *tsk-tsked* his finger in front of Sam's nose. "Your brother was a good man. A good man." Donald's eyes began watering and he reached for a tissue on the table beside his chair.

Sam silently measured his father. *Was* a good man . . . Throughout their conversation Donald Ford had been remarkably "sane." Yes, he fell into forgetfulness, but he seemed to be getting the information overall. He wondered, again, just how much of his father's dementia was manufactured.

Yeah, but you think everyone's faking what they know.

He tried to hold on to his patience. "Look, Dad, I don't think my brother tried to kill himself, but I don't think his death was an accident. I think it's connected to Joe's financial dealings. A lot of people invested with him, and I want to know about the ones who lost money, who maybe blamed Joe. I want to know who among them would kill him over it."

His father slowly sat back in his chair. "You need to talk to the whistle-blower."

"You brought him up before. Dennis Mulhaney?"

His father squinted at him. "You know him?"

"I heard he left Joe's company." He didn't add that Mulhaney had been missing for six weeks, according to Phoenix Delacourt.

"He worked for Joe . . . and Hapstell. Said he was gonna tell everybody they were crooks. They said fine and he quit, all mad. Joe said he kept going on and on about them hooked in with Cardaman, but it wasn't true."

The Cardaman file. Maybe it wasn't true. . . . Sam sure hoped it wasn't true.

His father blinked a couple of times, then shook his head in frustration. "Why'd you come by again?" he asked. "It wasn't just to talk about money, was it?"

Sam tamped down his frustration with an effort. "We were talking about Joe and his investment company."

"Uh-huh. Joe always protects his customer," his father said with a sage nod of his gray head. "That's why everybody invests with him."

Donald was looking at the clock and clucking his tongue, so Sam let him get up and ready for breakfast. Though he had cognitive difficulties, Donald was a fairly young man for the clientele at Sea and Sunset; he brought the mean age way down. But he'd been eager to move in, so here he was.

He walked with his father down the hall toward the dining area, then peeled off at the main set of doors and pushed his way outside, heading to his truck. He dialed the sheriff as he climbed inside, but learned from Brenda, the dispatcher, that Vandra wasn't around. Could someone else help him?

"What about Detective Stone? He there?"

"I can put you through."

Stone sounded distracted when he answered, so Sam just started right in. "I'm trying to reach the sheriff. Joe didn't burn that boat. I don't care what the kid . . . Mayfield . . . said."

"You see Mayfield yet?" Stone asked.

"That's on today's agenda."

Stone exhaled slowly and said, "Vandra won't appreciate me giving you Mayfield's name. He doesn't like family interference during an investigation."

Sam sensed something in Stone's tone, a dissatisfaction, maybe? Definitely a caution. "Why'd you give it to me, then?"

"We could use more people looking into what happened, family or otherwise. Just my opinion."

And you and Detective Dunbar have had your hands tied by the sheriff's assertion that the fire was set by Joe.

"Who interviewed Mayfield?" Sam asked. "Was it just Vandra?"

"Yep."

"Is that usual? For the sheriff to conduct investigative interviews?"

"We all do the same work." The answer was short, his tone cool. Whatever Stone felt, he was keeping it to himself, but Sam sensed the detective thought there was more to be learned.

"I'll call you after I see Mayfield," Sam said, wondering if he could fit that in before picking up Jules. He needed to call the hospital and get some kind of idea about the anticipated time of her release. He also still needed to pick up that burner phone for Jules, since she was in no condition yet to fight it out with her cell phone carrier.

Staring through the dusty windshield, he placed the call to Tillamook Hospital, and after being routed around for a while, learned that Julia Ford was unlikely to be released before eleven. That gave him some time, so he hung up, fired up his truck, and drove to Seaside, where he purchased the disposable cell phone. Then he headed back down the coast. He put a call in to the marina, hoping to catch Mayfield and risking a ticket while he drove, as his Bluetooth wasn't working. Maybe the kid would be at the marina this early, or maybe not. Sam's nebulous plan had always been to just show up and take the kid unawares, make him tell his story without any rehearsal. But a call to the marina would at least tell him if Ryan Mayfield was on the premises.

"Yep?" an older male voice answered as an apparently usual form of greeting.

"Is this Bay Marina in Nehalem?"

"Sure is."

"Is Ryan Mayfield working today?"

"No sirree. Should be here tomorrow, though."

"Okay, thanks." Damn. He clicked off before the man could ask who wanted to know. Now, what?

He wondered if he should track the kid down at his home. He could call Stone back and ask for an address, but sensed the detective had given him about as much help as he could without risking the sheriff deeming his actions total insubordination. Instead he called Griff. No answer. The call went straight to voice mail. Sam left a quick message: "Hey. This is Sam. Give me a call."

He was passing Salchuk when he decided to try the Spindrift again. It was still early enough for breakfast and he still hankered for the huevos ranchcros he'd seen on their menu yesterday. Sam's appetite had come back with a vengeance, and he'd almost stayed and breakfasted with his father, but he'd been too antsy.

There was a parking spot right in front of the restaurant, which he zipped into. Inside, he was shown to a seat in one of the booths and ordered the huevos and a cup of black coffee as soon as the waitress appeared. His mind was circling back to the circumstances of his brother's death and, of course to Jules. Always Jules.

When his breakfast arrived, it smelled and looked delicious, both refried and black beans circled two eggs smothered in melted cheddar and simmering in red ranchero sauce. He tucked into the flour tortilla, forking up the beans, eggs, and sauce, feeling better than he had since he'd learned about Joe. The deep heaviness from the loss was still inside him, but he was better than yesterday.

One step at a time, he told himself, already thinking about his next move as he drained his coffee. He couldn't sit still too long, had to keep on track and find out what the hell had happened to Joe. Suicide? No way. But what about murder? If Joe had planned on torching the boat himself, to end it all, why take Jules? It just didn't make sense and it pissed him off big-time that the sheriff would even entertain such a notion.

He paid for the breakfast, dropping a healthy tip on the young girl who'd served him—a different waitress from yesterday's, this one a little nicer—telling her it was the best meal he'd had in a long, long time.

"Thank you!" she said with a bright smile. "I'll tell the cook."

As he drove back toward Highway 101, summer sun glinting off the hood of his truck, he took a quick turn to circle by his brother's office. He needed to do a more thorough search of Jules's house and find the extra keys. Meanwhile, there had to be a way into the office. If he could just keep Officer Bolles off his back and maybe get some cooperation, then—

Sam looked over at the small house Joe had rented and immediately screeched to a stop. A cold frisson slid down his spine and pooled in the small of his back. The front door of Joe's office was thrown wide open. Through the door Sam could see papers strewn across the floor, drawers tossed on the floor, a lamp overturned.

Someone was there.

Heart pounding, he jumped out of the truck, left it running, and ran pell-mell toward the office door. One step inside and his worst fears were confirmed. The place had been completely trashed. Every drawer in the desk and credenza had been yanked open, most of the contents spilled on the floor, cushions of a small couch dumped and slashed, stuffing visible, plaques and pictures ripped from the walls and smashed on the floor.

What the hell?

On full alert, he did a quick run-through of the three rooms, a back break room with a counter, microwave, and minifridge, the bathroom, and the main office. No one. He took a deep breath. Mentally cursed the intruder, felt his anger mount. Whoever'd been there was gone. He waited for his racing pulse to slow down. He'd had a moment where he'd automatically reached for his gun, which he no longer carried, his hand swiping dead air near the hip where his holster had held his Glock.

Back in the main office he righted a chair and looked at the drawers and papers scattered every which way on the floor. Someone had tossed the place but good. Obviously searching for something. Something important. Something to do with the reason Joe was killed. Telling himself to remain calm, to survey the damage as a cop, not Joe's brother, he let his eyes travel over the space without moving for several minutes, taking everything in, but understanding little. Eventually, he headed back down the short hall.

In the kitchen, cabinet doors were thrown open and everything was tossed in a pile on the floor; paper plates, plasticware, coffee bags slit and spilled, a couple of apples, and a small container of half-and-half made up most of the mess. He took a few steps and stood in the doorway of the bathroom, where toilet paper, cleansers, soap, and various and sundry medicine cabinet supplies—Band-Aids, throat lozenges, aspirin, and mouthwash— had been thrown about the small room.

Disgusted and seeing nothing that would explain why the place had been ransacked, he returned to the main room— *Joe's office*, he thought with a pang. Pushing thoughts of his brother aside, he bent down to the papers, examining them without touching them. He shifted a few with the toe of his sneaker. They were mostly skinny manuals, financial circulars, and a scratch pad with a number of doodles. "SKY HARBOR" was spelled out in all caps, and below it the letters "CF." Sam committed both to memory and realized the writing looked like the same on the missing Cardaman note. "Sky Harbor" sounded familiar, but it wasn't anywhere he knew on the Oregon coast. He picked up a pencil from one of the open drawers and, using the eraser, leaned down to push other pages aside. There appeared to be no work files among the papers. Nothing to do with Joe's business beyond general information pertaining to financial companies.

"CF" . . . Could that refer to the Cardaman file? Like the note had?

He thought about it awhile, thought it might be right. It seemed Joe had written the note, left it at his house, but who had taken it? And why?

Joe's work files were on the missing computer, he

concluded, or uploaded to a secure site. There might be paper files somewhere, but there were no file drawers in the office. He saw Wi-Fi paraphernalia tucked on a shelf to one side of the desk, and a desk phone, but there was no computer of any kind. So where the hell was it? Back at the house? He hadn't noticed it. On the boat with Joe when it burned and sank? Or had it already been stolen by whoever was behind the mess in this office? Sam spied a power cord for charging a laptop, but said laptop was no longer on the desk. Had the intruder stolen it along with a desktop, or had it still been in Joe's possession, tucked away somewhere, when he'd gotten on the boat? He sure hoped it was the latter.

He'd just straightened when he heard an approaching engine and shortly thereafter, a step on the outside porch.

He waited and froze in place when the muzzle of a Glock edged around the doorframe, followed quickly by Officer Bolles. The gun was aimed straight at Sam's midsection.

"Whoa, now," Sam said.

"Hands up," Bolles growled, and Sam immediately complied. "Put that down," the cop snapped, and Sam realized Bolles meant the pencil he was still holding.

Sam had been a cop long enough to recognize that Bolles was so nervous he might make a serious mistake. "All right." Sam lowered his right arm and eased the pencil to the desk where it rolled toward Bolles before falling off the edge and bouncing onto the floor.

"Careful, there," Bolles warned.

Sam put both arms up again, palms out. He wasn't going to give this bohunk cop any reason to shoot first and answer questions later, which he sensed was a real possibility.

"What're you looking for, Mr. Ford?" Bolles demanded.

"I'm not sure, but I didn't break in. The door was open and I could see papers on the floor. Looked like the place had been burgled."

"Yeah?"

"Yeah."

"Everything was hunky-dory this morning," he said.

"What time was that?" Sam questioned.

"Earlier."

"You said you were going to keep an eye on my brother's office, yet . . ." He looked over the mess on the floor.

Bolles's face suffused with color. Sam worried for a second that he'd pushed the man too far. "Okay, smart guy. I think we'd better go down to the station and see the chief."

The chief? The police department in Salchuk couldn't be more than five people. "I look forward to meeting him or her," Sam said.

"Him," Bolles hissed.

"All right."

"You head back out that door and I'll follow behind you."

Sam did as he was told, but his temper was rising. He told himself to let the situation just play out. Not give Bolles any reason to do something stupid. But as the officer marched him outside, he couldn't resist saying, "You know, your sorry ass is gonna be in a sling when it comes out that you let someone break into my brother's office."

"I didn't *let* them, asshole!"

"You're the one who told me you would be patrolling, so this is your problem, Officer Bolles."

"Just get in the goddamn car."

He meant his patrol car, the same dark blue Ford Explorer with "Salchuk Police" swept up the side of it in white letters.

"Mind if I turn off my truck first?" Sam asked. Its engine was still rumbling away, the driver's door wide open.

"Fine."

He could hear Bolles holster his gun, which was comforting as he walked to his truck. No good getting into a pissing contest with Bolles, whose mental skills didn't seem to rise above average. He was lucky the officer hadn't decided to handcuff him. He reached into the truck, switched off the ignition, and pocketed his keys.

As he climbed into the back of Bolles's Explorer, Bolles got behind the wheel and said, "I'll have Cesar, our maintenance guy, come and secure this place."

Then he drove the three blocks to the station.

Chapter Twelve

Jules lay in the hospital bed, her body stiff, her mind still on her stint hiding beneath the mattress, concealed by the bedclothes. She sensed things could have played out far differently last night. Jesus God, who was that man who had stolen into her room? What had he intended to do to her? *Nothing good. Nothing good at all.* She still couldn't control the shiver beneath her skin, but it made her feel safer to hear the sounds of the day staff outside her room, telephones ringing, voices talking, elevator cars opening and closing.

The night nurse had come into her room shortly after the intruder had left, summoned by her call, but his attitude had been brusque and impatient and Jules hadn't been able to bring herself to reveal what had happened. She'd been too freaked out, and too certain by the nurse's attitude that he wouldn't have believed her, would have thought she'd been dreaming, having a nightmare. Worse yet, he might have suspected her mental condition had morphed from amnesia to paranoia. She wanted to tell Sam. Only Sam. Even though she knew he already had trouble believing she was struggling with her memory. Maybe he would think she *was* paranoid. She had no proof that the man had come into her room.

Did this hospital have cameras in the hallways? Was that

a real thing? Or was it just on television? The facility was old, but could it have been retrofitted? Was there evidence somewhere?

A man had been here last night, she was sure of it. There had been real danger in the room. Whoever had stepped inside had been looking for her. Had intended to do her harm.

The shiver became an outward shudder. She drew in a shaking breath and let it out slowly. Something bad was going on. Something she'd deliberately shut down. She had to get out of here.

That thought galvanized her and she realized with a bark of laughter that she had no clothes. The ones from two days earlier were in a bag in the closet. Wet, sandy, and cut from her body, they were in shreds. She had to tell Sam to bring her some or she would be walking bare-assed out of the hospital in her hospital gown. If she wasn't so frightened, it might be funny.

But she was frightened—nearly scared to damned death. Deep down in the core of who she was, her innermost self. She tried to remember why she was so certain someone was after her, but immediately the oppressive gray veil came down on her. She understood, now, that it was a kind of protection, something her own mind had created.

But protecting her from *what*?

Carefully, she tried to pull back that gray curtain, but nothing happened. She struggled harder, but the more effort she put into it, the more it seemed to turn to iron, heavy, hard, impossible to lift.

Good.

The thought popped in from nowhere, and she knew it was her true feeling. She was scared to remember, and she was making sure she didn't.

How's that for crazy, huh, Jules? What you don't know can't hurt you, right?

Frustrated, she turned her mind to the here and now. How

long would it be before Sam showed up? She felt trapped and vulnerable. He'd said he would come get her, hadn't he? A panicked moment. What if he forgot? What it he didn't want to get her? He didn't believe she couldn't remember anything. What if he just left her to figure it out on her own?

Knock, knock.

She jumped about a foot, gasping, then relaxed when she saw Dr. Lillard push open her door. "Didn't mean to scare you," he said. "How are you doing?"

"I'm . . . fine."

"You sure?"

"I think so. I'm ready to go home."

"How's your memory coming along?"

"It's coming . . . slowly." She didn't want to tell him it was still practically nonexistent.

"There's no blanket rule about when it'll return. Just relax and take it easy. Dr. Werkel's office will be calling you for a follow-up visit."

She nodded, but she didn't know how that was going to happen. She didn't have a phone. She'd lost it in the ocean when she'd gone overboard.

She froze in shock. *I remember going overboard!*

". . . your brother-in-law's picking you up?" the doctor was asking.

She recalled the water closing over her head. The panic she'd felt. For a moment there was a rushing in her ears.

"Julia?"

She came back to the moment slowly, her heart pounding. "I'm sorry, what?"

"Your brother-in-law, Mr. Ford, is picking you up, I understand?"

Jules nodded. Sam was all she had, apparently. Her husband was gone and her brother had died young. Her mother and father were gone as well, and she had no memory of the friends Sam had spoken of who lived near her on a canal.

The doctor left her and she looked at the telephone on her night table. She should have gotten Sam's number.

As if she'd willed it to ring, the phone suddenly jangled loudly, making her jump again. Damn. Her nerves were shot. Carefully, she picked up the receiver. "Hello?"

"Hey, Jules, it's Sam. I'm tied up for a while. Have they released you yet?"

"I think it's just a matter of paperwork," she said, so relieved to hear his voice, she felt tears well. She wanted to blurt out about the intruder, but she was afraid he wouldn't believe her. She said instead, "Sam . . . I don't have any clothes."

"Ahhh . . . yes." That seemed to stop him for a moment. "I'll go to your house and find some things before I come to the hospital."

"Thank you," she said, her throat suddenly tight.

"But it looks like it'll be a little while. I'm currently on my way to the Salchuk Police station, waiting to talk to the chief. Joe's office was broken into. Somebody looking for something, apparently, and I was first on the scene, so . . . ah . . . they're making sure it wasn't me who broke in," he said dryly. "At least they're letting me use my phone."

The tone of his voice stirred something in the back of her mind, a distant memory, a feeling of déjà vu. And something stirred inside her, too . . . stretching and waking. Memories . . . of Sam . . . She tried to reach out and grab onto them but they faded away. Her mind was fractured a bit, and she had trouble tracking what he was saying. "But you didn't, did you? Break in?"

"Nope. Somebody did that for me. Joe's computer wasn't there, no desktop, but maybe he only had a laptop. That's what he was carrying around the last time I saw him. I don't know if it was stolen, or if it's somewhere else. Would he have taken it on the boat?" he mused, talking more to himself than her.

The laptop . . . she could almost see it.

"I'm hoping to get out of here soon," he added. "I'll see you as soon as I can," he assured her, and then he was gone.

She'd sat up to answer the phone and now she sank back against the pillows, her mind on their conversation. The movement brought a memory of sinking back against other pillows, laughter escaping from her lips as she pulled Sam's face down to kiss her. She could recall the feel of his lips, the stubble of his beard, the caress of his hand sliding down her rib cage. This time she didn't pull away in shock from the memory. This time she lay still and forced herself to relax, wanting more. *Don't think. Just let it come. Stop fighting.*

Sam . . . she thought. *Samuel Ford.* Couldn't remember his middle name. No, wait. She did remember! He didn't possess one. That was right, wasn't it?

Relax. Don't try. Just ease back. Be patient.

She closed her eyes. Could recall him kissing her neck and moving lower. She was naked and she could still feel the soft, moist line his lips formed as they moved ever downward. Her stomach muscles quivering as he slid lower, his tongue exploring her navel.

I love you, she'd thought, winding her fingers through his dark hair, her back arching as he moved dangerously close to the juncture of her thighs, his tongue exploring her secret depths in a way that had her groaning aloud and clutching the bedclothes.

"Oh, God," she whispered now, opening her eyes to the hospital room. Her heart was pounding, which set her head to pounding as well.

She suddenly wanted a shower. To clean up and be presentable. Sam had said he was going to be a while, so there was nothing stopping her from taking one right now . . . except the thought that someone could find her, naked and vulnerable.

Not in the light of day. Not with all this activity.

Sliding out of bed, she headed into the bathroom. It took a bit of effort to pull off the shoulder harness, but she managed, letting her right arm drop carefully before stripping out of her hospital gown, pulling back the shower curtain, and turning on the taps. Stepping beneath the spray, she had another memory, so vivid she almost slipped. She recalled Sam and her being entwined beneath cascading water, making love, laughing at the awkwardness, half drowning themselves as they grappled to bring each other nearer, her back pressed against the shower stall tiles.

Now she carefully put her head beneath the water, aware of the bandage on her temple. They'd given her instructions on taking it off and replacing it, but she also knew the injury was more an abrasion and bump rather than a laceration. The bump had been strong enough to knock her senseless, and drop out her memories, but, from every test the doctors had run, not enough to do permanent damage.

She ripped the bandage off again and let her hair fall down.

Bolles had taken Sam inside the Salchuk Police Department, which was little more than an anteroom attached to a garage with four bays, and through a counter-height swinging door where a female officer in her midthirties, black hair scraped back from her face into a bun, her uniform tight on her small frame, sat in front of a computer screen. Her name tag read Malkers, and she looked askance at Sam. "What have we got here?" she asked.

"I'm not sure," Sam answered, beating Bolles to the punch. "Maybe check with him. He's the one who held me at gunpoint."

Bolles sputtered, "Joe Ford's office was broken into and trashed, and this guy was standing in the middle of the mess, so I brought him on down here to have a talk with the chief."

"Pendergast isn't in yet," she said.

Sam explained, "This 'guy' is Sam Ford. Joe Ford's brother. Joe lost his life in the boating accident the other day."

"I know about it," she said, her tone carefully neutral.

Bolles said quickly, "And we don't know what went down out there on that boat. Could be anything. Chief's talking to Sheriff Vandra about it all. That's probably where he is now. I was patrolling, and I came around the corner and there he was"—he pointed to Sam—"and his truck's running and he's inside, and I can see the place is completely tossed."

Malkers said, "The chief's talking to the mayor about the development on Summit Ridge."

Summit Ridge. Sam said, "My truck was running because I saw the door was wide open to my brother's office. I thought someone was inside, so I just ran in."

"To confront them?" she asked.

"Yeah, maybe. I'd been inside about five minutes when Officer Bolles showed up and held a gun on me. There was quite a bit of destruction inside. Before that I was at the Spindrift, having huevos rancheros. You can ask the waitress, the one in her twenties, if you want to check my story. I didn't have time to do all that damage. Someone was looking for something, but it wasn't me."

"Save it for the chief," Bolles snapped.

"I've got a lot of things to do today, so I'd like to make this quick. I'm picking up Joe's widow at the hospital this morning."

"The office door was open?" Malkers asked.

"Yes."

Malkers's eyes were on Bolles and Sam sensed her deep impatience with the other officer. "It could be a little while before the chief gets here."

"I'll contact him." Bolles flushed, aware Malkers wasn't

buying any of his posturing. He whipped out a cell phone and placed a call, got nowhere, and clicked off in annoyance.

"Maybe I should wait in one of those," Sam suggested, pointing to the other side of the counter where two white, plastic, visitors chairs were arranged against the wall. There was nowhere to sit on this side of the counter, apart from Malkers's desk chair.

As if on cue a portly man strode into the Salchuk Police station at that moment wearing a uniform like Malkers and Bolles. He flicked a look toward Sam as he pushed open the swinging door to the inner office area. He fit the stereotypical image of a small-town lawman caricature to a T: thirty pounds overweight, stuffed with self-importance, swaggering like he owned the place. All he was missing was a cowboy hat and a toothpick in the corner of his mouth.

"You must be Mr. Ford," he said, regarding Sam carefully. His voice was genial, but his expression said the jury was still out about Sam's innocence or involvement.

"And you're Chief Pendergast."

"Well, that's what they call me around here, but we're kind of small potatoes, y'know, so chief? Chief of what?"

"Chief of the Salchuk Police Department," Sam said.

He took a step back and looked Sam up and down, then shot a glance at Bolles, who was on one foot and then the other, practically panting to talk.

"I caught him breaking in to Joe's office. I had to bring him in—"

"I did not break in," Sam stated calmly.

"—because, well, there's still a lot we don't know about that boat accident."

"Who's sitting on his burgled office?" Pendergast asked.

"I told Cesar to go," Bolles said. "But I caught this guy on-site, riffling through some papers. The place was trashed. So, I brought him here, so we—you—could talk to him."

Pendergast turned to Sam. "Mr. Ford, you were with the Seaside Police Department, is that correct?"

"Yes."

"And you interviewed for a job with the Tillamook County Sheriff's Department."

"That's right."

"I spoke with Sheriff Vandra this morning and he vouched for you. Said you're doing some investigating into your brother's death yourself."

Vandra knew? Sam was surprised. The sheriff had made it pretty clear he didn't want any interference, so he'd half believed the man would throw him to the wolves if he learned Sam was investigating on his own. Stone must have told the sheriff what Sam intended, but Vandra appeared to have taken the news in stride. That was unexpected. "I don't think Joe's death was an accident," Sam admitted. "I mean to find out what really happened."

"You think his financial business is connected to his death."

Stone had really sold him out, he thought. Except Sam hadn't mentioned anything about Joe's financial business to the detective. "Is that what the sheriff said?"

"Just stands to reason, far as I can see. Come on back to my office," he invited, then added to Bolles, "Get back up to Joe Ford's business office and make sure Cesar is there. You shouldn't have left it unattended."

"Well, what was I supposed to do with him?" Bolles asked, nodding at Sam.

When Pendergast didn't respond, just headed down the hallway that led toward the garage bays, Bolles flung back the swinging door and marched out. Pendergast held an arm out toward the room he wanted Sam to walk into. Like Joe's office, there were only two other rooms, the kitchen/break room and the bathroom, aside from this office and the reception area. A gray metal desk took up the office's center and a picture of Haystack Rock in Cannon Beach was hung on the wall behind it. The desk was covered with papers in neat stacks positioned next to a PC desktop computer sporting another beach scene as its screen saver. Wires snaked out from the back of the computer to the wall.

"My office, but we all use it," Pendergast said, dropping his hefty frame into the desk chair. He motioned Sam into another of the white plastic chairs that appeared to be the department's only other furniture. "Why don't you tell me what you're thinking about your brother."

Sam glanced at the clock on the wall and debated. He didn't want to say anything to Pendergast until he knew more. Maybe it was his imagination, but it felt like he was being purposely stalled. "I think someone killed my brother. I told the sheriff the same thing."

"Hmmm. I understand your brother purchased several gallons of gasoline in a gas can before he went out on the boat."

"Sheriff Vandra tell you that?"

"We work together pretty closely on this part of the coast. You folks up in Seaside take care of yourselves, but we monitor the whole coastline."

"All the jurisdictions work together," Sam pointed out carefully. He didn't want to totally piss the guy off, but what the hell?

"Well, of course. We gotta uphold the law, don't we?" When Sam didn't answer, he asked, "Is that your plan, then? To join up with the Tillamook Sheriff's Department?"

Sam didn't immediately respond. He was processing the chief's words, trying to understand the meaning behind the meaning. He didn't like the whole tenor of this meeting. "I don't know. Look, I didn't break into my brother's office."

"Bolles thinks you did."

"Well, he's wrong."

Pendergast smiled. "He sometimes sees ghosts when it's just fog, y'know."

"In this case, it's just fog," Sam said. He glanced at the desk clock. If he didn't get going soon, Jules was going to be waiting over an hour.

But Pendergast was in no mood to put a rush on things. "You know how long this police department has been here in Salchuk? As long as the town. It's an institution. We're not big, but we've been here from the get-go."

"Mmm." Sam gazed at him with polite interest. *Really? This guy was giving him the touristy history tour when time was of the essence, when even now the burglar could be getting away, and Joe's killer . . . if it is a murder. You're not sure of that yet, despite what your gut says.*

"Salchuk comes from the Chinook word *salt chuck*, which means sea, and so Salchuk is by the sea," the chief rattled on, a bit of pride in his voice as he warmed to his topic. "We've become the cat's meow, the belle of the ball, the place to be. We're getting this influx of people, and there's a lot of construction."

Sam had enough of the small town information center rhetoric and abruptly changed the subject. "You were up at Summit Ridge."

The chief's brows raised in surprise, and then he said, "Ah. Malkers told you."

"I have somewhere to be, and no one knew exactly when you'd get here."

Pendergast looked about to argue, but thought better of it. "Okay, I won't keep you. I don't believe for a minute you broke into your brother's office. But I'm going to assume you believe the thieves were after something specific. That this wasn't a random hit."

"That's exactly what I think, given the timing."

"And you think it has something to do with your brother's death."

"Yes."

"A lot of people invested with Joe."

"Yes," Sam said patiently.

"The sheriff is leaning toward a different theory."

"He thinks Joe set fire to the boat himself, and either was suicidal, or got caught up in his own trap."

"Something like that."

"There's a big hole in that theory. Joe would never hurt his wife. And he wouldn't hurt himself. If there was a financial problem, he would face it. Solve it. Make it right."

"You sound pretty certain of yourself." Pendergast picked up a paper clip and began unbending it. "And, despite you once being a cop, I wouldn't say you were exactly impartial, you being Joe's brother and all."

"I'm going to find out what happened," Sam told him flatly, and held the bigger man's stare. "And now, if you have any more questions about the burglary, ask them. I'll answer whatever I can. But I'm on a timetable."

The chief wasn't about to be pushed. The features in his broad face pulled together thoughtfully. "A lot of Salchuk people invested with your brother, and now they're in this pickle, y'see. They want their money back. I'm going to make sure they get it."

Your people, Sam thought. Pendergast was one of those guys who thought he owned the Salchuk residents. Maybe Joe's decision to move here had offended him somehow.

The man's next words pretty much confirmed Sam's thoughts. "We don't need any flimflam around here, if you know what I mean."

"You think Joe was a financial flimflammer?" Sam asked coldly.

"Cardaman was. And the jury's still out on the Hapstells."

Sam's cell phone rang. He pulled it from his pocket and saw that it was Griff. "Am I free to go?" he asked.

Pendergast waved a hand at Sam, releasing him. "Just don't go too far away," he advised as Sam put the phone to his ear and walked out of the office, past Malkers, through the swinging door, and outside into coolish morning sunshine. "Hey, Griff," he said. "I've got a favor to ask."

"Yeah, man. We've been hearing rumors about Joe and Hapstell and Cardaman around here. Lots of questions."

"That's what I'm working on. I need your sister's number."

Griff choked out a laugh. "Really? Well, Sadie's sure thinking about you. Whatever did you do to her, my man?"

"I need someone to stay at the house with Jules. She's recovering. Broken collarbone, head injury . . . some trouble with memory. I don't know if she's safe. You told me that Sadie was between jobs."

"Yeah, like you. Hmm . . . Well, Sadie'll be disappointed, but she'll probably do it." He gave Sam the number. "So seriously, you really think Joe's wife's in danger?"

"It's a real possibility," he said, and cut off any chance for further speculation or conversation with, "Thanks, man," and clicked off. He jogged the few blocks to his truck, still where he'd left it at Joe's office. As he climbed inside he threw a glance to the heavyset man who stood at the doorway of the building. Cesar, he presumed.

Remembering at the last minute to pick up some clothes for Jules, he aimed the Chevy north toward Fisher Canal, where he would stop before heading south again to Tillamook. He drove without paying too much attention to the speed limit and was almost to the canal when his cell phone, sitting in the cup holder, rang. He saw it was Stone, calling him back.

He picked up the phone and answered, and the detective said, "Stone, here. Returning your call."

Sam didn't waste time. "I just came from Salchuk where

my brother's office was broken into." He quickly gave the detective a rundown of the break-in, Officer Bolles, and his meeting with Chief Pendergast. "There's something going on there. Pendergast made a point of how many people in Salchuk invested with Joe. I get the feeling Bolles and Pendergast, and maybe the sheriff, too, want to say Joe killed himself. They want to get a quick resolution so they can get their money back. Something like that."

The detective thought that over. "What are you planning to do?"

"Hell, I don't know. Pick up Jules Ford from the hospital and think it all over. Joe didn't kill himself." He thought about telling Stone about meeting the Fishers, but he had nothing but impressions. "When I figure out what that is, I'll call you back."

"Keep me informed."

"Yep."

Keep me *informed. Not the sheriff.*

He'd barely clicked off when the phone rang again. He glanced at the screen. Didn't recognize the number. Screw it, he thought, pushing the on button. This time he hit speaker so he was hands free. "Sam Ford," he answered.

"Mr. Ford, this is James Fairbanks from the Fairbanks and Vincent Law Firm. First of all, let me say how sorry we are for the loss of your brother." He paused for a second, then said, "Carlton Vincent and I are the executors for your brother's estate and would like you to come in to our firm to go over his will and the dispensation of his assets."

Sam's mouth went dry. "Ah, yes. You're going to want his widow, Julia Ford, as well?"

"Yes, we've left messages on her phone."

"If that number's her cell phone, it's unlikely she's going to answer anytime soon as it's missing, probably have to be replaced. She's in the hospital, but being released today.

For now, just use my number. I'll get you one for her as soon as possible."

"Thank you." He sounded relieved. "Can we expect the two of you on Monday? Two o'clock?"

"I can make it, but I'm not sure about Jules yet. I'll tell her," he said, picturing what that meeting would be like if Jules truly had amnesia.

"Very good," Fairbanks said.

Sam parked in Joe and Jules's driveway and then let himself into the house with the key Tutti had given him. Still feeling a little weird about being in Joe's home, he went into the kitchen, searching once more for the Cardaman note, but it was a fruitless task. No surprise there. Could the person who had ransacked Joe's office have broken in here and snagged it? But then left the rest of the house untouched? He remembered the chaos that was the office and it seemed unlikely. Still . . . He headed into the master bedroom where he felt like a perverted thief as he searched through the drawers, pulling out skimpy pale pink panties and a nude underwire bra. Swallowing hard at the sight of the bra, he remembered a similar one, a pink scrap of lace and silk that he'd helped her out of, gaily tossing it across his first apartment bedroom where it had gotten hung up on the lamp. They'd both fallen into a fit of the giggles.

Stop it. Don't go there.

He opened several more drawers but those held men's clothes. Joe's. He then turned to the closet where he found a pair of jeans Jules's size, neatly folded on a shelf, and a sweatshirt that said, "By the Beautiful Sea." He was walking out when he realized the sweatshirt wasn't going to work. She wouldn't be able to pull it over her head. So he returned to the closet and ended up with a royal blue blouse with silver buttons that she could slide her arm into easier. His eye caught sight of a pair of black flipflops and he grabbed them, too.

On the way to the hospital he put the cell on speaker and called Griff again. "What now?" Griff answered.

"Can you find out the address for a Ryan Mayfield? He works as an attendant down at Bay Marina in Nehalem."

"This for Joe?"

"Yep."

"You know the rules around here about handing out information."

"I know the rules. That's why I'm asking you to break them, Griff. I need some help and fast. This Mayfield told the Sheriff's Department that my brother bought five gallons of gas from the marina right before he took off on the boat. The sheriff's trying to make a case that Joe set the blaze himself, and it's bullshit."

"Okay, give me a minute."

He clicked off and Sam waited while Griff accessed Mayfield's records. It took a few moments, then Griff came back on and rattled off an address in Salchuk.

Everybody moving to Salchuk . . . his father had said.

"Don't let this come back on me," Griff warned.

"Don't worry."

Sam glanced at the dashboard clock. Eleven-fifteen. It felt like an eternity since he'd stopped in to see his father this morning.

Chapter Thirteen

Phoenix strolled out of Perfect Cup and into the newspaper offices. She ignored a couple members of the staff as she headed to her back desk. She was friendly when she needed to be, but she was dedicated to whatever story she was on, much to others' amusement because they still saw her as a small, newsy, folksy kind of gal. She ignored them. So, they didn't believe in her. So what else was new? She'd fought those same opinions all her life.

Besides, she'd been working on her own angle of the Cardaman story awhile and it was catching fire.

Unlocking the bottom drawer to her desk, she pulled out the file that Julia Ford had handed to her five days earlier. What was funny was there was nothing in it that warranted all the drama, as far as Phoenix could see. Yes, it proved that Cardaman had sold and resold certain parcels of real estate to multiple investors at the same time, a blatant Ponzi scheme, but there had been no connection to Joseph Ford's clients, or so it seemed, though Julia had taken it off her husband's computer. Phoenix had been following up on Cardaman because he was a slimy thief who'd stolen peoples' hard-earned money and put the cash into his own pocket.

Coast people. Her people. She'd cheered when he'd gone to jail.

She hadn't known about any connections to Joseph Ford or the Hapstells until Denny Mulhaney had shown up at her office, ready for bear. "I want to report a crime," he'd announced, to which Phoenix had hooked a thumb east and said, "You're about a mile and a half away from the Sheriff's Department."

"I've been to the police," he'd snapped back. "They're all bought off by Cardaman. Every last one of those low-life cops."

Phoenix had invited Mulhaney to sit down. She knew a number of members of local law enforcement and suspected that his claims were patently untrue. "'All' is a pretty big number," she'd pointed out, but she'd listened to bigger whoppers in her time, so she'd also added, "Wha'cha got?"

Mulhaney proceeded to name Joe Ford, among others, as someone who'd made tons of investments, many of which had turned to shit for his trusting clients. Not only had Joe Ford taken these "loser investors" but he'd skimmed off huge fees before letting the poor fools know their portfolios were full of worthless stocks, bonds, deals, whatever. Mulhaney made himself out as the hero, fighting the good fight, but he let Phoenix know that he, too, had taken it in the shorts along with other clients, losing a minor fortune in the process, as well as his job, and he wanted payback. Phoenix had heard the anger in his voice, the thirst for revenge. He was a bookkeeper by profession, and had worked for Ford in the Seaside office before it was closed down.

"I've got the information you need to bring Ford down," he'd insisted.

"Well, let's see it," Phoenix had responded.

But when called upon to deliver, Mulhaney couldn't really produce the data. He'd just kept insisting that he was right, and that she needed to investigate it.

She'd mentally written him off, until he said, "I can get you the Cardaman file."

"You have a file on Cardaman?"

"Joe does. It'll prove I'm right."

"Get me a copy of it," Phoenix had ordered, her interest finally piqued.

Mulhaney had then started rambling on about subprime investments and risky ventures of all kinds without giving specifics, and Phoenix had grown impatient.

Sensing he'd lost her, he'd snapped out, "I'll bring you a file next week. Then you'll see."

But he hadn't. He'd returned a number of times with more bluster, but no facts.

The last time she'd seen him, he'd yelled, "They owe me!" loud enough to be heard in the outer office, but there was still no file. Mulhaney had gone on to complain about Walter Hapstell, both Senior and Junior, as he had investments with them, too. It was all twisted together and Phoenix suspected there might be shady dealings in there somewhere, but it sounded like maybe something for the SEC to investigate, which she suggested.

That suggestion had put him over the edge. "You're in on it, too, aren't you?" he'd screeched.

She'd then told him to calm down, take a breath. She'd been thoroughly annoyed. Mulhaney was just one of those guys who threw blame around like confetti. He also looked like he could use an electrical shock to reset all those screaming nerves.

"You're saying that Joe Ford has lost you, and other investors, money by putting your assets into risky deals. I don't see how that's a crime, unless he invested in criminal ventures."

"Cardaman's was criminal!"

She'd tried again. "You're saying Joseph Ford knowingly put investors' funds into Cardaman's illegal deals."

"Yes!"

"This is where you need to bring me proof."

Mulhaney had then collapsed in on himself, a hulk of a middle-aged man, dispirited and upset. Head in his hands, he'd moaned, "Can't you just write about it? Kick start them a little, y'know? Worry them?"

She'd felt a little sorry for him, her Achilles' heel. "I'll see what I dig up."

So, she'd blindly started nosing around, asking questions of Joe Ford and Walter Hapstell Junior and Senior and others. She'd tried to talk to Cardaman, but his lawyers weren't interested and neither was he. She noted that Joe Ford's wife, Julia, was employed at Joseph Ford Investments, and learned that Julia had worked part-time there for some time, long before a disgruntled Denny Mulhaney left in a huff. Phoenix had asked Joe why Mulhaney was no longer there, and Joe had told her easily enough that Denny wanted to be more involved with the whole company, not just work in bookkeeping. When he was told that wasn't going to happen, he'd quit.

"Was he able to get all of his investment money returned?" she'd tried, but Joe had said he couldn't reveal anything concerning his clients' private accounts.

In any case, it had all been a far cry from the tale of financial shenanigans Mulhaney had wanted exposed. There was no doubt Cardaman was a crook, in Phoenix's opinion, but the jury was still out on Joe Ford and the Hapstells.

And then Denny had disappeared. Relocated to Portland without telling her. She'd followed up enough to learn that Denny Mulhaney had moved into a slightly rundown apartment on Portland's west side and had taken a bookkeeping job at a local electrical company. When she'd contacted him, he hadn't been interested in talking to her any longer. She'd asked him if he'd gotten his investment back, and he'd snorted and said it was more like a payoff than a return.

Hmmm . . . That had sounded suspiciously like sour grapes, so she'd put the story on the back burner.

Until Julia Ford showed up with the Cardaman file. Joe's wife had clearly believed the file held information Phoenix needed to know about. Denny had warned her about her husband's dealings with Cardaman, but she'd ignored him, until she'd found the file on Joe's computer. She'd known Mulhaney had been talking to Phoenix—Denny wasn't exactly a paragon of discretion—and so she'd brought her the file. Phoenix had pressed her for more information, but had gotten nowhere. Follow-up calls had gone unanswered.

Then the boating accident . . . and now Julia's amnesia.

A little too convenient.

Phoenix had examined the Cardaman file with a hard eye, but the list of names of people who'd invested with both Joe Ford and Ike Cardaman was hardly damning. They were just people. A lot of them around Salchuk. A lot of them from Portland, the Northwest, and even one who lived in São Paulo, Brazil. She had their addresses and had begun to check with them, asking general questions, as she was on a fishing trip, seeing what would pop up. She wasn't clear on what they could tell her that would amount to a story beyond the fact Cardaman had taken them, something that had already been all over the news. If Ford had taken them in some way, too, she didn't have any information to support it, and none of the Cardaman investors was blaming him.

So nothing. To date. Except that Joseph Ford was dead.

The answers, if there were any, were floating around in Julia Ford's head.

Now Phoenix picked up the file and looked at it once more. Anyone remotely involved in the Cardaman fiasco was doing some serious ass-covering. Cardaman was in jail, and that's where it stood. Millions of dollars lost.

The houses Cardaman had sold to hoodwinked investors twenty times over were sitting fallow along Summit Ridge Road in Salchuk. Cardaman had sold them sight unseen to people across the country based on beautiful renderings in a brochure. Someone had discovered the crime and reported it and investors were reeling. Those same investors had also been seduced by double digit investment interest and had offered up hundreds of thousands of dollars that had been since seized by government-regulating industries, now that Cardaman was found out.

But Joe Ford's biggest crime, as far as Phoenix could see, was that he'd initially believed in Cardaman, as had the Hapstells. Cardaman, the flimflam man, had hoodwinked investors and friends alike. Investment fraud was laid at his doorstep, but there was no hint of it outside of Ike Cardaman, no matter what Denny Mulhaney believed.

"Joe Ford is dead, though," Phoenix said to herself.

Was it an accident? The brother, Samuel Ford, believed it was foul play, but maybe that was grief talking. Still, the man had been a police officer, and he seemed levelheaded and thoughtful. Phoenix was leaning his way.

And if it was foul play, then what had happened? Joe Ford must have learned something, she felt, something damaging, maybe something that would further nail Cardaman's coffin closed. Or, maybe Ford learned something else entirely. She'd posed as much to Sheriff Vandra when she'd stopped into the Sheriff's Department after the accident. He'd told her she'd better not publicize her "half-baked, inflammatory" ideas. She in turn told him it really wasn't up to him, what she reported on.

She caught herself tapping her pencil on her desk, so she put it between her teeth and leaned back in her chair, hands behind her head, staring up at the ceiling, thinking.

She needed answers from Julia Ford. She'd pushed her some, but maybe she needed to push her a little harder.

She glanced down at the open Cardaman file on her desk, examining the list of investors' names. She was about to call the next one, which was about halfway down the list, a Mr. P. J. Simpson, but changed her mind. Instead she scrolled through her contact list on her cell phone, found the number for Tillamook Hospital, dialed, and asked to be connected with Julia Ford.

Jules sat tensely in her bed. The clock on the wall showed it was climbing toward noon. She'd been released. All the tests had been done. All the paperwork was ready. She just needed Sam to get here with her clothes. . . .

Sam. She was remembering him more and more. It made her feel guilty as hell that she didn't remember Joe, her husband, the same way.

Brrriinnngg!

She about leapt out of her skin at the sound of the telephone. Sam. Thank God! She snatched up the receiver and said eagerly, "Hello?"

"Julia? Hi, it's Phoenix Delacourt."

Her heart sank. "Oh, hi."

"I was hoping I'd catch you before you left the hospital. I've got the Cardaman file open in front of me. I've been going down the list, calling some of these investors. I'm about two-thirds through it. So far, no one in this file has blamed your husband for any wrongdoing."

"Good."

"I know Dennis Mulhaney made you worry something illegal was going on, but I've no indication of that."

"Okay."

"I'd like to come by your house and talk to you later about the boat accident."

"I don't remember it," she said tightly.

"I know that. I also know your brother-in-law doesn't think it was an accident, and I'm inclined to agree with him."

"I wish I could help you, but I can't." Her pulse was starting to race again and she glanced at the door. Was someone out there? Someone waiting for *her*?

Stop. Don't panic. There's no one there.

You're okay. You're okay. . . .

She had a sudden memory of Sam and her at a diner . . . French fries . . . sand in her hair and on her face, in her mouth . . . her father upset at the time she got home because her mother was . . . was . . . acting oddly.

". . . you there?" Phoenix asked.

"Yes, yes . . . sorry," Jules said into the phone. She was breathing rapidly.

More fries, Sandy? Sam asked.

No, no, I'm stuffed . . . Sandy, she answered. I've got to get home or there'll be hell to pay.

They called each other Sandy.

Footsteps sounded in the hall and she turned in fear, dropping the receiver.

The door pushed inward and Sam, holding a duffel bag in one hand, appeared. Her clothes, she realized.

"Julia? Julia? Are you there?"

Phoenix's tinny voice brought her back to the moment. She grabbed the telephone cord and hauled up the receiver. "I can't talk now," she said.

"I've got an appointment with one of the names on the list. I'll stop by your house later."

Her eyes were on Sam. "Okay . . . and wait . . . when you come by? Bring the Cardaman file."

She hung up before Phoenix could say anything else, but Sam was staring at her, frozen.

"The Cardaman file?" he repeated. "What do you mean? You have the Cardaman file?"

"Phoenix said I gave it to her. She's been going over it."

"Phoenix? Wait. Phoenix Delacourt, the reporter? She has it? You gave it to her? My God . . ." He shook his head. "Did Joe know?"

He'd stopped just inside the door and now she reached an arm toward him, beckoning him forward. "My clothes . . . I really appreciate you bringing them."

He stepped forward and handed her the bag, distracted. "Joe wrote out that note about the Cardaman file. The one that's missing. Right?"

"Maybe . . . I don't know. . . . Phoenix acts like I took the file without his knowing."

"That was his handwriting," he said positively, but she could tell that wheels were turning in his mind; he was trying to cobble something together. "I saw a sample of it in his office. Oh, damn. *Sky Harbor.* Jesus. That's the name of the Phoenix airport. Joe was referencing Phoenix Delacourt in some kind of code. Why? What was going on?"

Sky Harbor . . . ? Jules sensed tiny pieces were trying to break through the fog. They'd poke up out of it, then disappear again.

"Why did Phoenix call you?" he demanded. "What's she doing?"

"She said she was going over the Cardaman file, which is apparently a list of names. She's calling each one of them and talking to them about Joe and Cardaman and . . . I don't know. Whatever else."

"She says you gave her the file?"

"Yes. She said I met her at the coffee shop next door to the newspaper office."

"She didn't say a word about this when I talked to her."

"Maybe you should talk to her again," Jules suggested.

He zeroed in on her, his intense appraisal making her

swallow hard. The thoughts she'd been having about him, the memories, still swirled around in her mind. "What else is in the file besides a list of names?"

"She just said the names."

"You don't remember?"

"If I did, I would tell you," she snapped, then caught herself and took a deep breath, tried to calm down. "Some things are coming back. Dr. Lillard was right. But there's still the gray fog."

"What's coming back? What have you remembered?"

Jules couldn't tell him that she was recalling their relationship . . . how they'd been walking on the beach . . . calling each other Sandy . . . making love on his father's couch. . . . She could almost see it, *feel* it.

But she was afraid. Afraid to recall too much. Something was there that she didn't want to remember.

A look passed between them and she wondered if he, too, remembered those days long ago, if . . . Oh, Lord. *Get real, Jules. That was a lifetime ago.* . . . She gave herself a quick mental shake.

"Anything about Joe? The boat? What happened two days ago?" He threw the questions at her fast and furiously.

"No!"

Sam drew a deep breath and exhaled it slowly. "Fine. Good. I'll let you get dressed," he said, turning away.

"I'm not lying about this."

"Yeah."

He didn't sound like he believed her, which pissed her off. "The paperwork for my release is ready. It's at administration."

"I'll take care of it."

He left without looking back. Jules sat for a moment, aware that she felt alone and unnerved as soon as he disappeared. *You should have told him about the man in your room. Why didn't you? Afraid he was a figment of your imagination?*

She took her time easing out of the bed one last time. Unzipping the duffel, she pulled out a dark blue blouse, feeling the lush silk between her fingers. Her favorite blouse, she realized.

And suddenly she remembered Joe, her husband, the man she'd turned to when her mother spiraled downward and her father had drawn away from her.

Joe . . . gray haired like Phoenix, with blue eyes like Sam's. Her heart ached in her chest as she finally recalled her husband, could see his careful smile.

Joe . . .

She felt almost sick with emotion. She'd worn this blouse to a dinner meeting with him, teaming it with a black skirt that swept over knee-high boots. It had been winter and they were at a function, a fund-raiser at a Seaside hotel for victims of an autumn storm that had ripped off roofs and collapsed houses. They'd been having drinks and Joe introduced her to a florid-faced, heavyset man, who shook her hand, his grip sweaty and tight, a man who breathed hard and loud through his nose, and seemed to undress her with his eyes. "Ike Cardaman," he said in a gravelly voice. "Pleased to meet you, Mrs. Ford. . ."

He'd been off-putting, and she'd worried that Joe was involved with him somehow, even before Ike had been indicted. Joe had sworn he wasn't, but she hadn't believed him. She'd worried and fretted, and listened to crazy Denny, who'd felt there were conspiracies afoot in every direction.

She'd stolen the file from Joe's computer. . . .

Jules came back to the present. She was crushing the fabric of the blouse in her hands and she quickly set it down and tried to smooth the wrinkles with her hand. She ripped off the hospital gown and gingerly took her right arm out of its sling, then lifted the blouse over her head with her left hand. Carefully she slid her right arm into its sleeve, then tried to put on the sling once more, but it was too difficult. With a sound of annoyance, she tossed the sling aside and finished sliding into the blouse and working on the buttons, her mind tripping to the thought that Sam had clearly had to go through her drawers and select her underclothes.

"Not the hot issue," she reminded herself through her teeth.

She was dressed and ready and sitting in the chair when Sam returned half an hour later. He looked at her and she looked back.

"Thanks," she said.

"What about that?" he asked, pointing to the sling.

"I can't get it on by myself."

He hesitated a moment, then picked it up and carefully helped put it over her head and settle her arm inside it. She could smell him, a familiar musky scent that brought goose bumps on her arms.

"Okay, let's go," he said brusquely, picking up her empty duffel. She thought she heard him mutter, "Jesus Christ," and wasn't sure what he meant by that.

One of the nurses was just arriving with a wheelchair. When Jules tried to deny it, the nurse insisted it was hospital policy, so Jules was settled into the chair. Sam pushed her into the elevator, and then back out again on the main floor, the nurse walking alongside.

"I'm going to bring my truck around," Sam said, leaving her with the nurse.

Jules looked through the sliding glass doors, watching Sam as he half jogged to his blue, decidedly beat-up truck. He climbed inside and wheeled it around to park in front of the doors. Her heart clutched a bit as he came around the front of the vehicle, his hair lifting in the stiff breeze.

The sun was obscured by dark clouds that promised rain

and the temperature had dropped to an unseasonably cool temperature as Sam pushed her toward his vehicle. At the truck, she stood up and the nurse took the wheelchair away. Sam opened the passenger door. The breeze played havoc with her own hair and she reached up with her left hand to corral it as she climbed inside. The second she was in her seat, Sam slammed the door, hurried to the driver's side and without a word, started the ignition.

They were on the road and had driven a few miles in silence, when she said, "I'm remembering a few things."

"The Cardaman file?"

"No. Other things."

"The accident?"

"No."

His expression grew grim. Again there was silence, no word spoken. Jules stared out the window, to the winding road cut between the cliffs and the sea. She recognized the terrain, she realized. Her memory was definitely coming back.

As they made a turn off the highway, past the houses along the waterway, flashes of sunlit water glistening as they drove by, she suddenly knew they were almost home.

Home . . . the canal . . . the house . . . Through the houses, she spied boats moored on private docks, kayaks and rafts on lawns. Seagulls crying, flying against a cloudy summer sky, and somewhere a dog . . . no, more than one dog, was barking loudly.

A flood of emotions, some good, some not so good, washed over her, and she bit her lip. She lived here, on this canal, with . . . with neighbors and friends and . . . something more.

When Sam pulled into the driveway, her driveway, she was gripped by a wave of fear so intense that she shuddered. Her heart began to pound and her throat turned to dust. Oh, God.

Something had happened at the house . . . something she didn't want to remember. No . . . not something, some*one*!

"Wait . . . *wait* . . ." she whispered.

"What?"

"I don't know. I just . . . there was someone there. Someone in the house. He . . . he . . . he . . . scared me." She broke off in confusion.

Get to the boat!

She could see Joe, his tense face, ordering her to move. She could remember tearing out to the dock, running frantically, tripping down the few steps, catching herself, stumbling onto the boat, Joe behind her.

Now, Sam switched off the ignition and turned toward her. His eyes were sober, his face grim, and she knew that he sensed she was remembering. "Okay," he said with measured calm, "just tell me what you remember from that day. I need to find out what happened on that boat. Why my brother's dead. I've got a couple leads that I need to follow up, but my first priority is getting you home and safe. I don't want to leave you here by yourself. I put a call in to a friend, Sadie McClesky. She's the sister of a guy I worked with at the department, Griff. He's still there. If you need anything, he's a phone call away."

"Wait. What? You're leaving?" She felt a surge of panic. "Where are you going?"

"I've got to see the guy who says Joe bought five gallons of gas and took it on the boat that day."

"You think he's lying?" She tried to remember, everything. But the details were elusive, the bits of memory lying beneath the fog.

"You don't remember anything about that boat trip?"

"No. I just . . . I remember getting on the boat, that's all." She told him of the quick flash of recall she'd just had. Shaking, her fear palpable, she stared at the house, her home, and felt herself shrink inside. "Something happened here . . . somebody came. . . ." She felt she was getting close to some kind of breakthrough and her breath came fast. The gray curtain was pressing down on her, hurting her head.

"Who?"

"I don't know. I'm afraid to know," she admitted. "I just know we had to get away."

"Away from what?"

"I don't know!"

"Think, Jules!"

"I'm trying! I'm really trying."

"Someone threatened you?"

"Yes. I think so. I don't know!"

"Well, what do you know?" he demanded in frustration. "Goddamn it, Jules. I know you're trying, but I need you to remember!"

"I don't remember anything else. I'm sorry!" She buried her head in her hands and wanted to scream. "I can't remember! I barely remember Joe. All I really remember is *you*."

Chapter Fourteen

Sam just stared at her. Tears were threatening her eyes and she looked wretched. He dragged his gaze away and gazed through the windshield. He sensed how vulnerable he was to her. But could feel time elapsing. He had too much to do. He had no faith that Sheriff Vandra would take the investigation into Joe's death any further. The man believed Joe had purposely set the boat afire.

And though it flattered him that she could only remember him—really flattered him, actually—he needed to keep focused on finding out what had happened to Joe.

"Okay, let's start over," he said. "Let me tell you what's going on, as far as I know. After I identified Joe's body, I met with Sheriff Vandra of the Tillamook County Sheriff's Department. Initially, the sheriff seemed to think foul play was involved, but since that time he's of the opinion that Joe set fire to the boat himself, that possibly it was a suicide, although you were there with him and that flies in the face of who my brother was.

"So, I'm planning to have a talk with the guy who says Joe bought the gas right before that last boat trip. I want to hear what he says for myself. Meanwhile, Joe's Salchuk office has been broken in to, and his computer's missing.

Probably a laptop. I've been thinking it was because of a link to Cardaman, but now that Phoenix has the file, I'm not so sure."

Jules seemed to pull herself together a bit, but she still made no move to get out of the truck.

"My father said 'it's all about the money,' when I told him about the boat accident and Joe's death. He's not the most reliable source these days, but he was in the same business as Joe and he knows the same people." Sam thought again about what Donald had said about Jules's father and kept that to himself. "Something's going on in Salchuk, probably has to do with Summit Ridge, houses Cardaman was building and selling twenty times over or so. Officer Bolles and his superior, Chief Pendergast, didn't seem to want me anywhere near Joe's office this morning. Bolles caught me inside and was itching for me to give him a reason to shoot. As I mentioned on the phone, he hauled me to the station where I had an odd talk with Pendergast, who gave me a rundown on the town, basically letting me see that he was in charge. Meanwhile, Phoenix Delacourt apparently has the Cardaman file. By the way, if I repeat myself on any of this, just let me run with it. I want to get it straight in my head."

Jules nodded. "Yes, please. I want to hear it all."

"When I first went into your house there was a note in the kitchen in Joe's handwriting that said 'Cardaman file,' and later it wasn't there. Someone took it. Someone who didn't want me thinking about Cardaman in relation to my brother. Someone who may have a key to your house. Which makes me wonder how many are floating around. The key I have is from Tutti, and apparently Georgie has one and may have passed it to some of her friends, so I don't know who got it. I'm thinking we should change the locks. What I do know is that it feels a helluva lot like everyone is two steps ahead of me and making sure I don't catch up.

They don't want me to find out what happened to Joe. That's the person I want to find. That's the person who killed my brother."

Jules nodded again, slowly. "I want to help you. I'm remembering a few things, but there's a block."

"A block," he repeated.

"Something I may be doing to myself because I don't want to remember."

"Is that what you think?"

"Maybe," she said cautiously. "I'd like to believe differently." She cleared her throat. "But there's something else I want to tell you."

"What?"

"Last night . . . I think someone came for me."

"What do you mean 'came for you'?" Sam asked sharply, his eyes narrowing as he stared at her.

"There was a man, I think. My door was open and I heard him in the hall in the middle of the night. There was something about the way he was walking, carefully, quietly. I heard him coming toward my room and I hit the call button, but then I slipped under the bed and hid. I think he wanted to . . . do me harm. He came in, but then he heard someone in the hallway so he froze and waited. I barely breathed. I thought he might hear my heart pounding; it was like a surf in my ears. But then he left when he thought the coast was clear. I swear he was looking for me," she added, but a note of doubt had entered her voice.

"Why didn't you tell me this?"

"I thought you might think I was making it up. Like you thought I've been faking my memory problems . . ."

"My God, Jules." He shook his head. "Vandra never should have pulled that guard!"

"So you believe me?"

"Yes. Of course. And I don't think you're faking. I think you're . . ."

"What?" she asked, when he trailed off.

"I think you're just having a hard time." It was an unsatisfactory answer, but it was all he had. "But now I'm doubly glad Sadie's going to be here. She said she'd be here this afternoon, and I'll stick around till she shows. I don't even like the idea of leaving you with her, but it's all I've got, for now."

With that Sam got out of the truck and came around to Jules's side, helping her from the vehicle. He was following Jules to the front door when a car pulled into the driveway next to his pickup. An Audi, new, gray, and unfamiliar.

"Who is that?" Jules asked, a faint quiver in her voice.

"I don't know. I don't think it's Sadie." Instinctively he put himself protectively between Jules and the car just as the passenger door blew open and a girl threw herself into the early afternoon sunshine. She ran toward him, sobbing.

Georgie.

Joe's stepdaughter.

She ran into Sam's arms, nearly knocking him back with the force, surprising him as he'd never been that close to her. He wrapped his arms around her and held her tightly. The driver's door slammed shut and a woman with long, blondish hair clipped at her nape, wearing a champagne silk blouse, skintight blue jeans, and matching champagne sandals with three-inch heels headed their way. She glanced up at the sky, as if expecting rain, then made her way toward them. Gwen. Sam looked from her no-hair-out-of-place appearance to Jules, who looked young and vulnerable, her right arm folded in its sling, her brownish hair stirring around her face as the wind kicked up.

"Hullo, Sam," Gwen Ford greeted him. "Hi, Julia," she added in the same carefully modulated tone.

"Hi, Gwen," he said.

Georgie lifted her head to see Jules, then pushed off Sam to throw herself into Jules's arms next. Jules held her with her left one. She looked slightly stricken, but she offered comfort to the devastated, crying girl.

"Georgie," Gwen said sharply.

"It's okay," Jules answered.

Sam said, "I'm just bringing Jules home from the hospital."

"I can see that," Gwen said.

Georgie, a gangly, dark-haired tween who seemed to be all arms and legs, lifted her tearstained face to glare at her mother. "I'm staying here. This is my home."

"Yes, well . . ." Gwen just managed to keep from rolling her eyes.

"Let's go inside," Sam said, glancing toward Jules.

"Before the rain starts," Gwen agreed, and they all headed into the house.

Sam hadn't counted on Georgie returning, but now that she was here, the girl clearly intended to stay, though she'd been spending the summer with her mother.

"I can't believe what's happened," Gwen said. "I'm just numb."

"Yeah," Sam said as he unlocked the door and they all headed inside.

"Georgie insisted on coming, and I thought, well, okay, we can pick up some more of her things since she'll be living with me full-time now."

"What? I'm not living with you!" Georgie turned a horrified face to Jules. "Oh, my God. Please. I can't live with her."

"Georgie." Gwen clamped her lips together, as if to stop herself from saying more.

"Let's table this for right now," Sam said.

"No!" Georgie took several steps away from her mother. "I won't go back. Please, Julia, tell her I'm staying with you."

"Georgie, stop. She's just out of the hospital—" Gwen started in.

"Of course you can stay, if you want to," Jules said at the same time.

Sam started to say something, but decided it was not his place.

Gwen frowned, and said, "Julia, I'm certainly not putting her on you at a time like this. She's fine with me for the summer. I'll figure out the school year when it happens."

"NO! Julia, please!" Georgie, sobbing, begged Jules.

"Actually, Gwen, I'd like the company," Jules said, and Sam looked at her closely. It seemed like she was telling the truth. He thought for a minute that she might be remembering Gwen, but he'd actually spoken her name aloud, so maybe she'd just picked it up from him. He wondered what Jules and Gwen's relationship had been like the past few years. Gwen and Joe hadn't had a happy marriage, from what he'd seen. It had been a mistake, much like his own.

A raft of protests were falling from Gwen's lips, but they were kind of halfhearted, Sam realized.

Jules cut in by saying, "Please, let her stay. I could use someone here with me." She threw Sam a look, daring him to mention that he'd already arranged for his friend to come. He didn't.

"What about Sam?" Gwen lifted an eyebrow at him.

"I can't be here the whole time. I've got a lot of work to do, and I live at the cabin," Sam answered. But he was wondering about that—now that Jules had said someone had sneaked into her room, that she feared he meant to do her harm. Sam didn't want to put Jules or Georgie in harm's way, and leaving them felt wrong, but certainly the more people around Julia the better. Georgie would be safe; Julia would see to it.

One of Gwen's eyebrows raised. "I just thought that now that Julia is . . . needs help . . . you might be moving in."

There was something about her tone that irked Sam. "Nope," he said, and didn't elaborate. If he felt Jules and Georgie needed him here, then, of course, he'd make it happen.

"I would like Georgie to stay," Jules said.

Gwen shrugged. "Well, if you're sure . . ."

"I'm sure." Jules was firm.

"Yes!" Georgie pumped her fist, elated, her tears dried and forgotten.

It took another twenty minutes for Gwen to decide Jules really meant what she said and get back out the door to her car. The woman could barely disguise her relief at being unshackled from her own daughter.

"I hate her," Georgie stated as the car drove out of sight.

"No, you don't," Jules said automatically, and both Jules and Sam looked at each other, recognizing how quickly she'd fallen into the parenting pattern.

"I'm gonna call Xena and tell her I'm back," Georgie said, yanking a cell phone from her pocket and heading toward the privacy of her bedroom.

Sam said, "I've got a cell phone for you, too. It's in the car. I'll go get it."

When he returned to the house with the burner, Jules was standing in the kitchen, looking out toward the dock. The rain that had worried Gwen was falling lightly, spattering against the wooden boards.

"You remember Georgie?" Sam asked as he put the phone on the counter. He needed scissors to open the plastic pack and he pulled a pair from a plastic container that was bristling with wooden spoons, tongs, several wire whisks, and various other kitchen tools.

"Yes. And Gwen. It just hit me as soon as I saw them. It's a relief. I just want it to all come back at once."

"You and me both. Sure you want an 'almost teen' to take care of?" He cut away the plastic and examined the phone.

"I guess we'll see who takes care of whom."

He looked up and caught her smile, the first one since she'd survived the boat accident.

She added, "But . . . I have to admit. I don't really want you to leave."

"Sadie should be here soon."

"I'd rather have you."

The words wrapped around Sam's heart and he had to break eye contact. He told himself Jules was feeling insecure and wanted a man around. It didn't necessarily have to be him. "I'll come back as soon as I can," he told her. "I'll pick up a pizza or something on the way."

"Am I going to figure out how to use that thing?" She nodded to the phone.

"They're easy. I'll show you."

There wasn't much to learn. Jules knew how to operate a cell phone and this one was pretty basic. They were standing in the kitchen and Jules opened a drawer, reached in, and pulled out a notepad and pen. "What's your cell number?"

He stared at the notepad. It was the same one from which the Cardaman file note had come. He gave her his number and watched her write it down. Her printing was far different from Joe's, far different from what had been on the note. If he needed more evidence that Joe had written the note, this was it. He just wished he knew why.

"Call me and it'll give me your number," Sam said. "Make sure all the doors stay locked and the windows are shut." He glanced at his niece. "I don't know how you'll contain her."

"I'm on it . . . Sandy."

He'd been turning away but his head whipped back toward her. "You remember that?"

"I told you. What came back first is my memory of you. What that says about me, I don't even know if I want to know." She lifted her scraped chin. "Maybe it's just a time in my life when I felt the safest."

Sam didn't know what to say to that and he was saved from explaining when there was a knock on the door and he looked through the front window to see Sadie standing on the porch. She was tall and rangy, built like her brother, with a much prettier face than Griff. When he let her in, she looked over Sam with a hungry look, but then broke into a smile.

"Oh, I know you just want me for my babysitting skills, not for my body. Okay, okay. Fine. I'll take what I can get."

"Thanks, Sadie," Sam said. He introduced her to Jules, adding, "I wouldn't call it babysitting. More like body-guarding. Jules can bring you up to speed on everything. I've got to get going."

"Bodyguarding," she mused, taking in Jules's bruised and scraped chin, her funky hair that flopped over the cut and knot on her head. Then she seemed to remember the cir-cumstances and said seriously, "I'm so sorry about your husband. Let me know what I can do to help."

Sam left them getting to know each other and headed to his truck. He told himself to keep his mind on his mission, but he kept hearing Jules's words play back like a tape on a loop. . . . *I'd rather have you. . . . I rather have you. . . . I'd rather have you. . . .*

Julia Ford wanted the Cardaman file back.

Well, hell. It was her file, so she had a right to it. Phoenix had reluctantly pulled the document from her locked drawers. She'd already copied it and sent it to the cloud. Normally, she didn't much trust the Internet and electronics in general, though she had a smartphone, a computer, and an iPad. There was no getting around technology. You had to move with it, or get left in the dust. But there were trolls out there, and WikiLeaks and hackers and God knew what. Phoenix preferred hard copy, something she could write on and pick up and smell and feel. She would run off a copy for herself later, but for now she would take the file with her and drop it off to Julia after she'd had a chance to settle in at home. Meanwhile, she had a meeting with one of the investors. Kind of a surprise, really, as most of them had only reluctantly talked to her. They really wanted nothing to do with the whole thing. Their lawyers were dealing with the Cardaman fiasco, working to unfreeze their assets, whatever was left of them. They didn't need any reporter pouring salt into their wounds.

But P. J. Simpson had sounded first worried that she was calling about Cardaman, and then eager to talk to her. He asked if she could meet him in Seaside, which she could, so she was making the trip north. She wondered if he was one of the ones who'd been rooked by the Summit Ridge deal in Salchuk. Probably not, because that particular scam only worked if the investors lived far enough away that they couldn't just drop in and see their "property." More likely he'd just given Cardaman free rein with his money and was desperately working to get it back.

Phoenix looked out the window. There was some light rain coming down, but the weather was clearing up. It was supposed to warm up, too. Get back to summer. She stopped in at Perfect Cup, picked up a double espresso, then headed out to the lot behind the office and her blue and white Mini.

Sam called Phoenix Delacourt as soon as he was on Highway 101 heading to Salchuk. He didn't expect her to answer and was surprised when she did. He could tell she was driving.

"Hi, Phoenix, it's Sam Ford."

"Hey, Sam," she responded easily enough, almost as if she'd been expecting his call.

He cut right to the chase. "You interviewed my brother several times, right?"

"Yes, I've interviewed a lot of people connected to the Cardaman case. I'm on my way to interview another right now."

"Sky Harbor," he said.

"Uh . . . the Phoenix airport?"

"My brother had 'Sky Harbor' written on a note by the letters 'CF.' I figure the 'CF' stands for the Cardaman file, but I thought 'Sky Harbor' might stand for you."

"You sound upset."

"Does 'Sky Harbor' stand for you? That's what I'm asking."

She thought about it briefly. "Probably. He called me that once, sort of jokingly, sort of not. He wasn't keen on some of the questions I asked about his business."

Sam could well imagine Joe might resent Phoenix's probing ways.

"But I was under the impression he didn't know Julia had given me the file, so I'm surprised my name was linked to it."

"In a kind of code," Sam reminded.

"I can't help you there . . . unless maybe he'd learned his wife had taken a copy of the file and was thinking over what to do about it. He might not want my name attached to any Cardaman information. I'm just guessing. I didn't really know your brother."

The words Joe had written had been outside any file, almost like a doodle, and doodling was part of Joe's makeup. He'd been known for it in their family. Sam could well imagine that if Joe had learned of Julia's duplicity regarding the Cardaman file, he might sit down to think it through, doodling away in the process.

He could have been angry at Julia. He could have taken her on the boat to have a heart to heart. . . .

But he would have never hurt her. That much Sam believed with total certainty.

"Julia asked you to bring the file back," he reminded.

"And I'm going to. Soon as I'm done with the Simpson interview, I'll stop by Julia's house and drop it off on the way back. . . ."

"And I imagine you have a copy."

"Of course," she said on a laugh, ignoring his cool tone. "See you later, Sam Ford."

He half smiled as he clicked off. He almost liked Phoenix, despite the fact she was working her own agenda.

Sam turned off the highway onto Fifth Street, Salchuk's main street and only commercial district. He'd plugged Ryan Mayfield's address into Google Maps and learned that Mayfield lived on Moolok Lane, residing in an apartment in an older home with two units on each of its three floors. Sam parked across the street, his eye following up Moolok as it meandered toward the headland and Summit Ridge, the location of the Cardaman homes that Hap hoped to purchase.

Mayfield's unit was on the top floor, and as Sam approached he saw the building looked in serious need of maintenance repair. It had once been a dignified house, part of the first wave of Salchuk construction built when the town was new. All of the homes that climbed toward the headland had fabulous views of the sea, or *salt chuck,* as Chief Pendergast had made such a point of letting him know.

His cell phone rang and he swept it from his pocket and checked the caller ID. A number he didn't recognize. "Sam Ford," he answered. "Jules?"

"Yeah, it's me. So now you've got my number."

"So now I've got your number."

He could hear the smile in his own voice and it annoyed him.

"Good," she said, a smile in her voice, too, though she also sounded tired.

"Take care of yourself. I'll check back later."

"You too. Oh, and Sadie's calling a locksmith."

"Tell her we want them ASAP."

"I think she knows, but I will. See you soon. . . ."

Sam said good-bye and clicked off, his mind full of Jules's image. It was with a supreme effort that he pushed her from his thoughts and concentrated on the job at hand. Ahead of him and up the cliff road, Sam could see a few of the newer homes built by Cardaman, and others that were in various stages of construction, though it looked as if work had been halted indefinitely. Grayed boards, piled gravel with weeds climbing through it, and discarded wrappers, cans, and water bottles littered the construction site. A NO TRESPASSING sign was tilted against one half-finished wall and written over with graffiti: a squinched-up face sticking out a tongue accompanied by colorful messages about what the vanished builders could go do to themselves.

It would be quite a project for Hap, if he ever got it. And it would cost a bundle to finish.

Sam stepped out to cracked asphalt in danger of breaking off and cascading down the cliffs into the ocean. As he crossed a derelict plank board entry to the front door he could smell the skunklike scent of marijuana and hear someone picking an occasional note on an acoustic guitar. He walked into the main foyer and saw doors with numbers scratched into their wood. Apartment four was upstairs in the back. He stepped past the guitar music and climbed the stairs. Outside Mayfield's door he could hear the laugh track from some television program.

He knocked and, when there was no immediate answer, knocked more forcefully. The television sound was turned down, so he rapped one more time, hard and fast.

"Shit, man. I'm comin'," a male voice muttered.

The door was thrown open and a sleepy-eyed guy with a shock of red hair currently tied into a man-bun stood in front of him. Swayed in front of him, more like it.

A cloud of smoke boiled out of the room and Sam struggled not to inhale.

"Who're you?" the guy asked, trying to straighten up and act sober, to little effect.

"You Ryan Mayfield?"

"Uh . . . depends who's askin'."

"Sam Ford."

They stared at each other and Sam could practically track the message moving from the guy's ears toward his brain, making some kind of dull connection, then moving away again, back down the optic nerve as Ryan's eyes slowly widened.

"Who?" He cocked his head as if he didn't understand, but his face had given him away.

"Joe Ford's brother. And I know for a fact that you didn't sell him five gallons of gasoline from the marina."

"Wha'cha talkin' about, man?"

"You told Sheriff Vandra you sold Joe the gasoline, but you didn't. The sheriff knows you lied." Sam figured his own little falsehood might speed the interview along

"I didn't lie! The guy *was* Joe Ford. He said he was. I didn't ask him, or anything. He just told me!"

"He paid cash?"

"Yeah, man," he said belligerently. "He paid cash. Said he was Joe Ford."

"What did he look like?"

"I dunno . . . baseball cap and windbreaker . . . dark color, maybe . . . uh . . . jeans?"

Sam could tell he was making it up on the spot. "He never told you he was Joe."

"He did!"

Sam was growing angry. "We all know you're lying. Who'd you sell the gas to?"

"Joe, man!"

"Someone tell you to say it was Joe?"

"NO! He said he was Joe! I swear I didn't do anything!"

"What do you mean? What didn't you do?"

Mayfield stepped back from the door, nearly tripped over his own feet. He'd given something away, Sam realized, and now he was literally backtracking. "Just get the hell outta here and leave me alone!"

He sought to slam the door but Sam's foot was in the way. "You did something. What was it? The boat?"

"NO!" he shrieked. "No way! I wouldn't do that. Your brother killed himself with the gas, not me."

"You're lying about something, you piece of shit," Sam said tautly, purposely pushing him. If he kept ratcheting up the pressure, the guy might crack.

"Not the boat! Not the boat!" He moaned, holding his head.

Sam sensed this was the truth. He cast about for another answer. What else could he have done? It came to him a moment later. "You broke into Joe's office!"

"Nooooo . . ." But this time it was a wail of fear.

"Why? Somebody put you up to it?"

"You're putting words in my mouth! I didn't do nothing," he moaned.

"What were you looking for? What did you take?"

The laptop.

"Nothing! Nothing! Go away. I'm calling Officer Bolles!"

"You know Officer Bolles?"

For an answer he made a squeak of protest, then yanked his cell phone out of the pocket of his loose-hanging jeans. "I'm calling my lawyer," he declared. "You don't want to get arrested, get the fuck out!"

His lawyer? Mayfield didn't look like a man who could afford a public defender, let alone a lawyer. "I'm going to find out who put you up to this," Sam warned with a hard edge. "When I do, your ass is mine."

"Hello? Hello?" Mayfield was practically shrieking into his phone.

Sam stepped back and let Mayfield slam the door. He'd gotten enough for the moment, at least enough to go back to the sheriff with. Ryan Mayfield had lied to Vandra about who'd purchased the gas, he was sure of it. And Mayfield had also trashed his brother's office and taken the laptop. Had to be. It stood to reason that Mayfield had already passed the laptop off to whoever had wanted it in the first place. There was someone moving behind the scenes on all this, and it was time Sam threw it all in Vandra's lap, even if it meant getting cut from the investigation.

He went downstairs and headed back to his pickup. The guitar picker had given up his tune. Sam's lips tightened as he checked the time, torn between wanting to keep going and feeling he should return to Jules.

As he waited to catch back into the highway traffic his cell phone rang. Glancing at the screen, he saw it was Griff.

"Just checking in, see how you're doing," Griff said, when Sam answered. "Sadie get there all right?"

"Yep. She's with Jules now."

"Good. Maybe you can sneak away one of these nights and join me at the Seagull? Place is becoming a hot spot for the college crowd on weekends, and well, Friday's here."

"When things settle down," Sam said. "Right now, I've got too much to do."

"Okay, Sammy. Watch out for my sister. She's a shark."

Sam clicked off, then headed south on 101 toward Fisher Canal. He placed his cell in the cup holder, then put it on speaker and called the sheriff. This time he finally answered with a brusque, "This is Vandra."

"Sam Ford. I just had a talk with Ryan Mayfield. He lied to you. He didn't sell the gas to my brother."

There was a moment of silence, maybe surprise, on the sheriff's end. "You talked to Mayfield yourself?" He sounded like he was getting pissed.

"I sure did. Mayfield lied to you. There's something else going on. I think someone told him to lie about Joe. I want to know why."

"You saw Mayfield at the marina?" he snapped out.

"Nope. I went to his apartment where he was enjoying the freedom of legal marijuana."

"How'd you know where he lived?" he demanded.

"I asked around." He sure as hell wasn't going to get Griff in trouble. "Everybody knows everybody around here. And here's something else: My brother's office was broken into and I think whoever did it stole Joe's laptop."

"You think, or you know that for a fact?" he shot back, rapid-fire.

"What I know is Mayfield's up to his eyeballs in this. The laptop's missing. A little more pressure, and he'll break."

"You're not part of this investigation, Ford. You're not a cop any longer, and this is your brother. You're family. You stay out of it."

"Which is why I called you to let you know what I found out."

Vandra launched into a diatribe about why Sam should stay out of the investigation, and Sam listened with half an ear. Vandra wasn't wrong, but Sam just didn't care. He wanted Joe's killer brought to justice, and he was going to do whatever he could to make that happen, no matter what the sheriff said.

As if he could read Sam's mind, Vandra doubled his efforts to get him off the case. His voice rose with the effort.

But all it did was convince Sam to go back to Mayfield and press him himself. Even if the sheriff did as he'd requested, he wasn't going to keep Sam in the loop. That was evident. As soon as Sam got the sheriff off the phone, he looked for a place to turn around and head back toward Salchuk. Ryan probably wouldn't let him in a second time, but Sam figured he'd sort it out when he got there. If the guy'd been bought once, he could be bought again. Just a matter of finding the right buttons to push.

Sam parked in his same spot, locked his car, and pocketed his keys. It had been about forty minutes round-trip since he'd been there. Since he was no longer a cop, he no longer carried a gun, but he figured he could scare the shit out of Mayfield anyway—he'd already done it once—and that might get him results.

He took the stairs two at a time. When he got to Mayfield's door it was cracked open.

Immediately he froze. The guy had been barricading himself in when Sam left earlier. Had he decided to get the hell out and leave the door open?

He used his elbow to ease the door open wider.

Ryan Mayfield lay on the floor, eyes open, a look of dumb surprise on his face. A gun lay beside his right hand, as if he'd used it.

Sam looked closer.

No one would believe he actually shot himself in the chest four times.

As Sam stared down at him he heard clambering footsteps coming through the outside door and then up the stairs. Less than a minute later he was once again looking at the dark circle at the end of the barrel of Officer Bolles's Glock.

Chapter Fifteen

Sam carefully raised his hands and stared into Bolles's eyes, needing to make sure the man saw him, didn't shoot him. Bolles looked about to jump out of his skin. His eyes rolled from Mayfield's corpse to Sam, then back again.

"I didn't kill him," Sam said carefully. "Check the gun. I didn't touch it."

"You coulda wiped it," he charged, his gaze drawn like a magnet back to Mayfield's bloody and bullet-ridden chest.

"I just got here," Sam said. "I don't know when this happened, but it wasn't in the last five minutes, which is about how long I've been here."

Bolles looked like he wanted to argue, but he kept his mouth closed. Possibly because he knew Sam was right, based on what time the call had come in and alerted him.

Sam added, "I'm guessing someone called in about shots fired. Maybe someone from one of these apartments. That someone may be able to tell you that I pulled up after the fact. Or you could check any of the traffic cams or security cams in the area."

"If there are any. Besides, you were here earlier, too," Bolles said belligerently.

"How did you know that?"

"I don't have to tell you anything."

"Ah . . . Sheriff Vandra."

"Mayfield called us and complained!" he shot back, unable to stop himself. "Sheriff didn't appreciate it much, and neither did the chief!"

"I told Vandra where I'd been. It wasn't a secret."

"I'm not standing here arguing with you anymore." Bolles started reaching for his handcuffs, a bit disconcerted when he had to hold Sam at gunpoint and manage the cuffs as well.

"Just don't shoot me," Sam said.

He was saved by the arrival of Chief Pendergast, who hurried up the steps as fast as his short legs would carry him. Quickly observing the situation, he barked at Bolles, "For God's sake, put your gun down! He didn't kill Mayfield unless he was in two places at the same time!"

Bolles reluctantly lowered his weapon and Sam exhaled a pent-up breath. Held at gunpoint twice in two days. Holy mother of God.

"Sheriff Vandra's on his way, and we got the ME coming." Pendergast threw a quick peek into the room, like he didn't really want to look, but had to. "Goddamn it," he said wearily. "We don't have killings in Salchuk."

Sam pointed out, "Well, you got one now."

"What were you doing here?" he questioned Sam.

"Asking Mayfield a few questions. The sheriff and I talked about it."

"Goddamn it," he said again.

Sheriff Vandra showed up a few moments later. Pendergast didn't seem to mind having the sheriff on his turf and Sam sensed there might be some kind of underlying partnership between them. Bolles stood by tensely, as if he expected trouble. It took about twenty minutes more for the ME to show up, since he was coming from Tillamook. No one was exactly sure when the crime scene team would arrive, but they'd been alerted and were on their way.

Sheriff Vandra, Pendergast, Bolles, and Sam moved away from Mayfield's door, heading down the stairs to the first floor entryway and outside into the afternoon sunshine. Sam inhaled the fresh, briny scent of the sea, welcome after the skunky smell of Mayfield's weed.

"Who killed him?" the sheriff asked.

Sam didn't immediately respond, since he thought the question was for the group at large, but then he saw that Vandra was looking at him, squinting in the sunlight. "You're asking me?"

The sheriff nodded once, curtly.

"Then I'd say it's whoever killed my brother."

"That's a leap, son," Pendergast said.

"Joe didn't buy the gas from Mayfield. Somebody else did and said he was Joe. Or, maybe Mayfield was lying about that, too. An embellishment to cover his own crimes."

"What crimes?" Vandra asked.

"I think Mayfield was put up to break into my brother's office. Somebody wants some information that may or may not have been there. Joe didn't have hard copies at his office. He probably keeps everything on his computer or the cloud. Whoever did it may have taken his laptop. I don't know. I'm not much of a conspiracy theorist, but a lot of the people I've talked to recently had invested with Joe. There's a lot of tension now."

The sheriff, the chief, and Bolles stood in silence for a few minutes. Sam waited for one of them to speak. It was Vandra who squinted up at the sun, then leveled a look at Sam. "Suicide never really fit with your brother's profile. I thought I'd let Mayfield think I believed him. Hell, I wanted to believe him. I didn't want to think that someone set out to kill Joe and his wife. Someone . . . from around here."

Sam was a little surprised by Vandra's honesty. The sheriff

hadn't exactly been transparent to date. He didn't want the local investors, anyone he knew, to be involved in a crime of this magnitude.

"You sure about all this?" Pendergast asked Vandra. He, too, wanted to protect "his townfolk."

Vandra snapped, "I'm not sure of anything, except that Sam Ford didn't kill Ryan Mayfield."

Bolles ignored the sheriff's temper. "You think Mayfield's killer was the same guy who set the boat on fire?"

Vandra pressed his lips together, got hold of himself. "We need to find out. There aren't many cameras down by the marina, but there are some on nearby houses. We've checked and there's no one on 'em in the last few days buying a can of gas, as far as we can see. We talked to some of the locals, fishermen and people at the marina. No one seems to remember anything out of the ordinary."

"That was a fiction by Mayfield, then," Sam concluded. "And you'd better check the hospital cameras outside Jules Ford's room last night, if there are any. Someone came in to harm her," Sam said. He'd planned to put Stone on that one, but hadn't yet called the detective. However, since the sheriff seemed more amenable now, he threw it out at him.

"Someone came into her room last night?" the sheriff demanded.

"That's what Jules said. After the guard was pulled," he pointed out, sticking it to Vandra a little. "She was lucky he was interrupted before anything bad happened."

"Goddamn it," Vandra growled.

Sam should have been relieved that the three officers had finally come around to his way of thinking, but mostly he was angry. Angry that it had taken them so long to get on the same page. "Whoever killed my brother blamed Joe for losing his investment money, whether it was true or not. This guy brought the gas to the boat, killed Joe, meant to kill Julia, then he burned the whole damn thing, probably hoping it would burn to nothing. Then he got Mayfield to break into Joe's office, steal the laptop or whatever he could find that might incriminate him. He always planned to kill Mayfield because Mayfield could identify him. Then last night, this guy went after Jules, probably for the same reason. I have someone with her now. I'm not leaving her alone anymore," he added. "But whoever did it, did it for money. That's your motive. Money."

Pendergast rubbed his chin. "One guy for all. That's quite a theory. You have anything to support it?"

"Not a damn thing. Yet."

"Any idea who we're talking about?" Vandra asked.

Sam's mind flashed on Walter Hapstell Junior, but he immediately pushed that thought down. He didn't believe Hap had what it took to be a cold-blooded killer. He was too . . . weak. His father, Walter Hapstell Senior, however, was another story entirely, but Sam had no reason to suspect him other than he was a powerful man who may have risked a lot of money. "Jules is damn lucky to be alive," he said instead of answering.

Sam stuck around with the other law enforcement officers while the ME processed the body. After being treated like a criminal, Sam seemed to have passed the litmus test and been accepted as one of their own again, even without a badge. It was a relief to be working on the same side, though he wasn't going to quit investigating, which he knew was the tacit request.

It was after four o'clock by the time the crime scene investigators had arrived and had roped off the area. Everyone was wrapping up. Sam headed to his truck and found Sheriff Vandra trying to keep up with his longer strides. "Have you thought anymore about the job offer?" the sheriff asked.

"I haven't thought about anything beyond finding my brother's killer."

"You've been helpful, thinking right, but you need to leave it up to us now."

"Sheriff, I can't do that."

"We have the resources, and you're family, and—"

"I know all the reasons. But if your brother was murdered, would you be able to just sit by?"

His lips tightened. "I would hope I had the good sense to leave it to the authorities."

Sam snorted his disbelief. "What I want to know is how that killer got on the boat with the gas. Did he stash it there before? Was he a stowaway, or maybe someone Joe knew? Joe was supposed to meet me on his dock, but he went out in the boat instead. Was he trying to escape some kind of danger? Or did someone force him onto the boat? Was that why Jules was onboard? Because the killer set the stage?"

"We'll look into everything."

"You do that, Sheriff. And I will, too."

"That is a bad idea, Mr. Ford."

"Won't be my first one, nor my last."

When her phone rang Bridget snatched it up and saw that her hands were shaking. "Where the fuck are you?" she hissed when she realized it was Tom.

"Seaside. Got things to do. Gotta show that I'm working on the job, talk to people, establish an alibi."

"What did you do?" she asked, feeling a jolt of fear . . . well, more like anticipation, really.

"I took care of the man's problem. But shit, I damn near got seen."

"Oh, God . . ." She sank onto a chair. She'd worked this morning but had come home early, her mind on Julia Ford. They needed to take care of her. *He* needed to take care of her. She couldn't understand why he was so lackadaisical about the fact that she could identify him. He seemed to get off on the danger, and it was not the kind of danger that she craved.

". . . that damn Ford," he was saying in a voice laced with anger. "He showed up and talked to Mayfield. I damn near passed out from shock. Thought Mayfield was going to crack open like a goddamn egg and tell him everything. I was ready to blow both their heads off and damn the consequences, but Mayfield managed to hold Ford off. But after Ford left, fucking Mayfield called the police himself and complained about harassment! Jesus Christ, what a moron. I listened at his door and heard him on the phone. I barely got out of there before that fucking guitar player called nine-one-one. Jesus."

"What guitar player? What are you talking about?" Her voice was shrill. She was freaking out, imagining him being hauled in by the cops.

"In one of the apartments. I was in the back, on the basement stairs that led to the outside. After Ford left and I'd listened at the door, I had to calm myself down, think it through. I had the gun from the gun show. Untraceable to me. I had gloves. It was simple. I just kicked open the door and plugged Mayfield. *Bam, bam, bam, bam!* Then I put the gun near his hand and got the fuck out the back way. No cameras."

"No cameras," she repeated. It was like a mantra with them. They were always looking around, checking for cameras. The whole damn country had turned into a bunch of pansy-ass voyeurs. "Nobody's going to believe he shot himself four times!"

"Let 'em think Ford did it. I sure as hell didn't expect him to turn around and come right back. Holy mother! I'd just pulled out on the highway, heading north, and he turns onto Fifth, into Salchuk! We like, pass each other. Holy shit. May have to do something about him," he mused.

"What about Julia? What about *her*?"

"I told you, the word from the hospital is she has amnesia."

"Well, that's damn convenient."

"I'm gonna do it. Just trying to get our hundred thousand, babe."

"When's that going to happen? Have you even seen one dime of this fucker's money yet?"

"It's all gonna happen very, very soon." His voice lowered. "Then we're gonna have some fun, you and me."

"If we're not in prison."

"You gotta relax a bit. Get zen, or whatever the fuck." He laughed and then he drawled, "You know what I see? I see you naked, on your back, legs spread, mouth open."

She rolled her eyes. Half the time she asked herself what she was doing with him.

"Or, how about tied up? My hostage . . . and you're lying on a pile of money. Hundred-dollar bills. A *thousand* hundred-dollar bills. You're covered in them. And then I'm on you, and we're rolling around getting dirty in dirty money."

A wave of heat enveloped her in spite of herself. She could see it, too, and a thrill ran through her. She wasn't quite as money motivated as he was, but he could sure paint a picture for her. And she did love him. She did. Most of the time . . . well, sometimes . . .

"I'm thinking about being inside you right now," he purred. "God, I'm high."

She wanted that same high. She wanted him inside her. But they had things to do. Loose ends to tie up. Then they could screw themselves silly, maybe go after another mark, kill him or her, someone not picked by "the man," whoever the fuck he was. She didn't even want to know.

"Come to Seaside right now," he said. "I'm horny as hell."

"I can't leave the kids."

"Bullshit, you can't."

"Bad things could happen, and then what? And you've got to take care of Julia Ford. She's home right now, you asshole. If you don't do something about her, I will."

"Maybe we could do her together."

The thought sent an icy chill down her spine, fear mixed with a dangerous desire.

"Maybe," she said cautiously.

"Scope it out, sweetheart. Do a little reconnaissance and maybe tonight . . . ?"

She hung up on him, but dangerous thoughts circled her mind. She would have to be sure she could get away unseen, and Julia had to be as dead as Joe Ford was, no fuckups this time, because Bridget was not going to jail ever. Nuh-uh. She'd take down anyone in her path if she was caught, and that meant all those nosy neighbors on the canal. The Fishers. It wouldn't be such a bad idea to thin them out anyway. The world would certainly be a better place without them.

She walked through the house to the slider that led to her deck. Clasping her hands together in the shape of a gun, she lifted them to eye height and aimed through the window at each house on the canal. *Bam.* You're dead. *Bam . . .* you, too, fuckers. *BAM.* Especially you guys! *Bam, bam, bam!* She shot every house on her side of the canal and across the way, too.

She pulled back her "gun" and blew across the top of it, thinking about the real gun that she owned herself, the small one Tom didn't know about. Like his, it was untraceable to her. She had it squirreled away for that day she might need it.

A thrill swooped down her spine and she shivered. Maybe she should search out her vibrator. She hadn't needed it in a while, but now might be a good time. While she was thinking about taking 'em all out.

Making the world a better place.

Jules checked the clock in her bedroom. Four p.m. She'd tried to stay up and talk to Sadie and Georgie, but Georgie had been with her friend Xena, and hadn't been interested in any more sad conversation about Joe or anything else. Sadie had taken a look at Jules and told her she'd better lie down before she fell down. From that, Jules had walked into the bedroom that she'd shared with Joe, had lain down on the right side of the bed, her side, and had fallen into dreamless slumber.

But now she was awake.

She got up and wandered down the hall. The door to Georgie's room was closed and she and Xena seemed to be watching something on TV or their iPads. She ran a blueprint of the house through her mind, seeking to reacquaint herself with her life before the boating accident, and was pleased that most of those memories were back in place. She knew the house and her surroundings. It almost felt like home. Almost.

She headed into the kitchen and looked around, could name what was in every closet and cupboard. Her memory problem was hard to define. Sometimes she just blanked out and was gone. She would surface fairly quickly, but it always felt like she had to reboot her mind.

Those moments happened whenever she got too close to the accident. Then the gray curtain would slam down on her and she would miss pieces, and when she came to completely, she wanted to gulp in air as if she were being suffocated.

She hadn't seen Sadie in the living room and she wasn't in the kitchen. Jules looked out the window over the sink and saw that Sadie was lying on a lounge chair. She'd rolled her capris up to her knees and unbuttoned her shirt down to her bra. It didn't look that warm out, but Sadie was soaking up the sun, a pair of sunglasses on her nose.

Good. Jules wasn't ready to get into conversation just yet. She checked the refrigerator, more out of habit than anything else, and found a fresh pitcher of iced tea. She shot a grateful glance outside, which Sadie couldn't see from her angle, as she poured herself a glass.

Even though she enjoyed her privacy she was glad she wasn't alone, glad she had both Georgie and Sadie, though she was looking forward to Sam coming back.

As she was taking her first sip, she heard Georgie's door open and slam shut, then footsteps march down the hall to stop suddenly. She pictured Georgie standing outside Jules's bedroom door. Then the footsteps resumed and came back down the hall to the kitchen. Jules turned as Georgie appeared by the white kitchen table, her eyes hollow, face drained of color.

Before Jules could ask what was wrong, Georgie declared, "Xena's mom said that somebody killed Daddy."

Jules had a flash of memory. *Joanie Bledsoe.* Brown hair clipped at the nape. Favored shapeless, loose-fitting dresses. Divorced. A helicopter parent hovering over her two daughters. It was a surprise Xena was here without Joanie. Damn the woman for shooting off her mouth. "Oh, Georgie," she said, her heart pained for Joe's daughter. "We don't know what happened yet. Sam's looking into it."

"You were there," she accused.

"Yes, I know, but . . . Georgie, I can't remember what happened. I only know what people have told me."

Georgie frowned, looking a lot like Gwen in that moment. Jules didn't have to be told that she and Gwen had never gotten along well. Gwen was the ex-wife and Jules had been the current one, and never the twain shall meet.

"Did you kill him?" Georgie asked flatly.

"What? God, no!" she answered in shock.

"Then why is he dead and you're still alive!" Her eyes suddenly filled with tears and she angrily dashed them away. Sniffing loudly, she glared at Julia. "How come you made it and he didn't?"

"I don't know. I wish your father was here more than you could possibly know."

Georgie swallowed several times, the tears still coming. "You miss him?"

"Yes." She couldn't remember him as well as she should, though she sensed she'd been thinking about him. Maybe her sleep had not been as dreamless as she'd thought.

"You always wanted to be alone before," Georgie said.

"Did I?"

"Yes. Don't you remember?"

"As I said, I'm kind of struggling with my memory."

"You said that you and Dad fell out of love," she offered up belligerently.

Jules would have liked to argue, but the words sounded right, like something she might've said. "If I could, I'd reset the clock, get him back, make sure we're all safe," Jules said with some heat, despite how much she felt for the girl's pain at the loss of her father. "But I just can't."

Georgie seemed to accept that.

"Xena doesn't have a dad. He's not around, anyway," Georgie said. "It's just her mom and her and her sister, Alexa. I don't want to be like them. I want to be a whole family." Now the tears started falling in earnest, but when Jules made a move to comfort her, Georgie backed sharply away.

"I'm sorry, Georgie. I'm really sorry." Jules's words were heartfelt.

"I want him back." She could barely get the words out.

Jules nodded. "Do you want me to call your mother?" she asked, searching for a way to comfort the girl.

"NO! No! I told you. I want to be with you." She looked half panicked, and Jules remembered suddenly how strained Gwen and Georgie's relationship was. "I just want Dad to be here, too, and I don't want anybody taking his place."

"No one's going to take his place."

"What about Uncle Sam?"

Jules had picked up her glass and taken another sip, but started choking a bit.

"I don't want you sleeping with my uncle. I like him, but don't do that, okay?" Georgie said, sounding a lot older than her years.

Sleeping with the enemy . . . That phrase seemed to haunt her mind and it made her head hurt. "I'm not sleeping with anybody," she stated firmly. Where was this coming from? Surely nothing the girl had observed. Then from Gwen? Or Joanie . . . or *whom*?

"You dated Uncle Sam before you married Dad," Georgie said stubbornly.

"Who told you that? Joanie Bledsoe?"

"Is it true?"

"It was a long time ago."

"But you remember it?"

Jules was saved from answering when the door to her bedroom opened again and Xena called plaintively, "Are you coming back, Georgie, or should I go home?"

"I'm coming," Georgie yelled over her shoulder. She held Jules's eyes, seemed to want to say something else, but then she headed back to her room.

Deciding it was best to let the girl work things out for now, Jules carried her iced tea to the kitchen table and sank into one of the chairs. Good Lord. She'd had a pretty good relationship with Georgie; she could recall that. But she could see the girl half blamed her for Joe's death.

She sipped at her tea and gazed through the slider across the canal to Tutti's house. She could just see Sadie's painted toes and legs to the right of her vision.

Get to the boat!

She half rose from her chair. Joe's voice. Warning her. She heard it as if he'd just spoken.

Her heart was pounding, but there was no one there. She

sat back down, tense. Her mind slipped back to the night before, when she'd hidden under her bed. Someone had come for her, someone who meant her harm.

What if they were still coming?

She almost called Sadie back inside, but then decided she was being foolish. She wanted Sam to return. She felt safer with him around, but Georgie's perception about him had been disturbing.

After a few moments, she poured the remains of her melted ice down the sink, left her glass, then headed back to the bedroom. She tried to think about Joe as she entered the bedroom, but he seemed on the edge of her vision. Every time she tried to look directly at him he slipped away.

Relax . . . don't fight it . . . ease into it. . . .

Had they grown out of love? Georgie seemed to think so, and she couldn't come up with anything inside herself that said differently. She'd blocked Joe from her mind because something was wrong there. When she tried to think of him she felt panic, like if she remembered it all, the whole world would fall apart.

But she needed to remember. Sam needed her to remember.

She lay down on the bed again and closed her eyes, her mind drifting to Joe. Maybe if she could remember just one thing about him. Some detail. What was it that had attracted her to him in the first place? How had they gotten together?

You met him when you were with Sam. . . .

That was right. The first time she'd met Joe was the first time she'd also met Sam. After a football game and party at Hap's house. Hap, her sort of boyfriend at the time.

Her brain started to clamp down again and she forced herself to relax once more, counted her breaths. She could remember Hap, the spoiled, rich boy who'd chosen her over Martina Montgomery. Memories suddenly broke free, flooding her brain, and she had to struggle to stay calm and just let it happen.

Their three families were the triumvirate, she recalled. The three families with the most money, the most power, the most influence in the area. Her father and Conrad Montgomery and Walter Hapstell Senior. They had businesses in Portland, but were slowly spreading their interests throughout the coast, north to Astoria, south to Tillamook and beyond. Hap had decided there was no other girl for him other than either Martina Montgomery or Jules St. James, and he'd zeroed in on Jules.

She'd been flattered. She could recall enjoying being the center of attention at school, the object of envy and jealousy as she walked down the halls. It had been nice. Great, even. A much-needed bolster because of what was going on with Mama and Dad. Fights . . . lots of fights at first . . . her father threatening to leave. But those fights had turned into long, lethal silences as her mother's "spells" grew to become the norm.

She hung out with Hap and his friends to get away from her parents, though she grew to disdain them all. Her problems were adult problems, family problems, so much bigger than who'd stolen whose boyfriend and who'd slept with whom. She didn't care, but she didn't let them know. It wouldn't have done her high school rep any good to have her true feelings show through. She would have been ostracized, and the girls who envied her would gladly have turned their backs on her and flounced away. It had been important to her to be accepted.

But the toll it took to be a happy cheerleader, the effort to *rah-rah-rah* it while her parents' marriage disintegrated, nearly broke her. Mama had never forgiven her for letting her little brother die, even though Jules had been too young to be responsible for him that day on the beach, even though it was entirely unfair, that it was as much Mama's fault as anybody's. Jules began cracking under the strain. Her father, who'd been her champion when she was little, had seemed to be fading away from her, too.

And then Samuel Ford called out to her on a lonely beach, while he'd struggled with a pair of crutches. Had he not had the crutches, she would have probably just kept on walking, running maybe, putting distance between herself and Hap and Martina and the party.

But he'd been helpless and therefore harmless, and she'd waited for him, and he'd smiled, and his hair was tossed by the wind, and his eyes were nice. She'd donned her social armor—her courage, such as it was—and pretended she was just like everybody else, that she cared about the same things as all her classmates. She and Sam had then fought their way through the wind and blowing sand, had started calling each other Sandy, and had ended up bantering over French fries at Brest's.

Her heart began to pound as the memories came, faster and faster. She had to slow them down. Concentrate. As clear as if it had been yesterday, she remembered that she and Sam had started dating. With Sam it was easy to pretend, easy to forget the fact that her family was imploding. He didn't go to the same high school as she did, and though he knew Hap and his gang, he was a step out. And even though his father, Donald Ford, was in the same business, or had been, as the triumverate, he wasn't in the same league, apparently, and so Sam's family and hers had not run in the same social circle.

At Brest's that night, Jules had decided they were made for each other. Sam knew a lot about her, it turned out, at least the Jules that everyone else knew, and she'd realized he'd been aware of her for a while. It was flattering, a little stalker-esque, she'd told him, which embarrassed the hell out of him and only made him all the more attractive to her.

That night he'd stepped outside himself in order to meet her, and that had meant something, too.

She'd fallen in love with him, and she'd thought he loved her, too. Instead of dreading going home after school to find her mother staring out the window and her father gone on another week or month or God knew how long business trip, she would race home and call Sam and then he would drive into Seaside from his father's cabin in the woods, pick her up, and they would spend every afternoon together, almost every evening.

But when high school ended Sam went to a police academy in Salem, while Jules's situation worsened at home. By then her father was rarely home, and it was up to Jules to take care of her mother. Her father could handle neither his wife's illness nor the pressures of his job, which seemed the lesser problem at first, but then had grown into something terrible. . . .

Her mind suddenly tried to shut down and Jules eased back, taking deep breaths, counting first to ten, and then to twenty. There was nothing to be scared about. Her mother was gone, and her father was gone, and there was nothing inside those memories other than a long felt grief.

And then had come Sam's betrayal. In the midst of her family's disintegration, while her father became a ghost and her mother grew more distant, Lena St. James's moments of awareness turning to mere glimmers before being extinguished completely, Sam took up with Martina Montgomery.

How could he? When the rest of her world was in shambles, how could he, the one steady influence in her life, the boy she was certain she loved . . . how could he betray her? Jules's bitterness knew no bounds. All the things they'd laughed at, everything they'd shared, it was all a joke. Meaningless. When he'd tried to explain, she'd told him it was over, that they were through. She meant it, but the words had come from a well of pain. Martina had actually made the trip to Jules's house, pretending to apologize, but in truth she'd just wanted to know if Jules and Sam were really done. Jules had given Martina an emphatic, "Yes," which she'd learned to regret, as Sam and Tina began seeing each other in earnest.

Jules's mother had finally ended up in a nursing home, unable to recognize anyone she'd once known. Jules, freed from her caretaker job, had hardly known what to do. She'd ended up attending Portland State and that's where she'd run into Joe Ford, who'd been finishing up an MBA. Joe had chosen the same financial arena as his father, investments, making money with other people's money, the same as the triumvirate. Martina's father had retired by then, and Hap had started taking over most of the reins of Hapstell, Ltd. Devastated by his wife's mental and physical downward spiral, Jules's father had sold his business to Joe, and soon after Jules's mother passed away, he'd killed himself . . . thrown himself off a bridge into deep water, never having learned to swim. . . .

Her eyes flew open and she pulled in a shuddering breath. She was sweating and breathing hard. She rolled over and felt something hard beneath the mattress on Joe's side of the bed. A board?

She got to her feet on her side, then walked around to Joe's, reaching her left arm between the top mattress and box springs.

Her hand encountered the edge of something hard and metallic, and it only took a second for her to make the connection. *The laptop!* Joe's laptop!

She eagerly slid it out and stared down at the silver Dell. Setting it on the bed, she opened the lid and hit the start button. It flickered on and within seconds asked for the password.

The password . . . She'd known it once before, hadn't she? She'd gotten the Cardaman file off his computer. Squeezing her eyes closed, she thought hard, pressing her palm to her forehead to fight the pain that always came.

Easy does it . . . relax . . . let it come to you.

She decided to lie down on the bed again, and placed the open laptop on her abdomen. Tried to think about Joe, his office, anything connected . . .

What *was* the password?

Georgie.

Immediately she inputted Georgie's name.

Incorrect password. Try again.

Damn. She'd been so sure. Her fingers hovered over the keyboard, then she tried her own name, both Julia and Jules. Nope.

Joe was mad at you for taking the file. Not mad, disappointed. He thought you'd betrayed him. He came home with the laptop on Wednesday. . . .

And suddenly she remembered Joe fully. He'd burst in the door, upset and distracted. He'd barely spoken, just showed her the note in his own handwriting that read 'Cardaman file,' as they'd stood in the living room. She'd been sick with guilt. Felt like Benedict Arnold. When he'd asked, "Where is it?" she'd admitted that she'd given the file to Phoenix Delacourt, ready for any punishment he handed out.

And Joe had been . . . relieved?

Was that right?

Her head felt like a surf was crashing through it.

There's more, Jules. . . . There's more. . . .

She heard the sound of the sliding glass door opening. "Julia?" Sadie's voice called, sounding concerned.

She switched off the laptop, scrambled from the bed, slid the computer back beneath the mattress.

The motion sent another memory: Joe shoving the laptop between the mattress and box springs. A sound outside that had him rushing to the front room, Jules on his heels.

Joe had looked out the front window and recoiled in shock. *What?* she'd asked. *What is it? Is someone there? Get to the boat!*

"Julia, a boat just pulled up to your dock," Sadie called. *Someone was at the house. Joe sent you to the boat because someone came to the house!*

"What?" Jules asked Sadie, her voice trembling, panic surging through her. "What?" she demanded, her pulse pounding in her ears. It was as if Joe were here now, yelling out a warning: *Get to the boat!* Frantic, telling herself she was overreacting but unable to stop the fear coursing through her veins, she stumbled down the hallway toward Sadie. A weapon. She needed a weapon.

He was coming for her. A knife. She needed a knife.

There were knives in the kitchen.

Sadie had backed up and was standing in the living room at the end of the hall. Jules nearly ran into her as she barreled forward, stopping short at the last second. Sadie's gaze was focused on whoever had arrived at their dock. Jules wanted to yell at her, warn her to hide or to run. Just get out of the way!

But then Sadie asked, "Should I stop them?" *Them?*

Jules's shaking legs managed to carry her to where Sadie was standing. Outside, a motorboat was just docking, a trim woman at the helm. Jules could count six women and a girl inside, each holding a potluck dish. When they saw her, they waved frantically, then helped each other out of the boat.

"It looks like dinner has arrived," Sadie said, lifting her brows at Jules, silently asking her what she wanted to do.

Chapter Sixteen

The neighbors. The Fishers . . .

"It's all right," Jules said, trying to still her heart, to calm down. It was nothing. She'd panicked for no reason. Sadie was staring at her as if she'd lost her mind, which wasn't that far from the truth. Jules managed a smile. "It's . . . fine." Then she turned to the window and lifted her left arm to hail the group as they came en masse toward her sliding glass door. Joanie Bledsoe and her daughter Alexa were in the front, the rest packed behind them. "I remember them."

"Want me to be your taster?" Sadie asked as she stepped forward to unlatch the door.

"Maybe," Jules said, only half joking. Like high school, she'd never been all that close to the Fishers, but she'd always put on a good front.

"Should I call Sam?" A thread of eagerness had entered Sadie's voice.

"Uh . . . yeah, maybe. Did you call a locksmith?" They'd discussed Sam's directive to get the locks changed, and Sadie said she would make the call as she'd shooed Jules off to bed.

"Yup. Guy from Doorworks coming Monday. Earliest he could." Sadie was walking away, putting her phone to her ear. Her interest in Sam was pretty clear. Maybe Sam felt the same about her, Jules thought, not liking the idea at all.

Joanie Bledsoe was the first Fisher through, Alexa right on her heels. Joanie carried a salad in a clear plastic bowl with a lid and Alexa held a square, glass pan with corn bread, the aroma filling the room, reminding Jules of Thanksgiving and the stuffing her mother had made with crumbled, day-old corn bread. The memory was oddly disquieting.

"I couldn't leave Alexa home alone, so I brought her along," Joanie said. "I hope you don't mind." She shifted her salad bowl to one side and gave Jules a half hug, mindful of her sling. "Julia, oh, my gosh, we've been so worried about you. Are you okay? It's all so terrible. Joe . . . dear God, Joe . . ."

Joanie had always fashioned herself as Jules's good friend, but there was an insincerity to her sweetness that had caused Zoey to dub her "Phony Joanie."

Now, Joanie looked past Jules, searching the room. "Where are Xena and Georgie? Aren't they here?"

"They're in Georgie's room. You can join them," Jules added to Alexa. "It's right down the hall."

"I know where it is," Alexa said. She hastily set the corn bread on the counter and hurried away, as if she couldn't wait to beat feet away from them.

Zoey stepped around Joanie and said, "Girl, you look like hell," to which Joanie gasped, "Don't say that!"

Zoey Rivera was still as pert and sassy as she'd been when they were in high school. Jules hadn't known her well. She'd been a Hawk, not a Triton, but all the guys had been acutely aware of her. Her dark hair was short now and clipped back. Real estate agent, Jules recalled. Her husband was in real estate development . . . not husband, *boyfriend*. Brian . . . nope, Byron. Byron Blanchette . . . and they'd moved to the canal around the same time she and Joe had, about a year earlier. Now Zoey, ignoring Joanie, held out an opaque cream casserole dish with a snug plastic lid toward Julia. The unmistakable scent of baked beans wafted into the room as Zoey asked, "Where can I put this?"

"On the counter, or the stove top if it's too hot?" Jules responded.

"Not too hot anymore. Counter's fine. You know what I meant about how you look, right? That you look just like you should, like you've been through hell, because you have." Zoey set the beans beside the corn bread and gave Joanie a *look*, before adding, "We all decided on a Texas barbecue kind of thing, and Tutti said we should all descend on you at once."

"I said no such thing! I said we should go together so Julia knows we're all thinking of her!" an aggrieved voice behind Zoey declared.

Tutti Anderson. Real name, Kathy. She lived directly across the canal. Her two sons were just a little older than Georgie and obsessed with video games. Their father, Tutti's ex, was in insurance . . . or something like that, and Tutti said she couldn't stand him . . . the bastard . . . except she talked about him all the time.

"You really didn't have to go to all this trouble," Jules started to say.

"Of course we did," Tutti responded. "I've got the skirt steak, and it's done up right. I had to practically rap Sean and Devon's hands with the back of my wooden spoon to keep them from eating it all before I got it over here. They're monsters, that's what they are, with monster stomachs," she said affectionately as she set a large metal pan covered with foil across several stove top burners.

Jules was beginning to feel a bit overwhelmed and it didn't help that Sadie was laughing and joking on the phone to Sam.

"We were told you were having trouble remembering things," Joanie said, drawing close to Jules.

". . . don't worry, she's fine," Sadie's voice was saying warmly. "We're good. The neighbors just brought enough food to feed an army. . . ."

"The accident's still a blur, but it's all coming back," Jules told Joanie. That was a bit of a stretch, but it seemed important that she keep up the fiction of being back to herself as much as possible.

Bette Ezra was next, her closest neighbor to the south, owner of the dogs, she thought. Mutt and Jeff . . . no, More and Less. Yeah, that was right. She was the woman who'd been at the helm of the motorboat. But . . . there was something wrong there. The boat, Jules was certain, belonged to another couple. Bette was compact with smooth skin and a toned body. Yoga instructor, Jules remembered. Bette said, "You know me, if it isn't store bought, it just isn't. This is gluten free." She was carrying a lemon meringue pie.

Jules thanked her and then looked past her to the red-headed woman who was diffidently entering the house, carrying a brown paper sack from which the necks of several bottles sprouted up. *Martina Montgomery* . . . Sam's ex-wife. Jules's heart sank. She remembered Tina all right . . . and she remembered Joe saying Hap's girlfriend was moving in with him. She hadn't known who that girlfriend was until Tina had walked onto Hap's deck in the skimpiest of bikinis, her body still as taut and sculpted as when she'd been on the squad with Julia.

Some things in life were just not fair.

And what the hell was she doing here tonight? She and Jules weren't friends. Hadn't been since she'd moved in on Sam.

"Hey, Julia. Hope you're feeling better," Tina said a bit sheepishly, holding up the sack. "Tequila and triple sec and lime juice."

"Patrón?" Zoey asked, interested.

"Yes, I was thinking of you, Zoey," Tina said dryly, moving into the kitchen. She seemed as uncomfortable as Jules was.

"Only the best for our Zoey," the last woman said with a tight smile. She wore a skintight black tank top with equally skintight workout pants, which she'd teamed with silver high heels. Jules struggled with her name for a second, but it all came back as she turned her head and Jules caught her in profile. *Jackie Illingsworth.* Unhappy . . . working on being a full-blown alcoholic . . . possible affair with . . . *Stuart Ezra.* Jackie and her husband—what was his name?—*Rob.* That was it. Jackie and Rob owned the boat that Bette had driven to Jules's dock.

Jules suddenly had a knife-sharp memory. Jackie snuggled up to Stuart Ezra underneath the overhang of the Ezra eave, just beyond Jules's deck. "Shhhh . . ." his voice had warned, and then the rustle of clothing and a soft mewl from Jackie's lips. . . .

Jules returned to the moment to find Jackie squeezing her hand, saying, ". . . terrible, just terrible. You need anything, anything at all, you hear? Rob and I are here for you."

Rob Illingsworth, Jackie's husband. In a quicksilver flash, Jules remembered Zoey telling her in an aside, "Byron's got this development deal that Rob wants to go in on, but Jackie holds the purse strings. Rob tells everyone that he sold his family's dairy farm, but Jackie's the one with the family moola. If I was really catty I'd tell you that's why he married her, but I'll save that story for another day."

Bette was saying to Martina, ". . . take them to Dina's Doggy Day Care in Rockaway. They've got that red and white building with the paw prints painted all over the siding, just off the highway."

"Sounds horrifying," Tina drawled.

Bette shrugged. "Hey, I'm grateful because they take Less and More and I know they can be a handful sometimes."

"Those German shepherds are rabid beasts," Jackie said with a brittle smile. It was supposed to be a joke, but Bette's return gaze was glacial.

"They're just big pussycats. They've never hurt anybody, and they absolutely love Georgie," Bette retorted, turning away and sharing a "Can you believe her?" look with both Tina and Tutti, who seemed kind of embarrassed to be caught in a quiet conversation betwen themselves as if they were gossiping.

And Jules had another spark of memory, Joe telling Georgie, "All I'm saying is be careful. The dogs respect you, but they're huge, and strong, and Bette and Stuart make excuses for them." Georgie had been incensed by Joe's assessment, but Jules could see the dogs in her mind's eye and Joe hadn't been wrong.

Jackie was holding an appetizer tray with salsa, guacamole, and corn chips, and for the first time Jules noticed that Jackie seemed to be fighting tears as she crowded into the kitchen with the others. She met Jules's eyes and then, as if embarassed, stiffened her spine and joined a conversation with Tutti.

Strange, Jules thought, just as Sadie came to Jules's elbow and said, "Sam said he's uncomfortable having them in the house. He wants me to stay. What do you think?"

A little shiver of fear slid through Jules's blood and her mind tripped to the man who'd come for her in the hospital. Could he be one of these women's husbands? Boyfriends? But why? And who? And . . . weren't they all acquaintances, if not friends? Still, she didn't feel a real connection to any of them and she couldn't shake the feeling that something was very wrong.

An unfamiliar ringtone filled the air and Jules realized it was her new cell. Sam. Had to be.

"Uh, yes, please stick around," she told Sadie, then she took the call and headed down the hall to her bedroom. She closed the door behind her and pressed the answer button. "Sam?" she asked.

"Yeah, it's me. I just got a call from Sadie. She says your neighbors are there."

"With food. Yes."

"I told Sadie I'm on my way, but I asked her to stay."

"Good . . . um, Sam? One of them's Martina."

"Yeah, I learned that last night at Tutti's barbecue. They said they were going to bring you food. I didn't know they were going to come all together."

"You knew Martina was on the canal?"

"Well, I learned it yesterday. And that she's cohabitating with Hap."

"Does that bother you?" she couldn't help asking, and looked out the window to the canal, the water clear and rippling just beyond their dock. Calm. Peaceful. And seeming right now to be such a lie. Jules felt there was nothing calm and peaceful on this slow-moving waterway.

"Nope. She's my ex for a reason. But, Jules . . . if you're remembering that, it sounds like your memory has really returned."

"It's coming," she admitted.

"Anything about the accident?"

She hated dashing his hopes. "Not yet. And I can't talk long. They're all in the kitchen, getting everything ready, some kind of Texas potluck, Zoey told me." Still gazing out the window, her eye caught an osprey circling over the water, searching the depths, looking for prey. The bird suddenly folded its wings and dove. It surfaced in a spray of water, a wriggling fish caught in its talons. She shuddered as she watched it flap its great wings and fly away. "How soon will you be here? Should I tell them to wait? Martina brought tequila and I think they'll be here awhile."

"Whose idea was it to make it a party when you're just getting out of the hospital?" he asked, sounding annoyed and not waiting for an answer. "I'll be there soon."

"Okay. Oh, and Sam, I found Joe's laptop. Not sure if he had another computer, but this is one he slid between the mattress and box springs."

"Good! Great. I was certain Mayfield took it, but maybe not. Funny he put it under the mattress."

"I think he thought something bad was coming."

Get to the boat!

"Hmm. Okay. See you soon. None of the husbands are there, right? Of the neighbor women?"

"No." Maybe he was thinking the same way she was, that it was a man who'd sneaked into her room at the hospital.

"Keep it that way. If one of 'em shows up, call me immediately."

"But you're on your way, right?"

"Be there within minutes."

Phoenix drove her Mini through Seaside, heading north toward Astoria. She'd just wrapped up her meeting with Mr. P. J. Simpson, an odd duck if there ever was one. Now she was on her way to try and meet with Walter Hapstell Senior at one of his properties. Outside the city limits, she wound down a back road and meandered east and into the Coast Range foothills, keeping one eye on her phone where Google Maps was displaying her route.

Simpson had asked her to meet him at an old chowder house in Seaside that had nothing much to recommend it, especially not the food. Located on a narrow dead end street at the edge of a residential district, the restaurant was an old coastal institution that had lost customers and appeal long before, but it was his choice, so she figured, what the hell. She'd agreed to meet him out of curiosity, and had walked in to find him seated in a booth at the back, a middle-aged man with a shock of gray hair and a dark, nearly black, Magnum P.I. mustache that Phoenix hadn't been able to take her eyes off.

A waitress who looked as if she'd been with the place since its inception had taken their orders without much interest, and had actually frowned when neither of them had wanted more than coffee. "Coming right up," she'd said in a voice raspy from cigarette smoke. She'd brought the coffee, then left them alone.

During the course of their short conversation Phoenix had then determined that the mustache was a fake. In fact, Simpson had all the earmarks of a fugitive: the way he kept watching the door, the nervous manner in which he clenched and unclenched his fists, his careful conversation, the way she could almost see him study each question she asked, turning it over in his mind for a full minute before responding. She'd almost called him out on the disguise and whatever else he might be hiding, but she'd decided instead to hear him out, listen to whatever story he'd spun, and take it all with a grain of salt.

What she'd learned, as she'd sipped her watery coffee and taken notes, was that he knew next to nothing about Joe Ford, Ike Cardaman, or anything to do with the widening financial scandal. He just wanted his money back. And he wanted it back yesterday.

"Joe Ford stole all my money," he'd insisted in a whispery voice.

"But you invested with Ike Cardaman," Phoenix had reminded him. "Your name's in a file with other Cardaman investors. That's how I found you."

"What file?" he demanded, for once raising his voice above a whisper and reacting instantly, half rising out of his seat in alarm.

"The file I told you about. The reason I called you." Phoenix had then reiterated how she'd come to have the file from an unknown source, and how she'd been going down the list and had just come to his name.

"That's confidential information!"

"Yes, it is."

"How do you have it?"

"Through research," she said, trying to fob him off. She also didn't tell him that he was the only investor she'd actually met in person. Most just wanted to complain about Cardaman and/or eagerly ask if she could help them recover their savings, either via e-mail, text, or phone calls. Nothing face to face. She'd asked Simpson, "So, were all your investments with Cardaman, or were some with Joseph Ford Investments?"

"I'd like to see this file."

"Like you said, it's confidential."

That had put them at a stalemate. Simpson had blustered and said how heads would roll if that information got into the wrong hands, and Phoenix had tried to assure him she was just trying to find out if Joe Ford and Walter Hapstell were as guilty as Cardaman about misusing funds.

Finally, Simpson had stopped grousing and come to some kind of decision. He said, "The real crook is Walter Hapstell Senior. He got his young pup of a son to make some shaky deals and kept all the money. Joe Ford was in on it, too, but he's gone. Died in that boat accident the other day."

"There's an ongoing investigation into that accident," Phoenix had said.

"There should be," he harrumphed. "Boat exploding. Something wrong there."

"There are theories that it might not have been an accident. That Ford's death could be related to the very investment tangle we're discussing."

"Poppycock." He peered at her intently. "Who says that?"

"If it hasn't been reported on the news yet, it will be. It's a prevailing theory."

She'd been kind of winging it by then, sensing Simpson had something to say but just couldn't get it out. Several times he'd started to say something, then stopped, his eyes darting around the nearly empty restaurant where only a handful of patrons occupied tables and the waitstaff was practically nonexistent.

"Do they have this list? The one you have?"

"No one has the list but me, and of course, Joe Ford Investments."

"Joe Ford's the one who gave it to you. Lie all you want. The blame starts with him."

She'd shaken her head and assured him, "No one's going to give away confidential information, certainly not me."

Simpson had thought that over for another long minute, then asked, "What about the wife? She survived the accident. What if she puts it out there?"

"There are laws made to protect investors. No sensitive information will be revealed."

"So says the reporter." He'd pulled out a piece of paper at that time and had slid it across the table to her. "That's Walter Hapstell's home address. Backwater kinda place he's at now, hiding out with all of our money. You go talk to him," he'd advised. "If you can help me get my money back, I'll get you a finder's fee."

Phoenix had laughed. There was just something so old-time gangster about the man. "I appreciate it, but no. I'm just trying to get to the story."

"He's home now," Simpson had insisted as if he hadn't heard her. "You could go see him today and you might get some answers, more than you know."

She'd regarded him with some amusement. "What do you want me to ask him?"

"What do you think? I want him to give me my money back!"

Phoenix had had no intention of calling on Walter Hapstell Senior. P. J. Simpson, like a number of the investors she'd spoken to, had made some risky investments and now wanted to point blame.

But . . . Walter Hapstell Senior was very difficult to get hold of and though she questioned whether odd and gruff Mr. Simpson really knew what he was talking about, she decided to give it a try. Then again, he hadn't missed much. She'd left, wondering if he'd pick up the tab and noting he hadn't so much as touched the now cold cup of coffee.

Now as she was driving, the town of Seaside far behind her, she stared through the windshield and turned everything he'd said over in her mind. The road wasn't well traveled as it followed the meandering course of a stream. She met only an occasional car or truck as the evergreen forest thickened the hillside. After double-checking Google Maps to make certain she was on the right route, she put a call into Glencoe Electric, the company Denny Mulhaney had worked for before he'd disappeared. A few weeks earlier she'd talked to several people who worked there, but no one had been able to give her any definitive answers as to what had happened to him. It seemed, at the time, as if everyone had been scratching their heads about what had happened to their bookkeeper. Phoenix had made a mental note to herself to call back some of the employees she hadn't been able to reach after they returned from vacation, which should be about now. She was worried about Mulhaney because he'd fallen off the grid. She'd even thought about filing a missing person's report with the Laurelton Police Department, where Denny had lived after leaving Seaside, but it had seemed premature. The man could have just walked away from his job. It wasn't that unusual and, from what she could tell, Denny wasn't the most stable of characters.

Bluetooth kicked in and she heard the line ringing. A few seconds later an older, female voice said, "Glencoe Electric."

"Hi, this is Phoenix Delacourt with the *North Coast Spirit.* I came by a few weeks ago and—"

"You wanted to know about Dennis Mulhaney," she cut Phoenix off briskly. "Yes, I have a note to call you. Pearl Enos is back from vacation and wants to talk to you."

"Okay . . . good." This, at least, sounded promising. "Is Pearl there now?"

"I'll connect you."

The line buzzed a couple of times, and then another female voice answered, "Warehouse. This is Pearl."

Phoenix was glancing down at her phone, seeing how far she was from the turnoff to Hapstell's property. About a quarter mile. "Hi, this is Phoenix Delacourt from the *North Coast Spirit.* I was at Glencoe Electric a couple of weeks ago asking about Dennis Mulhaney."

"Oh, *Denny.*" Her voice was suddenly fraught with worry. "He's just disappeared. Hasn't been to work. Hasn't been home. Hasn't been to Tiny Tim's."

"Tiny Tim's?"

Google Maps let her know she was nearing a turn. Squinting, she spied a break in the tall fir trees and slowed, easing her Mini onto what had once been a gravel lane and now was little more than ruts cutting through wooded acres. Dry weeds scraped the undercarriage of her little car and her tires bounced over potholes and rocks even as she slowed. Little sunlight pierced through the canopy of boughs overhead and the area seemed as if no one had been there in months, maybe years. It sure didn't look like a place for Walter Hapstell. She'd met the man once and had seen him a number of times, and this . . . backwater spot didn't fit with his slick, reptilian appearance. But he was a developer. Maybe there was a decent house at the end of the drive.

"Me and Denny had a few drinks there a couple of times," Pearl was saying longingly. "He was a friend. Sad, y'know? Things hadn't worked out too good for him. There was like all this money stolen from him. Do you think they found him . . . those criminals who took his money? I've been so worried. Maybe they were more than swindlers and con artists? Oh, Lord. Maybe they were much worse!"

That was a bit of a leap, Phoenix thought. From thieves to, what? Kidnappers or worse? But she let the woman ramble on as she tried to keep her shimmying car on the ever-dimishing lane.

". . . been so worried," she was saying. "It was really hard to enjoy the annual camping trip with Sheryl and Ray, even though Ray brought the big tent this year and we stayed in a campground with toilets, which was really great. . . ."

Phoenix had eased up on the accelerator, slowing to a crawl to keep her little car from bouncing. Had she turned at the wrong place? No. Not according to Google Maps. Had P. J. Simpson sent her on a wild goose chase? Whatever the case, this didn't bode well.

". . . last year, when we were out in the boonies and there was nothing. No water, no toilets, just awful. That's really too much nature for me. . . ."

"Pearl, when did you last see Denny?" Phoenix asked, trying to get the woman back on point. The Mini was coming to a clearing, where the old-growth timbers had parted, high on a hillside with an edge that she couldn't see over. A dip down to a small valley? There was no house in sight. At least not here. Weird. This whole place was so remote . . . a little unsettling.

"Ummm . . . it was in June. Around Flag Day, I remember. Is that the fourteenth? I think it was around the fourteenth. We had these little flags to wave, and I was—"

A sudden roar echoed through the hills, reverberating through her Mini. A truck engine revved up high. She jerked in surprise and, pulse quickening, looked in her rearview. Her heart nearly stopped. A massive black monster vehicle with a huge silver grill, churning tires, was charging right at her!

"—thinking how great it was, y'know and then . . . What's that noise?"

Phoenix hit the gas. The roar filled her ears, deafening her. No! Damn it! No!

Her little car leapt forward. She slewed to the left, running along the edge of the drop-off. Her phone flew across the seat and down the passenger side of the car, disappearing from view.

What the hell is going on!

She shot another glance in the mirror. The truck was right on her tail!

"Mrs. Phoenix?" Pearl asked in a tinny voice.

She was on the lip of what she now saw was a ravine. The silvery waters of a creek bed flashed by, snaking through the canyon a long way down. *He set me up*, she thought, in disbelief. *That prick Simpson, in the weirdo disguise, set me up! God, Phoenix, why didn't you listen to your instincts?*

But there was no time for second-guessing. At that moment the black truck caught her left back fender, spinning her around. Frantic, Phoenix fought for control, her hands tight on the steering wheel, but the Mini's right rear tire slipped over the edge. She was losing traction, the Mini straining on three wheels. The truck roared past her and turned a tight circle. Aimed for a head-on shot.

"Call the Seaside Police!" Phoenix screamed, hoping Pearl would hear. "Pearl! Call the damned police! Ask for Sam Ford! SAM FORD!" Phoenix shrieked. She yanked the wheel, desperately hit the gas, trying to get out of the truck's path. But it charged like an angry beast, smashing into her right headlight, sending her little car shimmying backward, tumbling into the narrow valley and creek far below.

"Sam Ford?" she heard dimly. "Mrs. Phoenix . . . ? You there . . . ?"

And that's all she knew.

Sam parked and raced toward his brother's house to pound on the door. He had no key as he'd given the one he'd received from Tutti to Jules, the key that Tutti had given him. He *thunked* his fist against the panels until Sadie let him into the house. "They're on the back deck," she said, eyeing him in a way that made him realize his own fears must be etched on his face. He tried to relax. Couldn't. "Julia's about wiped out, but she's trying to be nice."

"It's just the women?" Sam asked again.

"Yes. Joanie's getting ready to leave because her younger daughter, Alexa, got thrown out of Georgie's bedroom by the older girls, Georgie and Xena. Lots of crying and yelling." Sadie rolled her eyes. "Joanie doesn't want to go, but she's going to have to, and since she lives across the canal, the whole group thinks they might have to take the boat, although someone suggested Jules lend Joanie her canoe to just get rid of her. Nice, huh?" She took a breath and went on, "Bette and Zoey can just walk home, as they live on this side. Some alcohol's been consumed, but not as much as you'd think, though Jackie seems to be consuming her fair share. Tutti just keeps looking over at her own property, as if she'd rather be there. Her boys are home and playing video games, apparently at an ear-bleeding level, because we can hear the music from here."

"How's Jules?"

Sadie inclined her head toward the deck. "Okay, I guess. She's pretending to drink a margarita, and doing a piss poor job of it, I might add. Think she just wants them all to evaporate. Mostly, the neighbor women are hugging and sorrowful one minute, mean and spiteful to each other the next. It's kinda weird they're all together. Maybe it's just because they live so close, but I don't think these people like each other much."

Sam was at the back slider before Sadie finished her report and, from his vantage point, could see through the glass to all the women standing on the deck or sitting on folding chairs. Jackie Illingsworth was swaying on her heels again. Bette Ezra was looking at her house and holding up a finger to her dogs, who were sitting on the edge of their deck, staring at her, awaiting a command. Zoey had a margarita in one hand and was doing some kind of dance to the video game music. Tutti was yelling that it was one of those kill everybody games her boys loved to play, and Martina stood aloofly from the group. Her gaze was zeroed in on Jules, who was sitting in a chair, holding a drink in her left hand, facing the canal.

Sam slid open the door and Martina shifted her gaze to him. Immediately she put on a smile and came his way. "You got here just as we have to leave. Some teen, or pre-teen, girl thing." She inclined her head to Alexa, presumably, from Sadie's report, who was standing by her mother, her face red from crying. Joanie was trying to get her to buck up, but the girl wasn't having it. The older two girls, Georgie and Xena, apparently, were at the far end of the dock, being exclusive.

Jules glanced around to see Sam, and the look of relief and joy that came over her face melted his heart. He hadn't realized how scared he was for her until he could see for himself that she was alive and well. Sadie stepped through the door to stand beside him, and he said with meaning, "Thanks."

"You're welcome. And you owe me."

"Yeah?" He hadn't taken his eyes off Jules, who had stood up and was walking their way.

"I was going to ask for a date, but I can see that ain't gonna work," Sadie said on an exaggerated sigh. "Goddamn you good-looking single men who are in love with someone else."

"I'm not . . ." He trailed off because, well, Sadie might be right, and she wasn't listening anymore anyway.

"I'm glad you're back," Jules greeted him, and he noticed how the sunlight played in her hair. Though he hadn't asked, she said, "It's been fine, really. The party. Nice. And everyone's been great. . . ." She smiled. "I'm really glad you're back."

He wanted to pull her to him and kiss her. There was something about her that just reached inside him and made him want to hug her, hold her, protect her. He fought the urge to place his palm on the side of her face and trace the curve of her scraped jaw and noticed the other women were approaching.

"Ahem," Zoey said, dancing her way over to them. "You guys should get a room. Wait. There's one just down the hall."

"Zoey." Tutti rolled her eyes.

Joanie said, "Okay, we're going. I guess we can't have any more fun, because the girls can't get along."

"Oh, Mom," Xena groaned, glancing at Georgie for support.

"Can I go with them?" Georgie asked.

"No," Jules and Sam said at the same time. Then they looked at each other.

"Sorry," Sam said, lifting his hands. "Not my place."

"You sounded just like Dad," Georgie grumbled, but suddenly seemed as if she was about to cry again.

The party broke up after that, with everyone leaving. Sam, Jules, and Georgie watched the women and two girls get into the boat, which Bette drove expertly down the canal and back, dropping everyone at their respective homes, leaving the motorboat at Jackie's dock. Jackie was already stumbling toward the house as Bette slipped into a kayak and paddled back across to her house. Sam, Jules, and Georgie went back inside the house where Sadie had started to help clean up.

Jules shooed her away. "We've got this. Thanks for everything."

"Will I be back tomorrow?" Sadie asked, looking at Sam. "You're spending the night, right?"

"Yes," he said without hesitation. He wasn't going to leave Jules and Georgie alone.

"Where're you going to sleep?" Georgie asked. Then, before Sam could struggle for an answer, she said, "You can have my room. I'll sleep with Julia, if that's okay . . . ?" She looked at Jules.

"Fine," Jules said automatically, then added, "Sure. Good."

Jules seemed distracted and Sam worried that maybe she didn't want him, but he wasn't going to be talked out of it. She'd been pretty scared the night before at the hospital, so maybe she wasn't unhappy that he was planning to stay, but rather was caught up in some inner thoughts, perhaps memories slowly surfacing.

Sadie left a few moments later, and Georgie said to Jules, "Can we all watch one of those old movies you like? The rom-coms?"

Jules's gaze flicked toward Sam. He recalled nights on his father's couch, the only light in the room from the television screen as he and Jules made love. He wondered if she was thinking the same thing.

"I don't know. Maybe," Jules said. "Let's finish cleaning up the kitchen and we'll think about it." Georgie groaned, and Sam was surprised when Jules added, "You don't have to help this time, Georgie." Her gaze touched his for the briefest of seconds. "I think Sam and I can handle it. This time."

Georgie looked suspiciously at Jules, then at Sam. "You sure?"

"Yes."

Appearing about to argue, Georgie seemed to think better of it, and before Jules could change her mind, she shrugged and headed back to her room. When they heard the door close, Jules said, "I put the laptop back beneath the mattress, but I don't want it there if Georgie sleeps with me tonight."

"Ahh, yes . . ."

"I wish I could remember the password."

"Maybe it's written down somewhere."

"Unlikely. Joe was too careful. He memorized everything and I . . ." She stopped herself and finished in a surprised voice, "I'm terrible at remembering."

"You remembered that about Joe," he pointed out.

"Yeah, I did." She gazed up at him, smiling just a bit.

God, she was beautiful. *And your brother's widow, remember that. Even though you dated her first, a lifetime ago, Jules was still married to Joe.*

Sam's cell phone rang, pulling him out of his reverie. He dragged his gaze from her and looked down at the screen. "It's Griff. I gotta take this."

"I'll get the laptop."

Jules, breaking the spell that seemed to come over her, a problem where Sam was concerned, hurried to the bedroom and reached under the mattress for the laptop. She'd just closed her hand around the sleek computer and was pulling it out when she heard Sam's voice shot with tension.

"What hospital?" he demanded. "*Shit.* I'm on my way. I don't give a damn, Griff! When she wakes up, I need to talk to her."

Jules ran back down the hall, cradling the laptop in her left arm. "Where are you going?" she asked fearfully.

"Seaside Hospital. Phoenix Delacourt was in an accident. A bad one. Someone ran her off a cliff into a creek. You're coming with me. Call Joanie—do you know her number? We'll leave Georgie with her. . . ."

Chapter Seventeen

Sam drove fast and sure, his face set. Jules sat huddled in the passenger seat of his truck. She'd grabbed a jacket before they'd driven around the canal to drop Georgie off at Joanie's, a wasted extra twenty minutes, but there was no choice unless they wanted to paddle her across in a canoe or swim.

As soon as Georgie was with the Bledsoes, Sam finally explained, "Griff called. A woman phoned the station asking for me. She said she'd been instructed to ask for me, that a Mrs. Phoenix had called, and she thought there was an accident. She was so insistent that they gave the call to Griff and he figured out she meant Phoenix Delacourt. He tracked Phoenix's phone, through her GPS, the phone being still on. They found her car in a creek bed at the bottom of a deep ditch on property about to be a housing development, just south of Astoria. She was rescued and taken to Seaside Hospital. Preliminary findings say it appears as if her car was pushed over the edge by another vehicle."

"Oh, my God." Jules felt her face drain of color. "Is she all right?"

"She's in ICU."

"And somebody did this on purpose?"

"Looks that way. Phoenix was screaming my name, according to this woman, who could hear a roaring sound—the second vehicle's engine, probably a truck if it was as loud as she says. Shoved Phoenix's Mini over the edge of the cliff. Crime techs'll figure it out."

"She's lucky to be alive," Jules whispered, shaken. Who would do this? And why?

"Yes." He shook his head as if to clear it. "She knew I wasn't with the department any longer. She asked for me because whoever did this is attached to the investigation into Joe's death. That has to be it. She found something out and somebody felt they had to silence her."

Oh, God. "Something about the Cardaman file?"

"Gotta be related in some way. She said she had an interview. She said the name, but I can't think of it right now."

"I asked her to bring the file to me," Jules reminded, but she also remembered she was the person who had given the information to the reporter before the accident. If Phoenix had been targeted because of the file . . . Jules swallowed hard, felt more than a little guilt niggle through her brain. She gazed down at her lap where the slim, silver computer rested. She hadn't let go of it. "But it's probably on her. Should I carry this into the hospital?"

He thought about that as he slowed slightly for a curve. "Griff'll be there. We'll give it to him, have him take it to the station. Lock it up. Too many people can get into your house and maybe one of them has the password. I don't trust it in my truck."

They drove in tense silence after that. Jules's tiredness had disappeared as soon as Sam had shown up. She'd wanted all the women to leave. She'd wanted to be alone in her bedroom. She'd wanted to allow herself to think, remember. The laptop had lifted the gray veil a bit, allowing a swirl of memories before her brain shut down again, but there were still big holes, curtained thoughts that she couldn't quite bring to the surface. They teased her, tested her, frustrated the hell out of her. If she could just remember everything.

What then?

She didn't know, but it had to be better than feeling part of her life was shrouded in some self-protective fog. Or, was the past so terrifying that she was better off not knowing?

Georgie's request to watch a romantic comedy had brought a knot to her stomach she was still trying to figure out. She associated those kinds of films with Sam, which brought on good feelings, but there was something else that her mind shied away from, some memory that had to do with . . . Thanksgiving again?

She lay her head back on the seat and closed her eyes. She saw the candles, the cornucopia . . . the sweet potatoes swimming in a syrup of butter, brown sugar, and miniature marshmallows, the metal pan being lifted from a red-hot oven by hands in long mitts that came to Mama's elbows. . . .

Mama's? When is this memory? How old? Long before Sam.

She could almost see her mother and her father. She heard her father talking to someone. A man. And Clem was there, looking up at the other person. They were at a cabin . . . *the cabin in the snow. . . .*

Jules awoke with a gasp.

"You all right?" Sam asked, looking over at her with concern. They were pulling into the hospital parking lot.

"Yeah, I just . . . I just had some real memories. I didn't realize I'd drifted off. I keep thinking about Thanksgiving for some reason, but now I realize I've been mixing up memories. I thought all of them were from the same year, that year you and I were first . . . dating, but some of them are from when I was a kid. My brother was still alive. We were at a cabin . . . like your father's, kind of, but . . . huh . . ." She struggled to recall. "Maybe it was . . ." She trailed off.

"No, finish. What were you going to say?"

Sam threw the truck into park and reached across for the laptop, while Jules unhooked her seat belt. They both got out of the vehicle and slammed their doors, then walked quickly toward the hospital's front entrance.

"I don't know. I think maybe it was my uncle's cabin, for some reason—my mother's brother—but he's been gone a long time. He lived like a hermit. Off the grid in a cabin in the Cascades, I think. My father called him Crazy Paul. We visited him once . . . the Thanksgiving before Clem died, maybe? That's right! It was a *woodstove,*" she said on a note of discovery. "That's what it was. I can remember Mama pulling a pan of sweet potatoes from the embers of a fire. There was no electricity there. We were basically camping inside the cabin. We had turkey, but it was kind of burned on the bottom. Wow, I haven't thought about that in years." She exhaled heavily. "I don't get why Georgie's mention of romantic comedies triggered it, but it did."

"You've always liked rom-coms," he reminded, then, "I've watched a few with you."

So, he remembered, too. She gave him a quick smile, then pushed aside the warm feeling that had engendered and said, "But I couldn't have been watching them at that cabin at that time. Like I said, we had no electricity, and I was pretty young. *Pretty Woman* and *Sleeping with the Enemy* . . . I would have seen them a lot later. But somehow Thanksgiving and rom-coms seem connected."

"I don't know *Sleeping with the Enemy,*" he said, holding open one of the front doors for her with one hand, gripping tightly onto the laptop with the other.

"It's more of a thriller, but it's a Julia Roberts film. It's . . ."

She trailed off as they stepped into the hospital reception area and she was assailed by the scents, sounds, and smells of the place. She'd just been released from the hospital herself, but her mind traveled back to Clem's death nonetheless, like a needle in a groove. Now at least she understood her aversion. Those memories had returned in full.

A uniformed officer saw Sam, and Sam spotted him at the same moment. They both picked up their pace and Jules had to hurry to keep up, but the officer motioned toward a hallway, heading that way himself, already speaking in low tones as Sam fell into step with him. This had to be Griff, Jules presumed.

". . . in ICU . . . unconscious . . ." Griff was saying. He looked back at Julia, as if finally realizing she was following them, and his steps slowed.

"I'm sorry. This is Jules Ford," Sam introduced, apparently waking up to the fact that they'd never met. "My brother's . . . widow."

He looked at her closely, making Jules wonder what had been said about her. "I don't know if the hospital will allow her into ICU. And, well, between you and me"—he cast a glance in Jules's direction—"this is looking like attempted murder. . . ."

"She stays within eyeshot of me," Sam stated firmly. He held out the laptop to Griff. "Take this when we leave here. Lock it up at the station. It's my brother's, and I want to keep it safe."

Griff accepted the laptop. "What's on it?" he asked, his voice lowering further still as the elevator doors whispered open and an orderly pushing a wheelchair passed in the other direction. His patient was midforties, probably, wearing a huge, padded hospital boot on one foot while holding a potted plant with a half-deflated balloon tied to the pot and trailing behind them.

Once they rounded a corner, Sam said, "No idea what's on the laptop. Maybe nothing. Maybe what got my brother killed. We don't know the password."

Griff grunted and clamped the laptop a little tighter. To

Jules, he said, "You might have to wait outside the door to Phoenix's room."

"That'll be fine. I'll be okay," she said when Sam seemed about to protest again.

Griff nodded curtly, and they walked on.

ICU was on the second floor at the end of a hall with several glass doors that whispered open as they approached. As Griff had predicted, they were stopped outside Phoenix's room. Jules could see the monitors and tubes and lights that regulated Phoenix's vitals. Jules's head throbbed, as if in commiseration, and she shifted her right arm in its sling, earning a jab of pain from her collarbone.

Griff and Sam were allowed inside and Jules stood right outside the windowed enclosure. Seeing her, a nurse drew a curtain and Jules was cut off. She looked around herself a bit nervously. Maybe the guy who'd come after her had worked at the hospital?

No, he came there specifically for you. Don't be paranoid. It's still light out; there's a full staff of nurses, doctors, volunteers, and interns. Sam's just on the other side of the curtain, with Griff, a Seaside cop, no less. You're fine.

But she couldn't stop the knot of worry fisting in her stomach. She hunched her shoulders, drawing in on herself, and kept searching the area, cataloguing the nurses and hospital staff nearest to her. Better to be safe than sorry.

Sam reappeared within minutes, looking grim, carrying the laptop again. He was moving and she fell in step beside him. "Phoenix is still unconscious. Broken limbs. Head trauma, which they're monitoring, bruised kidney, but no internal bleeding, so that's good."

"Is she going to be all right?" Jules asked. They reached the elevator and Sam slapped his palm against the button.

"I hope so. No one's saying she won't be."

"I hope so, too." They entered the elevator car and she observed, "You have the laptop."

"Thought it over. If it goes to the station, and someone thinks it's connected to my brother's death, we might not get it back. Griff's not the problem, but up the chain of command could be. Griff's allowing me more information than he probably should because the woman who alerted them about Phoenix asked for me specifically, but if someone shuts him down, he can't help me anymore. He's got a job to protect."

The elevator opened on the first floor. "Okay. What now?" She could tell Sam had something in mind.

"Phoenix was going to meet someone. Maybe that person's involved with this, maybe not. I'll have to think about that. But meanwhile there's something I can do, and I'm going to run with it."

"What?"

He pushed open the door to outside and they were greeted by an orange and pink gathering sunset. "Are you up for a trip to Portland? Actually, around Laurelton?"

"When? Tonight?" Laurelton was one of the westernmost suburbs of Portland, but it was an hour and a half's drive from Seaside.

"It's eight-thirty. We could be there by ten p.m. I'll have to trust the laptop in the truck, shove it under the seat," he thought aloud, then seemed to come to himself. "I don't want to overtax you, but I don't want to leave you alone, either."

"No, don't leave me alone," she agreed immediately.

"I could check with Sadie. She seemed ready—"

"Hell, no, Sandy. I'm going with you."

He flashed a smile as they got into his truck, and her heart somersaulted. *Oh, you've got it bad. You always had it bad. You married Joe for all the wrong reasons; it was Sam you wanted.*

She immediately sobered, thinking about Joe. Had she

loved him, or had she just been grateful that he'd been there during one of the hardest times of her life?

Sam was saying, ". . . her name's Pearl Enos. Griff talked to her awhile, and I gave her a call. She's employed at Glencoe Electric, where Dennis Mulhaney worked until about six weeks ago. Phoenix said she went to see Mulhaney at the company, and then went again a few weeks later, but he was no longer there. Nobody knows what happened to him. Pearl was first out sick, then on vacation, so she didn't know about Phoenix's second visit till today, when Phoenix called. Not long into the conversation, she heard strange sounds, a loud roar, and then Phoenix yelling as if from a distance to call me, probably just at the time Phoenix's car was being shoved into the creek. Pearl's worried about Mulhaney. They had some kind of relationship and met a few times at a bar called Tiny Tim's. That's where we're meeting her."

"Okay, let's go."

With that, Sam pulled onto the highway and headed to the turnoff that would take them to Highway 26 and all points west.

P. J. Simpson looked at himself in the mirror and peeled off the thick mustache. There was a faint tremor in his hand and once the mustache was removed he opened and closed his fist several times. The tremor was the aftermath of adrenaline.

He'd killed that woman . . . that reporter. He'd known he was going to do it when she'd called him and wanted to ask some questions. Panic had flooded through his system and it was all he could do to react normally. He'd talked her into a face-to-face and chosen the old chowder house because it was off the beaten track and damn near forgotten. He hadn't been worried about being recognized himself, but she was well-known up and down the coast. A nosy, quirky personality who'd come from money and then thumbed her nose at it. Stupid woman. No one ever gave up that much money unless they were touched in the head.

He'd never met her personally. Phoenix Delacourt. But he knew of the family before he'd left the area and become the hermit he'd chosen to be.

He sighed. Life had been a total shit bucket for too long. All his careful planning going up in smoke. These dire circumstances had brought him back to the beach, and he'd found he'd missed it, though he couldn't afford to stay here long. He needed to be here just long enough to get his money back. Ike Cardaman, the venal scoundrel, had jeopardized everything of importance in his life. Suddenly all his money was at risk and then gone! Everything he'd worked so hard for, given up so much for, pretended and acted and lied for.

He'd raised holy hell in those first few months after the Ike Cardaman story broke. He'd fallen for the scam hook, line, and sinker. *Him.* A man who knew the game! Jesus. He wanted to put his head in his hands and weep.

He'd needed an ally, someone to help him. A man on the inside who could move his money for him. He'd promised Denny Mulhaney buckets of cash, and Mulhaney had gone to bat for him. Yes, he'd known Mulhaney was a sour, grudging loser who was quick to blame everyone but himself, but he was all he could get. The only other employee at Joseph Ford Investments had been Julia St. James Ford, and that was never going to work.

But his alliance with Denny broke down almost immediately. Mulhaney had started whining and making demands of Joe Ford himself. Mulhaney hadn't been able to make the transfers, not enough power. And then the fool had gone to the reporter! What an idiot. Worst of all, he'd awoken Joe's interest in P. J. Simpson and then P. J. knew it was only a matter of time until everything unraveled.

And it sure as hell had.

He shuddered from head to toe. He'd had to build another alliance with a thrill-killer, actually a dynamic duo, though neither of them realized he knew about the female half of the couple. P. J. had done years of research on anything to do with his money. Every aspect, and that included the thrill-killers. He also knew about as much about Joseph Ford Investments as Joseph Ford himself. And he'd kept tabs on Ford, too. Joe Ford was smart. He'd personally invested in homes along Fisher Canal, taking the slow and steady route rather than the big kill, like Summit Ridge. What a cluster-fuck that was. It hurt P. J.'s head to think about it.

P. J. had followed Ford's investment on the canal closely, intending to follow suit, but his money had been tied up with Cardaman, and that whiner, Mulhaney, hadn't been able to get it out. It stuck in P. J.'s craw that Joe had actually cautioned his investors about the risks of going with Cardaman and he hadn't listened.

Too smart for your own good, huh?

High risk, high reward, baby. His whole life had been a risky venture, because you don't make money playing it safe.

But if you don't play it safe, you could lose everything.

And then P. J. had had a complete meltdown, had called up Ford personally and screamed at the man, demanding his money back.

And Joe Ford, who'd absorbed Peter St. James's clients, of which P. J. was one, into his own company without looking at them closely, started going over them with a fine-toothed comb. If he figured out what P. J. had done . . .

It didn't bear thinking about. All of a sudden, everything had become at risk and that's when he'd hired the thrill-killers.

Except Joe figured out the investment scam anyway and then a frantic plan B had gone into effect, which had damn near killed Julia. P. J. had mixed feelings about her survival. He didn't want to hurt her, but she knew too much.

And then *Phoenix* . . . that damn reporter. He hadn't trusted the thrill-killers. They'd botched things up good, and the police were all over Joe's death. He'd had to act himself, and so he'd driven her into the ravine. The Mini had rolled twice and landed upside down on its roof. He'd raced down the ridge after it and looked inside. Phoenix had been been unconscious, bleeding, at death's door. A soft briefcase of sorts was *right there,* lying on the crumpled roof of the car by her head. He reached through the broken window and took it.

The Cardaman file.

He'd wanted to roar with triumph, had carried his bounty back to his truck—the one he'd bought with cash two months earlier from a teenaged drug dealer who was desperate for money, the one he hadn't yet changed the title on—and had driven back to the motel. He'd checked the grill on the front of the truck, but there was barely any damage to the hulking beast of a vehicle, so he'd felt safe as he'd hurried inside and opened the file.

A list of names and phone numbers. No addresses. No other information. Nothing that would lead them to him. *Nothing.*

He'd killed Phoenix Delacourt for *nothing.*

Not that he still didn't have other problems. Julia Ford was still alive and if, or when, her memory returned in full . . . but the file wasn't the confidential disaster he'd blown it up to be in his mind.

So, now what?

If you hadn't confronted Joe. If you'd let everything lie . . . then you'd be safe.

And dead broke.

But you did confront Joe. Julia wasn't supposed to be

*there. And she survived the boat accident and could wake
up at any moment and point fingers.*

God, what a disaster.

He raked his hands through his hair. Could he trust the
thrill-killers to finish the job with Julia? Did he want them
to? Yes . . . yes . . . it had to be done. He'd promised them a
small fortune to do the job. What a laugh. If he couldn't
get his money back, none of them was going to get paid.

Sam's cell rang as he was approaching the outskirts of
Laurelton. He glanced at the screen, saw it was Griff, and
swept the phone up, putting the call on speaker.

"Some new information," Griff said without preamble.
"There was a note in the car with the address of the property. Checking the handwriting. Doesn't look like hers.
Someone wrote the note out for her, and get this: That property is owned by Walter Hapstell Senior. We contacted him.
He purchased it with the thought of developing it. He's been
waiting for the right time, and now there are preliminary
plans in to the city. And the developer? One of Joe's neighbors, Byron Blanchette, lives on the same canal."

Jules sucked in a breath and Sam's blood ran cold.
"Doesn't necessarily mean they were involved in whoever
ran Phoenix off the road," Sam said cautiously.

"No, but it's a hell of a coincidence."

"For sure. Did you find a file in the car?" Sam asked.

"No. Just the note. Look, I gotta run. All hell's breaking
loose here. Just wanted to get you up to speed."

"Okay, thanks."

"Phoenix said she was bringing me the Cardaman file,"
Jules reminded.

"I know. I don't like the note, like someone sent her there."

"I don't either," Jules said thoughtfully.

"Maybe she forgot to put the file in her car."

He didn't sound convinced, and Jules asked, "Do you think someone took it? Whoever ran into her? That maybe . . . they were after the *file*?"

Sam shook his head. "I don't know. Maybe. Or maybe it was something else entirely. Phoenix pushed people and they didn't like it. The police will be on it, and if Phoenix recovers, she might be able to tell us."

"If?"

"When," he corrected himself grimly. "The police are already looking for a vehicle with front end damage. They'll find it."

"And if it's Walter Hapstell's, or Byron Blanchette's . . . or *Rob Illingsworth's?*" she suggested. "Zoey told me Rob was trying to get involved in a land development project with Byron—maybe this is the one."

"When did she tell you this?"

"I don't know. A while ago? I just remembered it when I saw her earlier today with all the women. I remembered a lot of things about all of them, actually."

"Like what?"

"Well, let me see . . ." And she told him all the things she'd recalled about the Fishers.

Chapter Eighteen

Tiny Tim's was a low-slung building with neon beer signs sparkling in the windows in colors of red, white, and blue, the cheeriest thing about the place. Scraggly plants were stuck in boxes beneath the windows and a number of cars were nosed up to a cracked sidewalk. There was more parking behind the bar, accessed by a gravel drive around the side, but there were still a few places out front, so Sam pulled into an empty spot, three cars from the front door. A chain-link fence separated the bar from buildings on either side, and a line of trees around the periphery offered the illusion of privacy in the middle of the city.

Jules, shivering a little even though the temperature was warmer in the Willamette Valley than it had been on the coast, let herself out of the vehicle and met Sam at the front door.

"Need a jacket?" he asked.

"No, I'm fine."

"C'mon, let's get inside and find Pearl."

The interior of the bar was dark, lit only by a few more neon signs against the walls and some undercounter lighting at the bar. The bartender moved toward them, a rotund guy whose waist was the widest part of him. At the end of the bar was a woman in her thirties, about ten pounds overweight, squeezed into a tight, flowered sundress. She looked up like she was expecting someone, but didn't move.

Sam walked toward her and Jules followed. "Pearl Enos?" Sam asked.

"Oh. I thought . . . I didn't know you were bringing someone," Pearl said. She examined Jules's sling and the abrasions on her chin.

Sam made introductions, then said, "This is where you and Dennis Mulhaney met for drinks?"

"Right here," she said, gesturing around the end of the bar. "This is where we always sat."

"You were here a lot with him?" Sam asked.

Even in the dim lighting, he could tell she blushed. "A few times. It was kind of his place and I . . . would stop in." She shook her head and said, "He stopped coming to work. I've been to his apartment over and over again, but he's not there. His car's there. Hasn't moved. It's all dusty now, but Denny hasn't been there for weeks."

The bartender had been methodically wiping a glass. Now he edged his way down the bar to them, listening hard. Sam looked over at him and said, "We're looking for Dennis Mulhaney, who was a semiregular here, it sounds like. He's been missing awhile."

The bartender looked him up and down. "You a cop?"

"Not anymore," Sam said.

He thrust out his hand and shook with Sam. "I'm Tim. Tiny Tim."

"Sam Ford."

Pearl said, "I've called and called Denny's cell, but he's never answered. I texted. E-mailed. Even tried to find him on social media. Facebook. Twitter. Instagram. Nothing.

The boss finally hired somebody else. I thought it was mean to just give up on him."

"I think I saw him here with you a time or two," Tim said to Pearl. "He always sat at this end of the bar."

"Yes," Pearl said eagerly. "Have you seen him? I mean, recently?" She sounded hopeful.

"Uh-uh. Hasn't been here for a couple months, maybe. No . . . about six weeks."

He met Sam's eyes meaningfully, and Sam realized he had something else he wanted to say.

Sam pulled out his wallet and laid some bills on the counter near Pearl. "Jules, can you get Pearl a glass of wine, or whatever she might like?"

Jules looked from Sam, then over to Tiny Tim, who'd wandered to the far end of the bar. "Sure. Pearl, what's your drink?"

"A chi-chi?" she asked, suddenly teary eyed. "I thought maybe Denny was still coming here . . . without me, but now I don't know. You think something bad happened to him?"

"That's what we're trying to find out." Sam moved down the bar to join Tim, leaving Jules to commiserate with the unhappy woman. "You have something you want to say?" Sam asked, when he and the bartender were out of earshot.

Tim bent down to an undercounter refrigerator and pulled out cans of coconut syrup and pineapple juice. "The last time I saw the guy, there was a man and a woman in here, sitting at the bar. I'd never seen either one of 'em before. She was a looker, but just smelled like trouble, y'know? Came on to the other guy. Told him she was stepping out on her husband, who sounded like he was bad news. The guy didn't pick up on her, so she moved down the way to your guy, Denny." Tim dumped the cans in a blender along with vodka and ice and turned it on. Sam waited out the loud whirring noise as Jules continued commiserating with Pearl.

A half minute later Tim stopped the blender, grabbed a tall glass, and poured the white concoction into it. "Denny told everybody his troubles. Life had run him down, y'know? He'd been cheated and stomped on, promised things that never panned out, the whole nine yards. Meanwhile, this woman gets all huffy with the other guy and says she's gonna be with him, meaning Denny. She struts on down to Denny, who thinks he's won the lottery. The other guy sits there for a bit, then pays for his beer and goes out the back. A little while later—this woman is all over Denny by now—she and Denny stumble out the back, too."

Tiny Tim stuck a straw in the drink and took it to Pearl, who looked up gratefully. He came back to Sam, and said, "She always orders chi-chis. Not the usual drink around here. Don't want to crush her, but Denny just put up with her, y'know? You could just tell."

"Did they ever come back in? The woman and Denny, or the other man?"

"Nope. Not that I saw." Tim was frowning, shaking his head as he swabbed at a spot on the bar. "The woman and Denny both used the front door when they arrived, but they went out the back. Didn't see how the other guy entered— I was busy with customers—but I know he went out the back, too. He sat right there in the center of the bar. Once the woman moved on to Denny, he couldn't take his eyes off her." Tim huffed out a laugh. "Gotta admit, I couldn't either. She had Denny by the balls, damn near literally, when they headed out. It had been getting pretty damn hot in here, while she was stroking and rubbing. I swear the temperature dropped ten degrees once they were gone. I wanted a cigarette something bad, but I gave those cancer sticks up six years ago. Anyway, that was the last time I saw Denny."

"And the man and woman?"

"Nope. Never been back. Paid cash and were gone . . ."

He snapped his fingers and blew out as if they'd disappeared into dust motes.

"You think they had something to do with Denny's disappearance?"

"I didn't know he'd disappeared till I heard her say it." He nodded toward Pearl. "But yeah, I'd say so. They both seemed . . . wise, y'know? Like they were playing a game and made up all the rules themselves. It just seemed off . . . role playing, that's what it was. I've sorta thought about it off and on."

"All three of them went out the back and never came back in," Sam reiterated.

"That's right. It got a little busier around here after they left, but I was kind of looking for them, y'know? I even went out back and looked around a bit when I had the chance, but there was nothing to see. Nobody there."

"Can you describe them, the woman and other man?"

Tim thought it over. "The guy was cheap with his money, barely left a tip. I saw in his wallet briefly, when he took the cash out. License right out in front. He tried to put his hand over it, but he was careless, pretty turned on by what the woman was doing to Denny. No surprise. I've seen a lot of shit around here, but she wasn't even trying to hide what she was doing at all, and she kept looking at the other guy, like daring him to stop her. I wanted to know who the hell the guy was, so I looked at his license. Whole thing just felt like some kinda setup."

"You saw his name?"

"Not really," he admitted regretfully. "Started with an E or a B. Short one, like Eric or Evan, or Brian or Bob, maybe? Take your pick. He was in his thirties somewhere, I'd say. Maybe a little taller than average. But it's her I remember. She had ample breasts, very nice, y'know. Big enough, like I said, ample, damn near spilling them out on the bar. Dark hair, but it coulda been a wig. Good body.

Denny's tongue was hanging out and why not, with that massage going on beneath the bar."

Sam asked a few more questions, but that was about all Tiny Tim had. "You some kind of private investigator?" he wondered then.

"More like I've got a personal stake," Sam said. He gave Tim his cell phone number, in case he remembered anything else, and he inputted the bar's number into his cell contact list, then walked back to where Jules was just getting to her feet, having seen Sam's interview with Tim had ended. "I'm going to take a look outside," he told her.

Jules nodded and said to Pearl, "We'll do what we can to find him."

"You'll let me know?" she asked, clutching her glass with the last swallow of her chi-chi separating in the bottom.

"Yes."

Jules followed Sam through the back door and they stepped into a moonless evening. There had still been a faint glow to the west as they'd driven east, but since they'd been inside the bar it had grown very dark. There was one outdoor light, but it was at the far end of the lot and gave out a minimal pool of illumination. There were no cars in the back lot. It was quiet and secluded. "No cameras," he observed.

"You think something happened out here?" Jules asked.

He brought her up to date on the man and the woman in the bar the last time Denny had been seen at Tiny Tim's. "None of them ever came back inside through the rear door, so they either got into vehicles here, or walked around to the front. Doesn't sound like he had his car here, from what Pearl said about it not moving."

"Pearl said he always used Uber. Didn't like to drink and drive."

"So, did they come out here for privacy? Sex? Was the other guy still here, and did they roll him?"

"You said Tiny Tim felt like it was a setup."

Sam nodded. "Yeah."

Sam started walking up the gravel drive around the building, and then past the front parking lot, all the way to the street. He looked up and down it. "There's a camera on that cell phone tower," he observed. "I'll ask Griff if he can pull some records from around that date, check with the Laurelton Police. I should've pinned Pearl down on dates and found out what kind of cell phone Mulhaney had."

"Apple, and sometime after Flag Day. That was their last date and he didn't show up for work after that."

He gazed down at her admiringly. "Nice going." A breeze was blowing her hair across her lips and he automatically reached forward and pulled the silken strands away. She stayed very still and he dropped his hand. "We'd better get back," he said gruffly.

Jules sat in the passenger seat and watched the miles pass beneath the wheels of Sam's truck. They hadn't talked much on the way back to the coast, each lost in their own thoughts. Finally, when they'd passed the halfway mark, Sam said, "We've got to figure out the password to the laptop and find out what's in that file."

"I thought it was 'Georgie,' but maybe Joe changed it." Memory tickled, but wouldn't coalesce. So frustrating.

"Where does Mulhaney fit in?" Sam mused. "Phoenix was contacted by him. He wanted her to investigate Joe. He blamed Joe for mishandling investors' money. He quit his job and moved to Laurelton. Started a new job, then a month or two later, disappeared."

"And who are this man and this woman?" Jules posed.

"They targeted Mulhaney. I believe Tiny Tim on that. What did Mulhaney do for Joe? Did he have access to the Cardaman file?"

He looked at Jules, who said, "I don't know. I knew the password to Joe's computer and he dealt with the records from the company all the time, so Mulhaney must've had it, too, to access company records."

"Mulhaney was stirring up trouble. He wanted to shine a light on Joe's business dealings and that included his investors. Maybe someone didn't want his or her name to come to light. Someone with an inside track to Joe's business. Someone who knew about the Cardaman file." He looked at her. "Remember, somebody took that note from your house."

"So, somebody with access." It gave her a cold feeling in the pit of her stomach. "I'm glad Georgie's with Joanie and her daughters tonight. I don't want her at the house."

"Joanie seems okay, and I don't want you there, either. Maybe we should go to my dad's cabin. I put in Wi-Fi there. We can try to break into Joe's laptop."

"Okay."

"And let's go over the Fishers. Bette said she has a key, and everybody acts like Georgie passed hers around. Somebody got into your house, and maybe they tested the kitchen window like I did, found a way in that way, but however they did it, it's someone familiar with your house. They knew you weren't there . . . and maybe knew I wasn't there, when they went inside and took the note, because it was taken between the time I was first at your place and after you were rescued."

"After you rescued me," she reminded.

"Among others." In the dash light she could see his brief smile, but then he sobered and went on, "Someone has a close eye on your house."

"Or, someones? A man and a woman?"

Sam grunted an assent. "What do you think? Do any of the Fishers sound some kind of alarm inside your head?"

"They all do, kind of," Jules admitted. "When Sadie said

someone was coming I had a moment of real terror. It felt like déjà vu. And then I thought of Joe, and the laptop, and the note. . . ." She took a breath, wanting to make sure her head didn't start hurting, then continued, "Joe said, 'Get to the boat!' He saw something out the front window that scared the bejesus out of him. I remember that pretty clearly now. So I ran, but I fell, hit my head . . . maybe that's when it happened? The head injury. But then Joe was right there, and that's all I remember until the hospital."

Sam said, "When I found you on the beach, you said, 'You're dead.'"

"Was I talking about Joe?" she asked helplessly. "I just don't know."

He nodded, then went back to his train of thought. "You'd think one of the Fishers would have seen the boat leave. Tutti said she was picking up her sons, which was unusual on a Wednesday. Bette and Stuart Ezra were at work. So were Zoey and Byron, Rob Illingsworth, Joanie, and maybe Scott Keppler—don't know about him. And Hap and Tina, where were they? Hap's job sounds like it's what he makes it."

"Tina works for both Hap and Walter Senior some, I think. I don't know doing what."

"What about Jackie? I've never heard she has a job."

"She doesn't . . . I don't think . . ."

Sam grunted. "Tomorrow, I'd like to nail down where all of them were on Wednesday. Maybe Griff will know something more about Walter Senior and the land development deal."

"Well, there's one thing. . . ."

"What?"

"If the man and woman who targeted Dennis Mulhaney are connected to the Fishers, or are the Fishers, we can count out Zoey and Joanie for the women because neither of them have 'ample' breasts."

"Well, that's a good point," he said.

Half an hour later they pulled into Sam's father's cabin. Jules remembered it immediately. She'd been here a number of times since that first Thanksgiving with Sam.

It felt cold as they entered, so Sam immediately went to the short hallway in search of the thermostat. Julia looked around, reacquainting herself, her gaze lingering on the couch where she'd first made love to Sam. She dragged her eyes away with an effort and walked over to the television, seeing the stack of DVDs on the shelf beneath it, recognizing so many of the familiar titles.

When Sam returned, he stopped at the edge of the living room. "You want anything to eat? I don't know what's in the refrigerator, but I could probably find something."

"No, thanks, I'm fine. I have a refrigerator full of leftovers the Fishers brought over earlier. Doubt I'll ever eat them. Just don't have any appetite."

"I'm going to dig up some peanut butter," he said, and headed into the kitchen. "Want a drink? Soda, water, wine? A beer?"

"I'm all right."

She sat on the couch gingerly. She was afraid to stir up her memories of Sam, which were so readily accessible, a pisser when the others were so hard to reach.

He returned with a beer and a plate of saltine crackers slathered with peanut butter and sat down on the couch beside her, apparently unaffected by the memories of their shared past. Despite what she'd just thought, her stomach rumbled a little and she nibbled on a few of the crackers with him.

"They say you can't whistle with saltines in your mouth," Sam observed as he set the empty plate aside.

"I can't whistle anyway."

"Oh, come on. Sure you can."

"No, I can't."

"Give it a try."

She smiled. "No."

"'You just put your lips together and blow.'"

She lifted her brows. "Quoting Lauren Bacall, huh?"

"I watched a lot of those movies with you." He waved a hand at the DVDs.

"Those don't go any further back than the nineties. You just knew that phrase."

"Maybe," he admitted.

"No maybes."

She smiled at him and he smiled back at her. Slowly, the smile fell from her lips. The same happened to him.

She didn't look away. "The first time we ever made love was on this couch," she said, a catch in her throat, her fingers running over the worn fabric of the cushions.

There was a moment of silence, then he reached forward and gently cupped her bruised chin in his hand. "A long time ago."

"A lifetime," she agreed.

"But it seems like . . ."

"Yesterday," she finished, and in her mind's eye she saw the two of them, naked, the television's flickering light the only illumination. Her throat turned to dust and she yearned for those simpler days, those magical nights. She wondered how it would feel to relive those moments, then shut the thought down.

As if he'd read her mind, he said, "I've wanted to do that all day. Didn't want to hurt you."

"You aren't." Her heart had started a slow, hard beat. They stared at each other a good long time, then she took the bull by the horns, leaning forward to brush her lips against his.

After a few moments, he gathered her close, and she

made an involuntary sound of protest as she had to shift her damn arm. He let go of her immediately, but she said, "Help me take my arm out of the sling."

"You sure?"

"Yes."

He unhooked it and pulled it off her shoulder. Her arm dropped as if it had no strength. "Maybe this isn't a good idea. . . ."

She lifted the arm and carefully dropped it again. "I don't care. I don't want this to stop."

When he kissed her again it was with respect for her arm. Jules just wanted to crush him closer to her. She wanted *him*. Had wanted him forever, it felt like, and whatever had transpired between then and now had no meaning. Not in this moment.

He helped her off with her clothes, and then she did the same for him. In minutes they were lying on the couch, him atop her, grappling for each other as if this was their last chance. Briefly, Jules realized she was breaking her promise to Georgie, but she didn't care. Sam started to say something and she cut him off with kisses. *No talking. No spoiling it. Please, Sam, don't say anything!*

And then he was inside her and they were moving together, their bodies one. She felt on fire and arched up and gasped, distantly aware of her arm, every little bruise, scrape, and ache, the throb in her head, but she didn't give a damn. She craved him like an addict. All she wanted was Sam and the pleasure he was building in her.

Jules wrapped her fingers in his hair, holding him tightly, feeling his thrusts grow faster, harder, while she strained to meet him, gasping, crying, holding in a silent scream of desire until she suddenly felt him come inside her.

Sam . . . And then she was cascading over the edge, awash in pleasure, her chest heaving, her mind splintering.

I love you. . . . I've always, always loved you. . . . I don't ever want this to end. . . .

He drove his SUV to the lot where he kept his "For Sale" Honda Civic. He didn't like leaving his good car there, but he'd done it before when he needed some anonymity. A new wrinkle had occurred that had nearly knocked the breath out of him. Someone had run Phoenix Delacourt off the road! He'd seen it on the ten o'clock news. Had the man done that himself? Or had he hired someone new?

And what did that mean about the money he owed them?

He was on his way to meet the man, and had caught himself driving about ten miles over the speed limit in his anxiety. Luckily, no cop had been around. Couldn't be caught with this car.

And if that wasn't enough, she was becoming a problem. Somehow, in their relationship, she'd started thinking she called all the shots. Like she was the Queen of Sheba. Well, fuck her and the horse she rode in on. He didn't need her. He'd never needed her, and he was damn well better off without her.

Now he waited at their appointed meeting spot in Seaside, tapping his fingers on the steering wheel, expecting to see the man drive up in his black Dodge Ram with the silver grill at any moment. What a vehicle for the old fool. He'd only met him in person a couple of times, which was just as well because the man was fucking crazy and paranoid and a whole lot else. But he had money and lots of it; he'd seen his statement from Joseph Ford Investments, which had a whole lot of zeroes . . . a whole lot of zeroes. Unfortunately, the man couldn't access those zeroes unless Joe Ford was dead.

So, okay, there'd been that deal, which he had yet to be

paid for, and now Ryan Mayfield, and of course, Julia Ford. . . . Probably worth a lot more than he was getting paid. He'd tried to get her tonight, but that damn house had been dark and no one was there. He knew Georgie was with Joanie, that rod-up-her-ass hausfrau who couldn't keep a man if her life depended on it, and neither Julia, nor Joe's younger look-alike, Sammy boy, had been around.

If Julia finally remembered him, it was going to be a problem. He'd have to lie. Bluff his way out. Her word against his.

But where was the man? He was late. What the fuck?

He checked the time on his phone. Twenty minutes past their meeting. He called him, no answer, then called right back. Still no answer. He damn well wasn't going to leave a voice mail, something that someone could definitely track to him.

A sudden frisson of fear. Maybe the man *had* pushed Phoenix Delacourt's car over, and maybe he'd been caught! No, the man was smarter than that. Smart enough to make a fortune.

Fuck it. He'd catch up with the man later. He had somewhere he had to be.

He drove the Civic to the Seagull, his dick twitching at the thought that there might be more coeds there. It was the weekend, after all; could be lots more action.

And then across the darkened parking lot he saw *her* standing by the door, teetering on her heels, a scarf around her neck and wearing a teensy skirt that made his mind go to what was between those legs.

But she was going to betray him. He could feel it.

Fucking Jezebel.

He cruised up and rolled down the passenger window. Spying him, her lips curled into a smile and she strutted over and leaned inside like a streetwalker. A game she loved. Everything was a game. Even the drinking. "Hey, baby," she whispered. "Where'd you get this piece of shit? Maybe I should wait for someone else?"

"What are you doing out here? You trying to get caught?" he demanded, his anger exploding.

"Oh, come on. Don't be that way."

"Get in, Jackie," he told her flatly. "Before someone sees you."

Their relationship had just come to its inevitable end.

Chapter Nineteen

Jules awoke on a cry of terror, and Sam rolled away from her in the dark, instantly on his feet.

"What?" he asked tensely.

Immediately she remembered where she was. At Sam's cabin. In Sam's bed, where they'd moved after their initial lovemaking. "Nothing . . . just dreams . . ."

He slid back under the covers with her, his warm arms pulling her close to his body. It was only faintly light outside, about five a.m.

They'd talked into the night, discussing her neighbors, the laptop password, Mulhaney's disappearance and the man and woman he'd last been seen with, the boat accident and Joe's death, Ike Cardaman and the Summit Ridge development, Jules's slowly returning memory, and Phoenix's state of health.

They'd also made love twice more by mutual consent. Jules seesawed from elation over this night with Sam, unwilling to look ahead to the future and worry about what it meant, to a low-grade fear over what, and who, was lurking outside the safety of the cabin, someone, or ones, who wished her harm.

Now, curling next to him in the rumpled bedding, she

said, "I'm going to have to go back this morning and collect Georgie. Joanie told me she's got work today, and she's been leaving Xena sort of in charge of Alexa. She has Jackie check in on them, just in case they fight. You know, the whole teenage girl thing, so I don't want Georgie spending the day there." He kissed her hair as she sighed and added, "I owe Joanie for taking her on short notice."

"Okay." Was there a hint of regret in his voice? She didn't blame him; she felt it, too, the desire to throw the covers over their heads and make love all day, tune the rest of the world out and hide in their cocoon, here, away from the world. Which, of course, was impossible. "I'll take you back as soon as we get up. Sadie said she was available, so I'll call her and reconfirm."

Sam had said he was planning to meet with Griff and go over the case. He also wanted to check on Phoenix. If it hadn't been for Georgie, Jules would have gone with him. Already she didn't like the idea of them being separated.

"C'mon, darlin'. Much as I'd like to, we can't stay in bed all day." He kissed her cheek and she turned to him. "Uh-uh. Don't make this any harder than it is." He rolled out of bed, grabbed her hand, and led her to the bathroom.

"Hey!" she cried, almost in protest. "What d'you think you're doing?" But she knew, before he reached into the shower and twisted on the taps and steam began to roll toward the ceiling. "You're bad."

"Just bad enough." He pulled her under the spray, grabbed a bar of soap and, before she could argue, kissed her, holding her tight with one hand while he lathered her back with the other.

Slick, hot, wet, they kissed hungrily, as if they hadn't made love in years instead of hours, and as he lifted her up, she carefully wrapped her arm around him and threw her head back, lost in the feel and touch of him making love beneath the needle-sharp spray. Jules never wanted this moment to end and was sorry when she had to re-dress in the jeans and navy blouse that Sam had brought her yesterday. Seemed like a lifetime ago. So many things had happened in a short period of time.

Less than an hour later, as they were driving back down the coast, Jules opened a window, letting the salt air dry her hair. The patchy part that had been shaved to allow stitches was blown away from her face and she pulled it back in place, slightly embarrassed. Silly to be so consumed with her looks with everything that was going on, but she didn't want to look like a haggard mess in front of Sam.

At Salchuk, they stopped in for breakfast at the Spindrift. Sam recommended the huevos rancheros and Jules managed to make her way through most of her meal, savoring the spicey sauce, trying not to stare at Sam across the table. She was all too aware of him and wondered, fleetingly, what would have happened had they never broken up? Would they be married, have children now? Or would their relationship have eventually dissolved or become old and tired? And what about Joe? Too many questions, she thought, pushing her plate away and realizing her feelings for Joe had never run this deep. Guilt chased through her brain, but she firmly pushed it away. Joe was gone, and he would want her to find happiness. That much she knew.

"Ready?" Sam said, and she thought for a second, as he held her gaze, that he might have read her thoughts. Ridiculous.

They held hands on the way back to his truck, Jules aware how much she never wanted the contact to end. Sam made her feel safe, and loved. Joe had, too, she realized as she climbed into the passenger seat, feeling sadness at the loss, elation at the rekindling of her romance with Sam, and beneath it all an underlying sense of fear. Whoever had murdered Joe and maimed both her and Phoenix was still out there. Waiting. Lurking. One step ahead.

They'd barely got going again, the road stretching out

ahead, when Sam's cell rang and Jules handed it to him. He looked at the number, said, "It's Detective Stone," then clicked it on to speaker and placed it in the cup holder, as he said, "Sam Ford. I'm here with Jules Ford. You're on speaker."

"Stone, here. You got the sheriff on board with your theories yesterday," he said. "Didn't know if that was gonna happen, but it did. We doubled our efforts on the cameras nearby the marina and hospital and finally picked up somebody buying gas in a can from Mayfield about five days ago. He's in a hoodie and jeans. Also got a picture from the hospital, same thing. Guy in a hoodie and jeans. Can't really see who he is, but I'm texting both shots to your phone."

"Great work. Thanks." He clicked off and said, "So Mayfield did sell someone gas, but it wasn't on Wednesday."

They heard the *ding* of an incoming text and Sam asked Jules to scroll through to the correct screen while he kept driving. She touched the most recent text and pulled up several black and white pictures. She focused on the one from the hospital camera first. It looked like the man in the hoodie had been aware of the camera from the way he ducked his head. His nose stuck out, but that was all she could see of his face. Her eye traveled over his build, and she felt a buzz of recognition, but couldn't put it together. She'd seen him somewhere. Maybe knew him. She was sure of it.

Quickly, she scrolled to the next photo. In it a young man in shorts and a T-shirt was standing on the marina dock, handing a gas can to another man who wore an identical hoodie and jeans to the man in the hospital photo. Though the sun was bright and the water sparkled, the man reaching for the can was covered head to toe. A disguise, she thought, again feeling that tantalizing zing of forgotten memory.

"He look familiar?" Sam asked, glancing at the phone, then looking back at the road.

Jules stared at the hoodie. Gray. She couldn't see a label. She went back and forth between the two photos, enlarging them to get a closer look at his face, but it was hidden. Still . . . the jeans . . . and those sneakers . . . She narrowed her gaze at them. Dark Nikes, maybe, probably black.

With silver . . . on the boat . . . walking toward her as she lay on the deck . . .

"You weren't supposed to be here, Julia."

She sucked in a startled breath and nearly dropped the phone.

"Who?" Sam asked before she could even speak.

"Those shoes . . . the guy on the boat wore those shoes . . . and a hoodie," she said in a shocked voice, her heart drumming wildly, fear curling in her stomach. "I remember I saw him. . . . *I saw him*. . . . He came at me. Oh, holy God, it's *Stuart Ezra . . . !"*

P. J. Simpson was having a crisis of conscience. He was staring slack jawed at the morning news. She survived? Phoenix Delacourt *survived*? She'd looked so dead that it hadn't even crossed his mind that she could live.

He sat at the end of the motel bed and stared down at his toes in abject misery. He'd confronted Joe and that hadn't worked. And he'd tried to kill Phoenix—which he couldn't even believe now!—and that hadn't worked.

What did you expect? And Joe was never going to give you the money anyway.

He shook his head. Thought of all the years he'd spent playing the role of the pauper, waiting for that big win. Maybe he could've taken out his money when Joe went out on his own, but questions would have been raised, and anyway, he'd had tons more money to make. He'd known he could do it. Transform thousands into a million, one million into two, two into three, four, five, *ten* . . . !

You got greedy.

He choked out a sob. After all the shit he'd put up with? All the terrible years? All the sideways looks and raised eyebrows by people who considered him a lesser being?

And then that phone call last night, where that lowlife *Tom* accused him of misrepresenting himself. Misrepresenting himself? All he had to do was get his hands on *his own money* and he could afford whatever he wanted. He just *couldn't do it!*

God, it was FRUSTRATING!

In a fit of fury he stood up and stalked to the bathroom, ripping off the mustache he'd painstakingly applied just a few minutes earlier. What good was a disguise when Phoenix would remember who she'd met with right before she was pushed into the ditch! Everything would unravel. He couldn't count on her having lost memories like Julia. Lightning never struck twice. No, Phoenix would remember him, all right, and she'd be on his trail like a bloodhound.

There was only one course of action and that was to approach Julia directly, be as honest as he dared.

Killing her now wouldn't help, and he didn't want to anyway. She held the purse strings and if she was gone . . . who would be in charge of Joseph Ford Investments? Who would be in charge of his money? Not Joe's adopted daughter; she was too young. A much more likely candidate would be Joe's brother, Samuel Ford, and he already knew that was a nonstarter. The man had been a cop, and there was no negotiating with cops unless they were dirty, and even then it was a risky proposition. And from all accounts Sam Ford was squeaky clean.

Fuck! He shook his head woefully. No, he had to confront Julia. Alone. And hope she made the right decision.

* * *

Stuart Ezra? Sam wrenched the wheel and pulled off the highway at a wide spot in the road when Jules made her announcement.

"Stuart Ezra. You're certain?" he demanded as he stopped the truck on the side of Fifth Street and threw it into park.

"Yes . . . yes . . . pretty sure."

"Pretty sure?" he questioned sharply.

"No, sure. Completely sure . . ." Her mind was reeling, images tumbling one after another. "He was on the boat. Oh, my God, Sam. He was on the boat!"

"With you and Joe?"

"Yes!"

"Stuart Ezra was on the boat with you and Joe when it caught fire," he clarified. "You remember it?"

"Yes. Yes, I do. And it's a real memory."

"Jesus. Stuart Ezra . . ." He went silent, thinking hard. *You weren't supposed to be here, Julia. . . .*

"He was surprised to see me. He thought Joe would be alone on the boat."

"How did he get on the boat?"

"He . . ." She squeezed her eyes closed, pushing it, needing to know. She was lying on the deck . . . his black Nikes coming toward her, and Joe . . . Joe's body was in a heap in her line of vision, blood pooling on the deck, mixing with water. . . .

"He . . . Stuart . . . was having trouble with his boat . . . a small speedboat. . . . I don't think I've ever seen it before, at his house. . . . I don't . . ."

"He was in a speedboat out on the water," Sam said, seeking to corral her thoughts.

"Yes. He had a gas can, but he said his boat wasn't running. Something else wrong with it. He needed help. He asked to come aboard."

Permission to come aboard, Captain Ford, he'd said jauntily.

Jules's eyes filled with tears. The gray veil had lifted, and the memories were coming fast and hard. "Joe let him on our boat. Helped him on. My head was hurting. . . . I had an ice pack, I think. When Stuart came aboard he had the gas can . . . which was weird. Joe said to just leave it, but he swung it and hit Joe across the head, threw him to the deck. . . ."

"He purposely hit my brother with the gas can?" Sam repeated in a hard voice.

"Yes. He went down and Stuart hit him again. I screamed and then . . . then Stuart looked at me. I'd been sitting and I scrambled to my feet and then I slipped, fell to the deck. I'd fallen before. . . ."

She could see the Nikes coming at her. Was powerless to get up. Behind those feet, Joe moving . . . staggering to his feet. . . .

"Stuart grabbed me, yanked me up . . . k-k-kissed me . . . pressed me against the rail . . . and then he upended me. . . . Threw me overboard. . . ."

The shock of ice cold water covering her head. The taste of salt in her mouth. "I was in the water . . . swimming . . . and there was a life preserver. . . ."

Joe. Joe had thrown it to her. She could see him climbing to his feet, stumbling toward her as Stuart pressed against her, ran his hands over her body. Joe failing to reach her in time, the life preserver his last effort to save her. . . . "He killed Joe, Sam," she said, voice quavering. "Stuart killed Joe."

Sam's face was set. Without a word he rammed the truck in drive again, turned around and got back on the highway heading south toward Fisher Canal, his eyes lasered on the ribbon of road in front of him. He muttered, "Where's Ezra now? His job . . . he's in sales of some kind . . ."

"Medical-equipment sales. Why . . . why did *he* do it?" she asked.

"I bet it's about the money. People wanted to believe it was Joe's fault they lost money." He drove with a kind of controlled ferocity. "Was Stuart's name in the Cardaman file?"

"I—I don't know. I never looked it over closely. It was just a bunch of names and numbers. I gave it to Phoenix. I wanted her to fix it all."

"Ezra must've blamed Joe for losing his money, just like everyone else did. The difference is, he acted on it. Took it to another level. Killed him because of it." Sam's voice was flint hard. "We need to know about the Ezras' finances. And we need to know where he is right now!"

"He came to the hospital to finish the job," Jules realized. "He never thought I'd survive. I shouldn't have survived."

"Thank God you did." He slipped her a warm look. "Jesus, the Ezras live right next to you, Jules. I shouldn't take you anywhere near there!"

"No, we have to go back! I've got to get Georgie!" She felt a new panic now, tried to stay calm, but the horror of that day on the boat, the knowledge that Stuart had deliberately killed Joe, who had tried to save her. . . . She swallowed against tears, refused to back down as Sam drove, hands clenched over the steering wheel, jaw set hard.

"I know. We will. We'll go to Joanie's and pick her up. Use my phone. Call Georgie and tell her we're on our way. Make sure she's ready to go. Then I'll call Griff, put him on finding Ezra. . . ."

It had been a long, long night and he was filled with an underlying fear that had shaped his life since he was a kid. Fear of his old man beating him for screwing his stepmother . . . fear of being caught breaking into homes around the neighborhood and stealing drugs . . . fear of being found cheating his way through community college courses . . . But the fear in itself was a high. He loved balancing on the knife's edge of danger. Knowing he could be found out at any moment. It was an added sexual thrill he craved like an addict.

It was barely light out as Stuart slid from the bed and looked at the woman lying on the pillows, her dark hair fanned out around her face. Jackie Illingsworth . . . ah, man . . . His mind traveled along the pathways of their relationship, including last night when they'd screwed for the last few times, culminating in the scarf that he'd wound tightly around her neck.

He touched his own throat where that blood-red scarf now hung as he dragged on his jeans, pulled his T-shirt over his head, put on the gray hoodie that his wife had tried to throw away once. He'd had to fight himself from beating her senseless over his lucky sweatshirt. Luckily, he'd just managed to keep control, hang on to his facade. He was like Batman, by day a mild-mannered sales rep, chatting up the women he met on his job, shaking hands with the men, clapping them on the back, using his spare time to work out, making friends with everyone at the club where he'd met his lovely wife, Bette, watching her through the window into the yoga studio. He'd wooed her with everything he had. He'd desired her toned body, her flexibility. She'd been perfect for him and he'd had to have her. He'd even thought being with her might be enough. Everybody, but everybody, loved him, and for a time, he'd traveled the straight and narrow, lived a so-called normal life.

But . . . the old need for fear, danger, to heighten the senses was an addiction that had never let him go.

So he'd started fooling around. A woman here, another there. When Bette had wanted to move to the canal, he'd balked. Too suburban. Too removed from his hunting grounds, which were small enough in Seaside already. He needed a bigger city, like Portland, or Seattle, or maybe south to San Francisco or Los Angeles, where the pickings were plentiful.

But Bette had started to suspect something, had wanted the move, so he'd had no choice but to go along with it. Luckily, there were unhappy women living all around him. Tutti had come on strong and he'd thought about hitting that, but Jackie was a better prospect. She was unhappy with her life, too. Bored with her husband, Rob, father of the year. Jackie felt disenfranchised from Rob and the boys, but she didn't go on and on about Rob the way Tutti did about "the bastard," her ex, Dirk Anderson.

He and Jackie had started a little tickle. Nothing much. It just kind of waxed and waned. Rob had begun to suspect something was going on between them, he knew, and Tutti, jealous, had picked up on their sexual chemistry and started rumors. Stuart had been pissed about that. Had wanted to confront Tutti, maybe give her what she was begging for, but she was always unavailable, with her two sons, the video game morons, whereas Jackie's boys were quieter, more well behaved. The whole Illingsworth family was worried about Jackie's drinking and bonding together over the problem, forcing her away from them with their "good intentions." Stuart had half expected some kind of intervention, and he'd backed off from Jackie, big-time. Too messy. He'd basically ended their affair and had his eye out for someone else, something new.

But then . . . that day at the lookout, and the matching Hofstetters, Jerry and Jeri. Holy God! His life had changed in one second. His old pal fear had reentered big-time and he'd welcomed the shivery sensation as he helped push those annoying tourists over the edge. He'd never been so high.

But now . . . a serious problem.

He threw a glance at Jackie, her face white with death. They'd used the scarf on each other, first on him, then on her, ostensibly to increase her sexual pleasure, and after she'd choked, fought, and stilled, he'd pulled the scarf from around her neck and wrapped it around his own, trying fruitlessly to yank it tight enough to limit oxygen while masturbating, but it just hadn't worked. He'd desperately wanted to regain the high she'd just given him by damn near strangling him with it in the midst of sex.

The problem was, she'd really intended to strangle him! He'd seen it in her eyes as she rode him. She'd screamed loud enough at her own climax to get the guy in the room next to them to bang on the wall, which had her laughing like a banshee. But the shock of her intent had nearly ruined his enjoyment. Luckily, he'd managed to finish before she actually asphyxiated him. Furious, he'd shoved her off him and dragged in a long, tortured gasp of air, his lungs near to bursting. She'd tried to laugh it off, tell him that she would never have let it go that far, but he'd seen her eyes and knew differently. That's when he'd removed the scarf from his own neck and wrapped it around hers, yanking and pulling and twisting while she bucked and struggled beneath him, her eyes bulging, her fingernails raking the skin on his hands till he bled.

Which was a damn nuisance because now there was blood on the sheets. His DNA-rich blood.

He'd just been so angry! Not only at her but at the man, that fucker P. J. Simpson, a goddamn charlatan! The bastard had tried to take out Phoenix himself. Unbelievable! And he'd done a piss poor job of it to boot. And now . . . all the money P. J. owed Stuart was at risk.

Stuart knew. He'd talked to P. J. On the phone last night the guy had sounded like he was coming undone. He hadn't met with Stuart because he didn't have the money he owed him, and he'd whined about his failure with Phoenix, moaning that he'd fucked things up so much, it looked like he was never going to get his money. Stuart had worried P. J. was going to actually break down and cry. Some *man,* all right.

"I've got one more play, though," P. J. had told him, pulling himself together at the last minute. "Julia Ford."

Stuart had wanted to reach through the phone line and throttle him. He'd respected the man. Believed in him. And he'd been taken by him.

Nobody took Stuart Ezra.

"I said I'd do it," Stuart had growled. "How the fuck are you going to take care of her? You failed with Phoenix already!"

"I'm not going to kill Julia, *Tom,*" he'd sneered, growing some balls. "And it's lucky you didn't, either."

There was unspoken blame inside his words that had made Stuart burn with rage. His daily affable persona had been stripped away. He'd decided right then and there that P. J. had to go, too, and he would love nothing better than to rip the man's head off.

And so he'd taken his frustration out on Jackie. She'd pissed him off, too, and now . . . now . . . what the hell was he going to do with her? Maybe he could cram her in the Civic's trunk, maybe not. And what about security cameras? This motel Jackie had chosen wasn't top drawer, by a long shot, but there were bound to be a few security cameras around. There always were.

It was a hell of a conundrum and he didn't have tons of time. How was he supposed to get Jackie's body out of here? If only he had a wheelchair . . . He also needed to wipe the place down and get rid of the sheets, make sure there was no trace of DNA.

Jackie had paid cash. He'd watched her from the car. But she'd had to give the older woman with the caftan and the seen-it-all expression a credit card number for incidentals. Incidentals, in this fleabag motel? They were lucky they hadn't gotten bedbugs, but Jackie loved the lowness of it. She was like that. A rich bitch who got off on getting dirty. Still, it added a layer of secrecy that helped keep him anonymous, and he needed to keep it that way.

He went out to the Civic to get the bottle of bleach he always kept on hand in a plastic grocery bag inside the trunk, grabbing it from where it was caught beneath the shovel that he also kept handy. But as he returned to the room and turned the corner of the hall, his neighbor from the room next door appeared. What the fuck was he doing up this early? Stuart's heart pumped madly, and he walked directly past his own room; he didn't want the man to see him, know he was the occupant of the room that he'd banged on the wall. But the guy, fiftyish, sent him a wolfish smile anyway. "Quite a woman you got there," he said, not fooled for a minute as he strolled back the way Stuart had come.

Shit.

As soon as the guy was out of sight, Stuart reversed and beelined to his room. He had to get Jackie out of here!

He nearly had a heart attack when he opened the door and she was sitting up on the bed and staring at him as he walked in.

"Jackie!" he burst out, closing the door behind him as quickly as possible. Oh, shit. Oh, God. Oh, fuck.

She didn't move other than to blink.

"Jackie?" he asked cautiously.

She opened her mouth and said, "Wha—wha—wha . . ."

He froze for a moment, eyeing her from across the room. Something wrong there. Lack of oxygen to the brain.

"Can you get up, sweetheart?" he asked, moving toward her, his brain whirling. Her clothes were on the floor and he picked up the scrap of underwear and push-up bra.

"Wha . . ." she said. The ligature mark around her neck was clear. He suspected he might look the same way.

"Gotta get dressed, babe. Get outta here. Rob's gonna be wondering where you are. And the boys. Gotta get back to the kids, right?" She'd told him that Rob had taken the boys on a camping trip, more family bonding, and Jackie was supposedly staying with her sister in Astoria and going to some concert with her. She was apparently due to be back early this morning to babysit for Joanie Bledsoe's nubile preteens, but then she'd *died* . . . so that wasn't going to happen. Except she wasn't quite dead.

He handed her the bra but she looked like she didn't know what to do with it. Feeling time ticking by, Stuart fumbled around until he got the damn thing on. He was a helluva lot better at taking them off than putting them on. After the bra, the panties and finally the dress. He eyed the high heels. She teetered in them at the best of times, even with only a couple of drinks. They would be no use to him now.

Dressed, she just sat on the edge of the bed. He placed the scarf back around her neck, covering the red line around her throat, the pièce de résistance.

Then he pulled out the bleach, and with breaks to shoot constant looks at her, making sure she was still sitting there, which she was, he cleaned the bathroom.

He moved from the bathroom to the bedroom, wiping off the surfaces as he went, while Jackie just sat passively by. His own throat was sore where she'd wrapped the scarf around her hand and yanked hard, teeth clenched. He rubbed it, and felt angry all over again.

Tossing the rag in the garbage bag, he growled, "Let's get you out of here," pulling her to her feet and walking her to the door.

"Wha—wha—" she said.

He almost felt bad for her, and kind of elated. He stood her by the door, then stripped the bed, wrapping up the bedding into a huge ball. How to get Jackie and the bedding out the door? He would have to take two trips.

So thinking, he walked her back to the bed and sat her down. He tightened the ball of bedding into as small a wad as he could make it, then carried it under his arm and ducked out to the Civic, which was parked at the back of the motel. He didn't see any cameras on this side. Maybe they only had them in the front of the motel? There was nothing back here . . . at least he hoped so.

He returned for Jackie, who had fallen over on her side. He sat her up again, annoyed, and starting to get buzzy with fear. What was he going to do with her? He got her to her feet, then grabbed her cell phone where it was lying on the nightstand, made sure it was still powered off, and slipped it back into her purse. Then he snagged her high heels and the purse, which was damn heavy. Damn heavy . . . hmmm.

He looked inside and got another distinct shock. A gun. She had a gun?

He pulled the small firearm from the bag, saw that it was loaded. "Jesus Christ, Jackie, what were you thinking!" he demanded furiously. He slipped the gun back inside the purse and hefted its strap over his shoulder. Deceitful bitch.

He gave a last look around the space, making sure there was nothing left. At the last minute, he remembered the bleach, and had to leave Jackie standing there, staring at the door, to go back into the bathroom for it. He put it back into its grocery bag, which he'd left by the tub, rolled the top closed, and held it under his arm.

Then he came back for Jackie. Her hair was a mess and her makeup was smeary. He patted her hair down a little bit.

It still held that "I've been rode hard" look. Still, that was as good as it was going to get.

They headed out to the car, him guiding her with his right hand, her purse over his left arm, the garbage bag beneath it, his fingers dangling the heels. It was tricky stuff because Jackie wasn't walking too well. One leg was a little wiggly. Had to move slow. He held the outside door for her, inwardly begging her to hurry, hurry, *hurry* the fuck up!

At the car, he opened the Civic's back door and dumped the shoes, garbage bag, and her purse inside—thought better about the purse and hung on to it. Then, he helped Jackie into the passenger seat, belting her in. "Don't want anything to happen to you," he said with a wink. He tucked the purse into the footwell, positioning it so it was easy for him to grab from the driver's side.

As they drove out of the motel, he saw the security camera. He ducked his head as they passed under it, but was afraid maybe he hadn't been quite quick enough. And Jackie sure didn't know how to hide her identity.

Stuart sighed, his gut gnawing at him. What about the guy in the next room with his smug attitude? He'd sure got a good look at him.

Immediately he shook his head. Nope. There was nothing to worry about. Things had been going his way, like they always had and they always would. He was a winner. He got things done. *He* was the man, not that old fart!

And then he knew what he would do with Jackie.

He drove through Seaside and onto Highway 26, heading east.

"Got just the place for you, babe," he said. No one had found Denny Mulhaney yet, so why not add Jackie to the mix?

She said, "Wha—"

"You just keep saying that. He's not much of a conversationalist, either," Stuart said, relaxing a tiny bit. He was going to have to get rid of this stolen license plate. Find a new one. Maybe get rid of the Civic entirely.

But it was amazing how good he felt. Once he got rid of Jackie, and the car—God he wished he could hang on to it, but ah, well—he would be home free. He would take the Civic back to the For Sale lot and switch to his Trailblazer. With P. J. failing him, he might have to come up with a new plan for achieving his goals, but overall, he was golden. Nobody could touch him.

Except . . .

What the hell had P. J. meant when he brought up Julia Ford?

I've got one more play, he'd said.

Somehow that sounded like a bad, bad idea. What was in P. J.'s mind? Did he think he could use Julia to wangle his money back . . . ? Talk her into opening the vault, or whatever the fuck he thought she could do? Not likely. Whatever the case, Julia was on Stuart's kill list no matter what the man . . . the *old* man thought.

Forty minutes later he turned onto the road that led to Mulhaney's burial ground and nearly ran over a couple of early morning hikers who screamed at him, one of them lifting her pole at him like an insect trying to ward him off.

He slammed on the brakes and Jackie's forehead hit the dash. What the fuck had happened to the seat belt? Damned thing had jammed before. Shit. What good was it?

Immediately the hikers came to help. They rapped on the passenger window as Stuart, pulse roaring in his ears, pulled Jackie back into position.

"She okay?" one of the women asked. Middle-aged. Looked like the kind who just was itching to call 911 over any goddamn thing.

"Whaaaaaaa . . ." Jackie said, looking at them.

"Hit her head," Stuart called back to her. He wanted to run the nosy fuckers over. Jesus. Jackie had barely touched the damn thing, and now they probably thought she needed help. Shit! What was he going to do now? "Nothing serious." He offered what he hoped was a reassuring smile. "She's okay."

While they eyed him through the windshield, he leaned over and kissed Jackie on the cheek. *Pay attention, fuckers. We're in love.* To his delight, Jackie chose that moment to lean into him.

He nodded to the hikers. See?

They seemed satisfied, sort of, and he surreptitiously straightened Jackie in her seat, then patted her hand and waved off the hikers, before backing out the way he'd come in. The hikers stood in the road, watching him disappear. Once on the highway, he continued east toward Portland, taking his time. Half an hour later he doubled back, returning to the road. The hikers were nowhere to be seen now, luckily, but as he drove carefully and slowly, the Civic bumping down the ruts, he tried to remember exactly where he'd dropped off Denny. Here, in the sun-dappled woods, where old-growth Douglas firs and scraggly pines dominated, everything was looking the same. Where the hell had they ditched the body? He began to sweat. Worried. Thinking for a millisecond that it might have been found by hikers or tree huggers, like the two he'd just seen.

Calm down. Think. He's here, damn it.

It took him a while to find anything that looked familiar when he spied a stump that he thought he'd seen before. He decided to search on foot and had to leave Jackie in the car while he scoured the forest. Nervous at leaving her alone, swatting at a fly that buzzed around his neck, perspiring despite the shade of the forest floor, he tromped around the woods searching, feeling the pressure of time ticking by. Then he found the familiar, slight mound. Looked better than he'd thought, and nothing had been disturbed since they'd dropped Mulhaney. He let out a pent-up breath. So far so good.

And now for Jackie.

He hurried back to the spot where he parked and sucked in a shocked breath when he spied her, standing outside the car.

Holy. Shit.

She was a silent statue, staring at him across the vehicle's hood. A slight smile curved her lips. For a split second he saw his life flash before his eyes.

He stood frozen. A deer in the headlights as she slowly lifted her hand. He saw the gun. Waited to be shot point blank.

"Wha—" she said.

He closed his eyes. Braced for the shot.

And nothing happened.

He opened his eyes again, his gaze dropping to her hand. No gun. His fucking imagination had nearly given him a heart attack.

"Jesus," he muttered, then grabbed the motel blankets and sheets from inside the car, intending to bury them, too. He hooked his arm through Jackie's and half walked, half dragged her to Mulhaney's grave. He laid the blankets atop the slight mound, then made Jackie lie down atop them. He thought he saw worry in her eyes.

"We're just going to pick up where we left off," he whispered, unbuckling his jeans and getting between her legs, pulling off her panties. When he was settled atop her, he kissed her lips.

"Wh—" she started to say, but he wrapped his hands in the scarf, twisting again.

"No time to talk," he crooned, kissing her straining neck, as he twisted and twisted. *Die, bitch, just fucking die!*

She feebly clawed at his hands again, but there was no

real energy left as her eyes rolled back into her head. Stuart gave her the rocking and rollicking send-off she deserved, aware he was going to have to pull out the shovel and get to work, but what the hell? Almost better than working out at the gym.

Chapter Twenty

Georgie was waiting for them when Jules and Sam arrived at Joanie's, but so was Rob Illingsworth.

Jules had to contain her urgency as Joanie grabbed her before she'd taken one step from the truck. They were parked on the side of the house that led directly to the back deck, and Joanie practically dragged Jules toward the water. "Jackie's missing," Joanie declared. "She was supposed to come home after a concert last night, but she never did. Rob took their boys camping, but Jarrod, the younger one, got sick and threw up, so they came home about eleven."

She shot a glance at Rob, who was standing between Joanie's house and his, looking over the water.

Sam had gotten out of the driver's side and walked to Rob. "What time was she supposed to be back?" he asked tensely. He seemed to realize he was giving away his emotions and cleared his throat, visibly forcing himself to relax.

"Midnight or so?" Rob looked worried, but there was anger in his stance and fire in his eyes.

"You think she's with Stuart Ezra," Sam guessed.

"What makes you say that?" Rob demanded.

Joanie said, "Stop, stop. Girls, go back in the house." Xena, Alexa, and Georgie had come onto the deck, and she shooed her daughters inside, but Georgie planted herself by Jules.

"Can we go now?" Georgie half whispered to Jules. "I just want to go. Now."

"Why don't you get in the truck?" Jules suggested.

Georgie looked like she wanted to say something more, but she did as she was told and, visibly fuming, headed to Sam's truck.

"What makes you say that I think Jackie is with Stuart?" Rob demanded of Sam again, a little quieter this time. He was squinting against the afternoon sunlight, his lips compressed.

Jules answered, "I heard them together once. Outside the Ezras' house."

Rob stared up at the sky and said, "Fuck." Then he looked toward his own house. The faces of his two boys showed in the window. When they saw their father staring at them, they backed away. "Jarrod's better now. If we'd stayed camping, we might not have known. She coulda kept her secret a while longer and the boys might never have found out," he added bitterly.

"Except Jackie's supposed to be around to watch the girls today," Joanie reminded. "It's Saturday. Let me call and see if I can beg off, postpone some appointments. Won't be easy. Everybody wants their interior designer available on weekends. . . ."

"I've called her cell phone a dozen times," Rob said.

"I called it, too," Joanie threw over her shoulder as she walked away, slipping through the slider door, holding her cell phone to her ear. "But maybe this time she'll pick up." She disappeared into the house.

"I wouldn't bet on it," Rob said, almost to himself.

On the south of Joanie's house, the opposite side from the Illingsworths, the slider for Hap's place opened and Martina walked out onto her deck. "What's going on?" she asked, walking over to the rail. She wore a black bikini with a white overshirt, and was carrying a cup of coffee in one hand.

"Nothing," Rob said shortly, gazing across Joanie's deck to the one where Martina stood.

"Bullshit, nothing!" Martina wasn't buying it. "I've got ears, y'know. And it's not as if we live miles apart, for God's sake. Jackie's missing. I heard Joanie bitching and moaning about how late she was. So I came out here earlier and told Joanie to just leave, that I'd look after her little darlings." Perturbed, she took a swallow from her cup. "As I said, 'bullshit.'"

Jules almost felt like she was having an out-of-body experience. Why were they all just standing around, arguing about Jackie's cell phone and whereabouts? The memories of the boat and Stuart and the water filled her head. Stuart . . . they had to find Stuart. . . . Where was he? They needed to find him, call him. Without freaking out anyone else. "Could I get everybody's number?" she suddenly said. "I've lost my phone and I need the numbers."

"Good idea," Sam said, catching on. She could feel his eyes on her, worried, his jaw tight. They were both filled with urgency.

"I've got them," Martina said. "I'll be right over."

Jules had hoped Rob would step up, but he seemed to be going through his own inner turmoil, just staring at the water in the canal, which was spangled in sunlight and moving slowly toward the sea, sliding past grassy lawns and canoes tied to docks, splitting the two rows of homes where families lived and hid and laughed and lied.

Sam's cell rang, and he said, "Griff," and walked a few steps away to stand on the thick grass near the dock.

"For God's sake!" Joanie exploded from inside the house. "I've got to leave," she declared angrily, sticking her head back through the slider. "Can somebody watch the girls?"

At that moment Tina, who had already started toward the group, walked up Joanie's deck stairs. "I said I can do it, Joanie. No big deal." Then, seeing the look on her neighbor's face, added, "Oh, for the love of God. I'm not going to eat them."

Joanie threw up her hands and snapped, "Thank you," her feelings for Martina crystal clear.

"Drama queen," Martina muttered under her breath, out of Joanie's earshot as she sauntered across the deck, passing Jules. "Something's definitely off with her." Then she stepped onto the grass and sidled up to Sam, who was speaking in monosyllables to Griff, keeping his voice low, giving nothing away. Tina waited until he ended the call, then opened her phone. She went through her call list one by one, saying the name of each Fisher aloud and giving the number as Sam inputted them into his cell. When she came to Stuart's number, Sam's eyes lifted to briefly meet Jules's. She felt his tension. Knew he wanted to get the hell out of here as much as she did.

"Anything else?" Martina asked.

"No." As he finished inputting the last number, he said to Jules, "Let's roll."

Across the canal and a few houses north, Bette Ezra suddenly stepped onto her dock. Clad in workout gear, she shaded her eyes and looked over at them. "You guys having a powwow out here or something?" she called.

Rob, who'd turned his anger inward and had returned to his own deck by now, glared over at her. "Where's your husband?" he demanded.

"Stuart? I don't know." She dropped her hand from her eyes and gazed over at him, puzzled. "Why? What's wrong?"

"Did he come home last night?" Rob sneered.

She didn't answer, but the way she stiffened made Jules realize that Rob's query had hit pay dirt. The dogs, as if sensing all was not right, rushed outside to stand on either side of Bette, hackles stiffening as they growled at Rob. He flapped a hand at them and stalked angrily into his house, slamming the slider behind him.

"Thanks for the numbers, Tina," Martina singsonged as Sam and Jules hurried back to the truck.

Sam lifted a hand to her. "Yes, thanks."

"Hey, remember, I'm not the enemy here," she called as Sam and Jules slammed into his truck.

"Should we talk to Bette?" Jules asked, leaning past Georgie who'd scooted into the middle, to meet Sam's eyes. He nodded. "What did Griff say?"

"Tell you later." He shot a glance at Georgie, who was staring through the windshield at Martina. She was watching Tina in a fixed way that got both of their attentions. "Something wrong?" he asked Georgie as he did a quick three-point turn and they started the twenty-minute trek that would take them back over the bridge and around to the other side of the canal.

Georgie kept her eyes on Sam's ex till the last moment, twisting around in her seat to look out the back until Martina was out of sight. "Uh, no . . . I just . . ."

She seemed to come to herself and suddenly turned on Jules. "You left me at Joanie's last night. Just left me! You know I don't like her!"

"What?" Julia was taken aback. This tirade seemed to be coming out of left field. "Now wait. You didn't mind last night. You said you wanted to be with Xena," Jules sputtered, momentarily surprised out of her fear and anxiety by the unexpected attack.

"Joanie's a bitch."

"Georgie!" Jules couldn't believe it. She might not remember everything about her stepdaughter, but she'd never heard Georgie talk that way about another adult.

"Well, she is," she said stubbornly, then bit down on her thumbnail, worrying it with her teeth. "So's Tutti, sort of, but not as bad. . . . She's just, she used to be terrible, but now that she's with Devon and Sean's dad again, she's better."

"What are you saying? Tutti's with her ex?" Jules asked. She would have loved to share eye contact with Sam over this news, but Georgie was leaning forward between them and Sam seemed to be concentrating on driving.

"Uh-huh. They're like sneaking around. . . . I guess like Jackie and Stuart, huh?" she suggested daringly.

Jules felt weary all over. There was so much on her mind—Stuart, the boat, and Joe kept replaying in a loop—and she could feel the results of a sleepless night, a night full of lovemaking, and Georgie being difficult now was trying her patience. She held on to her tongue with an effort.

"Tutti thinks the boys don't know," Georgie was going on. "But she's always leaving them alone, so she can be with their dad, which is fine with them, but geez, both of their parents are acting stupid. They just want their parents to leave them alone." She sniffed. "They should just get remarried and stop acting so dumb. It's embarrassing. And it leaves Devon and Sean to get into all kinds of shit . . . er, stuff . . . that drone, y'know."

"I know the drone," Jules remembered.

"What have they been doing with it?" Sam asked.

When Georgie didn't immediately answer, Jules looked at her. She sensed there was more to come. "Georgie?"

Georgie was once again staring through the windshield, this time into the middle distance, obviously thinking hard. Finally, she said, "Okay, I've decided to tell you, but you can't *do* anything to get Devon and Sean in trouble. I promised I wouldn't tell."

"What?" Jules demanded.

"Well, they took some pictures of . . ."

Jules wanted to yank the words out of her throat. "Of what?"

"Of Martina, okay?" Her head swiveled to Sam.

"What kind of pictures?" Sam asked carefully.

"Naked ones. I mean, it wasn't really their fault," she rushed on. "She was on her deck, completely butt-ass naked. There's that screen they put up sometimes for privacy— you've seen it," she said in an aside to Jules. "But the drone flew right over and there she was."

Sam groaned, sounding exasperated.

"Where are these pictures now?" Jules demanded. "On their computer?"

"On their phones."

"Holy sh . . . Have they sent them to anyone?" Sam shot out.

"NO! I knew you'd get upset. Geez. It's *fine*. They know better than to send them all over the place. They know about *sexting*. I told them they were perverts. I mean, she's so *old*."

"I'm going to have to tell Tutti," Jules said on a sigh. This was the last thing she needed. "You know that, don't you? And Martina should know."

Jules expected the girl to have a conniption fit, but Georgie just sank back into her seat and folded her arms over her chest. "They'll never trust me again," she said, pouting. "I just wanted to know about the boat, y'know? I didn't ask them to show me the pictures of Martina. They just did."

"The boat?" Sam asked before Jules could.

"Dad's boat." Her voice caught. "You know. On that day . . ." Her face crumpled and she started to cry. Embarrassed, she pressed her hands to her face.

"They were using the drone the day Joe took the boat out?" Sam asked, clarifying. He looked over at Jules, who met his gaze in a sort of slow motion horror as between them, Georgie nodded her head. "Did they get any pictures?"

She shook her head, seeking to stop the gulping sobs that racked her. "Not really."

Jules wanted to collapse. It felt like she'd run a marathon, she was so wrung out.

"Only of the guy who came to the front door," Georgie then added. "They weren't supposed to be using the drone. They're supposed to take it to the beach, but Tutti was with their dad and they were home alone and so . . . they do it every time their parents go on a date."

"But they used it on Wednesday," Sam said, clarifying. "That's the day there was a guy at the front door."

"Yeah, the day Dad . . . died." She shuddered. "They wanted to show me the pictures, but they weren't very good of the boat. It was just at the dock. Nobody on it. So, then they showed me the ones of Martina, which they'd taken a few days before, I guess. I don't really care . . . except . . . I wanted them to have better pictures, y'know? I wanted . . . I thought . . . maybe I would see Dad one more time." Tears ran down her cheek. Jules reached for her and she turned her face into Jules's shoulder and cried, hard, racking sobs.

"Who was the guy at the front door?" Sam asked gently.

She lifted her head and wailed, "I don't know."

"You didn't recognize him?" Jules pressed. "Was he . . . wearing a hoodie? Could you see his face?"

"I don't know, no. . . ."

"It wasn't anyone from the canal?" Jules couldn't control herself.

"No, I told you!" She sniffed. "Why? Does this have something to do with Dad?"

"Could he have been in disguise?" Jules pushed.

"I don't know!"

Sam's attention had wandered from the road during this exchange, and he suddenly had to slam on the brakes a little harder than he'd intended. The laptop slid out from underneath the passenger seat. Georgie swiped at her eyes and looked down at it. "Is that . . . Dad's?" she asked tremulously.

Jules picked it up. "I'm sorry, Georgie. I'm not trying to press, I just . . ." She drew a breath. "Could the man in the picture have been Stuart Ezra?"

"No . . . He was old." She was shaking her head, rubbing her tears away with her fingers.

"This picture was definitely taken Wednesday, the same day of the boat accident?" Sam asked. "Taken that morning, before the boat went out?"

"I don't know. I guess. That's all I know. Why did you think it was Mr. Ezra?"

"We want to know what Mr. Ezra saw that day," Sam said.

"Well, the guy in the picture was old. And he had a mustache." Georgie gestured to the laptop, sniffing back tears. "What are you doing with it?"

"Trying to get into it," Sam admitted. "Hoping it would tell us something."

"I can open it for you," Georgie said, taking it from Jules.

"You can? You know the password?" Jules asked hopefully.

Georgie frowned at her. "So do you. It's what Dad always called me. You really can't remember that? Come on, Julia. You know that one!"

"Georgiegirl," Jules said softly.

"See? You do remember. You know, you just have to try harder, I think," Georgie said earnestly.

"Think you could open it for us now?" Sam asked.

"Sure." Sniffing back the last vestiges of her crying jag, she cleared her throat, then fired up the laptop and waited for the screen that asked for the password. When it appeared, she typed in: GEORGIEGIRL.

"I could remember 'Georgie,' but that was all," Jules murmured.

Sam gave her a swift look. "You okay?"

The gray veil was shifting, lifting more of the blocks to her memory, nearly overwhelming Jules, but she wanted to know. She was sick to death of not knowing. "I'm fine."

The laptop uploaded to a dark green screen, the desktop littered with file icons across its face. Jules looked them over, then pointed to one in the shape of a notebook, labeled "TCF."

Georgie used the mouse to click on it, and the Cardaman file opened up.

Stuart backed the Civic into its spot at the For Sale lot, grabbed the sign with his smeared phone number and placed it back on the inside of the windshield. He climbed out, sucked in a breath of salt-laden ocean air, then looked at the license plate. He was going to have to pick up one of the others he'd pilfered over the years, one of the ones hidden in the back of a cabinet of his garage, one with current tags. He'd been lazy about changing this one out, but just today alone it had to have been seen by the motel camera, and probably the hikers as well. That one old broad had probably memorized it and was calling 911 as he stood here! And then there was the guy from the motel.

Sloppy, Stuart. Very sloppy. But improvisation sometimes went that way.

He needed to get rid of the car, but first, the license plate had to be changed out ASAP.

So, that meant he had to go home.

He looked down at his dirty knees and hands. He opened the trunk, hoping he'd left a gym bag inside with a change of clothes. No such luck. He'd moved the garbage bag with the bleach, Jackie's heels, and her purse to the trunk, removing the gun. His stash of hypodermics was in the toolbox that sat next to the shovel, the end of which was still covered in mud. He'd tried to kick most of it off, but again, he'd been aware of time passing. Jackie's cell phone he'd smashed into pieces at the grave, making sure it was completely dead before tossing the remains into the hole with her. He'd done a slapdash job of burying her; her grave wasn't near deep enough. Later, when he had more time, he would go back and cover her up, conceal both her corpse and Mulhaney's a hell of a lot better.

Slamming the Civic's trunk, he pocketed the keys. Then he pulled out the ones for the Trailblazer and unlocked his SUV. He sat behind the steering wheel for a few minutes, thinking about what he should tell Bette. She had her suspicions about Jackie. He was going to have to spin one hell of a yarn, wasn't he? And what about this dirt all over him?

Car breakdown. Flat tire.

Good one, Stu.

He got out of the vehicle and dug underneath the chassis, found the crank hole to lower the spare. Pulled the tire out and ran it around in the dirt until it didn't look quite so damn clean, then pulled out his pocketknife and stabbed it hard.

He put it back and got behind the wheel again. Wondered why he felt so weary. Coming off a high. Like a bad hangover. He switched on the ignition and pulled away, his thoughts returning to Jackie.

Damn if he didn't miss her already.

Griff called again as Sam pulled into the driveway of Joe and Jules's home. As if on cue, both Sam and Jules looked over to the Ezras' house, while Georgie got out of the car, still holding the laptop open. The Ezras' front door was closed, the blinds drawn. They didn't know if Bette was still there or, by the way she'd been dressed, if she'd gone to her yoga class.

"Why don't you two go inside," Sam said as he pulled up his phone. "See what's on the laptop. I'll be in in a minute."

Georgie had already pulled out her keys as Jules headed up the front porch steps. She heard Sam connect with his friend and say in a low voice as he climbed back into his truck, "What have you got?"

Georgie had seated herself at the kitchen table, the laptop in front of her. "It's just a bunch of names and phone numbers," she said as Jules walked into the kitchen.

"I know."

"Who are they?" She looked over at Jules, then inhaled swiftly and asked in a whisper, "Did one of them kill Dad?"

"We don't know what happened," Jules said, searching through the cupboard for the tin of tea bags. She grabbed a mug and filled it with water, sticking it in the microwave. "You had breakfast at the Bledsoes'?"

"Yeah. Frozen waffles." She asked in a small voice, "Do you think Mr. Ezra did it?"

"Sam just wants to talk to Mr. Ezra."

Ezra . . . Jules's breath caught. She could hear Tiny Tim saying, "The name on the license started with an E, maybe a B. . . ." Not a first name, she realized. A *last* name. Stuart had been the man at Tiny Tim's and the woman had been Jackie. . . .

Her knees quivered. Stuart and Jackie had helped Dennis Mulhaney disappear! She nearly dropped her mug as she pulled it hot from the microwave. She dunked the tea bag, saw her hand was shaking.

"You do think he did it!" Georgie declared in alarm, jumping up from the table.

"Georgie, Sam's figuring it out! Don't do anything!" she added, as the girl was stumbling toward the front door.

"He killed Daddy, didn't he?" she accused, tears welling again.

"Georgie, please."

"Tell me! Tell me!"

"I'm starting to remember. I remembered Stuart on the boat."

"Oh, God . . . Does Mrs. Ezra know? I feed their dogs!"

"I shouldn't have said anything. Please, Georgie, wait for Sam. He's working with the police. He'll be here in a second—"

"What if Mr. Ezra comes here?" She backed away from the door, tears running down her face. "He'll kill Sam and you and me."

"Georgie, hold on. Just . . . wait. Sam's on it. Please. He's working on it. Okay?"

At that moment they heard a squeal of brakes outside. Georgie shrieked in fear and ran to her room and slammed the door. Jules raced to the front door, sick with fear as the engine to Sam's truck suddenly roared to life.

What?

Reaching for the door handle, she peered through the side lights and saw Sam behind the wheel, making a three-point turn, then tearing away from the canal toward the highway, gravel spraying from behind the truck's wheels. Her cell phone rang at that same moment and she tore back to where she'd left it on the counter. Had to be Sam. He was the only one who knew her number besides Georgie.

"Sam?" she answered anxiously.

"Ezra just showed up," Sam said tautly. "I'm in pursuit. Stay inside."

"Sam . . . Sam . . ." She gulped. "Ezra was the name on

the driver's license, Sam. That was the name Tiny Tim saw at that bar when Denny Mulhaney disappeared!"

He exhaled sharply. "Shit. Yes. I gotta go."

"Be careful. Sam." She sank against the edge of the kitchen counter. "Oh, God, be careful."

"You too. I'll call soon."

And he was gone.

Stuart's heart jumped and leaped in his chest, pounding so loud he was deaf, as he tore back toward the coast highway, the Trailblazer screeching and swerving onto Highway 101, heading north.

What had happened? What the hell had happened? Frantic, he checked his rearview mirror. Nothing. Still, he couldn't stop the thundering of his heart, the nervous sweat breaking out all over his body.

He'd pulled into his driveway and hit the button to lift the garage door, aware that the truck in the Fords' driveway belonged to the brother, Sam Ford. He hadn't been worried about it. Ford was hanging tight with Julia, probably wanted to get into her pants, which wouldn't be a bad place to be, he'd thought a bit jealously. He'd been wondering if there was a way to separate Ford from Julia and have some time with her himself before he had to kill her.

And then Bette had run outside, screaming at him about Jackie, looking like a wild woman.

At the same moment Sam Ford, cell phone pressed to his ear, had stepped from his vehicle, his gaze targeting Stuart like a laser, his manner grim and purposeful . . . like a cop on a takedown.

Bette had been still shrieking, but he'd been deaf to her.

One thought had crystalized in his brain: Sam Ford *knew*.

Ford had leapt into his truck and backed out in a rush. Stuart had taken off.

How? How the hell had Ford put it together?

He shouldn't have run . . . stupid . . . but nothing else to do. The end of the line.

No.

He could still get away. He could turn off before Ford found him. Make his way back to the Civic. Switch vehicles again. Fuck. No time for a new license plate. Fine. He'd steal one somewhere else.

He'd go south. Into Tillamook. Then east. Hole up in the Coast Range . . . somehow. . . .

Sam tore after Stuart Ezra. . . . Ezra . . . *shit.* That was the name on the damned driver's license. And Jackie. God. They'd killed Dennis Mulhaney together. He was certain of it. They'd killed him over the investment money. And Stuart had killed Joe for the same reason. *It's about the money.* His father had gotten it right.

He'd told Griff about suspecting Stuart Ezra, and Griff had been telling him of the Seaside Police's continuing talks with Walter Hapstell Senior, who'd been in a land deal with Byron Blanchette, and how Scott Keppler had worked both ends against the middle, pissing Joe off in the process, and that's what had ended their relationship. Griff was just talking about Hap, and how he and his father were at odds, which was why Hap was so hell-bent on the Summit Ridge properties, when Ezra had suddenly appeared. Then all hell had broken loose as Bette had run out of their house, Ezra had spotted Sam, peeled out of his driveway, and the chase was on. Sam had told Griff he was in hot pursuit and gotten off the phone, called Julia to warn her, and now he was at the junction to the highway.

He lurched to a stop. No sign of Ezra. Which way? North? South?

North. Toward Seaside and the turnoff onto Highway 26,

Portland and beyond. Ezra could pull off into a number of roads and try to hide. He wouldn't go on to Seaside because he'd get caught in traffic. Though he might go south. . . .

He put a quick call in to Detective Stone, who answered almost as if he'd been waiting for his call. Sam told him he was in pursuit of Stuart Ezra, Joe's possible murderer, and told him to check with the Seaside Police for more information.

Stone asked, "Ezra's the man in the pictures I sent you?"

"Yes," Sam said, advising him that Ezra had driven onto 101 and disappeared, no telling which direction.

"We're on it," Stone said, and hung up.

Sam drove north, looking down offshoot roads, searching for signs of Stuart's Trailblazer. He saw a flash of black as he looked down the road to Salchuk, and he made the turn himself with a squeal of tires and brakes, nearly missing the turn, fishtailing a bit as he regained control of the truck.

Maybe it was Ezra's SUV, maybe not.

And where's Jackie in all this? he wondered.

Jules paced the living room. She'd tried to talk to Georgie, but the girl had just wanted to be left alone, barricading herself in her room with her phone and iPad. Jules had let her be, and truthfully she needed time to think, to be in her own head.

Walking back and forth from the kitchen to the far side of the living room and back again for about five minutes, she'd gotten nowhere trying to piece together what had happened. "Come on, Jules, think!" she'd admonished, when her gaze landed on Joe's still open laptop. She slid onto the chair Georgie had vacated, her whole body feeling like there was an electric charge running through it. Waking the computer from sleep mode, she had to reenter the password, and then the screen opened to where Georgie had left it, the Cardaman file.

Names and names. Alphabetic. She ran her eyes down the list. Some she recognized. Anderson, Illingsworth . . . Rivera, Zoey . . . So Zoey had invested with Cardaman? She didn't see Byron Blanchette's name. Nor Scott Keppler's, nor the Ezras'. But there was Vandra, Burton . . . had to be the sheriff.

Then she saw a name she'd initially skipped over.

Simpson, P. J.

"Uncle Paul?" she said aloud. Well, no. He'd been dead for years.

She debated on whether to call Sam with this information. Bad idea. Had to wait for him to call her. And it had to be a coincidence anyway. Her uncle had been gone for over a decade.

But maybe she should send Sam a text, get his brain working on it.

"It has to be nothing," she muttered to herself as she wrote out: Cardaman file. P. J. Simpson. Same name as my deceased uncle. She pushed send, feeling a little sheepish almost immediately. She was seeing ghosts everywhere.

"Get a grip," she muttered just as she heard a sudden knock on the front door. Jules nearly leapt from her skin.

She looked around for a weapon, settled on a butcher knife. *Don't get paranoid. You live on a damned canal where neighbors drop by all the time. Especially now, with everything that is happening.*

She drew in a deep breath. It could be anybody. No one to be afraid of. Sam was in hot pursuit of Stuart Ezra. No need to worry.

But she kept the knife with her anyway.

She looked through the side light window. A man stood there. Head down. Huge mustache.

"Julia," he said, his voice muffled through the door. "Can I talk to you?"

The voice. Familar. The gray veil shifted further, and she heard Joe's voice again.

Get to the boat!

But this voice . . .

"I came by that day to talk to Joe. I saw you, too, but Joe told you to run and you slipped and fell. I wanted my money from Joe, but he couldn't give it to me. We'd met face to face and he assumed the worst of me."

That *voice.*

"Julia?"

Oh, God. Was it Uncle Paul? Was he still alive? Was he the man she'd seen who had spiraled her into such a panic that she'd blocked it from her memory?

"Julia?"

And then she knew. *She knew.*

She gripped the knife and threw the door open wide. Not Uncle Paul . . .

"Hi, Dad," she greeted him in a bitter, brittle voice.

Chapter Twenty-One

Braking hard, Sam started to turn onto the street where he thought he'd seen the SUV disappear. In his peripheral vision, he caught a glimpse of a black vehicle nose out from another side street. A Trailblazer. It had turned right, then left, then left again, and then a final left on Fifth Street again, heading back toward the highway.

Except Sam was in the way.

Jamming his truck into reverse, Sam hit the gas and backed across Fifth Street, angling his Chevy so no traffic could pass, but facing toward where Ezra would come. Then he waited, eyes focused down the street, his blood running cold as he thought about Stuart Ezra and how he'd killed Joe and nearly killed Julia.

Now, it was over.

Gotcha, asshole.

His gaze narrowed on the street as the Trailblazer had started his way and then stopped, fifteen feet away.

Stuart Ezra stared at him through his windshield, and Sam stared back. Sam desperately wished for his gun, but he hadn't carried it since he quit the force. He snagged his phone from the cup holder, intending to call Griff.

Ezra raised a small pistol, the barrel visible.

Sam ducked just as the gun went off, a flash of light, his windshield shattering. The bullet hit the headrest with a loud *pfft* sound.

Well, shit.

A squeal of tires and Sam risked a quick glance above the dash. The Trailblazer was zigging, aiming toward the road past Ryan Mayfield's apartment and on toward Summit Ridge. A boxed canyon.

"Perfect," Sam ground out, and trod on his accelerator, slewing after him.

Jules held the butcher knife in her left hand. Her right hand was no use to her, her arm tied up in its sling. Didn't matter. She could do quite a bit of damage with her left if need be.

Her father . . . who'd taken a swan dive? into the Columbia . . . the man who couldn't swim . . . Her father, who loved her, or at least had pretended he had.

She'd seen him on Wednesday, she knew now. Had felt like she was going to pass out in that first shock of recognition. Had heard the urgency in Joe's voice as he yelled at her to get to the boat. She'd stumbled, fallen down, hit her head.

She'd seen her father lunge for her—to help her or hurt her?—and Joe grabbing him and forcibly pushing him out of the house. Joe yelling at him to stay away, that he was turning her father in, that he'd always planned to but had to tell Julia first, that Peter St. James's embezzling was going to come to light. No way was Peter St. James pretending suicide . . . *pseudocide* . . . and assuming deceased P. J. Simpson's life.

"Julia," her father said to her now, his voice cracking as he stepped inside.

You're dead, she'd said to Sam on the beach. She'd meant her father, she realized now.

"I'm—" he started to say, but she cut him off.

"Don't come an inch closer. Sit in that chair. We'll wait till Sam gets back." Her voice was cold and hard. Didn't sound like her. Or maybe it did. The true Jules who'd never forgiven him for leaving her, saddling her with her dying mother who didn't recognize her anymore and needed constant care. She shut the door and steeled herself for what was sure to be an emotional roller coaster. Dad was alive. Alive! After all these years. Showing up now . . . Her stomach turned in on itself at what that could mean, the only thing it could mean—that he was involved. Oh. Dear. God.

"I left you some money for Lena. I didn't take it all," he said, before obeying her order and dropping into the nearest side chair.

She laughed harshly. "Oh, thanks very much."

"Sit down," he suggested.

"I'll stand." And she didn't let go of the knife.

He appeared about to argue, then cast a glance around the living room, the one she and Joe had shared. Almost imperceptibly, he shook his head. "Look, I messed up. I know it, but I couldn't deal with your mother's illness, Julia. You know that. I was weak, I admit it." He reached up and peeled off his dark mustache. With it, he'd looked almost clownish; without it, he was a gray, tired, old man. *Dad. The traitor. And what else?* Inside, she was shaking, hurt, incredibly wounded that he would let her believe he was dead, leave her with Mom, but she forced herself to outwardly be strong, not let him know how much it killed her to know that he'd lied to her and kept it up, letting her think he was dead.

"How did you take Uncle Paul's identity?" she asked tightly.

"He died in his cabin. You know he was a hermit. Barely anyone knew of him when he was alive. Then he stopped checking in at all. Became a total recluse. Your mother hadn't heard from him for nearly a year, and she was losing it, so I didn't listen to her fretting about him. But then time went on. Still no word. Your mother couldn't recall anything anymore, and she forgot about him, but I wondered about P. J., so I went to his cabin. All that was left were bones and ragged skin when I found him. Lying on the kitchen floor. Rats had found him, too." His features tightened at the memory. "Ugly scene. I—I don't know what he died of. I buried him under the cabin floorboards, and left. But his death made me think about things in a different way. How short life is. How you struggle so hard and never get anywhere, and then you're gone. It's all over and your life's worth nothing. Except . . ." He smiled faintly, sadly almost, a smile Jules didn't trust. "P. J. gave me a way out. It just seemed so . . . providential."

"Providential?" she snarled. "Such a grand word instead of cowardly."

He flinched, but she didn't care about his feelings, not now. "You know, *Dad*, you left everyone who cared about you, just up and pretended to die, never once checked in." She took a step forward, suddenly furious for all the years she'd grieved for a man who cared so little for her. Involuntarily, her fingers clenched over the handle of the knife. "But Joe found you out. That's what happened."

"I went to his office. I had to see him. I'd been living at the cabin for years, being P. J., living alone, dreaming of the day, very soon, when I would cash in and start the next phase of my life, knowing my nest egg was growing and accumulating in Joe's capable hands. I practically gave him my business, if you remember. He owed me."

"Owed you?" She choked. "You killed him!"

"I came here to reason with him!" he declared with a

flash of emotion. "Only to reason with him. He was your husband. My only daughter's husband. And he owed me!"

"You hired Stuart Ezra to kill Joe, burn the boat . . . kill me."

"No!"

"I don't believe you."

"I'm telling you the truth!"

"You've never told me the truth!" she charged. She was shaking all over. Her knees were jelly, threatening to collapse. She locked them in place, needing to stop the emotion, stay in complete control. "I recognized you, but then I couldn't remember. I wouldn't let myself remember because it was too terrible!"

"I never meant to hurt you," he insisted, his voice low. "You're my daughter."

"Go ahead and tell yourself that, all the way to prison," she snarled. "You don't care a lick about anyone but yourself, and that's the way it's always been."

"That's not true. I was devastated when Clem died." His face contorted with pain, fake or real, she couldn't tell. "Your mother had spells even then and she blamed it on you, when it was really her fault."

"You say that, but you almost believed her," she realized dimly. "You wanted to blame me, too."

"Not true." He dolefully shook his head.

He was telescoping away from her in her eyes. She was mentally putting distance between them. "How did you manage to survive the fall into the river?" she asked, feeling like she was losing control. She was worried . . . worried about Georgie . . . worried for Sam.

"Julia?" His voice sounded watery in her ears.

Was that a sound on the porch? Someone coming? Her imagination?

"You can't even swim . . ." she whispered.

And then she remembered the movie, *Sleeping with the*

Enemy, where Julia Roberts's character, who couldn't swim, taught herself to swim on the sly in order to pretend to be dead to escape her abusive husband. Pseudocide. Jules had been trying to remind herself of that since the accident, but her mind had been protecting her from the truth.

Now her vision had narrowed to where her father was all she could see. And he was looking at her in a hard way. "I need you to help me get my money back," he said.

Was that a threat?

In slow motion she saw him rise from the chair, come at her.

"I'm sorry, Julia, but you need to help me."

He grabbed at her arm, and she slashed down with the knife, but missed. "Get away from me!" she yelled.

And then Georgie's voice, shrieking behind her. Her father lunged at her, grabbing her hand, twisting her wrist, her fingers losing their grip on the knife. She caught a glimpse of Georgie frozen with fear, her mouth open, then the sound of the front door banging open.

"Run, Georgie!" Julia yelled, "Run!" But the kid couldn't move.

BLAM, BLAM, BLAM!

Gunshots thundered through the house, the smell of cordite filling the air.

Barking madly, two dogs rushed through the open door, leaping, snarling, and growling. Georgie screamed again as one shepherd clamped vicious teeth around Peter St. James's left leg, the other his arm. Growling, they held him fast, two muscular, furry, black and brown animals who wouldn't let go. Screaming with pain, he turned terrorized eyes on his daughter. "I'm shot . . . I'm shot," he muttered in disbelief. "Get them off me!"

"Georgie, get out of here. Get help!" Jules ordered, and turned toward the doorway, where the shooter was in silhouette. Oh, God. A knife against a gun. She was a dead woman.

"Julia!" Bette Ezra cried as she stepped into the room. Holding a gun at arm's length, she stared down at Peter in horror. "He was threatening you. Attacking you. I couldn't let him hurt you." Her hand was beginning to shake like mad as she still held the gun on him, as if there was any chance he would get up.

"Bette, please put the gun down."

"Who is he? Oh, God, I've shot him." Coming to herself, she called, "Less! More! Release! Back!"

As if by magic, the dogs let go of the wounded man and slunk to a spot behind Bette, near the door. She lowered the gun and gazed at Jules in shock.

Jules's eyes dropped to the man who'd betrayed his whole family.

Peter St. James stared right back at his daughter. For a moment it seemed like he was about to say something more, but then he passed from this world.

Sam opened the door to his truck, standing behind it for protection, his gaze fixed on Stuart's empty Trailblazer. Ezra, running out of a road to escape on, had stood on his brakes, letting the SUV slide sideways, and before it had stopped completely, bolted from behind the wheel, leaving the Trailblazer running.

As Sam had ground his pickup to a stop he'd spied Stuart dashing madly between two of the partially finished homes.

He has a gun and you don't.

Sam hesitated, but couldn't run the risk of losing the bastard. Too much was at stake. For now he was running on instinct. He'd never wanted to kill someone before, but he wanted to kill Stuart Ezra. He believed Jules one hundred percent. This man had premeditatedly murdered his brother. He wanted him to pay.

Crouching, using construction equipment and piles of lumber as cover, he darted toward one of the houses and slipped through an open window. Along with an empty box of nails and used cylinders of caulking material, there was scattered debris on the floor. He found a piece of two-by-four framing and picked it up, weighing it in his hand. Small enough to carry easily, strong enough to do serious damage.

He wanted to do serious damage.

Hearing the scrape of a shoe against the bare subfloor, he realized Ezra had just stepped into the same house. *Perfect.* He felt a savage urge run through his blood, tightening his muscles, getting him ready.

Silently he crept along a wall that was sheet-rocked, careful with each step.

I'm coming for you, you bastard!

Ears straining, fingers holding the two-by-four in a death grip, he edged along the hall wall to tuck himself into a shallow corner. If Ezra came from either direction, there would be a split second when Sam could launch forward and attack him before he could get a shot off.

At least he hoped to God that's the way it would play out.

Georgie's face was buried in the rough fur of one of the German shepherd's necks, Less or More, Jules couldn't say. The dog stood beside her like the guard dog it was. The other one sat a few paces away. They both were protecting Georgie as if she were her master, not Bette.

Bette was in a state of delayed shock. The gun clattered from her fingers and she collapsed on the floor. "He was trying to kill you. He was trying to kill you. And Sam . . . ?

He tore out after Stuart. What's happening? Julia, what's happening?"

Jules was looking for her phone, completely discombobulated. She felt she was on the verge of passing out, but she couldn't. "I need to call Sam."

They heard a car arriving outside and all tensed. Bette walked to the open door, and Jules saw her tense body nearly collapse. "It's Sadie," she said.

Sadie. God. Sam had called her.

Sadie greeted Bette suspiciously, "Well, hello. What are you doing here?"

"I'm . . ." Bette looked behind her to where Peter sprawled on the floor, his eyes open and staring.

"Holy Mother of God," Sadie said in shock. Her gaze flew to Jules. "You okay? What happened? You okay?"

"The phone . . . I'm . . . I need to call Sam."

Without further ado Sadie whipped out her own phone and dialed 911. "Who is he?" she asked before the dispatcher answered.

"My father," Jules responded, then she wobbled to the couch and collapsed.

"I know you're there, Ford."

Stuart Ezra's half-amused voice sounded to Sam's left, not far from the edge of his hiding niche.

Sam remained silent.

"I know you're hiding from me, but there's really nowhere to go. You might as well come on out now."

Sam tested his grip on the two-by-four. He couldn't make any noise. Not a breath. He needed one good shot.

"Joe shoulda kept better care of all our money, y'know? Shoulda warned us about Cardaman."

He did, asshole. You can't bait me into revealing myself.

Ezra's voice was coming closer. "Everyone thought he

was so great, but he was a bad guy. Just like the Hapstells and the Montgomerys and that fucker Ike Cardaman. Bloodsuckers. That's why it had to be done. Why I took the job."

A few more steps. Sam started counting in his head. *One . . .*

"P. J. Simpson promised a lot of dough, but he turned out to be just like the rest of them. He's the one who went after Phoenix. Don't blame that one on me."

Two . . .

"But you don't know who you're dealing with." He chortled. "You think your brother was the first? Tom and Bridget have been ridding the world of assholes for a long time. The tourists were first . . . and then that guy we choked to death—Bridget really got off on that one. . . . And then Monique." Ezra paused in his measured steps and Sam held his breath. "Mulhaney too. Your brother's lackey. Got him at a run-down bar in Laurelton. He was a paid kill. Buried him where you'll never find him. And now he's got a friend. . . ."

Something sounded in his voice. Regret? Sociopaths didn't feel regret.

Ezra took another step. He was right on the other side of the short wall. Sam readied the two-by-four.

"I'm going to get that little girlfriend of yours," Ezra said softly. "You've been with her, haven't you? Your brother's wife? My, my. Well, it's my turn next, just before I kill her. We're gonna have an awful good time."

Sam could see the toe of Ezra's black sneaker edging forward.

Three!

He leapt forward and swung the two-by-four blindly, but Ezra had leapt forward in the same moment.

BLAM!

The shot rang out and Sam shuddered, wondering where he'd been hit. He couldn't feel it.

Ezra looked at him in surprise, lifted the gun again, ready to take another shot.

BLAM, BLAM!!

The shots came from behind Ezra and Ezra turned, practically pirouetted on a toe, and fell over.

Sam stayed perfectly still, his hands in the air, as Officer Bolles, as jumpy as ever, slid into view, his Glock aimed at Sam.

Ezra had never gotten a shot off, Sam realized. It was all Bolles.

He stared at the officer, and Bolles stared back. For half a heartbeat, Sam wondered if Bolles was somehow involved as well, but then the officer relaxed his stance and wiped his brow.

"Never shot anyone before," he admitted, then, with a nod toward Stuart, "This the guy who killed your brother?"

"That would be the one," Sam said.

Chapter Twenty-Two

It was a blur to Jules until Sam got back to the house. It felt like hours had passed, and it had been a while, though maybe not as long as she thought. Relieved, she practically fell into his arms upon seeing him again, and once she'd finally calmed down, she could finally listen. To her horror, she learned that Sam had been embroiled in a gun battle of sorts of his own, although he had only been armed with a piece of wood. Her heart had turned to ice at the thought that she had come so close to losing him. But he was here. Alive. For that she was grateful.

The house was full of people. Police. Someone from the medical examiner's office. Griff. And Sadie, who was staying close to Georgie and the dogs at Jules's request. Detective Langdon Stone, who introduced himself to Jules, regarding her soberly as they shook hands. She tried to rally, but she really didn't have the energy, so she suspected her handshake didn't reflect how glad she was that the cavalry had come through.

And Bette Ezra, who'd clearly had the stuffing knocked out of her, was now on the couch beside Jules, her head in her hands, taking deep breaths and rocking back and forth. Not only had she killed Jules's father, shot him dead, but she also had to deal with the fact that her husband was a cold-blooded murderer. When Sam had called and the news reached them of Stuart's culpability and death, she fell into this near catatonic state. Her dogs came over and sniffed her, but she put up a hand to them, and they went back to Georgie, who greeted them emotionally, throwing her arms around them.

By the time Sam had actually arrived, Jules's father's body had already been stowed in the back of the medical examiner's van. Jules had heard the doors to the back of the vehicle being slammed shut, then the engine start as Sam walked in the room.

The stain of blood on the hardwood floor was all that remained to tell the tale.

Sam had walked into the house and beelined for Jules. He'd squatted in front of her and clasped her left hand. "You all right?"

She'd nodded. Then she'd swallowed several times, her throat tight. "I am now . . . Sandy," she'd managed to get out before flinging herself into his arms.

He'd smiled at her, one of pure relief as he'd gathered her close. "Thata girl, Sandy."

Now, Bette lifted her face from her hands and regarded Sam blankly. "Stuart's dead," she said.

"Yes."

"You killed him?"

"Actually, no, he was shot by a Salchuk police officer." Releasing Jules, Sam stood up and looked around. "Bette, would you like me to get you a glass of water? Something stronger?"

She shook her head. "Was he with Jackie? Stuart? I guess I always knew that they were having an affair, and I hoped . . . it would just run its course, but it didn't. It never would've. That's just the way he was made. But I don't believe he killed your brother." She swept a hand to the rest of the professionals in the room and said with both disdain and grief, "Joe was too good a guy, and Stuart could never have done anything like that."

Sam said kindly, "When you're ready, you can look at the evidence and decide for yourself."

She held his gaze for a long time, then her shoulders slumped. She looked over at Georgie and the dogs and said, "She really loves them, doesn't she?"

Jules stirred herself and murmured, "Maybe we need a dog of our own."

Bette laughed bitterly. "You can have mine. They were Stuart's at heart, and I could never leave them alone or they would bark all day."

Detective Stone stepped up and asked if he could take Jules's and Bette's preliminary statements for the record. He wanted to finish up and let them get back to their normal lives, whatever that was. Jules had already given a brief account, but now she gave him more details. She explained how her father had assumed her uncle's identity, how he'd either learned to swim on the sly, or maybe had lied and always been able to, how Sean and Devon had a picture from their drone, placing Peter St. James at their house on the day of the boat accident. However, she was certain that it had been Stuart she remembered who'd actually killed Joe, by first hitting him with the gas can, then fighting with him, which had apparently caused him to fall overboard into the sea and drown.

Bette watched her closely as she recounted those events, and seemed like she wanted to object, but she held herself back. She then told Stone that today she'd been getting ready to go to work when she'd talked to Rob Illingsworth, who'd intimated that her husband was with his wife, Jackie Illingsworth, the subtext being they were having an affair. Bette had been angry. She'd tried to contact Stuart's cell phone, but he'd never responded to her.

Then all of a sudden Stuart had pulled into the driveway and Bette had run outside. "I just lost it," Bette said, fresh tears welling. "I was crazy. I'd gotten my gun out and planned to confront him when he came home. I had it on the front table. I know. I shouldn't say that. I wouldn't have really hurt him, but I was just so *angry* and . . . hurt. When he pulled in I just ran out and screamed at him. But then Sam"—she glanced over at Sam now—"he . . . he was standing by his truck, talking on his cell, and he just looked over at us, and . . . and . . . I don't know. Stuart backed out of the driveway and tore away, and Sam jumped in his truck and chased him. I thought . . . I don't know . . . that it had something to do with Jackie. . . ." She broke off and shook her head. "I was going to ask Julia what it was about, but then this man showed up and walked to her door and I got a bad feeling, so I picked up the gun and came over. The door was open and there was a fight with a *knife*. And she . . ." Bette looked at Jules, her face full of pain. "She only had one good arm and he was really threatening her . . . and I shot him. Twice. Or maybe three times. I don't know. Can't . . . can't remember. All I know is that he was attacking her and I thought he was going to kill her or hurt her or . . . And I just . . . did it!"

She covered her face in her hands again, and Stone, after checking with Jules for corroboration of Bette's story, told them both, "Thank you. I've got all I need for now."

He seemed as relieved as they were to put the duty of making them relive the ugly incident to bed, at least for the meanwhile.

It took another hour before everyone cleared the house and Sam, Georgie, Sadie, Griff, and Jules were the only ones left, along with Less and More, whom Bette had allowed to stay with Georgie as long as Sam and Jules didn't mind. Sadie had been cleared to clean up the blood and refused help from anyone else.

Jules had recovered herself, for the most part, and had moved to the kitchen table, seating herself next to Sam. Sadie had made a pot of coffee and asked if anyone was hungry for lunch. She opened the refrigerator and pointed to the leftovers from the Fisher women's feast the night before. Griff, Sam, and Sadie managed to heat plates of food in the microwave for themselves, while Jules begged off. Georgie, in her room with the dogs, wasn't hungry, either.

Griff said, "Our detectives interviewed the Hapstells, Byron Blanchette, and Rob Illingsworth about the property where Phoenix was run off the road. They're all in a deal together apparently, which is moving forward. Nothing sinister there. Apparently Peter St. James knew about it and used it to his advantage. All of them have lost some money with Cardaman, but they expect to do well on this deal, so they didn't have any beef with Joe. One of our detectives, Jon Decker, said he got to see the dynamic between Walter Senior and Walter Junior, and almost felt sorry for Walt Junior. The old man denigrates the son in front of anyone who wants to see."

"Hap," Sam said. "Walter Junior goes by Hap. Did Decker think something about that? Why'd he bring it up?"

"Hap wanted everyone to invest with Cardaman, and a bunch of them did. Hap's the person they're all pointing the finger at as the one who offered bad investment advice, not Joe. Hap kind of spread the rumor that it was Joe's fault and people believed it. Now, he's got a hard-on for this one property and wants everyone to invest with him, but people are wary."

"Summit Ridge," Sam said.

"That's the one. Hap's got a big mouth, too. Talks too much. Can't seem to keep anything quiet."

Sadie snorted loudly.

Griff inclined his head toward her. "Some people have accused me of not being discreet enough—"

"You're not," Sadie said bluntly.

"But I'm a piker compared to Hap. Love you, too, sis," he added sarcastically, which she just shrugged off.

"What about Jackie?" Jules asked. Sadie had brought her a cup of coffee unasked, and Jules sipped at it gratefully. She needed a shot of caffeine.

"We're looking for her," Griff admitted. "Haven't found her yet. Bartender at the Seagull saw her last night, but she got in a car with someone and left. Several witnesses remember she was in a black dress with a red scarf and leaned into a small compact, maybe a Honda Civic, then climbed in."

"Could she be hiding out somewhere in Seaside?"

"We're checking the motels in Seaside, Warrenton, and Astoria. Stone's checking motels south. They spent the night somewhere and unless they had some regular love nest, it's likely to be a motel. If we can't find where they stayed on the coast, we'll start checking further afield. We've circulated her picture along with Ezra's. Someone will remember something."

They talked for a while more, then Griff and Sadie took their leave. When Sam and Jules were alone, they looked at each other in silence for a long moment. Then he got up from the table and held his arms out, and Jules rose to her feet and ran to his embrace.

"You're safe," he said into her hair.

As long as you're here, she thought.

At that moment Georgie's door opened and Jules and Sam broke apart as if they were teenagers caught sneaking around. They were both standing stiffly when Georgie appeared, the two German shepherds' toes clicking on the hardwood as they followed after her.

She stopped short upon seeing how guilty Sam and Jules

were acting. Her face crumpled, and she looked like she was about to cry again. She'd witnessed Peter's death and it had to have taken a huge toll. "You want to talk about . . . what happened?" Jules asked.

"No. No, I don't." She shot Jules a scared glance. "It was bad for you, too."

"Yeah, but it's better to talk about it sometimes."

"No. I'm okay." She reached a hand to the head of one of the dogs and stroked it. "I just wanted to say . . . Uncle Sam . . . that you can stay with us. I mean, overnight. I'd like that. And I know Julia would, too."

"I'd like it, too," Sam said, watching her, trying to read where this was going.

"Thank you for getting Mr. Ezra," she said soberly. Before Sam could respond, she turned to Julia. "You know what I said earlier? About you . . . and Uncle Sam and stuff?"

Jules nodded, fully aware Georgie hadn't wanted Jules to move on from Joe to Sam.

"Well, it's okay. If you want to, I mean. We're kind of a family now, right? We've got to stick together." She looked anxiously between Sam and Jules. "Right?"

Sam looked at Jules. "Right," he said.

"Right," Julia agreed.

The offices of Fairbanks and Vincent were on Seventh Street in Salchuk, about three blocks from Joe's office. Sam held the door for Julia and she walked ahead of him into a cozy reception area with overstuffed leather chairs, a walnut coffee table, and a glass and gold bar cart, which held a black coffee thermos and a collection of mugs with the Fairbanks and Vincent logo: the firm's name in block letters beneath a scale.

They were invited into a room with a large table where

James Fairbanks and Carlton Vincent sat across from each other, while a man with thinning hair, the accountant, sat to one side.

Introductions were made all around, and then Fairbanks gave them each a copy of Joe's will, explaining that the assets of the estate had been divided in half, half to Jules and half to Sam, with a healthy amount set aside for Georgie's college. Far from being the financial mess that had once been rumored, Joe's finances were solid.

Sam tried to protest about being in the will, but Jules assured the lawyers that they would honor Joe's wishes.

Carlton Vincent went on to explain that Joe had done everything he needed to keep his clients separated from both Ike Cardaman and Walter Hapstell Senior's investment opportunities. He hadn't trusted either of them.

"It was out of concern for his clients' financial well-being," Fairbanks went on to say. "Mr. Ford sent letters and e-mails to his clients explaining that he did not endorse investments with either company. We have copies of all the correspondence. Walter Hapstell threatened to sue him, but Mr. Ford held firm. When Mr. Cardaman's troubles came to light, certain panicked investors chose to blame Mr. Ford, but he had very clearly advised against any and all of Mr. Cardaman's investment opportunities."

Vincent picked up the thread. "Most of Mr. Ford's long-time investors listened to him. Their savings are intact. Others have varying amounts with Mr. Ford, Mr. Hapstell, Mr. Cardaman, and/or various other ventures. There is no criminal investigation into Mr. Hapstell's practices at this time, but the percentage of return on investments has gone steadily downward over the last year while Mr. Ford's has remained steady." He looked to the accountant for confirmation. The man nodded, then went on to explain the wealth that Joe had personally accumulated as well and named a figure that overwhelmed both Sam and Jules.

Hap had been right when he'd said Joe had split his estate between Sam and Jules. He'd known because Scott Keppler, Joe's original attorney, had been a little too loose-lipped with Walter Hapstell Senior, upon trying to woo some of Hapstell's business his way. Walt Senior had told Hap, and Hap, never known for discretion, blabbed all at Tutti's barbecue.

Sam and Jules left the meeting feeling slightly overwhelmed.

"I feel sick that I ever doubted him. That I took the Cardaman file," Jules said.

"Joe was already on to 'P. J. Simpson' and was probably glad, at some level, that Phoenix was on the story."

Jules remembered she'd thought Joe was relieved when he learned she'd given the file to Phoenix. "I'm glad Phoenix is going to be okay."

"Me too," Sam said with feeling. He exhaled heavily and smiled faintly at her. "This afternoon I'm heading down to Tillamook."

Sam had accepted the job with the Tillamook County Sheriff's Department. He was starting out as a deputy but everyone understood he was on the fast track to detective. Griff had begged him to come back to Seaside, but Sam had wanted to be closer to Jules and Georgie.

"What do you think about Bette leaving Georgie Less and More?" Sam asked. "How do you just give up your pets?"

Jules shook her head, equally puzzled. "All I can tell you is that she said they were more Stuart's than hers, that they've completely bonded with Georgie, and that she's breaking her lease and moving away. Who knew the Ezras were renting from Scott Keppler?"

"Keppler told me that he'd taken a page from Joe's book. He knew Joe had bought up properties along the canal. I guess he did, too."

They drove north to Seaside and walked together into the

Sea and Sunset Retirement Center. Sam led the way to Donald Ford's room and knocked loudly on the door panels. When there was no answer, he knocked again, louder yet.

"Well, c'mon in," came through the door, faintly annoyed.

Sam twisted the knob and they stepped inside. Donald Ford was seated in his favorite chair, a leather recliner. Jules had only visited him once with Joe since he'd moved into the assisted living center, but she recognized the chair from years earlier. "Good to see you, Donald," she greeted him, leaning down to kiss his cheek.

Donald smiled up at her, then shot a glance to his youngest son, as he greeted her, "Hello, Jules. So, now you're with the right Ford again, huh?"

"I . . ." She really didn't know how to answer that.

"I don't know what you mean by that, Dad," Sam said, examining his father closely. "Jules was married to Joe."

"I know that. You think I don't know that?" He looked from one to the other of them. "Glad at least one thing worked out right." He sighed. "Now, tell me again, have you made arrangements for Joe's memorial service?"

"Working on it," Sam answered.

"I might have to go and buy myself a new suit." He smiled sadly, then asked Jules, "Think you could take an old man shopping?"

"Whenever you like," Jules told him.

"How about tomorrow? Might as well be ready. Who knows? Could be needing it for a wedding sometime soon, as well," he added with a knowing nod.

"Tomorrow it is," Jules told him. She wasn't going to touch that last comment with a ten-foot pole, but she couldn't deny it was nice to hear Donald would have no trouble keeping her in the family, so to speak.

Later, Sam and Jules drove home in companionable silence, each lost in their own private thoughts. When Sam's cell rang and he saw it was Griff, he almost let it go to voice mail. If what Griff was calling about had anything to do with Joe's or Peters's deaths, he would have rather taken in the information alone and talk it over with Jules later.

"Aren't you going to get that?" she asked.

Which decided it for him, so he clicked on and put the cell on speaker. "You're on speaker, Griff," he said. "Jules and I are in the truck."

"Some interesting stuff developing. Think we found the motel where Stuart and Jackie stayed. Guy who thinks he was in the room next to them saw Stuart's picture on the news and says he was there. Checked the room. Didn't find anything, but the staff thought it was unusual that the people who had rented the room made off with all of the bedding and that the place, when the cleaning person arrived, reeked of bleach. That was confirmed by the manager."

Jules and Sam exchanged glances as Griff went on, "We went through the security tapes and Jackie came up, clear as a bell. Ezra ducked his head, but it's him. Here's the thing. They were in a Honda Civic, and the license plate number came up stolen. Same license plate number some hikers called in early that same morning, Saturday morning. Apparently that Civic drove onto the road, nearly ran them down, slammed on its brakes, and a woman passenger smacked her head into the dashboard and seemed dazed. By their description I'd say it's Jackie. The driver acted like no big deal and backed onto the highway again, but the hikers thought there was something off, so they took down the license plate number and called it in. Must be a reason Stuart chose that road, so we're searching the area now."

"Sounds like Jackie was injured." Sam didn't add that he thought it highly likely they would not be finding Jackie alive and well.

"And get this," Griff added. "That same license plate on a Honda Civic was seen in Portland. A witness called it in because she saw a man and woman getting it on inside the car like their lives depended on it. The car was parked in a lot not too far from where a homicide had taken place, that of a transvestite named Monique, who was strangled to death in a back alley. Portland PD ran the plate and realized it had been stolen from a car registered to a Seaside resident. They've been working on the assumption that the killer or killers probably lived at the coast, and now we think the couple was Stuart and Jackie."

"Why did they kill Monique?" Jules burst out. "Was she involved in the Cardaman mess, too?"

"Actually, detectives around here think Stuart and Jackie were thrill-killers. We're going over past cases now. They apparently killed for money, too, but . . . it looks like they killed for pleasure."

They talked a bit more about the aspects of the case, then Sam clicked off and looked at Jules. She reflected for a moment, then said, "My dad hired them to kill Joe. He knew what they were and he hired them. I won't feel completely safe until they find Jackie." When Sam didn't immediately respond, she said, "You think she's already dead, don't you?"

"Yeah."

"Why doesn't that make me feel better?"

"Because you've run up against pure evil. A quirk in a person's DNA. A soul-deep illness. Call it what you will. It's dangerous, and deadly. And I'm never letting you out of my sight again."

She actually laughed. "Thank you. And yes, don't let me out of your sight."

"Except I have to leave you to go down to the Sheriff's Department. But I won't be gone long."

"Okay. And I've got Georgie and the kids."

"The kids?" Sam asked.

"That's what Georgie calls the German shepherds. She said it's what Bette always called Less and More . . . the kids."

* * *

She drove into the outskirts of Portland, negotiating the traffic. She had only the basics of her belongings: a suitcase of clothes, some personal items, a stash of cold, hard cash. . . . She would have to pick up another gun, since hers had not been returned to her yet by the Tillamook County Sheriff's Department. When he'd interviewed her, that detective, Langdon Stone, had looked her over hard. She'd felt the heat right in the core of her sex, even though he'd been regarding her with suspicion, not lust. She'd had to give a five-star, Oscar-winning performance to make them believe she'd killed P. J. to save Julia. Like she cared about that doe-eyed bitch. She'd had to kill "the man" to permanently shut him up, and luckily, before he met his maker, Stuart had let her know Simpson was planning some kind of "last play" with Julia. She'd been infuriated that Stuart had not killed Julia from the get-go, had wondered if his bungling was more because he wanted to fuck her first, rather than total ineptitude. And then when Stuart called to tell her Simpson had stiffed them, her fury had known no bounds.

She'd about decided to shoot Stuart, had gotten her gun out to do just that, but had cooled off a little by the time the fool pulled into the driveway, then peeled out again after Sam Ford gave him the cold, hard stare. That's why she'd started screaming. Holy God! She'd been beside herself, knowing Stuart would give her up. Crazed with fear.

But then . . . "the man" had shown up right on cue. Better than she could have planned it. She'd had the gun out and loaded. She'd let the dogs out, just in case she needed help, but hadn't needed them. The old fool had stumbled to his feet and started menacingly toward Julia and she'd blasted him. *Pow. Pow. Pow.* Done! She'd been ready to kill Julia, too, but Georgie was there and the dogs ran to her and . . . well, it was a major cluster-fuck. She figured Georgie could have the dogs. They barked like idiots and she didn't want the responsibility of them in her new life. If she needed a dog for protection, she'd just get a new one. They were disposable in her mind. Stuart was the one who liked them.

Stuart . . . and Jackie. Luckily, all blame for the killings fell on Jackie. Just desserts. The bitch thought she was such a sex kitten. What a laugh. Stuart was just too easy. His tongue was always hanging out over a piece of ass. Just his way.

But Stuart was gone now, too. He couldn't give her away any longer.

She kissed two of her fingers and raised her hand skyward, looking up to thank him for keeping his damn trap shut. Well, actually, she probably should be looking down, shouldn't she, since that was definitely the more likely eternity for Stuart's black soul.

She smiled to herself. She would miss him, a little. That was a fact. Maybe she would prowl around Portland for a while, then move on to Seattle. Or, maybe she'd go the other way, head down to San Francisco, LA, San Diego. Arizona could be nice . . . hot weather, really hot in the summer. . . . She liked the heat.

She could legally change her name to Bridget and finally become the person she was meant to be.

So many possibilities . . .

Books by Bestselling Author
Fern Michaels

___The Jury	0-8217-7878-1	$6.99US/$9.99CAN
___Sweet Revenge	0-8217-7879-X	$6.99US/$9.99CAN
___Lethal Justice	0-8217-7880-3	$6.99US/$9.99CAN
___Free Fall	0-8217-7881-1	$6.99US/$9.99CAN
___Fool Me Once	0-8217-8071-9	$7.99US/$10.99CAN
___Vegas Rich	0-8217-8112-X	$7.99US/$10.99CAN
___Hide and Seek	1-4201-0184-6	$6.99US/$9.99CAN
___Hokus Pokus	1-4201-0185-4	$6.99US/$9.99CAN
___Fast Track	1-4201-0186-2	$6.99US/$9.99CAN
___Collateral Damage	1-4201-0187-0	$6.99US/$9.99CAN
___Final Justice	1-4201-0188-9	$6.99US/$9.99CAN
___Up Close and Personal	0-8217-7956-7	$7.99US/$9.99CAN
___Under the Radar	1-4201-0683-X	$6.99US/$9.99CAN
___Razor Sharp	1-4201-0684-8	$7.99US/$10.99CAN
___Yesterday	1-4201-1494-8	$5.99US/$6.99CAN
___Vanishing Act	1-4201-0685-6	$7.99US/$10.99CAN
___Sara's Song	1-4201-1493-X	$5.99US/$6.99CAN
___Deadly Deals	1-4201-0686-4	$7.99US/$10.99CAN
___Game Over	1-4201-0687-2	$7.99US/$10.99CAN
___Sins of Omission	1-4201-1153-1	$7.99US/$10.99CAN
___Sins of the Flesh	1-4201-1154-X	$7.99US/$10.99CAN
___Cross Roads	1-4201-1192-2	$7.99US/$10.99CAN

Available Wherever Books Are Sold!
Check out our website at **www.kensingtonbooks.com**